NEW PENGUIN SHAKESPEARE
GENERAL EDITOR: T. J. B. SPENCER
ASSOCIATE EDITOR: STANLEY WELLS

WILLIAM SHAKESPEARE

*

THE SECOND PART OF KING HENRY THE SIXTH

EDITED BY
NORMAN SANDERS

PENGUIN BOOKS

PENGUIN BOOKS

Published by the Penguin Group
27 Wrights Lane, London w8 5tz, England
Viking Penguin Inc., 40 West 23rd Street, New York, New York 10010, USA
Penguin Books Australia Ltd, Ringwood, Victoria, Australia
Penguin Books Canada Ltd, 2801 John Street, Markham, Ontario, Canada l3r 1b4
Penguin Books (NZ) Ltd, 182–190 Wairau Road, Auckland 10, New Zealand

Penguin Books Ltd, Registered Offices: Harmondsworth, Middlesex, England

This edition first published in Penguin Books 1981
3 5 7 9 10 8 6 4 2

All rights reserved

Made and printed in Great Britain by
Richard Clay Ltd, Bungay, Suffolk
Set in Monotype Ehrhardt

CONTENTS

INTRODUCTION

MOST Elizabethans would have been familiar with the Tudor bishops' formulation of God's design for a stable state as it is phrased in the *Homily Against Disobedience and Wilful Rebellion*:

> Besides the obedience due unto his majesty, He not only ordained that in families and households the wife should be obedient unto her husband, the children unto their parents, the servants unto their masters; but also, when mankind increased and spread itself more largely over the world, He by His holy word did constitute and ordain in cities and countries several and special governors and rulers unto whom the residue of His people should be obedient.

It is equally certain that many people in the audiences that attended the first performances of *Henry VI, Part Two* in the spring months of 1592 would have recognized that the dramatized history they were seeing illustrated the results of one nation's abandonment of these principles of orderly social stratification. For in this play a king is defied by his wife, nobility, and people; the rule of law breaks down; justice becomes a victim of whim and ambition; goodness is scorned in families and in the nation; and Christian virtue is seen to be impotent when opposed by vigorous self-interest and violence. Both in the large allegorical arrangement of the action and in the smallest details of characterization and language, the play offers a believable movement from the possibility of order to the reality of multiple division and civil war.

7

For the play's materials, as for those of *Part One*, Shakespeare went again to the English chronicles; but in this case his following of historical events is far more accurate. The changes he made in his sources – such as the blending of York's two uprisings into one, or the moving of York's fury against Somerset's release from the Tower two years back in time, or the introduction of Richard and Edward into happenings which took place historically while they were children – are all in the interests of shaping a well-ordered play about the breakdown of rule and its connexions with the personal qualities of those who jostle for political power.

The conditions necessary for right rule, and productive of the kind of harmony the *Homily* speaks of, are represented by two characters: Humphrey, Duke of Gloucester and Protector of the realm, and Henry VI. All that transpires is in reaction to the positive virtues these two men possess. The less complex of the two is Gloucester. He is a far remove from the fiercely partisan opponent of Cardinal Beaufort found in *Part One*, where his righteous antagonisms were seen as one element in the internal strife that caused the loss of the English possessions in France. For this later play Shakespeare clearly based his conception of the character on the admiring portrait he found in Edward Hall and Raphael Holinshed, where 'the good Duke Humphrey' is the very image of a pre-Renaissance humanist, a collector of classical manuscripts, a patron of scholars, an admirer of Italian architecture, a precursor of More, Erasmus, Elyot, and Pole.

But although this chronicle figure lies behind Shakespeare's creation, the dramatic focus is on the way Gloucester's human qualities issue into public service, on how one man's moral probity and his administered justice may be interdependent, on the possibility of

ideals being shrewdly applied. Yet this perfect governor is
no two-dimensional abstraction. While his role in the
play draws him close to his theatrical ancestors in the old
Morality drama, the method of his creation ensures a
credible mingling of transcendent ability, strong personal
emotion, political perceptivity, and ultimate helplessness
in the face of forces which operate outside the realms of
his own standards.

Gloucester, as the Protector to the son of Henry V, is
first a remnant of the older generation which shared the
triumphs of the hero-king, and which worked after his
death to make certain the empire he had won was efficiently
administered for England's benefit. Gloucester can
legitimately remind his fellow peers of Henry V's legacy:

> *And did my brother Bedford toil his wits*
> *To keep by policy what Henry got? . . .*
> *Or hath mine uncle Beaufort and myself,*
> *With all the learnèd Council of the realm,*
> *Studied so long, sat in the Council House*
> *Early and late, debating to and fro*
> *How France and Frenchmen might be kept in awe?*
>
> I.1.81-2, 86-90

More importantly, he is a seeker after truth and 'indifferent
justice' in the England of Henry VI. This central aspect
of his nature is displayed in a series of brilliantly realized
episodes. Alone among the nobles in the first scene, he is
free of self-interest in his castigation of Henry's marriage
to Margaret. His emotional response to the humiliating
conditions agreed to by Suffolk in the settlement causes
him to break off his reading of the articles; but it does not
blind him to the new political situation thus produced.
This shameful league and fatal match will indeed deface
the 'monuments of conquered France, | Undoing all,

9

as all had never been'. They will also produce a new power block at the English court centring on 'Suffolk, the new-made duke that rules the roast'; and raise financial problems as a result of the high taxes necessary to cover the costs and charges for Margaret's dowry.

In the discussion of the French Regency (I.3), Gloucester's judgement is carefully considered; and his obvious disinterestedness stands in sharp contrast to the vicious factionalism underlying the contribution of the other principals. The Cardinal and Warwick bicker like schoolboys over precedence and prowess, Margaret makes a bitchy reply to Salisbury's attempt to raise the tone of the discussion, York and Somerset are proudly defensive of their military records. Gloucester makes it clear that he sees his role as Protector not as a self-gratifying position but as one of public service: 'I am Protector of the realm, | And at his pleasure will resign my place'. His answer to the palpably unjust attacks on his administration is simply to make a dignified exit, in order to avoid the possibility of discussing national issues while his judgement is clouded by emotion. His first lines on his re-entry are an implicit condemnation of all the other nobles present:

> Now, lords, my choler being overblown
> With walking once about the quadrangle,
> I come to talk of commonwealth affairs.
> As for your spiteful false objections,
> Prove them, and I lie open to the law.

I.3.150–54

This respect for the law is at once demonstrated. Initially he thinks 'York is meetest man' to be Regent in France; but the suspicion that one of the Duke's servants is favourably discussing his master's right to the throne makes his appointment politically unsuitable; so Somerset is elected and Horner and Peter are sentenced to trial by combat. The rightness of these decisions proves true: we have already heard from York's own lips his royal ambitions and his plans for fulfilling them (1.1.237–57); and we are to see in II.3 that, against all our theatrical expectations, Horner turns out to be guilty of voicing York's treasonous claims.

The most dramatically effective display of Gloucester's shrewdness in the application of the law and the pursuit of truth is in the episode of Simpcox and the 'miracle' at Saint Albans in II.1. Step by step, in a demonstration of forensic skill, he probes the nature of Simpcox's claims about the recovery of his sight and reveals the outright fraud. The construction of this scene interestingly reflects its dramatic importance. The miracle is announced; Suffolk and the Cardinal establish their presence officiously by effecting the introduction of the beggar to the King; Henry and Margaret respond to the supposed cure respectfully. Then Gloucester proceeds with his examination. The other nobles remain silent during the cross-questioning; and it is only after the Protector has shown what is now obvious that the King, Queen, and Suffolk react in their characteristic manners. The exercise of deceit, the employment of the lie for personal gain, the unscrupulous battening on the human hope for some desired good, and the disguising of base motives by an appeal to higher principles all go undetected by the courtly manipulators of these very means at the national level; it is their ultimate victim alone whose skill and idealism can protect all from error but himself. He can also move the scene's lesson from the immediate context and hint at its function as a microcosm of that greater tragedy which the Simpcox qualities are to produce in England itself:

CARDINAL

Duke Humphrey has done a miracle today.

SUFFOLK

True; made the lame to leap and fly away.

GLOUCESTER

But you have done more miracles than I;
You made in a day, my lord, whole towns to fly.

II.1.156–9

Gloucester's faith in the law is tested on a personal as well as political level. His wife is the possessor of standards similar to those of her husband's enemies. Like the Cardinal and York, she is driven by an obsessive self-regard and pride of place; she is, like Margaret and Suffolk, incapable of separating an office from the particular holder of it; like them all, she can see national issues only in personal terms, never in a context of ideals divorced from individuals. She is haunted by dreams of the absolute power of the crown, and tantalized by Gloucester's dynastic closeness to the throne. In the domestic scene of her first appearance (I.2), she attributes to her husband her own narrow preoccupations; but she receives in return only his careful definition of the limits and privileges of her position at court:

O Nell, sweet Nell, if thou dost love thy lord,
Banish the canker of ambitious thoughts! . . .
Art thou not second woman in the realm,
And the Protector's wife, beloved of him?
Hast thou not worldly pleasure at command
Above the reach or compass of thy thought?

I.2.17–18, 43–6

But Eleanor can no more be satisfied with any glories less than those of the highest position than can York or Margaret; and, left to herself, she expresses her longings in that idiom which echoes York's and comes to its fully developed expressiveness in the mouth of Richard, the later and far different Duke of Gloucester:

> *Follow I must; I cannot go before*
> *While Gloucester bears this base and humble mind.*
> *Were I a man, a duke, and next of blood,*
> *I would remove these tedious stumbling-blocks*
> *And smooth my way upon their headless necks;*
> *And, being a woman, I will not be slack*
> *To play my part in Fortune's pageant.*   I.2.61–7

This determination for independent action, despite what she takes to be her husband's cowardice, serves only to demonstrate the validity of Gloucester's beliefs. She places herself in the hands of John Hume, who is an agent of Suffolk and the Cardinal, planted 'to undermine the Duchess' by exploiting the 'aspiring humour' Gloucester warned her against.

Eleanor's meddling with witchcraft for treasonous purposes is immediately, if subconsciously, recognized by Gloucester as the signal of his own downfall; as he says to his arch-enemy the Cardinal:

> *Sorrow and grief have vanquished all my powers;*
> *And, vanquished as I am, I yield to thee*
> *Or to the meanest groom.*   II.1.178–80

Yet this personal grief does not deflect him from his principles of service to the land and the law:

> *I banish her my bed and company,*
> *And give her as a prey to law and shame.*
>   II.1.192–3

The shame he witnesses on stage in II.4. Eleanor's reaction to her public penance is of a piece with her comportment in her days of prosperity: all the emphasis of her lines is on the public nature of her disgrace, the rabble's rejoicing in her tears, the inferior commons' being able to laugh at her pain; and the greatest part of her punishment is being able to recall her former pomp and her empty wish for 'this world's eternity'. Gloucester realizes there has been no change wrought in her by the experience; and he attempts to teach her true value for the last time:

> *Wouldst have me rescue thee from this reproach?*
> *Why, yet thy scandal were not wiped away,*
> *But I in danger for the breach of law.* II.4.64–6

At only one point in the play does Gloucester fall below the highest standards of political and personal behaviour: in his altercation with the Cardinal in the hawking scene at Saint Albans (II.1). This is an echo of the bitter enmity between the two men which in *Part One* helped divide the English court with such serious international repercussions. It portrays grotesquely two old men reverting to their youth, when differences could be settled by personal heroics in the single combat of the lists with their now antiquated 'two-hand swords'. As such it is a reminder of that age of the great captains, Talbot, Bedford, and Henry V himself, when strong conviction of right, commitment to public service, and noble utterance were a valid way of life. In the changed world of Henry VI's England, all that remains of those days are these irate ageing counsellors, whispering dares behind their hands, and the spectacle of a drunken armourer and his cowardly apprentice flailing at each other with poles and sandbags while a sneering nobility look on.

It is this archaic element in Gloucester's make-up that renders him, for all his gifts, powerless in the face of his enemies. His kind of truth and justice can operate only within a stable community; and it is based on the

faith that God will not allow evil to prosper in violation
of His law:

> *I must offend before I be attainted;*
> *And had I twenty times so many foes,*
> *And each of them had twenty times their power,*
> *All these could not procure me any scathe*
> *So long as I am loyal, true, and crimeless.*
>
> II.4.59–63

For his enemies, however, loyalty, truth, and innocence
are irrelevant when they stand in the way of ambition
and self-interest. Eleanor Cobham's view of the world
of the play is truer than her husband's; and she knows
instinctively what he can recognize only when it is too
late:

> *stir at nothing till the axe of death*
> *Hang over thee, as sure it shortly will;*
> *For Suffolk, he that can do all in all*
> *With her that hateth thee and hates us all,*
> *And York, and impious Beaufort, that false priest,*
> *Have all limed bushes to betray thy wings;*
> *And fly thou how thou canst, they'll tangle thee.*
> *But fear not thou until thy foot be snared,*
> *Nor never seek prevention of thy foes.*   II.4.49–57

The images of hunting, snaring, and trapping in these
lines are an apt vehicle for conveying the situation in
which Gloucester finds himself and by which he is
defeated. As Holinshed notes, Gloucester's foes, though
divided in all else, can come together for the purpose of
destroying the rule of law that hampers them: 'while the
one party sought to destroy the other, all care of the commonwealth was set aside, and justice and equity clearly
exiled' (III.237).

*

The finely constructed opening scene, by means of skilfully placed exits keyed to the progressive splintering of the court groupings, sets up for the audience the nature of the factionalism. The formal welcoming of the royal bride is performed by Henry, Suffolk, and Margaret in the first thirty-six lines and brought to a period by a flourish of trumpets to accompany the greetings of the kneeling court. Gloucester's 'sudden qualm' at reading of the loss of Anjou and Maine strikes an alien note, which is quickly covered when the Cardinal takes up the announcement of the marriage articles; and this in turn leads to the infatuated Henry's elevation of Suffolk to a dukedom. Gloucester's long lament for the loss of the French possessions and his diatribe against the humiliating conditions of the settlement swell to a communal threnody for England's lost glory, with each nobleman stressing one aspect of the Protector's total analysis. Salisbury perceives that the ceding of the two counties is a strategic military blunder which will lead to a weakening of Normandy; Warwick is personally affected by the giving away of lands he un-historically claims to have conquered; York is horrified at the blow to the pride of the English monarchy; and Gloucester himself notes the extra financial burden that will be placed on the taxpayer, before he leaves to prevent an outbreak of his 'ancient bickerings' with the Cardinal.

After this exit, Buckingham quickly aligns himself with the Cardinal's animosity against Gloucester, which takes as its public excuse the Protector's supposed royal ambitions; and Somerset's help is asked in Gloucester's downfall. As the Cardinal leaves to seek Suffolk's support, Somerset and Buckingham agree between themselves to side with the churchman only until the Protector is out of office, at which time they intend to divide the spoils of power between themselves. Warwick, Salisbury, and York watch these conspiracies take shape and, once left alone, form their own alliance with the intention of thwarting the ill effects of such pride and ambition in action:

> *Join we together for the public good,*
> *In what we can to bridle and suppress*
> *The pride of Suffolk and the Cardinal,*
> *With Somerset's and Buckingham's ambition;*
> *And, as we may, cherish Duke Humphrey's deeds*
> *While they do tend the profit of the land.*
>
> I.1.197–202

Finally, after the Nevils' departure on an ironic note of pompous self-dedication to the country's welfare, York is left to reveal his own far more wide-reaching plans in soliloquy.

Despite the variety of motivation within these groups and individuals, they can act unitedly against Gloucester because of characteristics they share. All of them recognize that the Protector represents a stability and ideal of service to the commonwealth that are no part of their own lives. For them England has become identified with self, so that, although they all offer lip-service to the national good, their lines convey to us only the way their political stances are rooted in deeply-felt personal antipathies. The Cardinal, for example, is almost an emblem of Pride and Envy; and one gathers from his words and actions that

> *Such men as he be never at heart's ease*
> *Whiles they behold a greater than themselves.*
>
> *Julius Caesar,* I.2.207–8

Salisbury hits the core of his nature accurately when he comments on the churchman's fusion of spite, hauteur, and pettiness:

> *Oft have I seen the haughty Cardinal,*
> *More like a soldier than a man o'th'church,*
> *As stout and proud as he were lord of all,*
> *Swear like a ruffian, and demean himself*
> *Unlike the ruler of a commonweal.*   I.1.183–7

For such a man as this to join the conspiracy against Gloucester is merely to turn personal rancour into gang violence. Somerset and Buckingham are but lay versions of the same stripe: ambitious, covetous of power for its own sake, unscrupulous, with Somerset bringing as a legacy from the chronicles his jealousy of York's martial achievements and a record of corruption and mismanagement during his tenure of the French Regency.

Margaret and Suffolk are allies in a sense the other plotters can never be. As we saw in *Part One*, Suffolk won Margaret by his personal charm, and calculated that her marriage to Henry would mean the possibility for himself of sexual indulgence and a position as effective ruler of England. His was the voice that provided the end of that play with its note of threat:

> *Thus Suffolk hath prevailed; and thus he goes,*
> *As did the youthful Paris once to Greece,*
> *With hope to find the like event in love*
> *But prosper better than the Trojan did.*
> *Margaret shall now be Queen, and rule the King;*
> *But I will rule both her, the King, and realm.*
>   *1 Henry VI*, V.5.103–8

He is characterized in *Part Two* as a man devoid of all sense of political responsibility. It is not that he allows personal considerations to override the demands of the public good; it is simply that for him there is no good but his own. In I.3, where he and the Queen are approached by the common petitioners, we are struck by his awareness of rank in the very vocabulary he uses ('sir knave', 'fellow') and are given information that he is already using his position for financial gain by 'enclosing the commons of Melford'. He appears incapable of taking seriously those people he considers 'rude unpolished hinds' or 'a sort of tinkers'; and in the scene of his death his self-regarding bombast emerges as a kind of blind courage. In a situation where even a modicum of common sense dictates temporizing, he persists in denying the danger of his position and angering his captors by the repeated assertions of his nobility:

> *Look on my George; I am a gentleman. . . .*
> *Jove sometime went disguised, and why not I? . . .*
> *Obscure and lousy swain, King Henry's blood,*
> *The honourable blood of Lancaster,*
> *Must not be shed by such a jaded groom.*
> *Hast thou not kissed thy hand and held my stirrup?*
> *Bareheaded plodded by my foot-cloth mule,*
> *And thought thee happy when I shook my head? . . .*
> *Suffolk's imperial tongue is stern and rough,*
> *Used to command, untaught to plead for favour.*
>
> IV.1.29, 48, 50–55, 123–4

He even goes to his sordid execution proclaiming the similarity between his end and those of Cicero, Brutus, Caesar, and Pompey. It is perfectly appropriate that among the conspirators he is the one who so readily undertakes the physical arrangements for Gloucester's murder; for he is the character so securely locked up in the dungeon of self that any accurate political calculation is impossible for him.

Suffolk is also a fit partner for Margaret in the early stages of her ambition. Her attitude of general resentment is based originally on a real disappointment of her expectations of being the first woman in England. To begin with, Henry is a sexual let-down for her, as most actresses who play the part make clear even before they speak in the opening scene.

> *I tell thee, Pole, when in the city Tours*
> *Thou rannest a tilt in honour of my love*
> *And stolest away the ladies' hearts of France,*
> *I thought King Henry had resembled thee*
> *In courage, courtship, and proportion.*
> *But all his mind is bent to holiness,*
> *To number Ave-Maries on his beads;*
> *His champions are the prophets and apostles,*
> *His weapons holy saws of sacred writ;*
> *His study is his tilt-yard, and his loves*
> *Are brazen images of canonized saints.*   I.3.48–58

A woman of Margaret's stamp could probably have borne (with Suffolk to hand) her husband's personal failings, if her position had provided her with the daily proofs of power and pre-eminence she craves; but she finds herself surrounded by noblemen, the least of whom 'can do more in England than the King'. The deeply egocentric response to public circumstances common to all Gloucester's enemies is most marked in her. None of the real limitations of her position as Queen vexes her half so much as

> *that proud dame, the Lord Protector's wife;*
> *She sweeps it through the court with troops of ladies,*
> *More like an empress than Duke Humphrey's wife.*
> *Strangers in court do take her for the queen,*
> *She bears a duke's revenues on her back,*
> *And in her heart she scorns our poverty.*
> *Shall I not live to be avenged on her?*   I.3.74–80

The same pettiness of mind leads her to open provocation of the Duchess as she boxes her ears (I.3.136); and while

20

Eleanor's disgrace is for her, as much as for the other plotters, an integral part of Gloucester's overthrow, only the Queen and her lover find pleasure in gloating on the painful nature of Gloucester's reaction:

QUEEN

> ... *And Humphrey Duke of Gloucester scarce himself,*
> *That bears so shrewd a maim; two pulls at once –*
> *His lady banished and a limb lopped off....*

SUFFOLK

> *Thus droops this lofty pine and hangs his sprays;*
> *Thus Eleanor's pride dies in her youngest days.*

II.3.40–42, 45–6

While Suffolk is alive, Margaret's dedication to her task of ruling the land with her lover through her pious husband has an air of hectic excitement about it. Convinced of the necessity for Gloucester's fall, she can bring all her formidable powers of persuasion to bear on Henry in a nice blending of the daily slights she is so sensitive to and a depiction of the alleged incipient dangers in the Protector:

> *But meet him now, and be it in the morn,*
> *When everyone will give the time of day,*
> *He knits his brow and shows an angry eye,*
> *And passeth by with stiff unbowèd knee,*
> *Disdaining duty that to us belongs....*
> *Now 'tis the spring, and weeds are shallow-rooted;*
> *Suffer them now and they'll o'ergrow the garden,*
> *And choke the herbs for want of husbandry.*

III.1.13–17, 31–3

She tries by means of a similar rhetoric to rescue Suffolk from banishment when the irate commons are at the palace gates after Gloucester's murder, but is choked off by the King (III.2.289–97). Here she is fighting for her hopes of a sexual fulfilment that can be combined with her political ambitions. Even the parting between the two, with its echoes of their Petrarchan wooing in *Part One*, is shot through with memories of a realized sensuality:

> *If I depart from thee I cannot live,*
> *And in thy sight to die, what were it else*
> *But like a pleasant slumber in thy lap?*
> *Here could I breathe my soul into the air,*
> *As mild and gentle as the cradle-babe*
> *Dying with mother's dug between its lips.*
>
> III.2.388–93

The final appearance of their special alliance is her lament as she gruesomely nurses Suffolk's severed head and reaffirms her faith in his political mastery:

> *Here may his head lie on my throbbing breast;*
> *But where's the body that I should embrace? . . .*
> *Ah, were the Duke of Suffolk now alive,*
> *These Kentish rebels would be soon appeased!*
>
> IV.4.5–6, 41–2

The Earls of Warwick and Salisbury are initially the least committed of the nobles to Gloucester's dismissal from his office. For Margaret, Suffolk, and the rest, the removing of the Protector is their sole aim for the first three acts of the play; this alone will bring the desired manipulation of the feeble king in which each one sees personal and political satisfaction. But the Nevils have early become aware of York's intentions and are therefore uniquely conscious that depriving the Protector of his staff is but one step towards robbing Henry of his crown. As we have seen, they stand unaligned in the developing divisions of the first scene, their initial inclination being only to bridle and suppress the vices of the other courtiers by cherishing 'Duke Humphrey's deeds | While they do tend the profit of the land' (I.1.201–2). Naturally they support York for the French Regency; but Warwick's arrogant confidence shows itself in his contributions to the debate, and his awareness of the larger stakes he is playing for is implied in his retort to Buckingham: 'Warwick may live to be the best of all' (I.3.110). In view of their easy acceptance of York's claims to be the rightful king of England and their calm reception of his vow to stain his sword 'With heart-blood of the house of Lancaster' (II.2.66), it is small wonder that they can wink at the narrower ambitions of the other peers and be grateful that they need only await the outcome of the plot against Gloucester, when their rivals for power will have

> *snared the shepherd of the flock,*
> *That virtuous prince, the good Duke Humphrey.*
> *'Tis that they seek; and they, in seeking that,*
> *Shall find their deaths, if York can prophesy.*
>
> II.2.73–6

To the schemers the sacrifice of even a virtuous individual is a minor matter when set against making 'the Duke of York a king' and 'the Earl of Warwick | The greatest man in England but the king' (II.2.79–82).

The centrepiece and turning-point of the play are the two great scenes of Gloucester's trial and death (III.1 and 2). Critics have noticed their structural debt to the Tudor Morality plays. Justice is assaulted by the forces of disorder before a helpless Commonwealth; and violence prevails, as Justice is denied and then strangled. The perspicacity Gloucester displayed in the matters of the Regency and the 'miracle' at Saint Albans is every bit as apparent in his analysis of the motives of his enemies and of the situation in which he finds himself. Just as he would not in the case of his own wife 'justify whom the law

23

condemns', so he is willing to give up his life if his death 'might make this island happy'. But he realizes that this is not what is at issue and that his death is only the prologue to a plotted tragedy of ambition inspired by strong destructive emotions:

> *Beaufort's red sparkling eyes blab his heart's malice,*
> *And Suffolk's cloudy brow his stormy hate;*
> *Sharp Buckingham unburdens with his tongue*
> *The envious load that lies upon his heart;*
> *And doggèd York, that reaches at the moon,*
> *Whose overweening arm I have plucked back,*
> *By false accuse doth level at my life.*
> *And you, my sovereign lady, with the rest,*
> *Causeless have laid disgraces on my head,*
> *And with your best endeavour have stirred up*
> *My liefest liege to be mine enemy.*   III.1.154–64

Gloucester's error is in believing that the guiltless need fear no danger, that his innocence will be proven by a diligent search for truth and the administration of an impartial justice:

> *thou shalt not see me blush,*
> *Nor change my countenance for this arrest;*
> *A heart unspotted is not easily daunted.*
> *The purest spring is not so free from mud*
> *As I am clear from treason to my sovereign.*
> *Who can accuse me? Wherein am I guilty?*
>   III.1.98–103

This is true enough in a court where Gloucester himself is the judge; but what operates now is the awful energy of unscrupulous self-interest, divided in its various mani-festations but united at this point in the purely negative urge to destroy him at any cost.

The form that Gloucester's trial takes is instructive and is based on a hint found in the chronicles: 'although the Duke sufficiently answered to all things against him objected, yet, because his death was determined, his wisdom and innocency nothing availed' (Holinshed, III.211). Suffolk, the entrapper of Eleanor Cobham, suggests that she began her 'devilish practices' by Gloucester's subornation; but then he realizes the stupidity of the charge and so qualifies it by stating that the Protector's closeness to the throne constituted a kind of instigation to his wife. The Queen is peeved that Gloucester is not sufficiently subservient in his manners towards her; and from this she deduces a 'rancorous mind' which, because of his popularity with the commons, will inevitably lead him to plan an insurrection. York's contribution to the indictment is to attribute to Gloucester the mismanagement in France he knows and has proclaimed Somerset to be responsible for; the Cardinal characteristically accuses his nephew of the maliciousness of mind he himself so abundantly possesses.

As Buckingham notes, such accusations will never do; and so he deflects the discussion towards large generalizations and the possibility of future disclosures of crimes in place of the search for present ones:

Tut, these are petty faults to faults unknown,
Which time will bring to light in smooth Duke Humphrey.
III.1.64–5

Each conspirator ransacks proverbial and fabular lore to express his conviction that Duke Humphrey's obvious goodness is a façade exceptional only in proportion to the enormity of potential for crime it conceals:

Small curs are not regarded when they grin,
But great men tremble when the lion roars . . . .

25

> *Smooth runs the water where the brook is deep. . . .*
>
> *The fox barks not when he would steal the lamb. . . .*
>
> *Seems he a dove? His feathers are but borrowed,*
> *For he's disposèd as the hateful raven.*
> *Is he a lamb? His skin is surely lent him,*
> *For he's inclined as is the ravenous wolves. . . .*
>
> *Gloucester's show*
> *Beguiles him as the mournful crocodile*
> *With sorrow snares relenting passengers;*
> *Or as the snake rolled in a flowering bank,*
> *With shining checkered slough, doth sting a child*
> *That for the beauty thinks it excellent.*
>
> III.1.18–19, 53, 55, 75–8, 225–30

Suffolk realizes, as does York, that the chance of
Gloucester's being 'condemned by course of law' is small,
in view of the King's favour, the commons' love, and the
triviality of the case they can allege against him. And so he
enunciates the standards of the animal world which have
been lurking behind the discussion throughout the
scene:

> *do not stand on quillets how to slay him;*
> *Be it by gins, by snares, by subtlety,*
> *Sleeping or waking, 'tis no matter how,*
> *So he be dead.*   III.1.261–4

Nothing can protect Gloucester against this decision of
brute dispatch. For all its courtly trappings, this action is
as mindless as Suffolk's own later murder by the pirates
and Cade's sentencing of Lord Say and the Clerk of
Chartham. All these killings are the consequence when
the law ceases and the personal whim of the momentarily
powerful is substituted for it, when

Virtue is choked with foul ambition,
And charity chased hence by rancour's hand;
Foul subornation is predominant,
And equity exiled your highness' land.   III.1.143–6

In the next scene (III.2), Shakespeare makes concrete for the audience the vision conveyed by these lines. The actual murder takes place offstage, so that its awful results can be displayed as Warwick provides his Grand Guignol commentary over the body of the one character in the play who really 'tugged for life, and was by strength subdued'.

This is the moment at which all possibility of order disappears from the England of the play. The temporary unity imposed on the factious peers by a shared antagonism vanishes. The Cardinal exits, to die in a hideous parody of Gloucester's end: 'So bad a death argues a monstrous life' (III.3.30). Warwick, the political manager, immediately seizes the opportunity to move against Suffolk. From the role of poet of charnel-house horror, he proceeds calmly to that of prosecuting counsel and deduces foul play from the physical evidence to accuse Suffolk in proverbial terms ironically similar to those used against the Protector:

Who finds the heifer dead and bleeding fresh,
And sees fast by a butcher with an axe,
But will suspect 'twas he that made the slaughter?
Who finds the partridge in the puttock's nest,
But may imagine how the bird was dead,
Although the kite soar with unbloodied beak?
                                        III.2.188–93

Warwick is not yet the 'arrogant controller' the Queen describes him as being; and he can be baited by her lover first into a slanging-match about his legitimacy and later into a symbolic drawing of his sword in the King's presence; but he is effective enough as York's agent in the scene.

The division released by Gloucester's death is seen to be generally infectious. The commons, whom the Queen had hypocritically feared as a potential force for commotion under Gloucester's rebellious leadership, now, simply because they lack their leader, 'scatter up and down | And care not who they sting in his revenge' (III.2.126–7). Even as Warwick assumed control of the investigation into the murder, so his father, Salisbury, appoints himself spokesman of the aroused mob, and makes the most of their undirected anger in order to make Suffolk's banishment the condition of its peace:

> Dread lord, the commons send you word by me,
> Unless Lord Suffolk straight be done to death,
> Or banishèd fair England's territories,
> They will by violence tear him from your palace
> And torture him with grievous lingering death.
> They say by him the good Duke Humphrey died;
> They say in him they fear your highness' death;
> And mere instinct of love and loyalty,
> Free from a stubborn opposite intent,
> As being thought to contradict your liking,
> Makes them thus forward in his banishment.
>
> III.2.243–53

What we are witnessing here is the skilful manipulation of popular unrest by both the Nevils, so that the most powerful nobleman of the Lancastrian party, and therefore the real threat to York's monarchical ambitions, will be removed from England. Suffolk himself is acute enough to see what Salisbury is about:

> *'Tis like the commons, rude unpolished hinds,*
> *Could send such message to their sovereign.*
> *But you, my lord, were glad to be employed,*
> *To show how quaint an orator you are.*

> III.2.271–4

The banishment of Margaret's paramour is thus as much a triumph of unscrupulous manoeuvre as was Gloucester's death. Together these events are a signal for the release of the powers which are able to threaten the throne itself. King Henry has been deprived at a blow of the man whose confident exercise of the law presupposed a stable royal authority and the man whose selfish power-lust required a royal authority sufficiently strong to be worth his management.

✳

With Gloucester's demise the King himself becomes the representative of his Protector's virtues; but he is a far more complex character, because he raises questions about the relationship between morality and government which go far beyond his uncle's principles of craftily applied justice.

It is easy to see Henry VI, as many critics have, as a religious and amatory sentimentalist, weak to the point of idiocy, and the most politically unfit of all Shakespeare's rulers. The portrait is clearly based on the character found in the chronicles; as Edward Hall (page 208) has it:

> *there could be none more chaste, more meek, more holy, nor a better creature. In him reigned shamefastness, modesty, integrity, and patience to be marvelled at. . . . He gaped not for honour, nor thirsted for riches, but studied only for the health of his soul, the saving whereof he esteemed to be the greatest wisdom and the loss thereof the extremest folly that could be.*

The Henry of the play is a genuinely religious man: not because of his consistently meek demeanour, or because he is conventionally pious, or because biblical echoes and quotations come readily to his mind. Rather it is because of the way in which the reality of the Godhead's existence is at the centre of his consciousness. He sees *all* human events in the context of a divinely ordered eternity and *all* moral choices in terms of truly eternal verities. This means that no political moment can have for him the terrible pressure it exercises on all other characters in the play. For Henry, human limitation is the only reality; and, whereas everyone else – from Eleanor, who, before her fall, wishes only perpetuation of this world's pleasures, to Suffolk, who is so incredulous of his fate – acts with the conviction that death is always for others, he alone sees in Gloucester's corpse 'my life in death'.

In the opening scene, Henry's obvious physical attraction to Margaret must, to be acceptable to him, be invested with some religious value:

> *I can express no kinder sign of love*
> *Than this kind kiss. O Lord that lends me life,*
> *Lend me a heart replete with thankfulness!*
> *For Thou hast given me in this beauteous face*
> *A world of earthly blessings to my soul.*

> I.1.18–22

The same cast of mind is obvious in his enjoyment of falconry principally as an example of God's natural design (II.1.5–7). At Saint Albans all his instincts strain to see Simpcox's 'miracle' as a divine ray of light sent to a sinful world (II.1.64–5); and his response to Gloucester's demonstration of fraud is real pain that God has been wronged (II.1.150), even as the news of Eleanor's witchcraft brings him only grief at the confusion the wicked heap on their own heads (II.1.181–2). In the face of the clearest evidence of guilt he refuses to judge the Cardinal, on the grounds that 'we are sinners all' (III.3.31); and he laments that Cade's rebels must perish by the sword, because even their treason is further proof of a simplicity and ignorance comparable to that of the crowds that mocked Christ at his crucifixion (IV.4.38).

This total religious conviction spreads naturally to the exercises of his kingly office. In someone who can take the loss of France merely as an expression of God's will, it is not surprising that his management of his jarring nobles is marked only by a belief that truth, loyalty, and innocence will prevail. Henry really means it when he says

> *What stronger breastplate than a heart untainted!*
> *Thrice is he armed that hath his quarrel just;*
> *And he but naked, though locked up in steel,*
> *Whose conscience with injustice is corrupted.*
>
> III.2.232–5

It is for this reason that he can commit Gloucester to trial confident that he can 'clear [himself] from all suspense' (III.1.140).

Henry VI is Shakespeare's dramatic portrayal of Christian belief in political action. Religion is not for him (as it was to be in Shakespeare's stage portrait of his father, Henry V) one weapon in the armoury of an effective ruler; it is rather consistent love, faith, and charity operating on a daily basis in the affairs of men. This is why he strikes so many students of the play as a fool; but he is the kind of fool Erasmus proved Christ to be in his *Praise of Folly*. All of the sharply-worded pictures we get of his ineffectual piety come from characters whose far different values we know well. Margaret's depiction of her husband as a man more fit to be pope than king (I.3.53–62) bears the stamp of a sexually disappointed

31

woman whose highest values are courtliness, proportion, and the sort of mindless courage Suffolk displays. York's scorn of Henry's 'church-like humours' and 'bookish rule' emanates from a mind which conceives kingship in terms of the labouring spider weaving snares to trap its enemies, of the stinging snake causing the deaths of those who cherish it, and of the energetic madman with sharp weapons in his irresponsible hands (III.1.339–47). Certainly one can contrast Henry with Gloucester to prove that goodness and ineffectiveness need not go together; yet the Protector's fate indicates that pragmatic shrewdness also has its limitations. In fact, Henry's career illustrates more clearly than Gloucester's fall that impasse analysed appropriately by Niccolò Machiavelli in *The Prince* (1513):

> *Our religion has given more glory to humble and contemplative men than to active ones. It has, besides, taught that the highest good consists in humility, lowliness, and contempt for human things. . . . If our religion does ask that you possess some courage, it prefers that you be ready to suffer rather than to do a courageous act. It seems, then, that this way of life has made the world feeble, and given it over as a prey to the wicked, who are able to control it in security, since the generality of men, in order to go to heaven, think more of enduring injuries than in defending themselves against them.*

When such a king as this is no longer protected by Gloucester, the progress to chaos is swift. York is clearly the most self-disciplined of his enemies. His early cautious use of circumstances not of his own making, but which can be turned to his advantage, is of a piece with his lurking behind active agents: Warwick and Salisbury at court, Jack Cade at large in the nation. It is to flesh out the necessarily shadowy figure thus produced that Shakespeare employs the two soliloquies at the ends of I.1 and III.1. This theatrical device by its very nature puts us in closer touch with the mind of York than with that of any other character; so that, when he reappears at the head of his Irish forces in V.1, after being absent from the stage since III.1, he has been sufficiently strongly characterized to be dramatically acceptable as the strong leader of a public challenge to royal authority. The first of these speeches is actually a proof of York's possession of all those faults that are later alleged against Gloucester: self-interested horror at the loss of Anjou and Maine and the humiliating marriage settlement, his ambition to be king because of a consciousness of his lineage, and his willingness to scheme and gather allies who will support his claim by rebellion. In the second speech, he rejoices at his unexpected good fortune in being presented with the military means to start a civil war; and he informs the audience that his surrogate while he is in Ireland will be Jack Cade.

It is to the Cade revolt that Shakespeare devotes the fourth act of the play, in which a succession of short scenes reflects structurally the national disintegration. These frightening scenes work on a number of levels; but, taken together they are a dramatization of the destructive forces unleashed by division, stripped bare of their courtly trappings, the pretensions to civilized behaviour, and the semblance of the legal process. Cade and his mob act out the full implications of a time when, in Gloucester's words, 'Foul subornation is predominant'.

Shakespeare makes sure that we realize that we are witnessing a crude burlesque both of the peers' better-phrased concern for the state and of York's monarchical claims. Even before Cade appears, his followers provide a comic counterpoint to the nobles' convictions about the inadequacy of established authority and the necessity for replacing it with their own myopically viewed version of acceptable rule:

BEVIS *O miserable age! Virtue is not regarded in handi-craftsmen.*

HOLLAND *The nobility think scorn to go in leather aprons.*

BEVIS *Nay, more; the King's Council are no good work-men.*

HOLLAND *True; and yet it is said 'Labour in thy vocation'; which is as much to say as 'Let the magistrates be labour-ing men'; and therefore should we be magistrates.*

IV.2.10–18

The nobles' coveting Gloucester's Protectorship of the realm is grotesquely reduced by Cade himself to this:

> *Go to, sirrah, tell the King from me that for his father's sake, Henry the Fifth, in whose time boys went to span-counter for French crowns, I am content he shall reign; but I'll be Protector over him.* IV.2.147–50

As well as being York's agent, Cade is also a *reductio ad absurdum* of him: the Duke's careful recital of his dynastic rights for Warwick and Salisbury in II.2 finds its counterpart in the rebel's ludicrous family history; York's emphasis on his military achievements is echoed by Cade's crude incitements to violence; the man of action's scorn for Henry's bookish rule is reduced to an ignoramus's horror at the monstrosity of a clerk's being able to 'write and read and cast accompt' (IV.2.80–81).

However, these scenes are more than a low-level actualization of the forces motivating York; they also offer the audience a glimpse of the society pictured by Ulysses where

> *Strength should be lord of imbecility. . . .*
> *Force should be right; or, rather, right and wrong –*
> *Between whose endless jar justice resides –*
> *Should lose their names, and so should justice too.*
> *Then everything includes itself in power,*
> *Power into will, will into appetite.*
>
> *Troilus and Cressida,* I.3.114, 116–20

Education in the person of the Clerk of Chartham and law in the form of Lord Say are pilloried and destroyed, the latter with the Gloucester-like sentiments on his lips:

> *The trust I have is in mine innocence,*
> *And therefore am I bold and resolute.*
>
> IV.4.59–60

The prisons are emptied of felons to swell Cade's following; nominal honours are distributed in accordance with the narrow ambitions of their recipients; individualism vanishes in the wild grouping of classes for the purpose of denigration; and the Swiftian extreme is reached when parliament becomes the stinking mouth of Cade himself.

It is noticeable that Shakespeare modified the picture of the Kentish rebel that he found in his sources, where he is treated with respect as an individual and his motivations are politically coherent. By drawing on the chronicles' account of the far more brutish Peasants' Revolt of 1381 as well as on his own ability to fuse in the character the qualities of clownishness and threat, Shakespeare achieved for the first time in his career something that was to be a hallmark of his later work: namely, an easy movement through the immediate dramatic situation and its special relevance for the plot to a basic human pattern. In this case, it is the one assumed when any demagogue is successful in persuading people to act as an uncritical

35

collective. Initially individuals in the mob, like Dick and Smith, can display a healthy common-sense scepticism about the whole proceedings, as their asides on Cade's claims to royal blood indicate:

CADE *My father was a Mortimer –*
DICK *(aside) He was an honest man and a good bricklayer.*
CADE *My mother a Plantagenet –*
DICK *(aside) I knew her well; she was a midwife.*
CADE *My wife descended of the Lacys –*
DICK *(aside) She was indeed a pedlar's daughter, and sold many laces.*
SMITH *(aside) But now of late, not able to travel with her furred pack, she washes bucks here at home.*

IV.2.37–45

But as their leader's vulgar energy and intellectual simplifications fulfil their limited desires and vindicate their deeply held prejudices, the drive towards senseless violence and destruction becomes inevitable.

Cade is defeated politically by Old Clifford's skilfully worded appeal and the promise of royal clemency. The speech is a blatant tapping of patriotic fervour in the face of a non-existent French invasion:

Were't not a shame, that whilst you live at jar,
The fearful French, whom you late vanquishèd,
Should make a start o'er seas and vanquish you?
Methinks already in this civil broil
I see them lording it in London streets,
Crying 'Villiago'! unto all they meet.
Better ten thousand base-born Cades miscarry
Than you should stoop unto a Frenchman's mercy.
To France! To France! And get what you have lost.

IV.8.40–48

This is successful not because it is true but because (as

Cade himself notes) the mob's capacity to be blown about like a feather is infinite.

Shakespeare also supplies a suitably symbolic end for Cade in the Kentish garden of Alexander Iden. This English squire represents the stability of society built into its traditional forms that Cade wished to destroy. He prefers the even tenor of peace to the excitements of strife and its possibilities; he is satisfied with his patrimony, and his little garden of state has remained uncorrupted by ambition:

> Lord, who would live turmoilèd in the court,
> And may enjoy such quiet walks as these?
> This small inheritance my father left me
> Contenteth me, and worth a monarchy.
> I seek not to wax great by others' waning,
> Or gather wealth I care not with what envy;
> Sufficeth that I have maintains my state,
> And sends the poor well pleasèd from my gate.
>
> IV.10.15–22

Nor would Cade himself have been turned away empty-handed. In a fine piece of emblematic writing, Shakespeare depicts Iden as a monolithic example of anonymous national sanity:

> Nay, it shall ne'er be said, while England stands,
> That Alexander Iden, an esquire of Kent,
> Took odds to combat a poor famished man.
> Oppose thy steadfast gazing eyes to mine,
> See if thou canst outface me with thy looks;
> Set limb to limb, and thou art far the lesser;
> Thy hand is but a finger to my fist;
> Thy leg a stick comparèd with this truncheon;
> My foot shall fight with all the strength thou hast;
> And if mine arm be heavèd in the air,
> Thy grave is digged already in the earth. IV.10.40–50

Cade is unable to accept either this opportunity or the figure offering it: the one he meets by recourse to the violence which has become his normal reaction to life, the other he attempts to devalue sneeringly as 'the most complete champion that ever I heard'.

*

With Cade's death, the open defiance of royal authority passes back to its originator – York. On his return from Ireland, his earlier caution and self-control have vanished. His machiavellian conviction that the only true king is an effective one can now be expressed openly:

> *Let them obey that knows not how to rule;*
> *This hand was made to handle naught but gold.*
> *I cannot give due action to my words,*
> *Except a sword or sceptre balance it. . . .*
> *'King' did I call thee? No, thou art not king;*
> *Not fit to govern and rule multitudes.*

V.1.6–9, 93–4

He is willing to back this theory of natural superiority by stirring up in England 'some black storm | Shall blow ten thousand souls to heaven or hell' until the golden circuit of the crown impales his head (III.1.348–54).

Shakespeare's arrangement of the scenes at the first Battle of Saint Albans ensures that the actual military confrontation is between Margaret and the Cliffords on the one hand and York and the Nevils on the other. Henry stands between them holding the crown until one or the other prevails. In the flyting before the battle, there are none of the conventional appeals to God, to the justness of a cause, no utterance of convinced moral rightness. The vocabulary seems deliberately chosen to convey a universal baseness: 'the bastard boys of York', 'blood-bespotted Neapolitan', 'Foul stigmatic', 'the bearard'

38

and 'the baiting-place', 'a hot o'erweening cur', 'heap of wrath, foul indigested lump'.

During the battle, a single moment of stillness is devised to sum up the end towards which the political manipulation, the ruthless ambition, the plotted tragedy of Gloucester, the depredations of Cade, and the obsessions of York have all been moving. Young Clifford finds his father's body mangled by 'ruffian battle' even in his chair-days. At first, he attempts to elevate his personal loss to the grand generality of doomsday:

> *O, let the vile world end,*
> *And the premised flames of the last day*
> *Knit earth and heaven together.*
> *Now let the general trumpet blow his blast.*
>
> V.2.40–43

However, the real effect of his filial passion is much more frightening, because it constitutes that human capacity to translate the political into terms of the individual which the play has shown to be the source of chaos and self-perpetuating strife:

> *My heart is turned to stone, and while 'tis mine*
> *It shall be stony. York not our old men spares;*
> *No more will I their babes; tears virginal*
> *Shall be to me even as the dew to fire;*
> *And beauty, that the tyrant oft reclaims,*
> *Shall to my flaming wrath be oil and flax.*
> *Henceforth, I will not have to do with pity.*
>
> V.2.50–56

On the Yorkist side, the same note is struck by Richard, who has only a small part in this play, but who brought to the stage from Thomas More's and the chronicles' caricatures of him a legend which loads his lines with more than their intrinsic malevolence:

> *Sword, hold thy temper; heart, be wrathful still;*
> *Priests pray for enemies, but princes kill.*   V.2.70–71

The final scene records the Yorkists' victory; but even they recognize that one victory does not mean that this war is won:

> *Well, lords, we have not got that which we have;*
> *'Tis not enough our foes are this time fled,*
> *Being opposites of such repairing nature.*   V.3.20–22

Salisbury is right in this. For the Lancastrians, Henry characteristically utters the providential truth: 'Can we outrun the heavens?' But Margaret's urging flight to London, 'where this breach now in our fortunes made | May readily be stopped' (V.2.73, 82–3), is a more accurate indicator of the impetus both sides share in the seesawing world of all-out civil war, where

> *The best lack all conviction, while the worst*
> *Are full of passionate intensity.*
>   W. B. Yeats, *The Second Coming*

FURTHER READING

GOOD surveys of scholarly and critical work done on the play
are those by Harold Jenkins in *Shakespeare Survey 6*
(Cambridge, 1953); by Ronald Berman in *A Reader's Guide to
Shakespeare's Plays* (second edition, New York, 1973); and by
A. R. Humphreys in *Shakespeare: Select Bibliographical
Guides*, edited by Stanley Wells (Oxford, 1974).

Text, Date, and Authorship
The best reproduction of the text in the first Folio is in *The
Norton Facsimile: The First Folio of Shakespeare*, prepared
by Charlton Hinman (New York, 1968), and the most detailed
analysis of it is in the same scholar's *The Printing and Proof-
reading of the First Folio of Shakespeare* (2 volumes, Oxford,
1963). A facsimile of the Quarto, *The First Part of the Contention
betwixt the Two Famous Houses of York and Lancaster*, was
prepared by J. S. Farmer for Tudor Facsimile Texts in 1913
(reprinted by AMS, New York, 1970). In 1790 Edmond
Malone claimed that Shakespeare had reworked this play into
2 Henry VI, a view which was accepted until 1928–9, when Peter
Alexander (*Shakespeare's 'Henry VI' and 'Richard III'*,
Cambridge, 1929) and Madeleine Doran (*'Henry VI, 2 and 3'*
in *University of Iowa Humanistic Studies*, VI, 4, 1928) proved it
to be a corrupt reported version of Shakespeare's original play.
Some scholars remained unconvinced by the work of Alexander
and Doran; examples of the arguments against it may be found
in J. Dover Wilson's New Cambridge edition of the play
(Cambridge, 1952) and Charles T. Prouty's *'The Contention'
and Shakespeare's '2 Henry VI'* (New Haven, Connecticut,
1954). There are valuable appraisals of the relationship
between the two texts by W. W. Greg (*The Shakespeare First
Folio*, Oxford, 1955) and by Andrew S. Cairncross in his
new Arden edition (London, 1957).

Adherents of the revision theory see the Folio text as being a mixture of the work of Shakespeare, Robert Greene, Thomas Nashe, and George Peele. The fullest treatment of the evidence for multiple authorship is found in Wilson's edition. Followers of Alexander and Doran view the play as totally by a young Shakespeare working under the influence of popular contemporary dramatists and gradually finding his own voice as he worked through the three parts. The play is variously dated between 1588 and 1592, according to the theories held about the authorship, the relationship between *The Contention* and the Folio text, and the companies that probably acted them. The most recent clear presentation of the dating evidence is Hanspeter Born's article, 'The Date of *2, 3 Henry VI*' (*Shakespeare Quarterly* 25 (1974), 323–34).

Sources

The chronicles of Edward Hall, Raphael Holinshed, Robert Fabyan, and Richard Grafton are available in early nineteenth-century reprints; the details are given at the head of the Commentary. There is a good general article on the use of the chronicles in all three parts of the play by R. A. Law in *Texas Studies in English* 33 (1955), 13–32. Geoffrey Bullough's introduction to his source selection in *Narrative and Dramatic Sources of Shakespeare* III (London, 1960), 89–100, is an invaluable balanced essay. In addition to his selections from the chronicles, Bullough also quotes the passages Shakespeare probably used in John Foxe's *Acts and Monuments* (1583).

Criticism

A number of useful books supply accounts of Elizabethan attitudes to history. E. M. W. Tillyard's influential *The Elizabethan World Picture* (London, 1943) gives a summary of the official theory of government, and there are full studies of the history plays of the period in Irving Ribner's *The English History Play in the Age of Shakespeare* (Princeton, N.J., 1957; revised edition London, 1965) and David M. Bevington's *Tudor Drama and Politics: A Critical Approach to Topical Meaning* (Cambridge, Mass., 1968).

Among studies of the history plays which see them as reflecting orthodox Elizabethan political beliefs are Tillyard's *Shakespeare's History Plays* (London, 1944), Lily B. Campbell's *Shakespeare's 'Histories': Mirrors of Elizabethan Policy* (San Marino, California, 1947), M. M. Reese's *The Cease of Majesty: A Study of Shakespeare's History Plays* (London, 1961), and S. C. Sen Gupta's *Shakespeare's Historical Plays* (Oxford, 1964). Recent critics have tended to find the plays less conservative in their political ideas. For example, Henry A. Kelly, in his *Divine Providence in the England of Shakespeare's Histories* (Cambridge, Mass., 1970), worked out freshly how Shakespeare treated the ideas he found in the chronicles; and Michael Manheim's *The Weak King Dilemma in the Shakespearean History Play* (Syracuse, N.Y., 1973) contains penetrating sympathetic analyses of Henry VI and the Duke of Gloucester.

There have been a number of full studies of the *Henry VI* sequence. R. B. Pierce examines the family–state correspondences in *Shakespeare's History Plays: The Family and the State* (Columbus, Ohio, 1971); E. W. Talbert's *Elizabethan Drama and Shakespeare's Early Plays* (Chapel Hill, North Carolina, 1963) shows a fine awareness of the problems of dramatizing history; David Riggs has some good comment on how the characters reflect political beliefs in *Shakespeare's Heroical Histories: 'Henry VI' and Its Literary Tradition* (Cambridge, Mass., 1971). Various studies emphasize particular aspects of the plays: Don M. Ricks in *Shakespeare's Emergent Form* (Logan, Utah, 1968) examines the structural principles; Robert Ornstein is perspicacious on character and style in *A Kingdom for a Stage: The Achievement of Shakespeare's History Plays* (Cambridge, Mass., 1972); Edward I. Berry's *Patterns of Decay: Shakespeare's Early Histories* (Charlottesville, Virginia, 1975) is a well-written exploration of the way central themes are embodied; and Robert Y. Turner's *Shakespeare's Apprenticeship* (Chicago, 1974) contains a subtle appreciation of aspects of the plays' dramaturgy. The most stimulating shorter essays on the sequence are J. P. Brockbank's in *Early Shakespeare* (Stratford-upon-Avon

43

Studies No. 3), edited by J. R. Brown and Bernard Harris (London, 1961), and A. C. Hamilton's in his *The Early Shakespeare* (San Marino, California, 1967). The fullest treatment of the imagery patterns in the plays is C. M. Kay's essay in *Studies in the Literary Imagination* 1 (1972), 1–26.

Accounts of how the plays have fared on the stage can be found in C. B. Young's notes in Dover Wilson's editions and in Arthur Colby Sprague's *Shakespeare's Histories: Plays for the Stage* (London, 1964). Particular productions are discussed in Sir Barry Jackson's 'On Producing *Henry VI*', *Shakespeare Survey* 6 (1953), and John Russell Brown's analysis of Peter Hall's and John Barton's version, *The Wars of the Roses*, in *Shakespeare's Plays in Performance* (London, 1966).

THE SECOND PART OF
KING HENRY THE SIXTH

THE CHARACTERS IN THE PLAY

KING HENRY THE SIXTH
Margaret, QUEEN of England, daughter of King Reignier
DUKE OF YORK, Richard Plantagenet
EDWARD ⎱ sons of the Duke of York
RICHARD ⎰
DUKE OF GLOUCESTER, Humphrey of Lancaster, Protector of England, uncle of the King
DUCHESS OF GLOUCESTER, Eleanor Cobham
CARDINAL BEAUFORT, Bishop of Winchester, great-uncle of the King
DUKE OF SUFFOLK, William de la Pole
DUKE OF SOMERSET, Edmund Beaufort
DUKE OF BUCKINGHAM, Humphrey Stafford
EARL OF SALISBURY, Richard Nevil
EARL OF WARWICK, Richard Nevil, son of the Earl of Salisbury
LORD CLIFFORD
YOUNG CLIFFORD, son of Lord Clifford
LORD SCALES
LORD SAY
SIR HUMPHREY STAFFORD
William Stafford, BROTHER of Sir Humphrey Stafford
SIR JOHN STANLEY
VAUX
ALEXANDER IDEN, a Kentish gentleman

JOHN HUME, a priest
JOHN SOUTHWELL, a priest
ROGER BOLINGBROKE, a conjurer

THE CHARACTERS IN THE PLAY

MARGERY JOURDAIN, a witch
A SPIRIT

THOMAS HORNER, an armourer
PETER THUMP, Horner's assistant
PETITIONERS
NEIGHBOURS
PRENTICES

SAUNDER SIMPCOX
WIFE of Simpcox
A MAN
MAYOR of Saint Albans
A BEADLE

JACK CADE
GEORGE BEVIS
JOHN HOLLAND
DICK, a butcher   } followers of Jack Cade
SMITH, a weaver
MICHAEL

A LIEUTENANT
A MASTER
A MASTER'S MATE
WALTER WHITMORE
Two GENTLEMEN, prisoners with Suffolk

MESSENGERS
SERVANTS
A HERALD
A SHERIFF
A POST
MURDERERS

COMMONS
CLERK OF CHARTHAM
A CITIZEN
A SOLDIER

Guards, soldiers, servants, attendants, falconers, aldermen, neighbours, prentices, officers, a sawyer, citizens, Matthew Gough

Flourish of trumpets, then hautboys. Enter the King, I.1
Gloucester, Salisbury, Warwick, and Cardinal
Beaufort on the one side; the Queen, Suffolk, York,
Somerset, and Buckingham on the other

SUFFOLK

As by your high imperial majesty
I had in charge at my depart for France,
As procurator to your excellence,
To marry Princess Margaret for your grace;
So, in the famous ancient city Tours,
In presence of the Kings of France and Sicil,
The Dukes of Orleans, Calaber, Bretagne, and Alençon,
Seven earls, twelve barons, and twenty reverend bishops,
I have performed my task and was espoused;
And humbly now upon my bended knee,   10
   (*He kneels*)
In sight of England and her lordly peers,
Deliver up my title in the Queen
To your most gracious hands, that are the substance
Of that great shadow I did represent –
The happiest gift that ever marquess gave,
The fairest queen that ever king received.

KING

Suffolk, arise. Welcome, Queen Margaret.
I can express no kinder sign of love
Than this kind kiss. O Lord that lends me life,
Lend me a heart replete with thankfulness!   20
For Thou hast given me in this beauteous face

A world of earthly blessings to my soul,
If sympathy of love unite our thoughts.

QUEEN

Great King of England and my gracious lord,
The mutual conference that my mind hath had
By day, by night, waking and in my dreams,
In courtly company or at my beads,
With you, mine alderliefest sovereign,
Makes me the bolder to salute my king

30   With ruder terms, such as my wit affords,
And overjoy of heart doth minister.

KING

Her sight did ravish, but her grace in speech,
Her words y-clad with wisdom's majesty,
Makes me from wondering fall to weeping joys,
Such is the fullness of my heart's content.
Lords, with one cheerful voice welcome my love.
        All kneel

ALL

Long live Queen Margaret, England's happiness!
        Flourish

QUEEN

We thank you all.

SUFFOLK

My Lord Protector, so it please your grace,

40   Here are the articles of contracted peace
Between our sovereign and the French King Charles,
For eighteen months concluded by consent.

GLOUCESTER (*reads*) *Imprimis, it is agreed between the
French King Charles and William de la Pole, Marquess of
Suffolk, ambassador for Henry King of England, that the
said Henry shall espouse the Lady Margaret, daughter
unto Reignier King of Naples, Sicilia, and Jerusalem,
and crown her Queen of England ere the thirtieth of May
next ensuing. Item, it is further agreed between them that*

the duchy of Anjou and the county of Maine shall be 50
released and delivered over to the King her father –
   (*Gloucester lets the contract fall*)

KING

Uncle, how now?

GLOUCESTER   Pardon me, gracious lord.
Some sudden qualm hath struck me at the heart
And dimmed mine eyes, that I can read no further.

KING

Uncle of Winchester, I pray read on.

CARDINAL (*reads*) *Item, it is further agreed between them*
that the duchy of Anjou and the county of Maine shall
be released and delivered over to the King her father,
and she sent over of the King of England's own proper
cost and charges, without having any dowry. 60

KING

They please us well. Lord Marquess, kneel down.
We here create thee the first Duke of Suffolk
And girt thee with the sword. Cousin of York,
We here discharge your grace from being Regent
I'the parts of France, till term of eighteen months
Be full expired. Thanks, uncle Winchester,
Gloucester, York, Buckingham, Somerset,
Salisbury, and Warwick.
We thank you all for this great favour done
In entertainment to my princely Queen. 70
Come, let us in, and with all speed provide
To see her coronation be performed.

              Exeunt King, Queen, and Suffolk
   Gloucester stays all the rest

GLOUCESTER

Brave peers of England, pillars of the state,
To you Duke Humphrey must unload his grief,
Your grief, the common grief of all the land.
What? Did my brother Henry spend his youth,

His valour, coin, and people in the wars?
Did he so often lodge in open field,
In winter's cold and summer's parching heat,
80 To conquer France, his true inheritance?
And did my brother Bedford toil his wits
To keep by policy what Henry got?
Have you yourselves, Somerset, Buckingham,
Brave York, Salisbury, and victorious Warwick,
Received deep scars in France and Normandy?
Or hath mine uncle Beaufort and myself,
With all the learnèd Council of the realm,
Studied so long, sat in the Council House
Early and late, debating to and fro
90 How France and Frenchmen might be kept in awe?
And had his highness in his infancy
Crownèd in Paris in despite of foes?
And shall these labours and these honours die?
Shall Henry's conquest, Bedford's vigilance,
Your deeds of war, and all our counsel die?
O peers of England, shameful is this league,
Fatal this marriage, cancelling your fame,
Blotting your names from books of memory,
Razing the characters of your renown,
100 Defacing monuments of conquered France,
Undoing all, as all had never been!

CARDINAL
Nephew, what means this passionate discourse,
This peroration with such circumstance?
For France, 'tis ours; and we will keep it still.

GLOUCESTER
Ay, uncle, we will keep it, if we can;
But now it is impossible we should.
Suffolk, the new-made duke that rules the roast,
Hath given the duchy of Anjou and Maine
Unto the poor King Reignier, whose large style

Agrees not with the leanness of his purse. 110

SALISBURY

Now by the death of Him that died for all,
These counties were the keys of Normandy.
But wherefore weeps Warwick, my valiant son?

WARWICK

For grief that they are past recovery;
For, were there hope to conquer them again,
My sword should shed hot blood, mine eyes no tears.
Anjou and Maine? Myself did win them both;
Those provinces these arms of mine did conquer;
And are the cities that I got with wounds
Delivered up again with peaceful words? 120
Mort Dieu!

YORK

For Suffolk's duke, may he be suffocate,
That dims the honour of this warlike isle!
France should have torn and rent my very heart
Before I would have yielded to this league.
I never read but England's kings have had
Large sums of gold and dowries with their wives;
And our King Henry gives away his own,
To match with her that brings no vantages.

GLOUCESTER

A proper jest, and never heard before, 130
That Suffolk should demand a whole fifteenth
For costs and charges in transporting her!
She should have stayed in France, and starved in France,
Before –

CARDINAL

My lord of Gloucester, now ye grow too hot;
It was the pleasure of my lord the King.

GLOUCESTER

My lord of Winchester, I know your mind;
'Tis not my speeches that you do mislike,

But 'tis my presence that doth trouble ye.
140 Rancour will out; proud prelate, in thy face
I see thy fury. If I longer stay,
We shall begin our ancient bickerings.
Lordings, farewell; and say, when I am gone,
I prophesied France will be lost ere long.

Exit Gloucester

CARDINAL
So there goes our Protector in a rage.
'Tis known to you he is mine enemy;
Nay more, an enemy unto you all,
And no great friend, I fear me, to the King.
Consider, lords, he is the next of blood
150 And heir apparent to the English crown.
Had Henry got an empire by his marriage,
And all the wealthy kingdoms of the west,
There's reason he should be displeased at it.
Look to it, lords; let not his smoothing words
Bewitch your hearts. Be wise and circumspect.
What though the common people favour him,
Calling him 'Humphrey, the good Duke of Gloucester',
Clapping their hands and crying with loud voice
'Jesu maintain your royal excellence!'
160 With 'God preserve the good Duke Humphrey!',
I fear me, lords, for all this flattering gloss,
He will be found a dangerous Protector.

BUCKINGHAM
Why should he then protect our sovereign,
He being of age to govern of himself?
Cousin of Somerset, join you with me,
And all together, with the Duke of Suffolk,
We'll quickly hoise Duke Humphrey from his seat.

CARDINAL
This weighty business will not brook delay;
I'll to the Duke of Suffolk presently.   *Exit*

SOMERSET
> Cousin of Buckingham, though Humphrey's pride   170
> And greatness of his place be grief to us,
> Yet let us watch the haughty Cardinal;
> His insolence is more intolerable
> Than all the princes' in the land beside.
> If Gloucester be displaced, he'll be Protector.

BUCKINGHAM
> Or thou or I, Somerset, will be Protector,
> Despite Duke Humphrey or the Cardinal.

> *Exeunt Buckingham and Somerset*

SALISBURY
> Pride went before; Ambition follows him.
> While these do labour for their own preferment,
> Behoves it us to labour for the realm.   180
> I never saw but Humphrey Duke of Gloucester
> Did bear him like a noble gentleman.
> Oft have I seen the haughty Cardinal,
> More like a soldier than a man o'th'church,
> As stout and proud as he were lord of all,
> Swear like a ruffian, and demean himself
> Unlike the ruler of a commonweal.
> Warwick, my son, the comfort of my age,
> Thy deeds, thy plainness, and thy house-keeping
> Hath won the greatest favour of the commons,   190
> Excepting none but good Duke Humphrey;
> And, brother York, thy acts in Ireland,
> In bringing them to civil discipline,
> Thy late exploits done in the heart of France,
> When thou wert Regent for our sovereign,
> Have made thee feared and honoured of the people.
> Join we together for the public good,
> In what we can to bridle and suppress
> The pride of Suffolk and the Cardinal,
> With Somerset's and Buckingham's ambition;   200

    And, as we may, cherish Duke Humphrey's deeds
    While they do tend the profit of the land.

WARWICK

    So God help Warwick, as he loves the land
    And common profit of his country!

YORK

    And so says York – (*aside*) for he hath greatest cause.

SALISBURY

    Then let's make haste away, and look unto the main.

WARWICK

    Unto the main! O father, Maine is lost!
    That Maine which by main force Warwick did win,
    And would have kept so long as breath did last!
210   Main chance, father, you meant; but I meant Maine,
    Which I will win from France or else be slain.

                  Exeunt Warwick and Salisbury

YORK

    Anjou and Maine are given to the French;
    Paris is lost; the state of Normandy
    Stands on a tickle point now they are gone.
    Suffolk concluded on the articles,
    The peers agreed, and Henry was well pleased
    To change two dukedoms for a duke's fair daughter.
    I cannot blame them all; what is't to them?
    'Tis thine they give away, and not their own.
220   Pirates may make cheap pennyworths of their pillage
    And purchase friends and give to courtesans,
    Still revelling like lords till all be gone;
    While as the silly owner of the goods
    Weeps over them, and wrings his hapless hands,
    And shakes his head, and trembling stands aloof,
    While all is shared and all is borne away,
    Ready to starve, and dare not touch his own.
    So York must sit and fret and bite his tongue,
    While his own lands are bargained for and sold.

Methinks the realms of England, France, and Ireland   230
Bear that proportion to my flesh and blood
As did the fatal brand Althaea burnt
Unto the Prince's heart of Calydon.
Anjou and Maine both given unto the French!
Cold news for me; for I had hope of France,
Even as I have of fertile England's soil.
A day will come when York shall claim his own,
And therefore I will take the Nevils' parts
And make a show of love to proud Duke Humphrey,
And, when I spy advantage, claim the crown,   240
For that's the golden mark I seek to hit.
Nor shall proud Lancaster usurp my right,
Nor hold the sceptre in his childish fist,
Nor wear the diadem upon his head,
Whose church-like humours fits not for a crown.
Then, York, be still awhile till time do serve;
Watch thou, and wake when others be asleep,
To pry into the secrets of the state,
Till Henry, surfeiting in joys of love
With his new bride and England's dear-bought queen,   250
And Humphrey with the peers be fallen at jars.
Then will I raise aloft the milk-white rose,
With whose sweet smell the air shall be perfumed,
And in my standard bear the arms of York,
To grapple with the house of Lancaster;
And force perforce I'll make him yield the crown,
Whose bookish rule hath pulled fair England down.

Exit

Enter the Duke of Gloucester and his wife the   I.2
Duchess

DUCHESS
Why droops my lord like over-ripened corn,
Hanging the head at Ceres' plenteous load?

59

Why doth the great Duke Humphrey knit his brows,
As frowning at the favours of the world?
Why are thine eyes fixed to the sullen earth,
Gazing on that which seems to dim thy sight?
What seest thou there? King Henry's diadem,
Enchased with all the honours of the world?
If so, gaze on, and grovel on thy face,
10 Until thy head be circled with the same.
Put forth thy hand, reach at the glorious gold.
What, is't too short? I'll lengthen it with mine;
And having both together heaved it up,
We'll both together lift our heads to heaven,
And never more abase our sight so low
As to vouchsafe one glance unto the ground.

GLOUCESTER

O Nell, sweet Nell, if thou dost love thy lord,
Banish the canker of ambitious thoughts!
And may that thought, when I imagine ill
20 Against my king and nephew, virtuous Henry,
Be my last breathing in this mortal world!
My troublous dreams this night doth make me sad.

DUCHESS

What dreamed my lord? Tell me, and I'll requite it
With sweet rehearsal of my morning's dream.

GLOUCESTER

Methought this staff, mine office-badge in court,
Was broke in twain – by whom I have forgot,
But, as I think, it was by the Cardinal –
And on the pieces of the broken wand
Were placed the heads of Edmund Duke of Somerset
30 And William de la Pole, first Duke of Suffolk.
This was my dream; what it doth bode, God knows.

DUCHESS

Tut, this was nothing but an argument
That he that breaks a stick of Gloucester's grove

Shall lose his head for his presumption.
But list to me, my Humphrey, my sweet Duke:
Methought I sat in seat of majesty
In the cathedral church of Westminster,
And in that chair where kings and queens were crowned,
Where Henry and Dame Margaret kneeled to me,
And on my head did set the diadem.   40

GLOUCESTER

Nay, Eleanor, then must I chide outright:
Presumptuous dame! Ill-nurtured Eleanor!
Art thou not second woman in the realm,
And the Protector's wife, beloved of him?
Hast thou not worldly pleasure at command
Above the reach or compass of thy thought?
And wilt thou still be hammering treachery,
To tumble down thy husband and thyself
From top of honour to disgrace's feet?
Away from me, and let me hear no more!   50

DUCHESS

What, what, my lord? Are you so choleric
With Eleanor, for telling but her dream?
Next time I'll keep my dreams unto myself,
And not be checked.

GLOUCESTER

Nay, be not angry; I am pleased again.
  Enter a Messenger

MESSENGER

My Lord Protector, 'tis his highness' pleasure
You do prepare to ride unto Saint Albans,
Where as the King and Queen do mean to hawk.

GLOUCESTER

I go. Come, Nell, thou wilt ride with us?

DUCHESS

Yes, my good lord, I'll follow presently.   60
  Exeunt Gloucester and Messenger

61

Follow I must; I cannot go before
While Gloucester bears this base and humble mind.
Were I a man, a duke, and next of blood,
I would remove these tedious stumbling-blocks
And smooth my way upon their headless necks;
And, being a woman, I will not be slack
To play my part in Fortune's pageant.
Where are you there? Sir John! Nay, fear not, man.
We are alone; here's none but thee and I.

Enter John Hume

HUME

70 Jesus preserve your royal majesty!

DUCHESS

What sayst thou? 'Majesty'! I am but 'grace'.

HUME

But, by the grace of God and Hume's advice,
Your grace's title shall be multiplied.

DUCHESS

What sayst thou, man? Hast thou as yet conferred
With Margery Jourdain, the cunning witch,
With Roger Bolingbroke, the conjurer?
And will they undertake to do me good?

HUME

This they have promised: to show your highness
A spirit raised from depth of under ground,

80 That shall make answer to such questions
As by your grace shall be propounded him.

DUCHESS

It is enough; I'll think upon the questions.
When from Saint Albans we do make return,
We'll see these things effected to the full.
Here, Hume, take this reward. Make merry, man,
With thy confederates in this weighty cause.   *Exit*

HUME

Hume must make merry with the Duchess' gold;
Marry, and shall. But how now, Sir John Hume?

Seal up your lips and give no words but mum;
The business asketh silent secrecy.   90
Dame Eleanor gives gold to bring the witch;
Gold cannot come amiss, were she a devil.
Yet have I gold flies from another coast –
I dare not say from the rich Cardinal
And from the great and new-made Duke of Suffolk.
Yet I do find it so; for, to be plain,
They, knowing Dame Eleanor's aspiring humour,
Have hired me to undermine the Duchess,
And buzz these conjurations in her brain.
They say 'A crafty knave does need no broker';   100
Yet am I Suffolk and the Cardinal's broker.
Hume, if you take not heed, you shall go near
To call them both a pair of crafty knaves.
Well, so it stands; and thus, I fear, at last
Hume's knavery will be the Duchess' wrack,
And her attainture will be Humphrey's fall.
Sort how it will, I shall have gold for all.   *Exit*

Enter four Petitioners, Peter, the armourer's man, I.3
being one

FIRST PETITIONER My masters, let's stand close. My
  Lord Protector will come this way by and by, and then
  we may deliver our supplications in the quill.
SECOND PETITIONER Marry, the Lord protect him,
  for he's a good man. Jesu bless him!
    Enter Suffolk and the Queen
PETER Here 'a comes, methinks, and the Queen with him.
  I'll be the first, sure.
SECOND PETITIONER Come back, fool. This is the Duke
  of Suffolk and not my Lord Protector.
SUFFOLK How now, fellow? Wouldst anything with me?   10
FIRST PETITIONER I pray, my lord, pardon me; I took ye
  for my Lord Protector.

QUEEN (*reads*) 'To my Lord Protector'? Are your supplications to his lordship? Let me see them. What is thine?

FIRST PETITIONER Mine is, an't please your grace,
against John Goodman, my lord Cardinal's man, for
keeping my house, and lands, and wife, and all, from me.

SUFFOLK Thy wife too! That's some wrong indeed. –
What's yours? What's here? (*Reads*) 'Against the Duke
20   of Suffolk, for enclosing the commons of Melford.'
How now, sir knave!

SECOND PETITIONER Alas, sir, I am but a poor petitioner
of our whole township.

PETER (*offering his petition*) Against my master, Thomas
Horner, for saying that the Duke of York was rightful
heir to the crown.

QUEEN What sayst thou? Did the Duke of York say he was
rightful heir to the crown?

PETER That my master was? No, forsooth; my master said
30   that he was, and that the King was an usurper.

SUFFOLK Who is there?

> *Enter a servant*

Take this fellow in, and send for his master with a pursuivant presently. We'll hear more of your matter before the King.   *Exit servant with Peter*

QUEEN
And as for you that love to be protected
Under the wings of our Protector's grace,
Begin your suits anew and sue to him.

> *She tears the supplications*

Away, base cullions! Suffolk, let them go.

ALL PETITIONERS Come, let's be gone.   *Exeunt*

QUEEN
40   My lord of Suffolk, say, is this the guise,
Is this the fashions in the court of England?
Is this the government of Britain's isle,
And this the royalty of Albion's king?

What, shall King Henry be a pupil still
Under the surly Gloucester's governance?
Am I a queen in title and in style,
And must be made a subject to a duke?
I tell thee, Pole, when in the city Tours
Thou rannest a tilt in honour of my love
And stolest away the ladies' hearts of France,   50
I thought King Henry had resembled thee
In courage, courtship, and proportion.
But all his mind is bent to holiness,
To number Ave-Maries on his beads;
His champions are the prophets and apostles,
His weapons holy saws of sacred writ;
His study is his tilt-yard, and his loves
Are brazen images of canonized saints.
I would the College of the Cardinals
Would choose him Pope, and carry him to Rome,   60
And set the triple crown upon his head –
That were a state fit for his holiness.

SUFFOLK

Madam, be patient. As I was cause
Your highness came to England, so will I
In England work your grace's full content.

QUEEN

Beside the haughty Protector have we Beaufort
The imperious churchman, Somerset, Buckingham,
And grumbling York; and not the least of these
But can do more in England than the King.

SUFFOLK

And he of these that can do most of all   70
Cannot do more in England than the Nevils;
Salisbury and Warwick are no simple peers.

QUEEN

Not all these lords do vex me half so much
As that proud dame, the Lord Protector's wife;

She sweeps it through the court with troops of ladies,
More like an empress than Duke Humphrey's wife.
Strangers in court do take her for the queen.
She bears a duke's revenues on her back,
And in her heart she scorns our poverty.
80 Shall I not live to be avenged on her?
Contemptuous base-born callet as she is,
She vaunted 'mongst her minions t'other day
The very train of her worst wearing gown
Was better worth than all my father's lands,
Till Suffolk gave two dukedoms for his daughter.

SUFFOLK
Madam, myself have limed a bush for her,
And placed a choir of such enticing birds
That she will light to listen to the lays,
And never mount to trouble you again.
90 So let her rest; and, madam, list to me,
For I am bold to counsel you in this:
Although we fancy not the Cardinal,
Yet must we join with him and with the lords
Till we have brought Duke Humphrey in disgrace.
As for the Duke of York, this late complaint
Will make but little for his benefit.
So one by one we'll weed them all at last,
And you yourself shall steer the happy helm.

*Sound a sennet. Enter the King, Gloucester, the
Cardinal, Buckingham, York, Salisbury, Warwick,
Somerset, and the Duchess of Gloucester*

KING
For my part, noble lords, I care not which;
100 Or Somerset or York, all's one to me.

YORK
If York have ill demeaned himself in France,
Then let him be denayed the Regentship.

SOMERSET
If Somerset be unworthy of the place,

Let York be Regent. I will yield to him.

WARWICK

Whether your grace be worthy, yea or no,
Dispute not that; York is the worthier.

CARDINAL

Ambitious Warwick, let thy betters speak.

WARWICK

The Cardinal's not my better in the field.

BUCKINGHAM

All in this presence are thy betters, Warwick.

WARWICK

Warwick may live to be the best of all.   110

SALISBURY

Peace, son; and show some reason, Buckingham,
Why Somerset should be preferred in this.

QUEEN

Because the King, forsooth, will have it so.

GLOUCESTER

Madam, the King is old enough himself
To give his censure. These are no women's matters.

QUEEN

If he be old enough, what needs your grace
To be Protector of his excellence?

GLOUCESTER

Madam, I am Protector of the realm,
And at his pleasure will resign my place.

SUFFOLK

Resign it then, and leave thine insolence.   120
Since thou wert king – as who is king but thou? –
The commonwealth hath daily run to wrack,
The Dauphin hath prevailed beyond the seas,
And all the peers and nobles of the realm
Have been as bondmen to thy sovereignty.

CARDINAL

The commons hast thou racked; the clergy's bags
Are lank and lean with thy extortions.

SOMERSET

  Thy sumptuous buildings and thy wife's attire
  Have cost a mass of public treasury.

BUCKINGHAM

130 Thy cruelty in execution
  Upon offenders hath exceeded law,
  And left thee to the mercy of the law.

QUEEN

  Thy sale of offices and towns in France,
  If they were known, as the suspect is great,
  Would make thee quickly hop without thy head.

Exit Gloucester

  The Queen lets fall her fan
  Give me my fan. What, minion, can ye not?
  She gives the Duchess of Gloucester a box on the ear
  I cry you mercy, madam; was it you?

DUCHESS

  Was't I? Yea, I it was, proud Frenchwoman.
  Could I come near your beauty with my nails,
140 I could set my ten commandments on your face.

KING

  Sweet aunt, be quiet; 'twas against her will.

DUCHESS

  Against her will, good King? Look to't in time.
  She'll hamper thee, and dandle thee like a baby.
  Though in this place most master wear no breeches,
  She shall not strike Dame Eleanor unrevenged. *Exit*

BUCKINGHAM

  Lord Cardinal, I will follow Eleanor,
  And listen after Humphrey, how he proceeds.
  She's tickled now; her fume needs no spurs,
  She'll gallop far enough to her destruction. *Exit*
  Enter Gloucester

GLOUCESTER

150 Now, lords, my choler being overblown

With walking once about the quadrangle,
I come to talk of commonwealth affairs.
As for your spiteful false objections,
Prove them, and I lie open to the law;
But God in mercy so deal with my soul
As I in duty love my king and country!
But to the matter that we have in hand:
I say, my sovereign, York is meetest man
To be your Regent in the realm of France.

SUFFOLK
Before we make election, give me leave   160
To show some reason of no little force
That York is most unmeet of any man.

YORK
I'll tell thee, Suffolk, why I am unmeet:
First, for I cannot flatter thee in pride;
Next, if I be appointed for the place,
My lord of Somerset will keep me here,
Without discharge, money, or furniture,
Till France be won into the Dauphin's hands.
Last time I danced attendance on his will
Till Paris was besieged, famished, and lost.   170

WARWICK
That can I witness, and a fouler fact
Did never traitor in the land commit.

SUFFOLK
Peace, headstrong Warwick!

WARWICK
Image of pride, why should I hold my peace?
          Enter Horner the armourer and his man Peter, guarded

SUFFOLK
Because here is a man accused of treason.
Pray God the Duke of York excuse himself!

YORK
Doth anyone accuse York for a traitor?

69

KING
> What meanest thou, Suffolk? Tell me, what are these?

SUFFOLK
> Please it your majesty, this is the man
> That doth accuse his master of high treason.
> His words were these: that Richard Duke of York
> Was rightful heir unto the English crown,
> And that your majesty was an usurper.

KING Say, man, were these thy words?

HORNER An't shall please your majesty, I never said nor
> thought any such matter. God is my witness, I am falsely
> accused by the villain.

PETER By these ten bones, my lords, he did speak them
> to me in the garret one night as we were scouring my
> lord of York's armour.

YORK
> Base dunghill villain and mechanical,
> I'll have thy head for this thy traitor's speech.
> I do beseech your royal majesty,
> Let him have all the rigour of the law.

HORNER Alas, my lord, hang me if ever I spake the words.
> My accuser is my prentice, and when I did correct him
> for his fault the other day, he did vow upon his knees
> he would be even with me. I have good witness of this;
> therefore I beseech your majesty, do not cast away an
> honest man for a villain's accusation.

KING
> Uncle, what shall we say to this in law?

GLOUCESTER
> This doom, my lord, if I may judge:
> Let Somerset be Regent o'er the French,
> Because in York this breeds suspicion;
> And let these have a day appointed them
> For single combat in convenient place,
> For he hath witness of his servant's malice.

This is the law, and this Duke Humphrey's doom.

SOMERSET

  I humbly thank your royal majesty.

HORNER

  And I accept the combat willingly.   210

PETER Alas, my lord, I cannot fight; for God's sake,
  pity my case. The spite of man prevaileth against me. O
  Lord, have mercy upon me! I never shall be able to fight
  a blow. O Lord, my heart!

GLOUCESTER

  Sirrah, or you must fight or else be hanged.

KING Away with them to prison; and the day of combat
  shall be the last of the next month. Come, Somerset,
  we'll see thee sent away!   *Flourish. Exeunt*

    Enter the witch, Margery Jourdain, the two priests, I.4
    Hume and Southwell, and Bolingbroke

HUME Come, my masters, the Duchess, I tell you, expects
  performance of your promises.

BOLINGBROKE Master Hume, we are therefore provided.
  Will her ladyship behold and hear our exorcisms?

HUME Ay, what else? Fear you not her courage.

BOLINGBROKE I have heard her reported to be a woman of
  an invincible spirit; but it shall be convenient, Master
  Hume, that you be by her aloft, while we be busy below;
  and so I pray you go in God's name, and leave us.

                        Exit Hume

  Mother Jourdain, be you prostrate and grovel on the 10
  earth. John Southwell, read you; and let us to our work.

    Enter the Duchess of Gloucester aloft, Hume following

DUCHESS Well said, my masters, and welcome all. To this
  gear the sooner the better.

BOLINGBROKE

  Patience, good lady; wizards know their times.

Deep night, dark night, the silent of the night,
The time of night when Troy was set on fire,
The time when screech-owls cry and ban-dogs howl,
And spirits walk, and ghosts break up their graves,
That time best fits the work we have in hand.
20   Madam, sit you and fear not. Whom we raise
We will make fast within a hallowed verge.

> *Here do the ceremonies belonging, and make the*
> *circle. Bolingbroke or Southwell reads 'Conjuro*
> *te' etc. It thunders and lightens terribly; then the*
> *Spirit riseth*

SPIRIT
Adsum.
JOURDAIN
Asmath!
By the eternal God, whose name and power
Thou tremblest at, answer that I shall ask;
For till thou speak, thou shalt not pass from hence.
SPIRIT
Ask what thou wilt. That I had said and done!
BOLINGBROKE (*reads*)
First, of the King: what shall of him become?
SPIRIT
The duke yet lives that Henry shall depose;
30   But him outlive, and die a violent death.

> *As the Spirit speaks, Bolingbroke writes the answer*

BOLINGBROKE (*reads*)
What fates await the Duke of Suffolk?
SPIRIT
By water shall he die, and take his end.
BOLINGBROKE (*reads*)
What shall befall the Duke of Somerset?
SPIRIT
Let him shun castles;
Safer shall he be upon the sandy plains

Than where castles mounted stand.
Have done, for more I hardly can endure.

BOLINGBROKE

Descend to darkness and the burning lake!
False fiend, avoid!

Thunder and lightning. Exit Spirit
Enter the Duke of York and the Duke of Buckingham
with their guard, Sir Humphrey Stafford as captain,
and break in

YORK

Lay hands upon these traitors and their trash.   40
Beldam, I think we watched you at an inch.
What, madam, are you there? The King and
          commonweal
Are deeply indebted for this piece of pains.
My Lord Protector will, I doubt it not,
See you well guerdoned for these good deserts.

DUCHESS

Not half so bad as thine to England's king,
Injurious duke, that threatest where's no cause.

BUCKINGHAM

True, madam, none at all. What call you this?
Away with them, let them be clapped up close,
And kept asunder. You, madam, shall with us.   50
Stafford, take her to thee.

          Exeunt above the Duchess and Hume, guarded
We'll see your trinkets here all forthcoming.
All away!   *Exeunt Jourdain, Southwell,*
                    Bolingbroke, escorted by Stafford
                    and the guard

YORK

Lord Buckingham, methinks you watched her well.
A pretty plot, well chosen to build upon!
Now pray, my lord, let's see the devil's writ.
What have we here?

73

(*Reads*) *The duke yet lives that Henry shall depose;*
But him outlive and die a violent death.

60   Why, this is just
  Aio te, Aeacida, Romanos vincere posse.
  Well, to the rest:
  Tell me what fate awaits the Duke of Suffolk?
  By water shall he die, and take his end.
  What shall befall the Duke of Somerset?
  Let him shun castles;
  Safer shall he be upon the sandy plains
  Than where castles mounted stand.
  Come, come, my lords, these oracles
70   Are hardly attained and hardly understood.
  The King is now in progress towards Saint Albans;
  With him the husband of this lovely lady.
  Thither goes these news, as fast as horse can carry them –
  A sorry breakfast for my Lord Protector.

BUCKINGHAM
  Your grace shall give me leave, my lord of York,
  To be the post, in hope of his reward.

YORK
  At your pleasure, my good lord. Who's within there, ho?
     Enter a servingman
  Invite my lords of Salisbury and Warwick
  To sup with me tomorrow night. Away!   *Exeunt*

*

II.1   *Enter the King, Queen, Gloucester, Cardinal, and*
       Suffolk, with falconers hallooing

QUEEN
  Believe me, lords, for flying at the brook,
  I saw not better sport these seven years' day;
  Yet, by your leave, the wind was very high,
  And, ten to one, old Joan had not gone out.

KING

 But what a point, my lord, your falcon made,
 And what a pitch she flew above the rest!
 To see how God in all his creatures works!
 Yea, man and birds are fain of climbing high.

SUFFOLK

 No marvel, an it like your majesty,
 My Lord Protector's hawks do tower so well;   10
 They know their master loves to be aloft,
 And bears his thoughts above his falcon's pitch.

GLOUCESTER

 My lord, 'tis but a base ignoble mind
 That mounts no higher than a bird can soar.

CARDINAL

 I thought as much; he would be above the clouds.

GLOUCESTER

 Ay, my lord Cardinal, how think you by that?
 Were it not good your grace could fly to heaven?

KING

 The treasury of everlasting joy.

CARDINAL

 Thy heaven is on earth; thine eyes and thoughts
 Beat on a crown, the treasure of thy heart,   20
 Pernicious Protector, dangerous peer,
 That smoothest it so with King and commonweal!

GLOUCESTER

 What, Cardinal? Is your priesthood grown peremptory?
 Tantaene animis coelestibus irae?
 Churchmen so hot? Good uncle, hide such malice;
 With such holiness can you do it?

SUFFOLK

 No malice, sir; no more than well becomes
 So good a quarrel and so bad a peer.

GLOUCESTER

 As who, my lord?

SUFFOLK   Why, as you, my lord,

30   An't like your lordly Lord's Protectorship.

GLOUCESTER
Why, Suffolk, England knows thine insolence.

QUEEN
And thy ambition, Gloucester.

KING   I prithee peace,
Good Queen, and whet not on these furious peers;
For blessèd are the peace-makers on earth.

CARDINAL
Let me be blessèd for the peace I make
Against this proud Protector with my sword!

GLOUCESTER (*aside to Cardinal*)
Faith, holy uncle, would 'twere come to that!

CARDINAL (*aside to Gloucester*)
Marry, when thou darest.

GLOUCESTER (*aside to Cardinal*)
Make up no factious numbers for the matter;

40   In thine own person answer thy abuse.

CARDINAL (*aside to Gloucester*)
Ay, where thou darest not peep; an if thou darest,
This evening on the east side of the grove.

KING
How now, my lords?

CARDINAL   Believe me, cousin Gloucester,
Had not your man put up the fowl so suddenly,
We had had more sport. (*Aside to Gloucester*) Come
      with thy two-hand sword.

GLOUCESTER
True, uncle.

CARDINAL (*aside to Gloucester*)
Are ye advised? The east side of the grove.

GLOUCESTER (*aside to Cardinal*)
Cardinal, I am with you.

KING   Why, how now, uncle Gloucester?

GLOUCESTER

Talking of hawking; nothing else, my lord.
(*Aside to Cardinal*)
Now, by God's mother, priest, I'll shave your crown
    for this,   50
Or all my fence shall fail.

CARDINAL (*aside to Gloucester*) *Medice, teipsum* –
Protector, see to't well; protect yourself.

KING

The winds grow high; so do your stomachs, lords.
How irksome is this music to my heart!
When such strings jar, what hope of harmony?
I pray, my lords, let me compound this strife.
    Enter a Man crying 'A miracle!'

GLOUCESTER

What means this noise?
Fellow, what miracle dost thou proclaim?

MAN

A miracle! A miracle!

SUFFOLK

Come to the King and tell him what miracle.   60

MAN

Forsooth, a blind man at Saint Alban's shrine
Within this half-hour hath received his sight,
A man that ne'er saw in his life before.

KING

Now God be praised, that to believing souls
Gives light in darkness, comfort in despair!
    Enter the Mayor of Saint Albans and his brethren,
    with music, bearing the man Simpcox between two
    in a chair; Simpcox's Wife and others following

CARDINAL

Here comes the townsmen, on procession,
To present your highness with the man.

KING

Great is his comfort in this earthly vale,
Although by his sight his sin be multiplied.

GLOUCESTER

70   Stand by, my masters; bring him near the King.
His highness' pleasure is to talk with him.

KING

Good fellow, tell us here the circumstance,
That we for thee may glorify the Lord.
What, hast thou been long blind and now restored?

SIMPCOX Born blind, an't please your grace.

WIFE Ay, indeed was he.

SUFFOLK What woman is this?

WIFE His wife, an't like your worship.

GLOUCESTER Hadst thou been his mother, thou couldst
80   have better told.

KING Where wert thou born?

SIMPCOX At Berwick in the north, an't like your grace.

KING

Poor soul, God's goodness hath been great to thee.
Let never day nor night unhallowed pass,
But still remember what the Lord hath done.

QUEEN

Tell me, good fellow, camest thou here by chance,
Or of devotion, to this holy shrine?

SIMPCOX

God knows, of pure devotion, being called
A hundred times and oftener, in my sleep,
90   By good Saint Alban, who said 'Simon, come;
Come, offer at my shrine, and I will help thee.'

WIFE

Most true, forsooth; and many time and oft
Myself have heard a voice to call him so.

CARDINAL

What, art thou lame?

SIMPCOX   Ay, God Almighty help me!
SUFFOLK
  How camest thou so?
SIMPCOX   A fall off of a tree.
WIFE
  A plum-tree, master.
GLOUCESTER   How long hast thou been blind?
SIMPCOX
  O, born so, master.
GLOUCESTER   What! And wouldst climb a tree?
SIMPCOX
  But that in all my life, when I was a youth.
WIFE
  Too true; and bought his climbing very dear.
GLOUCESTER
  Mass, thou loved'st plums well, that wouldst venture so.   100
SIMPCOX
  Alas, good master, my wife desired some damsons,
  And made me climb with danger of my life.
GLOUCESTER
  A subtle knave! But yet it shall not serve.
  Let me see thine eyes; wink now; now open them.
  In my opinion yet thou seest not well.
SIMPCOX Yes, master, clear as day, I thank God and
  Saint Alban.
GLOUCESTER
  Sayst thou me so? What colour is this cloak of?
SIMPCOX Red, master, red as blood.
GLOUCESTER
  Why, that's well said. What colour is my gown of?   110
SIMPCOX Black, forsooth, coal-black as jet.
KING
  Why then, thou knowest what colour jet is of?
SUFFOLK
  And yet, I think, jet did he never see.

GLOUCESTER
But cloaks and gowns before this day a many.

WIFE
Never, before this day, in all his life.

GLOUCESTER Tell me, sirrah, what's my name?

SIMPCOX Alas, master, I know not.

GLOUCESTER What's his name?

SIMPCOX I know not.

120 GLOUCESTER Nor his?

SIMPCOX No indeed, master.

GLOUCESTER What's thine own name?

SIMPCOX Saunder Simpcox, an if it please you, master.

GLOUCESTER Then, Saunder, sit there, the lyingest knave
in Christendom. If thou hadst been born blind, thou
mightst as well have known all our names as thus to
name the several colours we do wear. Sight may distin-
guish of colours; but suddenly to nominate them all, it
is impossible. My lords, Saint Alban here hath done a
130 miracle; and would ye not think his cunning to be great,
that could restore this cripple to his legs again?

SIMPCOX O master, that you could!

GLOUCESTER My masters of Saint Albans, have you not
beadles in your town, and things called whips?

MAYOR Yes, my lord, if it please your grace.

GLOUCESTER Then send for one presently.

MAYOR Sirrah, go fetch the beadle hither straight.

Exit an attendant

GLOUCESTER Now fetch me a stool hither by and by.
Now, sirrah, if you mean to save yourself from whipping,
140 leap me over this stool and run away.

SIMPCOX Alas, master, I am not able to stand alone. You
go about to torture me in vain.

Enter a Beadle with whips

GLOUCESTER Well, sir, we must have you find your legs.
Sirrah beadle, whip him till he leap over that same
stool.

BEADLE I will, my lord. Come on, sirrah, off with your
doublet quickly.

SIMPCOX Alas, master, what shall I do? I am not able
to stand.

> *After the Beadle hath hit him once, he leaps over the*
> *stool and runs away; and they follow and cry 'A*
> *miracle!'*

KING

O God, seest thou this, and bearest so long?   150

QUEEN

It made me laugh to see the villain run.

GLOUCESTER

Follow the knave, and take this drab away.

WIFE Alas, sir, we did it for pure need.

GLOUCESTER

Let them be whipped through every market-town
Till they come to Berwick, from whence they came.

> *Exeunt Mayor and townspeople,*
> *and the Beadle dragging Simpcox's Wife*

CARDINAL

Duke Humphrey has done a miracle today.

SUFFOLK

True; made the lame to leap and fly away.

GLOUCESTER

But you have done more miracles than I;
You made in a day, my lord, whole towns to fly.

> *Enter Buckingham*

KING

What tidings with our cousin Buckingham?   160

BUCKINGHAM

Such as my heart doth tremble to unfold:
A sort of naughty persons, lewdly bent,
Under the countenance and confederacy
Of Lady Eleanor, the Protector's wife,
The ringleader and head of all this rout,
Have practised dangerously against your state,

Dealing with witches and with conjurers,
Whom we have apprehended in the fact,
Raising up wicked spirits from under ground,
170 Demanding of King Henry's life and death,
And other of your highness' Privy Council,
As more at large your grace shall understand.

CARDINAL

And so, my Lord Protector, by this means
Your lady is forthcoming yet at London.
(*Aside to Gloucester*)
This news, I think, hath turned your weapon's edge;
'Tis like, my lord, you will not keep your hour.

GLOUCESTER

Ambitious churchman, leave to afflict my heart.
Sorrow and grief have vanquished all my powers;
And, vanquished as I am, I yield to thee
180 Or to the meanest groom.

KING

O God, what mischiefs work the wicked ones,
Heaping confusion on their own heads thereby!

QUEEN

Gloucester, see here the tainture of thy nest,
And look thyself be faultless, thou wert best.

GLOUCESTER

Madam, for myself, to heaven I do appeal,
How I have loved my king and commonweal;
And for my wife I know not how it stands.
Sorry I am to hear what I have heard.
Noble she is; but if she have forgot
190 Honour and virtue, and conversed with such
As, like to pitch, defile nobility,
I banish her my bed and company,
And give her as a prey to law and shame,
That hath dishonoured Gloucester's honest name.

KING

Well, for this night we will repose us here;

Tomorrow toward London back again,
To look into this business thoroughly,
And call these foul offenders to their answers,
And poise the cause in Justice' equal scales,
Whose beam stands sure, whose rightful cause prevails. 200
Flourish. Exeunt

Enter York, Salisbury, and Warwick II.2

YORK
Now, my good lords of Salisbury and Warwick,
Our simple supper ended, give me leave,
In this close walk, to satisfy myself
In craving your opinion of my title,
Which is infallible, to the English crown.

SALISBURY
My lord, I long to hear it at full.

WARWICK
Sweet York, begin; and if thy claim be good,
The Nevils are thy subjects to command.

YORK
Then thus:
Edward the Third, my lords, had seven sons: 10
The first, Edward the Black Prince, Prince of Wales;
The second, William of Hatfield; and the third,
Lionel Duke of Clarence; next to whom
Was John of Gaunt, the Duke of Lancaster;
The fifth was Edmund Langley, Duke of York;
The sixth was Thomas of Woodstock, Duke of
        Gloucester;
William of Windsor was the seventh and last.
Edward the Black Prince died before his father,
And left behind him Richard, his only son,
Who, after Edward the Third's death, reigned as king 20
Till Henry Bolingbroke, Duke of Lancaster,
The eldest son and heir of John of Gaunt,

Crowned by the name of Henry the Fourth,
Seized on the realm, deposed the rightful king,
Sent his poor queen to France, from whence she came,
And him to Pomfret; where, as all you know,
Harmless Richard was murdered traitorously.

WARWICK

Father, the Duke hath told the truth;
Thus got the house of Lancaster the crown.

YORK

30 Which now they hold by force and not by right;
For Richard, the first son's heir, being dead,
The issue of the next son should have reigned.

SALISBURY

But William of Hatfield died without an heir.

YORK

The third son, Duke of Clarence, from whose line
I claim the crown, had issue Philippe, a daughter,
Who married Edmund Mortimer, Earl of March;
Edmund had issue, Roger Earl of March;
Roger had issue, Edmund, Anne, and Eleanor.

SALISBURY

This Edmund, in the reign of Bolingbroke,
40 As I have read, laid claim unto the crown,
And, but for Owen Glendower, had been king,
Who kept him in captivity till he died.
But to the rest.

YORK   His eldest sister, Anne,
My mother, being heir unto the crown,
Married Richard Earl of Cambridge, who was
To Edmund Langley, Edward the Third's fifth son, son.
By her I claim the kingdom; she was heir
To Roger Earl of March, who was the son
Of Edmund Mortimer, who married Philippe,
50 Sole daughter unto Lionel Duke of Clarence;
So, if the issue of the elder son

Succeed before the younger, I am king.

WARWICK

What plain proceedings is more plain than this?
Henry doth claim the crown from John of Gaunt,
The fourth son; York claims it from the third.
Till Lionel's issue fails, his should not reign;
It fails not yet, but flourishes in thee,
And in thy sons, fair slips of such a stock.
Then, father Salisbury, kneel we together,
And in this private plot be we the first   60
That shall salute our rightful sovereign
With honour of his birthright to the crown.

WARWICK *and* SALISBURY

Long live our sovereign Richard, England's king!

YORK

We thank you, lords; but I am not your king
Till I be crowned, and that my sword be stained
With heart-blood of the house of Lancaster;
And that's not suddenly to be performed
But with advice and silent secrecy.
Do you as I do in these dangerous days,
Wink at the Duke of Suffolk's insolence,   70
At Beaufort's pride, at Somerset's ambition,
At Buckingham, and all the crew of them,
Till they have snared the shepherd of the flock,
That virtuous prince, the good Duke Humphrey.
'Tis that they seek; and they, in seeking that,
Shall find their deaths, if York can prophesy.

SALISBURY

My lord, break we off; we know your mind at full.

WARWICK

My heart assures me that the Earl of Warwick
Shall one day make the Duke of York a king.

YORK

And, Neville, this I do assure myself: 80

85

Richard shall live to make the Earl of Warwick
The greatest man in England but the king.   *Exeunt*

Sound trumpets. Enter the King, Queen, Gloucester,
York, Suffolk, and Salisbury; the Duchess of
Gloucester, Margery Jourdain, Southwell, Hume,
and Bolingbroke, guarded

KING

Stand forth, Dame Eleanor Cobham, Gloucester's wife.
In sight of God and us your guilt is great;
Receive the sentence of the law for sins
Such as by God's book are adjudged to death.
You four, from hence to prison back again;
From thence unto the place of execution.
The witch in Smithfield shall be burnt to ashes,
And you three shall be strangled on the gallows.
You, madam, for you are more nobly born,
10   Despoilèd of your honour in your life,
Shall, after three days' open penance done,
Live in your country here in banishment
With Sir John Stanley in the Isle of Man.

DUCHESS

Welcome is banishment; welcome were my death.

GLOUCESTER

Eleanor, the law, thou seest, hath judged thee;
I cannot justify whom the law condemns.
Mine eyes are full of tears, my heart of grief.
      Exeunt the Duchess and the other prisoners, guarded
Ah, Humphrey, this dishonour in thine age
Will bring thy head with sorrow to the ground!
20   I beseech your majesty give me leave to go;
Sorrow would solace, and mine age would ease.

KING

Stay, Humphrey Duke of Gloucester. Ere thou go,
Give up thy staff. Henry will to himself

86

Protector be; and God shall be my hope,
My stay, my guide, and lantern to my feet.
And go in peace, Humphrey, no less beloved
Than when thou wert Protector to thy King.

QUEEN

I see no reason why a king of years
Should be to be protected like a child.
God and King Henry govern England's realm! 30
Give up your staff, sir, and the King his realm.

GLOUCESTER

My staff? Here, noble Henry, is my staff;
As willingly do I the same resign
As ere thy father Henry made it mine;
And even as willingly at thy feet I leave it
As others would ambitiously receive it.
Farewell, good King. When I am dead and gone,
May honourable peace attend thy throne. *Exit*

QUEEN

Why, now is Henry King and Margaret Queen;
And Humphrey Duke of Gloucester scarce himself, 40
That bears so shrewd a maim; two pulls at once –
His lady banished and a limb lopped off.
This staff of honour raught, there let it stand
Where it best fits to be, in Henry's hand.

SUFFOLK

Thus droops this lofty pine and hangs his sprays;
Thus Eleanor's pride dies in her youngest days.

YORK

Lords, let him go. Please it your majesty,
This is the day appointed for the combat,
And ready are the appellant and defendant,
The armourer and his man, to enter the lists, 50
So please your highness to behold the fight.

QUEEN

Ay, good my lord; for purposely therefore
Left I the court to see this quarrel tried.

KING

A God's name, see the lists and all things fit;
Here let them end it, and God defend the right!

YORK

I never saw a fellow worse bestead,
Or more afraid to fight, than is the appellant,
The servant of this armourer, my lords.

*Enter at one door Horner the armourer and his
Neighbours, drinking to him so much that he is
drunk; and he enters with a drum before him and his
staff with a sand-bag fastened to it; and at the other
door Peter his man, with a drum and sand-bag, and
Prentices drinking to him*

FIRST NEIGHBOUR Here, neighbour Horner, I drink to
60 you in a cup of sack; and fear not, neighbour, you
shall do well enough.

SECOND NEIGHBOUR And here, neighbour, here's a cup
of charneco.

THIRD NEIGHBOUR And here's a pot of good double beer,
neighbour. Drink, and fear not your man.

HORNER Let it come, i'faith, and I'll pledge you all;
and a fig for Peter!

FIRST PRENTICE Here, Peter, I drink to thee; and be not
afraid.

70 **SECOND PRENTICE** Be merry, Peter, and fear not thy
master. Fight for the credit of the prentices.

PETER I thank you all. Drink and pray for me, I pray you,
for I think I have taken my last draught in this world.
Here, Robin, an if I die, I give thee my apron; and,
Will, thou shalt have my hammer; and here, Tom,
take all the money that I have. O Lord bless me, I pray
God, for I am never able to deal with my master, he hath
learnt so much fence already.

SALISBURY Come, leave your drinking and fall to blows.
Sirrah, what's thy name?   80

88

PETER Peter, forsooth.

SALISBURY Peter? What more?

PETER Thump.

SALISBURY Thump? Then see thou thump thy master well.

HORNER Masters, I am come hither, as it were, upon my man's instigation, to prove him a knave and myself an honest man; and touching the Duke of York, I will take my death I never meant him any ill, nor the King, nor the Queen; and therefore, Peter, have at thee with a downright blow. 90

YORK Dispatch; this knave's tongue begins to double. Sound, trumpets, alarum to the combatants.

Alarum; they fight and Peter strikes Horner down

HORNER Hold, Peter, hold! I confess, I confess treason.
He dies

YORK Take away his weapon. Fellow, thank God and the good wine in thy master's way.

PETER O God, have I overcome mine enemies in this presence? O Peter, thou hast prevailed in right!

KING
Go, take hence that traitor from our sight;
For by his death we do perceive his guilt,
And God in justice hath revealed to us 100
The truth and innocence of this poor fellow,
Which he had thought to have murdered wrongfully.
Come, fellow, follow us for thy reward.
Sound a flourish. Exeunt

Enter Gloucester and his men in mourning cloaks II.4

GLOUCESTER
Thus sometimes hath the brightest day a cloud;
And after summer evermore succeeds
Barren winter, with his wrathful nipping cold;

So cares and joys abound, as seasons fleet.
Sirs, what's o'clock?

SERVANT   Ten, my lord.

GLOUCESTER

Ten is the hour that was appointed me
To watch the coming of my punished duchess;
Uneath may she endure the flinty streets,
To tread them with her tender-feeling feet.
Sweet Nell, ill can thy noble mind abrook
The abject people gazing on thy face
With envious looks, laughing at thy shame,
That erst did follow thy proud chariot wheels
When thou didst ride in triumph through the streets.
But soft, I think she comes; and I'll prepare
My tear-stained eyes to see her miseries.

> *Enter the Duchess of Gloucester barefoot, in a white
> sheet and verses written on her back and pinned on and
> a taper burning in her hand, with Sir John Stanley,
> the Sheriff, and officers with bills and halberds*

SERVANT

So please your grace, we'll take her from the Sheriff.

GLOUCESTER

No, stir not for your lives; let her pass by.

DUCHESS

Come you, my lord, to see my open shame?
Now thou dost penance too. Look how they gaze!
See how the giddy multitude do point
And nod their heads and throw their eyes on thee.
Ah, Gloucester, hide thee from their hateful looks,
And, in thy closet pent up, rue my shame,
And ban thine enemies, both mine and thine.

GLOUCESTER

Be patient, gentle Nell; forget this grief.

DUCHESS

Ah, Gloucester, teach me to forget myself;

For whilst I think I am thy married wife,
And thou a prince, Protector of this land,
Methinks I should not thus be led along,   30
Mailed up in shame, with papers on my back,
And followed with a rabble that rejoice
To see my tears and hear my deep-fet groans.
The ruthless flint doth cut my tender feet,
And when I start, the envious people laugh
And bid me be advisèd how I tread.
Ah, Humphrey, can I bear this shameful yoke?
Trowest thou that e'er I'll look upon the world,
Or count them happy that enjoys the sun?
No, dark shall be my light, and night my day;   40
To think upon my pomp shall be my hell.
Sometime I'll say I am Duke Humphrey's wife,
And he a prince and ruler of the land;
Yet so he ruled and such a prince he was
As he stood by whilst I, his forlorn duchess,
Was made a wonder and a pointing-stock
To every idle rascal follower.
But be thou mild and blush not at my shame,
Nor stir at nothing till the axe of death
Hang over thee, as sure it shortly will;   50
For Suffolk, he that can do all in all
With her that hateth thee and hates us all,
And York, and impious Beaufort, that false priest,
Have all limed bushes to betray thy wings;
And fly thou how thou canst, they'll tangle thee.
But fear not thou until thy foot be snared,
Nor never seek prevention of thy foes.

GLOUCESTER

Ah, Nell, forbear! Thou aimest all awry;
I must offend before I be attainted;
And had I twenty times so many foes,   60
And each of them had twenty times their power,

All these could not procure me any scathe
So long as I am loyal, true, and crimeless.
Wouldst have me rescue thee from this reproach?
Why, yet thy scandal were not wiped away,
But I in danger for the breach of law.
Thy greatest help is quiet, gentle Nell.
I pray thee sort thy heart to patience;
These few days' wonder will be quickly worn.

Enter a Herald

HERALD
70   I summon your grace to his majesty's parliament,
Holden at Bury the first of this next month.

GLOUCESTER
And my consent ne'er asked herein before!
This is close dealing. Well, I will be there.

Exit Herald

My Nell, I take my leave; and, Master Sheriff,
Let not her penance exceed the King's commission.

SHERIFF
An't please your grace, here my commission stays,
And Sir John Stanley is appointed now
To take her with him to the Isle of Man.

GLOUCESTER
Must you, Sir John, protect my lady here?

STANLEY
80   So am I given in charge, may't please your grace.

GLOUCESTER
Entreat her not the worse in that I pray
You use her well. The world may laugh again;
And I may live to do you kindness if
You do it her. And so, Sir John, farewell.

DUCHESS
What, gone, my lord, and bid me not farewell?

GLOUCESTER
Witness my tears, I cannot stay to speak.

Exit Gloucester with his men

DUCHESS

    Art thou gone too? All comfort go with thee!

    For none abides with me; my joy is death –

    Death, at whose name I oft have been afeard,

    Because I wished this world's eternity.   90

    Stanley, I prithee, go and take me hence;

    I care not whither, for I beg no favour;

    Only convey me where thou art commanded.

STANLEY

    Why, madam, that is to the Isle of Man,

    There to be used according to your state.

DUCHESS

    That's bad enough, for I am but reproach;

    And shall I then be used reproachfully?

STANLEY

    Like to a duchess and Duke Humphrey's lady,

    According to that state you shall be used.

DUCHESS

    Sheriff, farewell, and better than I fare,   100

    Although thou hast been conduct of my shame.

SHERIFF

    It is my office; and, madam, pardon me.

DUCHESS

    Ay, ay, farewell; thy office is discharged.

    Come, Stanley, shall we go?

STANLEY

    Madam, your penance done, throw off this sheet,

    And go we to attire you for our journey.

DUCHESS

    My shame will not be shifted with my sheet.

    No; it will hang upon my richest robes

    And show itself, attire me how I can.

    Go, lead the way; I long to see my prison.   *Exeunt* 110

*

Sound a sennet. Enter the King, Queen, Cardinal,
Suffolk, York, Buckingham, Salisbury, and Warwick
to the parliament

KING

I muse my lord of Gloucester is not come;
'Tis not his wont to be the hindmost man,
Whate'er occasion keeps him from us now.

QUEEN

Can you not see? Or will ye not observe
The strangeness of his altered countenance?
With what a majesty he bears himself,
How insolent of late he is become,
How proud, how peremptory, and unlike himself?
We know the time since he was mild and affable,
10   And if we did but glance a far-off look,
Immediately he was upon his knee,
That all the court admired him for submission;
But meet him now, and be it in the morn,
When everyone will give the time of day,
He knits his brow and shows an angry eye,
And passeth by with stiff unbowèd knee,
Disdaining duty that to us belongs.
Small curs are not regarded when they grin,
But great men tremble when the lion roars;
20   And Humphrey is no little man in England.
First note that he is near you in descent,
And should you fall, he is the next will mount.
Me seemeth then it is no policy,
Respecting what a rancorous mind he bears
And his advantage following your decease,
That he should come about your royal person
Or be admitted to your highness' Council.
By flattery hath he won the commons' hearts,
And when he please to make commotion,
30   'Tis to be feared they all will follow him.

94

Now 'tis the spring, and weeds are shallow-rooted;
Suffer them now and they'll o'ergrow the garden,
And choke the herbs for want of husbandry.
The reverent care I bear unto my lord
Made me collect these dangers in the Duke.
If it be fond, call it a woman's fear;
Which fear if better reasons can supplant,
I will subscribe and say I wronged the Duke.
My lord of Suffolk, Buckingham, and York,
Reprove my allegation if you can;   40
Or else conclude my words effectual.

SUFFOLK

Well hath your highness seen into this Duke;
And had I first been put to speak my mind,
I think I should have told your grace's tale.
The Duchess by his subornation,
Upon my life, began her devilish practices;
Or if he were not privy to those faults,
Yet by reputing of his high descent,
As next the King he was successive heir,
And such high vaunts of his nobility,   50
Did instigate the bedlam brain-sick Duchess
By wicked means to frame our sovereign's fall.
Smooth runs the water where the brook is deep,
And in his simple show he harbours treason.
The fox barks not when he would steal the lamb.
No, no, my sovereign, Gloucester is a man
Unsounded yet and full of deep deceit.

CARDINAL

Did he not, contrary to form of law,
Devise strange deaths for small offences done?

YORK

And did he not, in his Protectorship,   60
Levy great sums of money through the realm
For soldiers' pay in France, and never sent it?

By means whereof the towns each day revolted.

BUCKINGHAM

Tut, these are petty faults to faults unknown,
Which time will bring to light in smooth Duke
      Humphrey.

KING

My lords, at once; the care you have of us,
To mow down thorns that would annoy our foot,
Is worthy praise; but, shall I speak my conscience,
Our kinsman Gloucester is as innocent
70 From meaning treason to our royal person
As is the sucking lamb or harmless dove.
The Duke is virtuous, mild, and too well given
To dream on evil or to work my downfall.

QUEEN

Ah, what's more dangerous than this fond affiance?
Seems he a dove? His feathers are but borrowed,
For he's disposèd as the hateful raven.
Is he a lamb? His skin is surely lent him,
For he's inclined as is the ravenous wolves.
Who cannot steal a shape that means deceit?
80 Take heed, my lord; the welfare of us all
Hangs on the cutting short that fraudful man.
    Enter Somerset

SOMERSET

All health unto my gracious sovereign!

KING

Welcome, Lord Somerset. What news from France?

SOMERSET

That all your interest in those territories
Is utterly bereft you; all is lost.

KING

Cold news, Lord Somerset; but God's will be done!

YORK (*aside*)

Cold news for me; for I had hope of France

As firmly as I hope for fertile England.
Thus are my blossoms blasted in the bud,
And caterpillars eat my leaves away;   90
But I will remedy this gear ere long,
Or sell my title for a glorious grave.

Enter Gloucester

GLOUCESTER
All happiness unto my lord the King!
Pardon, my liege, that I have stayed so long.

SUFFOLK
Nay, Gloucester, know that thou art come too soon,
Unless thou wert more loyal than thou art.
I do arrest thee of high treason here.

GLOUCESTER
Well, Suffolk, thou shalt not see me blush,
Nor change my countenance for this arrest;
A heart unspotted is not easily daunted.   100
The purest spring is not so free from mud
As I am clear from treason to my sovereign.
Who can accuse me? Wherein am I guilty?

YORK
'Tis thought, my lord, that you took bribes of France;
And, being Protector, stayed the soldiers' pay,
By means whereof his highness hath lost France.

GLOUCESTER
Is it but thought so? What are they that think it?
I never robbed the soldiers of their pay,
Nor ever had one penny bribe from France.
So help me God, as I have watched the night,   110
Ay, night by night, in studying good for England!
That doit that e'er I wrested from the King,
Or any groat I hoarded to my use,
Be brought against me at my trial day!
No, many a pound of mine own proper store,
Because I would not tax the needy commons,

Have I dispursèd to the garrisons,
And never asked for restitution.

CARDINAL

It serves you well, my lord, to say so much.

GLOUCESTER

120 I say no more than truth, so help me God!

YORK

In your Protectorship you did devise
Strange tortures for offenders, never heard of,
That England was defamed by tyranny.

GLOUCESTER

Why, 'tis well known that, whiles I was Protector,
Pity was all the fault that was in me;
For I should melt at an offender's tears,
And lowly words were ransom for their fault.
Unless it were a bloody murderer
Or foul felonious thief that fleeced poor passengers,
130 I never gave them condign punishment;
Murder indeed, that bloody sin, I tortured
Above the felon or what trespass else.

SUFFOLK

My lord, these faults are easy, quickly answered;
But mightier crimes are laid unto your charge,
Whereof you cannot easily purge yourself.
I do arrest you in his highness' name;
And here commit you to my lord Cardinal
To keep until your further time of trial.

KING

My lord of Gloucester, 'tis my special hope
140 That you will clear yourself from all suspense;
My conscience tells me you are innocent.

GLOUCESTER

Ah, gracious lord, these days are dangerous;
Virtue is choked with foul ambition,

And charity chased hence by rancour's hand;
Foul subornation is predominant,
And equity exiled your highness' land.
I know their complot is to have my life;
And if my death might make this island happy,
And prove the period of their tyranny,
I would expend it with all willingness.   150
But mine is made the prologue to their play;
For thousands more, that yet suspect no peril,
Will not conclude their plotted tragedy.
Beaufort's red sparkling eyes blab his heart's malice,
And Suffolk's cloudy brow his stormy hate;
Sharp Buckingham unburdens with his tongue
The envious load that lies upon his heart;
And dogged York, that reaches at the moon,
Whose overweening arm I have plucked back,
By false accuse doth level at my life.   160
And you, my sovereign lady, with the rest,
Causeless have laid disgraces on my head,
And with your best endeavour have stirred up
My liefest liege to be mine enemy.
Ay, all of you have laid your heads together –
Myself had notice of your conventicles –
And all to make away my guiltless life.
I shall not want false witness to condemn me,
Nor store of treasons to augment my guilt;
The ancient proverb will be well effected: 170
'A staff is quickly found to beat a dog.'

CARDINAL

My liege, his railing is intolerable.
If those that care to keep your royal person
From treason's secret knife and traitor's rage
Be thus upbraided, chid, and rated at,
And the offender granted scope of speech,

99

III.1

'Twill make them cool in zeal unto your grace.

SUFFOLK

Hath he not twit our sovereign lady here
With ignominious words, though clerkly couched,
180 As if she had suborned some to swear
False allegations to o'erthrow his state?

QUEEN

But I can give the loser leave to chide.

GLOUCESTER

Far truer spoke than meant. I lose indeed;
Beshrew the winners, for they played me false!
And well such losers may have leave to speak.

BUCKINGHAM

He'll wrest the sense and hold us here all day.
Lord Cardinal, he is your prisoner.

CARDINAL

Sirs, take away the Duke and guard him sure.

GLOUCESTER

Ah, thus King Henry throws away his crutch
190 Before his legs be firm to bear his body.
Thus is the shepherd beaten from thy side,
And wolves are gnarling who shall gnaw thee first.
Ah, that my fear were false; ah, that it were!
For, good King Henry, thy decay I fear.

Exit Gloucester, guarded by the Cardinal's men

KING

My lords, what to your wisdoms seemeth best
Do or undo, as if ourself were here.

QUEEN

What, will your highness leave the parliament?

KING

Ay, Margaret; my heart is drowned with grief,
Whose flood begins to flow within mine eyes,
200 My body round engirt with misery;
For what's more miserable than discontent?

Ah, uncle Humphrey, in thy face I see
The map of honour, truth, and loyalty;
And yet, good Humphrey, is the hour to come
That e'er I proved thee false or feared thy faith.
What lowering star now envies thy estate,
That these great lords, and Margaret our Queen,
Do seek subversion of thy harmless life?
Thou never didst them wrong, nor no man wrong;
And as the butcher takes away the calf,   210
And binds the wretch, and beats it when it strays,
Bearing it to the bloody slaughter-house,
Even so remorseless have they borne him hence;
And as the dam runs lowing up and down,
Looking the way her harmless young one went,
And can do naught but wail her darling's loss;
Even so myself bewails good Gloucester's case
With sad unhelpful tears, and with dimmed eyes
Look after him, and cannot do him good,
So mighty are his vowèd enemies.   220
His fortunes I will weep, and 'twixt each groan
Say 'Who's a traitor? Gloucester he is none.'
          Exit with Buckingham, Salisbury, and Warwick

QUEEN

Free lords, cold snow melts with the sun's hot beams:
Henry my lord is cold in great affairs,
Too full of foolish pity; and Gloucester's show
Beguiles him as the mournful crocodile
With sorrow snares relenting passengers;
Or as the snake rolled in a flowering bank,
With shining checkered slough, doth sting a child
That for the beauty thinks it excellent.   230
Believe me, lords, were none more wise than I –
And yet herein I judge mine own wit good –
This Gloucester should be quickly rid the world,
To rid us from the fear we have of him.

CARDINAL

    That he should die is worthy policy;

    But yet we want a colour for his death.

    'Tis meet he be condemned by course of law.

SUFFOLK

    But in my mind that were no policy.

    The King will labour still to save his life,

240   The commons haply rise to save his life;

    And yet we have but trivial argument,

    More than mistrust, that shows him worthy death.

YORK

    So that, by this, you would not have him die.

SUFFOLK

    Ah, York, no man alive so fain as I.

YORK

    'Tis York that hath more reason for his death.

    But, my lord Cardinal, and you, my lord of Suffolk,

    Say as you think, and speak it from your souls:

    Were't not all one, an empty eagle were set

    To guard the chicken from a hungry kite,

250   As place Duke Humphrey for the King's Protector?

QUEEN

    So the poor chicken should be sure of death.

SUFFOLK

    Madam, 'tis true; and were't not madness then

    To make the fox surveyor of the fold?

    Who being accused a crafty murderer,

    His guilt should be but idly posted over

    Because his purpose is not executed.

    No; let him die, in that he is a fox,

    By nature proved an enemy to the flock,

    Before his chaps be stained with crimson blood,

260   As Humphrey, proved by reasons, to my liege.

    And do not stand on quillets how to slay him;

    Be it by gins, by snares, by subtlety,

Sleeping or waking, 'tis no matter how,
So he be dead; for that is good deceit
Which mates him first that first intends deceit.

QUEEN

Thrice-noble Suffolk, 'tis resolutely spoke.

SUFFOLK

Not resolute, except so much were done;
For things are often spoke and seldom meant;
But that my heart accordeth with my tongue,
Seeing the deed is meritorious,   270
And to preserve my sovereign from his foe,
Say but the word and I will be his priest.

CARDINAL

But I would have him dead, my lord of Suffolk,
Ere you can take due orders for a priest.
Say you consent and censure well the deed,
And I'll provide his executioner;
I tender so the safety of my liege.

SUFFOLK

Here is my hand; the deed is worthy doing.

QUEEN

And so say I.

YORK

And I; and now we three have spoke it,   280
It skills not greatly who impugns our doom.

    Enter a Post

POST

Great lords, from Ireland am I come amain,
To signify that rebels there are up
And put the Englishmen unto the sword.
Send succours, lords, and stop the rage betime,
Before the wound do grow uncurable;
For, being green, there is great hope of help.

CARDINAL

A breach that craves a quick expedient stop!

What counsel give you in this weighty cause?

YORK

290 That Somerset be sent as Regent thither.
'Tis meet that lucky ruler be employed;
Witness the fortune he hath had in France.

SOMERSET

If York, with all his far-fet policy,
Had been the Regent there instead of me,
He never would have stayed in France so long.

YORK

No, not to lose it all, as thou hast done.
I rather would have lost my life betimes
Than bring a burden of dishonour home,
By staying there so long till all were lost.

300 Show me one scar charactered on thy skin;
Men's flesh preserved so whole do seldom win.

QUEEN

Nay then, this spark will prove a raging fire
If wind and fuel be brought to feed it with.
No more, good York; sweet Somerset, be still.
Thy fortune, York, hadst thou been Regent there,
Might happily have proved far worse than his.

YORK

What, worse than naught? Nay, then a shame take all!

SOMERSET

And, in the number, thee that wishest shame!

CARDINAL

My lord of York, try what your fortune is.

310 Th'uncivil kerns of Ireland are in arms
And temper clay with blood of Englishmen;
To Ireland will you lead a band of men,
Collected choicely, from each county some,
And try your hap against the Irishmen?

YORK

I will, my lord, so please his majesty.

SUFFOLK

    Why, our authority is his consent,

    And what we do establish he confirms.

    Then, noble York, take thou this task in hand.

YORK

    I am content. Provide me soldiers, lords,

    Whiles I take order for mine own affairs.   320

SUFFOLK

    A charge, Lord York, that I will see performed.

    But now return we to the false Duke Humphrey.

CARDINAL

    No more of him; for I will deal with him

    That henceforth he shall trouble us no more.

    And so break off, the day is almost spent.

    Lord Suffolk, you and I must talk of that event.

YORK

    My lord of Suffolk, within fourteen days

    At Bristow I expect my soldiers;

    For there I'll ship them all for Ireland.

SUFFOLK

    I'll see it truly done, my lord of York.   330

                        Exeunt all but York

YORK

    Now, York, or never, steel thy fearful thoughts,

    And change misdoubt to resolution;

    Be that thou hopest to be, or what thou art

    Resign to death; it is not worth th'enjoying.

    Let pale-faced fear keep with the mean-born man,

    And find no harbour in a royal heart.

    Faster than spring-time showers comes thought on

            thought,

    And not a thought but thinks on dignity.

    My brain, more busy than the labouring spider,

    Weaves tedious snares to trap mine enemies.   340

    Well, nobles, well; 'tis politicly done,

To send me packing with an host of men.
I fear me you but warm the starvèd snake,
Who, cherished in your breasts, will sting your hearts.
'Twas men I lacked, and you will give them me;
I take it kindly; yet be well assured
You put sharp weapons in a madman's hands.
Whiles I in Ireland nourish a mighty band,
I will stir up in England some black storm
350 Shall blow ten thousand souls to heaven or hell;
And this fell tempest shall not cease to rage
Until the golden circuit on my head,
Like to the glorious sun's transparent beams,
Do calm the fury of this mad-bred flaw.
And, for a minister of my intent,
I have seduced a headstrong Kentishman,
John Cade of Ashford,
To make commotion, as full well he can,
Under the title of John Mortimer.
360 In Ireland have I seen this stubborn Cade
Oppose himself against a troop of kerns,
And fought so long till that his thighs with darts
Were almost like a sharp-quilled porpentine;
And, in the end being rescued, I have seen
Him caper upright like a wild Morisco,
Shaking the bloody darts as he his bells.
Full often, like a shag-haired crafty kern,
Hath he conversèd with the enemy,
And undiscovered come to me again
370 And given me notice of their villainies.
This devil here shall be my substitute;
For that John Mortimer, which now is dead,
In face, in gait, in speech he doth resemble;
By this I shall perceive the commons' mind,
How they affect the house and claim of York.
Say he be taken, racked, and torturèd,

I know no pain they can inflict upon him
Will make him say I moved him to those arms.
Say that he thrive, as 'tis great like he will,
Why, then from Ireland come I with my strength,   380
And reap the harvest which that rascal sowed;
For Humphrey being dead, as he shall be,
And Henry put apart, the next for me.   *Exit*

      Enter two Murderers running over the stage from   III.2
      the murder of the Duke of Gloucester

FIRST MURDERER
Run to my lord of Suffolk; let him know
We have dispatched the Duke as he commanded.
SECOND MURDERER
O that it were to do! What have we done?
Didst ever hear a man so penitent?
    Enter Suffolk
FIRST MURDERER Here comes my lord.
SUFFOLK Now, sirs, have you dispatched this thing?
FIRST MURDERER Ay, my good lord, he's dead.
SUFFOLK
Why, that's well said. Go, get you to my house;
I will reward you for this venturous deed.
The King and all the peers are here at hand.   10
Have you laid fair the bed? Is all things well,
According as I gave directions?
FIRST MURDERER 'Tis, my good lord.
SUFFOLK Away, be gone!   *Exeunt Murderers*
    Sound trumpets. Enter the King, Queen, Cardinal,
    and Somerset, with attendants
KING
Go, call our uncle to our presence straight;
Say we intend to try his grace today
If he be guilty, as 'tis publishèd.

SUFFOLK

    I'll call him presently, my noble lord.   *Exit*

KING

    Lords, take your places; and, I pray you all,

20   Proceed no straiter 'gainst our uncle Gloucester

    Than from true evidence, of good esteem,

    He be approved in practice culpable.

QUEEN

    God forbid any malice should prevail

    That faultless may condemn a noble man!

    Pray God he may acquit him of suspicion!

KING

    I thank thee, Meg; these words content me much.

        Enter Suffolk

    How now? Why lookest thou so pale? Why tremblest

        thou?

    Where is our uncle? What's the matter, Suffolk?

SUFFOLK

    Dead in his bed, my lord. Gloucester is dead.

QUEEN

30   Marry, God forfend!

CARDINAL

    God's secret judgement; I did dream tonight

    The Duke was dumb and could not speak a word.

        The King swoons

QUEEN

    How fares my lord? Help, lords! The King is dead.

SOMERSET

    Rear up his body; wring him by the nose.

QUEEN

    Run, go, help, help! O Henry, ope thine eyes!

SUFFOLK

    He doth revive again. Madam, be patient.

KING

    O heavenly God!

QUEEN   How fares my gracious lord?
SUFFOLK
  Comfort, my sovereign! Gracious Henry, comfort!
KING
  What, doth my lord of Suffolk comfort me?
  Came he right now to sing a raven's note,   40
  Whose dismal tune bereft my vital powers;
  And thinks he that the chirping of a wren,
  By crying comfort from a hollow breast,
  Can chase away the first-conceivèd sound?
  Hide not thy poison with such sugared words;
  Lay not thy hands on me; forbear, I say;
  Their touch affrights me as a serpent's sting.
  Thou baleful messenger, out of my sight!
  Upon thy eyeballs murderous tyranny
  Sits in grim majesty to fright the world.   50
  Look not upon me, for thine eyes are wounding;
  Yet do not go away; come, basilisk,
  And kill the innocent gazer with thy sight;
  For in the shade of death I shall find joy,
  In life but double death, now Gloucester's dead.
QUEEN
  Why do you rate my lord of Suffolk thus?
  Although the Duke was enemy to him,
  Yet he, most Christian-like, laments his death;
  And for myself, foe as he was to me,
  Might liquid tears or heart-offending groans   60
  Or blood-consuming sighs recall his life,
  I would be blind with weeping, sick with groans,
  Look pale as primrose with blood-drinking sighs,
  And all to have the noble Duke alive.
  What know I how the world may deem of me?
  For it is known we were but hollow friends;
  It may be judged I made the Duke away;
  So shall my name with slander's tongue be wounded,

And princes' courts be filled with my reproach.
70   This get I by his death. Ay me, unhappy,
To be a queen and crowned with infamy!

KING

Ah, woe is me for Gloucester, wretched man!

QUEEN

Be woe for me, more wretched than he is.
What, dost thou turn away and hide thy face?
I am no loathsome leper; look on me.
What! Art thou like the adder waxen deaf?
Be poisonous too and kill thy forlorn Queen.
Is all thy comfort shut in Gloucester's tomb?
Why, then Dame Margaret was ne'er thy joy.
80   Erect his statue and worship it,
And make my image but an alehouse sign.
Was I for this nigh wrecked upon the sea,
And twice by awkward wind from England's bank
Drove back again unto my native clime?
What boded this, but well forewarning wind
Did seem to say 'Seek not a scorpion's nest,
Nor set no footing on this unkind shore'?
What did I then, but cursed the gentle gusts
And he that loosed them forth their brazen caves;
90   And bid them blow towards England's blessèd shore,
Or turn our stern upon a dreadful rock.
Yet Aeolus would not be a murderer,
But left that dreadful office unto thee;
The pretty vaulting sea refused to drown me,
Knowing that thou wouldst have me drowned on shore
With tears as salt as sea through thy unkindness.
The splitting rocks cowered in the sinking sands,
And would not dash me with their ragged sides,
Because thy flinty heart, more hard than they,
100   Might in thy palace perish Margaret.
As far as I could ken thy chalky cliffs,

When from thy shore the tempest beat us back,
I stood upon the hatches in the storm,
And when the dusky sky began to rob
My earnest-gaping sight of thy land's view,
I took a costly jewel from my neck –
A heart it was, bound in with diamonds –
And threw it towards thy land. The sea received it,
And so I wished thy body might my heart;
And even with this I lost fair England's view, 110
And bid mine eyes be packing with my heart,
And called them blind and dusky spectacles
For losing ken of Albion's wishèd coast.
How often have I tempted Suffolk's tongue –
The agent of thy foul inconstancy –
To sit and witch me, as Ascanius did
When he to madding Dido would unfold
His father's acts, commenced in burning Troy!
Am I not witched like her? Or thou not false like him?
Ay me! I can no more. Die, Margaret! 120
For Henry weeps that thou dost live so long.
    Noise within. Enter Warwick, Salisbury, and many
    commons

WARWICK
It is reported, mighty sovereign,
That good Duke Humphrey traitorously is murdered
By Suffolk and the Cardinal Beaufort's means.
The commons, like an angry hive of bees
That want their leader, scatter up and down
And care not who they sting in his revenge.
Myself have calmed their spleenful mutiny,
Until they hear the order of his death.

KING
That he is dead, good Warwick, 'tis too true; 130
But how he died God knows, not Henry.
Enter his chamber, view his breathless corpse,

And comment then upon his sudden death.

WARWICK

That shall I do, my liege. Stay, Salisbury,
With the rude multitude till I return.

Exeunt Warwick, then Salisbury
and the commons

KING

O Thou that judgest all things, stay my thoughts,
My thoughts that labour to persuade my soul
Some violent hands were laid on Humphrey's life.
If my suspect be false, forgive me, God,
140 For judgement only doth belong to Thee.
Fain would I go to chafe his paly lips
With twenty thousand kisses, and to drain
Upon his face an ocean of salt tears,
To tell my love unto his dumb deaf trunk,
And with my fingers feel his hand unfeeling;
But all in vain are these mean obsequies,
And to survey his dead and earthy image,
What were it but to make my sorrow greater?

Bed put forth with Gloucester's body in it. Enter
Warwick

WARWICK

Come hither, gracious sovereign, view this body.

KING

150 That is to see how deep my grave is made;
For with his soul fled all my worldly solace,
For, seeing him, I see my life in death.

WARWICK

As surely as my soul intends to live
With that dread King that took our state upon Him
To free us from His Father's wrathful curse,
I do believe that violent hands were laid
Upon the life of this thrice-famèd Duke.

SUFFOLK

A dreadful oath, sworn with a solemn tongue!
What instance gives Lord Warwick for his vow?

WARWICK

See how the blood is settled in his face.   160
Oft have I seen a timely-parted ghost
Of ashy semblance, meagre, pale, and bloodless,
Being all descended to the labouring heart;
Who, in the conflict that it holds with death,
Attracts the same for aidance 'gainst the enemy;
Which with the heart there cools, and ne'er returneth
To blush and beautify the cheek again.
But see, his face is black and full of blood,
His eyeballs further out than when he lived,
Staring full ghastly like a strangled man;   170
His hair upreared, his nostrils stretched with struggling;
His hands abroad displayed, as one that grasped
And tugged for life, and was by strength subdued.
Look, on the sheets his hair, you see, is sticking;
His well-proportioned beard made rough and rugged,
Like to the summer's corn by tempest lodged.
It cannot be but he was murdered here;
The least of all these signs were probable.

SUFFOLK

Why, Warwick, who should do the Duke to death?
Myself and Beaufort had him in protection;   180
And we, I hope, sir, are no murderers.

WARWICK

But both of you were vowed Duke Humphrey's foes,
And you, forsooth, had the good Duke to keep;
'Tis like you would not feast him like a friend,
And 'tis well seen he found an enemy.

QUEEN

Then you belike suspect these noblemen
As guilty of Duke Humphrey's timeless death.

WARWICK

Who finds the heifer dead and bleeding fresh,
And sees fast by a butcher with an axe,
190　But will suspect 'twas he that made the slaughter?
Who finds the partridge in the puttock's nest,
But may imagine how the bird was dead,
Although the kite soar with unbloodied beak?
Even so suspicious is this tragedy.

QUEEN

Are you the butcher, Suffolk? Where's your knife?
Is Beaufort termed a kite? Where are his talons?

SUFFOLK

I wear no knife to slaughter sleeping men;
But here's a vengeful sword, rusted with ease,
That shall be scourèd in his rancorous heart
200　That slanders me with murder's crimson badge.
Say, if thou darest, proud Lord of Warwickshire,
That I am faulty in Duke Humphrey's death.

Exit Cardinal

WARWICK

What dares not Warwick, if false Suffolk dare him?

QUEEN

He dares not calm his contumelious spirit,
Nor cease to be an arrogant controller,
Though Suffolk dare him twenty thousand times.

WARWICK

Madam, be still, with reverence may I say,
For every word you speak in his behalf
Is slander to your royal dignity.

SUFFOLK

210　Blunt-witted lord, ignoble in demeanour!
If ever lady wronged her lord so much,
Thy mother took into her blameful bed
Some stern untutored churl, and noble stock
Was graft with crabtree slip, whose fruit thou art,

And never of the Nevils' noble race.

WARWICK

But that the guilt of murder bucklers thee
And I should rob the deathsman of his fee,
Quitting thee thereby of ten thousand shames,
And that my sovereign's presence makes me mild,
I would, false murderous coward, on thy knee   220
Make thee beg pardon for thy passèd speech,
And say it was thy mother that thou meantest;
That thou thyself was born in bastardy;
And, after all this fearful homage done,
Give thee thy hire and send thy soul to hell,
Pernicious blood-sucker of sleeping men!

SUFFOLK

Thou shalt be waking while I shed thy blood,
If from this presence thou darest go with me.

WARWICK

Away even now, or I will drag thee hence.
Unworthy though thou art, I'll cope with thee,   230
And do some service to Duke Humphrey's ghost.

Exeunt Suffolk and Warwick

KING

What stronger breastplate than a heart untainted!
Thrice is he armed that hath his quarrel just;
And he but naked, though locked up in steel,
Whose conscience with injustice is corrupted.

A noise within

QUEEN

What noise is this?

*Enter Suffolk and Warwick with their weapons
drawn*

KING

Why, how now, lords! Your wrathful weapons drawn
Here in our presence? Dare you be so bold?
Why, what tumultuous clamour have we here?

SUFFOLK

240　　The traitorous Warwick, with the men of Bury,
　　　Set all upon me, mighty sovereign.

　　　　Enter Salisbury

SALISBURY (*to the commons within*)

　　　Sirs, stand apart; the King shall know your mind.
　　　Dread lord, the commons send you word by me,
　　　Unless Lord Suffolk straight be done to death,
　　　Or banishèd fair England's territories,
　　　They will by violence tear him from your palace
　　　And torture him with grievous lingering death.
　　　They say by him the good Duke Humphrey died;
　　　They say in him they fear your highness' death;
250　　And mere instinct of love and loyalty,
　　　Free from a stubborn opposite intent,
　　　As being thought to contradict your liking,
　　　Makes them thus forward in his banishment.
　　　They say, in care of your most royal person,
　　　That if your highness should intend to sleep,
　　　And charge that no man should disturb your rest
　　　In pain of your dislike, or pain of death,
　　　Yet, notwithstanding such a strait edict,
　　　Were there a serpent seen, with forkèd tongue,
260　　That slily glided towards your majesty,
　　　It were but necessary you were waked,
　　　Lest, being suffered in that harmful slumber,
　　　The mortal worm might make the sleep eternal;
　　　And therefore do they cry, though you forbid,
　　　That they will guard you, whe'er you will or no,
　　　From such fell serpents as false Suffolk is;
　　　With whose envenomèd and fatal sting,
　　　Your loving uncle, twenty times his worth,
　　　They say is shamefully bereft of life.

COMMONS (*within*)

270　　An answer from the King, my lord of Salisbury!

SUFFOLK

    'Tis like the commons, rude unpolished hinds,
    Could send such message to their sovereign.
    But you, my lord, were glad to be employed,
    To show how quaint an orator you are;
    But all the honour Salisbury hath won
    Is that he was the lord ambassador
    Sent from a sort of tinkers to the King.

COMMONS (*within*)

    An answer from the King, or we will all break in!

KING

    Go, Salisbury, and tell them all from me
    I thank them for their tender loving care;   280
    And had I not been cited so by them,
    Yet did I purpose as they do entreat;
    For sure my thoughts do hourly prophesy
    Mischance unto my state by Suffolk's means.
    And therefore by His majesty I swear
    Whose far unworthy deputy I am,
    He shall not breathe infection in this air
    But three days longer, on the pain of death.

                                  Exit Salisbury

QUEEN

    O Henry, let me plead for gentle Suffolk!

KING

    Ungentle Queen, to call him gentle Suffolk!   290
    No more, I say; if thou dost plead for him,
    Thou wilt but add increase unto my wrath.
    Had I but said, I would have kept my word;
    But when I swear, it is irrevocable.
    (*To Suffolk*)
    If after three days' space thou here beest found
    On any ground that I am ruler of,
    The world shall not be ransom for thy life.
    Come, Warwick, come, good Warwick, go with me;

I have great matters to impart to thee.

Exeunt all but the Queen and Suffolk

QUEEN

300 Mischance and sorrow go along with you!
Heart's discontent and sour affliction
Be playfellows to keep you company!
There's two of you, the devil make a third,
And threefold vengeance tend upon your steps!

SUFFOLK

Cease, gentle Queen, these execrations,
And let thy Suffolk take his heavy leave.

QUEEN

Fie, coward woman and soft-hearted wretch!
Hast thou not spirit to curse thine enemy?

SUFFOLK

A plague upon them! Wherefore should I curse them?

310 Would curses kill, as doth the mandrake's groan,
I would invent as bitter searching terms,
As curst, as harsh, and horrible to hear,
Delivered strongly through my fixèd teeth,
With full as many signs of deadly hate,
As lean-faced Envy in her loathsome cave.
My tongue should stumble in mine earnest words,
Mine eyes should sparkle like the beaten flint,
Mine hair be fixed on end, as one distract;
Ay, every joint should seem to curse and ban;

320 And even now my burdened heart would break,
Should I not curse them. Poison be their drink!
Gall, worse than gall, the daintiest that they taste!
Their sweetest shade, a grove of cypress trees!
Their chiefest prospect, murdering basilisks!
Their softest touch as smart as lizards' stings!
Their music frightful as the serpent's hiss,
And boding screech-owls make the consort full!
And the foul terrors in dark-seated hell –

QUEEN

Enough, sweet Suffolk; thou tormentest thyself,
And these dread curses, like the sun 'gainst glass,   330
Or like an overchargèd gun, recoil
And turns the force of them upon thyself.

SUFFOLK

You bade me ban, and will you bid me leave?
Now, by the ground that I am banished from,
Well could I curse away a winter's night,
Though standing naked on a mountain top,
Where biting cold would never let grass grow,
And think it but a minute spent in sport.

QUEEN

O, let me entreat thee cease. Give me thy hand
That I may dew it with my mournful tears;   340
Nor let the rain of heaven wet this place
To wash away my woeful monuments.
O, could this kiss be printed in thy hand,
That thou mightst think upon these by the seal,
Through whom a thousand sighs are breathed for thee.
So get thee gone, that I may know my grief;
'Tis but surmised whiles thou art standing by,
As one that surfeits thinking on a want.
I will repeal thee, or, be well assured,
Adventure to be banishèd myself;   350
And banishèd I am, if but from thee.
Go, speak not to me; even now be gone.
O, go not yet. Even thus two friends condemned
Embrace and kiss and take ten thousand leaves,
Loather a hundred times to part than die.
Yet now farewell, and farewell life with thee.

SUFFOLK

Thus is poor Suffolk ten times banishèd,
Once by the King and three times thrice by thee.
'Tis not the land I care for, wert thou thence;

360   A wilderness is populous enough,
So Suffolk had thy heavenly company;
For where thou art, there is the world itself,
With every several pleasure in the world;
And where thou art not, desolation.
I can no more. Live thou to joy thy life;
Myself no joy in naught but that thou livest.

Enter Vaux

QUEEN
Whither goes Vaux so fast? What news, I prithee?

VAUX
To signify unto his majesty
That Cardinal Beaufort is at point of death;
370   For suddenly a grievous sickness took him,
That makes him gasp, and stare, and catch the air,
Blaspheming God, and cursing men on earth.
Sometime he talks as if Duke Humphrey's ghost
Were by his side; sometime he calls the King,
And whispers to his pillow, as to him,
The secrets of his overchargèd soul;
And I am sent to tell his majesty
That even now he cries aloud for him.

QUEEN
Go tell this heavy message to the King.

Exit Vaux

380   Ay me! What is this world! What news are these!
But wherefore grieve I at an hour's poor loss,
Omitting Suffolk's exile, my soul's treasure?
Why only, Suffolk, mourn I not for thee,
And with the southern clouds contend in tears,
Theirs for the earth's increase, mine for my sorrows?
Now get thee hence; the King, thou knowest, is coming;
If thou be found by me thou art but dead.

SUFFOLK
If I depart from thee I cannot live,

And in thy sight to die, what were it else
But like a pleasant slumber in thy lap?   390
Here could I breathe my soul into the air,
As mild and gentle as the cradle-babe
Dying with mother's dug between its lips;
Where, from thy sight, I should be raging mad,
And cry out for thee to close up mine eyes,
To have thee with thy lips to stop my mouth;
So shouldst thou either turn my flying soul,
Or I should breathe it so into thy body,
And then it lived in sweet Elysium.
To die by thee were but to die in jest;   400
From thee to die were torture more than death.
O, let me stay, befall what may befall!

QUEEN
Away! Though parting be a fretful corrosive,
It is applièd to a deathful wound.
To France, sweet Suffolk! Let me hear from thee;
For wheresoe'er thou art in this world's globe,
I'll have an Iris that shall find thee out.

SUFFOLK
I go.
QUEEN And take my heart with thee.
        She kisseth him

SUFFOLK
A jewel, locked into the woefullest cask
That ever did contain a thing of worth.   410
Even as a splitted bark so sunder we;
This way fall I to death.
QUEEN   This way for me.
                        Exeunt in opposite directions

Enter the King, Salisbury, and Warwick, to the
Cardinal in bed

KING

How fares my lord? Speak, Beaufort, to thy sovereign.

CARDINAL

If thou beest Death, I'll give thee England's treasure,
Enough to purchase such another island,
So thou wilt let me live, and feel no pain.

KING

Ah, what a sign it is of evil life
Where death's approach is seen so terrible!

WARWICK

Beaufort, it is thy sovereign speaks to thee.

CARDINAL

Bring me unto my trial when you will.
Died he not in his bed? Where should he die?
10   Can I make men live whe'er they will or no?
O, torture me no more! I will confess.
Alive again? Then show me where he is;
I'll give a thousand pound to look upon him.
He hath no eyes; the dust hath blinded them.
Comb down his hair; look, look, it stands upright,
Like lime-twigs set to catch my wingèd soul.
Give me some drink; and bid the apothecary
Bring the strong poison that I bought of him.

KING

O Thou eternal mover of the heavens,
20   Look with a gentle eye upon this wretch;
O, beat away the busy meddling fiend
That lays strong siege unto this wretch's soul,
And from his bosom purge this black despair.

WARWICK

See how the pangs of death do make him grin!

SALISBURY

Disturb him not; let him pass peaceably.

KING

    Peace to his soul, if God's good pleasure be!
    Lord Cardinal, if thou thinkest on heaven's bliss,
    Hold up thy hand, make signal of thy hope.

                                  The Cardinal dies

    He dies and makes no sign. O God, forgive him!

WARWICK

    So bad a death argues a monstrous life.   30

KING

    Forbear to judge, for we are sinners all.
    Close up his eyes, and draw the curtain close;
    And let us all to meditation.   *Exeunt*

*

    Alarum. Fight at sea. Ordnance goes off. Enter a IV.1
    Lieutenant, a Master, a Master's Mate, Walter
    Whitmore, Suffolk, disguised, two Gentlemen
    prisoners, and soldiers

LIEUTENANT

    The gaudy, blabbing, and remorseful day
    Is crept into the bosom of the sea;
    And now loud howling wolves arouse the jades
    That drag the tragic melancholy night;
    Who with their drowsy, slow, and flagging wings
    Clip dead men's graves, and from their misty jaws
    Breathe foul contagious darkness in the air.
    Therefore bring forth the soldiers of our prize,
    For whilst our pinnace anchors in the Downs
    Here shall they make their ransom on the sand,   10
    Or with their blood stain this discoloured shore.
    Master, this prisoner freely give I thee;
    And thou that art his mate make boot of this;
    The other, Walter Whitmore, is thy share.

FIRST GENTLEMAN

What is my ransom, master? Let me know.

MASTER

A thousand crowns, or else lay down your head.

MATE

And so much shall you give, or off goes yours.

LIEUTENANT

What, think you much to pay two thousand crowns,
And bear the name and port of gentleman?
20   Cut both the villains' throats; for die you shall.
The lives of those which we have lost in fight
Be counterpoised with such a petty sum!

FIRST GENTLEMAN

I'll give it, sir; and therefore spare my life.

SECOND GENTLEMAN

And so will I, and write home for it straight.

WHITMORE

I lost mine eye in laying the prize aboard,
(*To Suffolk*) And therefore to revenge it shalt thou die;
And so should these, if I might have my will.

LIEUTENANT

Be not so rash. Take ransom; let him live.

SUFFOLK

Look on my George; I am a gentleman.
30   Rate me at what thou wilt, thou shalt be paid.

WHITMORE

And so am I; my name is Walter Whitmore.
How now! Why starts thou? What, doth death affright?

SUFFOLK

Thy name affrights me, in whose sound is death.
A cunning man did calculate my birth,
And told me that by water I should die.
Yet let not this make thee be bloody-minded;
Thy name is Gaultier, being rightly sounded.

124

WHITMORE

Gualtier or Walter, which it is I care not.
Never yet did base dishonour blur our name
But with our sword we wiped away the blot.   40
Therefore, when merchant-like I sell revenge,
Broke be my sword, my arms torn and defaced,
And I proclaimed a coward through the world.

SUFFOLK

Stay, Whitmore, for thy prisoner is a prince,
The Duke of Suffolk, William de la Pole.

WHITMORE

The Duke of Suffolk, muffled up in rags!

SUFFOLK

Ay, but these rags are no part of the Duke;
Jove sometime went disguised, and why not I?

LIEUTENANT

But Jove was never slain, as thou shalt be.

SUFFOLK

Obscure and lousy swain, King Henry's blood,   50
The honourable blood of Lancaster,
Must not be shed by such a jaded groom.
Hast thou not kissed thy hand and held my stirrup?
Bare-headed plodded by my foot-cloth mule,
And thought thee happy when I shook my head?
How often hast thou waited at my cup,
Fed from my trencher, kneeled down at the board,
When I have feasted with Queen Margaret?
Remember it and let it make thee crest-fallen,
Ay, and allay this thy abortive pride,   60
How in our voiding lobby hast thou stood
And duly waited for my coming forth.
This hand of mine hath writ in thy behalf,
And therefore shall it charm thy riotous tongue.

WHITMORE

Speak, captain, shall I stab the forlorn swain?

LIEUTENANT

First let my words stab him, as he hath me.

SUFFOLK

Base slave, thy words are blunt and so art thou.

LIEUTENANT

Convey him hence, and on our longboat's side
Strike off his head.

SUFFOLK   Thou darest not, for thy own.

LIEUTENANT

Yes, Poole.

SUFFOLK Poole?

70 **LIEUTENANT**   Poole! Sir Poole! Lord!
Ay, kennel, puddle, sink, whose filth and dirt
Troubles the silver spring where England drinks;
Now will I dam up this thy yawning mouth
For swallowing the treasure of the realm.
Thy lips that kissed the Queen shall sweep the ground;
And thou that smiled'st at good Duke Humphrey's
death
Against the senseless winds shalt grin in vain,
Who in contempt shall hiss at thee again;
And wedded be thou to the hags of hell,
80 For daring to affy a mighty lord
Unto the daughter of a worthless king,
Having neither subject, wealth, nor diadem.
By devilish policy art thou grown great,
And, like ambitious Sylla, overgorged
With gobbets of thy mother's bleeding heart.
By thee Anjou and Maine were sold to France,
The false revolting Normans thorough thee
Disdain to call us lord, and Picardy
Hath slain their governors, surprised our forts,
90 And sent the ragged soldiers wounded home.
The princely Warwick, and the Nevils all,
Whose dreadful swords were never drawn in vain,

As hating thee, are rising up in arms;
And now the house of York, thrust from the crown
By shameful murder of a guiltless king
And lofty, proud, encroaching tyranny,
Burns with revenging fire, whose hopeful colours
Advance our half-faced sun, striving to shine,
Under the which is writ '*Invitis nubibus*'
The commons here in Kent are up in arms; 100
And to conclude, reproach and beggary
Is crept into the palace of our King,
And all by thee. Away! Convey him hence.

SUFFOLK

O that I were a god, to shoot forth thunder
Upon these paltry, servile, abject drudges.
Small things make base men proud. This villain here,
Being captain of a pinnace, threatens more
Than Bargulus, the strong Illyrian pirate.
Drones suck not eagles' blood, but rob beehives.
It is impossible that I should die 110
By such a lowly vassal as thyself.
Thy words move rage and not remorse in me.

LIEUTENANT

Ay, but my deeds shall stay thy fury soon.

SUFFOLK

I go of message from the Queen to France;
I charge thee, waft me safely 'cross the Channel.

LIEUTENANT

Walter!

WHITMORE

Come, Suffolk, I must waft thee to thy death.

SUFFOLK

Pene gelidus timor occupat artus;
It is thee I fear.

WHITMORE

Thou shalt have cause to fear before I leave thee. 120

What, are ye daunted now? Now will ye stoop?

FIRST GENTLEMAN

My gracious lord, entreat him, speak him fair.

SUFFOLK

Suffolk's imperial tongue is stern and rough,
Used to command, untaught to plead for favour.
Far be it we should honour such as these
With humble suit. No, rather let my head
Stoop to the block than these knees bow to any
Save to the God of heaven, and to my king;
And sooner dance upon a bloody pole
130   Than stand uncovered to the vulgar groom.
True nobility is exempt from fear;
More can I bear than you dare execute.

LIEUTENANT

Hale him away, and let him talk no more.

SUFFOLK

Come, soldiers, show what cruelty ye can,
That this my death may never be forgot.
Great men oft die by vile Besonians:
A Roman sworder and banditto slave
Murdered sweet Tully; Brutus' bastard hand
Stabbed Julius Caesar; savage islanders
140   Pompey the Great; and Suffolk dies by pirates.

Exeunt Whitmore and soldiers
with Suffolk

LIEUTENANT

And as for these whose ransom we have set,
It is our pleasure one of them depart;
Therefore come you with us, and let him go.

Exeunt all but the First Gentleman
Enter Walter Whitmore with the body of Suffolk

WHITMORE

There let his head and lifeless body lie,
Until the Queen his mistress bury it.   *Exit*

FIRST GENTLEMAN

   O, barbarous and bloody spectacle!
   His body will I bear unto the King;
   If he revenge it not, yet will his friends;
   So will the Queen, that living held him dear.

                       Exit with the body

     Enter George Bevis and John Holland   IV.2

BEVIS Come, and get thee a sword, though made of a lath;
   they have been up these two days.

HOLLAND They have the more need to sleep now then.

BEVIS I tell thee, Jack Cade the clothier means to dress
   the commonwealth, and turn it, and set a new nap upon it.

HOLLAND So he had need, for 'tis threadbare. Well, I
   say it was never merry world in England since gentlemen came up.

BEVIS O miserable age! Virtue is not regarded in handi- 10
   craftsmen.

HOLLAND The nobility think scorn to go in leather aprons.

BEVIS Nay, more; the King's Council are no good work-
   men.

HOLLAND True; and yet it is said 'Labour in thy
   vocation'; which is as much to say as 'Let the magistrates be labouring men'; and therefore should we
   be magistrates.

BEVIS Thou hast hit it; for there's no better sign of a
   brave mind than a hard hand.   20

HOLLAND I see them, I see them! There's Best's son,
   the tanner of Wingham.

BEVIS He shall have the skins of our enemies to make
   dog's leather of.

HOLLAND And Dick the butcher.

BEVIS Then is sin struck down like an ox, and iniquity's throat cut like a calf.

HOLLAND And Smith the weaver.

BEVIS Argo, their thread of life is spun.

30 HOLLAND Come, come, let's fall in with them.

> *Drums. Enter Jack Cade, Dick the butcher, Smith the weaver, and a sawyer, with infinite numbers*

CADE We John Cade, so termed of our supposed father –

DICK *(aside)* Or rather of stealing a cade of herrings.

CADE For our enemies shall fall before us, inspired with the spirit of putting down kings and princes. Command silence.

DICK Silence!

CADE My father was a Mortimer –

DICK *(aside)* He was an honest man and a good bricklayer.

CADE My mother a Plantagenet –

40 DICK *(aside)* I knew her well; she was a midwife.

CADE My wife descended of the Lacys –

DICK *(aside)* She was indeed a pedlar's daughter, and sold many laces.

SMITH *(aside)* But now of late, not able to travel with her furred pack, she washes bucks here at home.

CADE Therefore am I of an honourable house.

DICK *(aside)* Ay, by my faith, the field is honourable, and there was he born, under a hedge; for his father had never a house but the cage.

50 CADE Valiant I am.

SMITH *(aside)* 'A must needs, for beggary is valiant.

CADE I am able to endure much.

DICK *(aside)* No question of that; for I have seen him whipped three market days together.

CADE I fear neither sword nor fire.

SMITH *(aside)* He need not fear the sword, for his coat is of proof.

DICK *(aside)* But methinks he should stand in fear of fire, being burnt i'th'hand for stealing of sheep.

CADE Be brave then; for your captain is brave, and vows 60
reformation. There shall be in England seven halfpenny
loaves sold for a penny; the three-hooped pot shall have
ten hoops; and I will make it felony to drink small beer.
All the realm shall be in common, and in Cheapside shall
my palfrey go to grass. And when I am king, as king I
will be –

ALL God save your majesty!

CADE I thank you, good people. There shall be no money;
all shall eat and drink on my score; and I will apparel
them all in one livery, that they may agree like brothers, 70
and worship me their lord.

DICK The first thing we do, let's kill all the lawyers.

CADE Nay, that I mean to do. Is not this a lamentable
thing, that the skin of an innocent lamb should be
made parchment? That parchment, being scribbled
o'er, should undo a man? Some say the bee stings, but I
say 'tis the bee's wax, for I did but seal once to a thing,
and I was never mine own man since. How now? Who's
there?

Enter some rebels with the Clerk of Chartham

SMITH The clerk of Chartham; he can write and read and 80
cast accompt.

CADE O, monstrous!

SMITH We took him setting of boys' copies.

CADE Here's a villain!

SMITH H'as a book in his pocket with red letters in't.

CADE Nay, then he is a conjurer.

DICK Nay, he can make obligations, and write court-hand.

CADE I am sorry for't. The man is a proper man, of mine
honour; unless I find him guilty, he shall not die. Come
hither, sirrah, I must examine thee. What is thy name? 90

CLERK Emmanuel.

DICK They use to write it on the top of letters. 'Twill go
hard with you.

CADE Let me alone. Dost thou use to write thy name?

131

Or hast thou a mark to thyself, like a honest plain-deal-
ing man?

CLERK Sir, I thank God I have been so well brought up
that I can write my name.

ALL He hath confessed; away with him! He's a villain
100 and a traitor.

CADE Away with him, I say; hang him with his pen and
inkhorn about his neck.

Exit one with the Clerk

Enter Michael

MICHAEL Where's our general?

CADE Here I am, thou particular fellow.

MICHAEL Fly, fly, fly! Sir Humphrey Stafford and his
brother are hard by, with the King's forces.

CADE Stand, villain, stand, or I'll fell thee down. He shall
be encountered with a man as good as himself. He is
but a knight, is 'a?

110 MICHAEL No.

CADE To equal him I will make myself a knight presently.
(*He kneels*) Rise up, Sir John Mortimer. (*He rises*) Now
have at him!

*Enter Sir Humphrey Stafford and his brother, with
drum and soldiers*

STAFFORD

Rebellious hinds, the filth and scum of Kent,
Marked for the gallows, lay your weapons down;
Home to your cottages, forsake this groom.
The King is merciful, if you revolt.

BROTHER

But angry, wrathful, and inclined to blood,
If you go forward; therefore yield, or die.

CADE

120 As for these silken-coated slaves, I pass not;
It is to you, good people, that I speak,
Over whom, in time to come, I hope to reign;

For I am rightful heir unto the crown.

STAFFORD

Villain, thy father was a plasterer;
And thou thyself a shearman, art thou not?

CADE

And Adam was a gardener.

BROTHER   And what of that?

CADE

Marry, this: Edmund Mortimer, Earl of March,
Married the Duke of Clarence' daughter, did he not?

STAFFORD

Ay, sir.

CADE

By her he had two children at one birth.   130

BROTHER

That's false.

CADE

Ay, there's the question; but I say 'tis true:
The elder of them, being put to nurse,
Was by a beggar-woman stolen away;
And, ignorant of his birth and parentage,
Became a bricklayer when he came to age.
His son am I; deny it if you can.

DICK

Nay, 'tis too true; therefore he shall be king.

SMITH Sir, he made a chimney in my father's house, and
the bricks are alive at this day to testify it; therefore deny   140
it not.

STAFFORD

And will you credit this base drudge's words,
That speaks he knows not what?

ALL

Ay, marry, will we; therefore get ye gone.

BROTHER

Jack Cade, the Duke of York hath taught you this.

CADE (*aside*) He lies, for I invented it myself. (*To Stafford*)
Go to, sirrah, tell the King from me that for his father's
sake, Henry the Fifth, in whose time boys went to span-
counter for French crowns, I am content he shall
150   reign; but I'll be Protector over him.

DICK And furthermore, we'll have the Lord Say's head
for selling the dukedom of Maine.

CADE And good reason; for thereby is England mained and
fain to go with a staff, but that my puissance holds it up.
Fellow kings, I tell you that that Lord Say hath gelded
the commonwealth and made it an eunuch; and more
than that, he can speak French; and therefore he is a
traitor.

STAFFORD O gross and miserable ignorance!

160   CADE Nay, answer if you can; the Frenchmen are our
enemies; go to, then, I ask but this: can he that speaks
with the tongue of an enemy be a good counsellor, or
no?

ALL No, no; and therefore we'll have his head.

BROTHER
Well, seeing gentle words will not prevail,
Assail them with the army of the King.

STAFFORD
Herald, away! And throughout every town
Proclaim them traitors that are up with Cade;
That those which fly before the battle ends
May, even in their wives' and children's sight,
170   Be hanged up for example at their doors.
And you that be the King's friends, follow me.
                    Exit with his brother and soldiers

CADE
And you that love the commons, follow me.
Now show yourselves men; 'tis for liberty.
We will not leave one lord, one gentleman;
Spare none but such as go in clouted shoon,

For they are thrifty honest men, and such
As would, but that they dare not, take our parts.

DICK They are all in order, and march toward us.

CADE But then are we in order when we are most out
of order. Come, march forward.   *Exeunt* 180

Alarums to the fight, wherein both the Staffords IV.3
are slain. Enter Cade and the rest

CADE Where's Dick, the butcher of Ashford?

DICK Here, sir.

CADE They fell before thee like sheep and oxen, and thou
behaved'st thyself as if thou hadst been in thine own
slaughter-house. Therefore thus will I reward thee:
the Lent shall be as long again as it is; and thou shalt have
a licence to kill for a hundred lacking one.

DICK I desire no more.

CADE And to speak truth, thou deservest no less.

He puts on Sir Humphrey Stafford's coat of mail
This monument of the victory will I bear; and the 10
bodies shall be dragged at my horse heels till I do
come to London, where we will have the Mayor's sword
borne before us.

DICK If we mean to thrive and do good, break open the
gaols and let out the prisoners.

CADE Fear not that, I warrant thee. Come, let's march
towards London.   *Exeunt*

Enter the King with a supplication, and the Queen IV.4
with Suffolk's head, the Duke of Buckingham, and
the Lord Say

QUEEN (*aside*)
Oft have I heard that grief softens the mind,
And makes it fearful and degenerate;

Think therefore on revenge and cease to weep.
But who can cease to weep and look on this?
Here may his head lie on my throbbing breast;
But where's the body that I should embrace?

BUCKINGHAM What answer makes your grace to the
rebels' supplication?

KING
I'll send some holy bishop to entreat;
For God forbid so many simple souls
Should perish by the sword! And I myself,
Rather than bloody war shall cut them short,
Will parley with Jack Cade their general.
But stay, I'll read it over once again.

QUEEN (*aside*)
Ah, barbarous villains! Hath this lovely face
Ruled like a wandering planet over me,
And could it not enforce them to relent,
That were unworthy to behold the same?

KING
Lord Say, Jack Cade hath sworn to have thy head.

SAY
Ay, but I hope your highness shall have his.

KING
How now, madam?
Still lamenting and mourning for Suffolk's death?
I fear me, love, if that I had been dead,
Thou wouldst not have mourned so much for me.

QUEEN
No, my love; I should not mourn, but die for thee.
Enter First Messenger

KING
How now? What news? Why comest thou in such
haste?

FIRST MESSENGER
The rebels are in Southwark; fly, my lord!

Jack Cade proclaims himself Lord Mortimer,
Descended from the Duke of Clarence' house,
And calls your grace usurper, openly,   30
And vows to crown himself in Westminster.
His army is a ragged multitude
Of hinds and peasants, rude and merciless;
Sir Humphrey Stafford and his brother's death
Hath given them heart and courage to proceed.
All scholars, lawyers, courtiers, gentlemen,
They call false caterpillars and intend their death.

KING

O, graceless men, they know not what they do.

BUCKINGHAM

My gracious lord, retire to Killingworth,
Until a power be raised to put them down.   40

QUEEN

Ah, were the Duke of Suffolk now alive,
These Kentish rebels would be soon appeased!

KING

Lord Say, the traitors hateth thee;
Therefore away with us to Killingworth.

SAY

So might your grace's person be in danger.
The sight of me is odious in their eyes;
And therefore in this city will I stay,
And live alone as secret as I may.
    Enter Second Messenger

SECOND MESSENGER

Jack Cade hath gotten London Bridge;
The citizens fly and forsake their houses;   50
The rascal people, thirsting after prey,
Join with the traitor; and they jointly swear
To spoil the city and your royal court.

BUCKINGHAM

Then linger not, my lord. Away! Take horse!

137

KING

Come, Margaret. God, our hope, will succour us.

QUEEN

My hope is gone, now Suffolk is deceased.

KING (*to Lord Say*)

Farewell, my lord. Trust not the Kentish rebels.

BUCKINGHAM

Trust nobody, for fear you be betrayed.

SAY

The trust I have is in mine innocence,

60 And therefore am I bold and resolute.   *Exeunt*

IV.5   *Enter Lord Scales upon the Tower, walking. Then
          enter three Citizens below*

SCALES How now? Is Jack Cade slain?

FIRST CITIZEN No, my lord, nor likely to be slain; for
they have won the bridge, killing all those that withstand them. The Lord Mayor craves aid of your honour
from the Tower to defend the city from the rebels.

SCALES

Such aid as I can spare you shall command,

But I am troubled here with them myself;

The rebels have assayed to win the Tower.

But get you to Smithfield and gather head,

10 And thither I will send you Matthew Gough.

Fight for your king, your country, and your lives;

And so farewell, for I must hence again.   *Exeunt*

IV.6   *Enter Jack Cade and the rest, and strikes his staff
          on London Stone*

CADE Now is Mortimer lord of this city. And here, sitting upon London Stone, I charge and command that,
of the city's cost, the Pissing Conduit run nothing
but claret wine this first year of our reign. And now

138

henceforward it shall be treason for any that calls me
other than Lord Mortimer.

Enter a Soldier, running

SOLDIER Jack Cade! Jack Cade!

CADE Knock him down there.

They kill him

SMITH If this fellow be wise, he'll never call ye Jack Cade
more; I think he hath a very fair warning.   10

DICK My lord, there's an army gathered together in
Smithfield.

CADE Come then, let's go fight with them. But first,
go and set London Bridge on fire, and, if you can, burn
down the Tower too. Come, let's away.   *Exeunt*

Alarums. Matthew Gough is slain, and all the rest.   IV.7
Then enter Jack Cade with his company

CADE So, sirs. Now go some and pull down the Savoy;
others to th'Inns of Court; down with them all.

DICK I have a suit unto your lordship.

CADE Be it a lordship, thou shalt have it for that word.

DICK Only that the laws of England may come out of your
mouth.

HOLLAND (*aside*) Mass, 'twill be sore law then, for he was
thrust in the mouth with a spear, and 'tis not whole yet.

SMITH (*aside to Holland*) Nay, John, it will be stinking
law, for his breath stinks with eating toasted cheese.   10

CADE I have thought upon it; it shall be so. Away! Burn
all the records of the realm; my mouth shall be the parliament of England.

HOLLAND (*aside*) Then we are like to have biting statutes,
unless his teeth be pulled out.

CADE And henceforward all things shall be in common.

Enter a Messenger

MESSENGER My lord, a prize, a prize! Here's the Lord

Say, which sold the towns in France; he that made us
pay one-and-twenty fifteens, and one shilling to the
20   pound, the last subsidy.

Enter George Bevis with the Lord Say

CADE Well, he shall be beheaded for it ten times. Ah,
thou say, thou serge, nay, thou buckram lord! Now art
thou within point-blank of our jurisdiction regal. What
canst thou answer to my majesty for giving up of
Normandy unto Mounsieur Basimecu, the Dolphin
of France? Be it known unto thee by these presence,
even the presence of Lord Mortimer, that I am the
besom that must sweep the court clean of such filth
as thou art. Thou hast most traitorously corrupted the
30   youth of the realm in erecting a grammar school; and
whereas, before, our forefathers had no other books
but the score and the tally, thou hast caused printing
to be used; and, contrary to the King his crown and
dignity, thou hast built a paper-mill. It will be proved
to thy face that thou hast men about thee that usually
talk of a noun and a verb, and such abominable words as
no Christian ear can endure to hear. Thou hast appointed
justices of the peace, to call poor men before them
about matters they were not able to answer. Moreover,
40   thou hast put them in prison; and because they could not
read, thou hast hanged them; when, indeed, only
for that cause they have been most worthy to live.
Thou dost ride in a foot-cloth, dost thou not?

SAY What of that?

CADE Marry, thou oughtest not to let thy horse wear a
cloak, when honester men than thou go in their hose and
doublets.

DICK And work in their shirt too; as myself, for example,
that am a butcher.

50   SAY You men of Kent –

DICK What say you of Kent?

SAY Nothing but this: 'tis *bona terra, mala gens.*

CADE Away with him! Away with him! He speaks Latin.

SAY

 Hear me but speak, and bear me where you will.
 Kent, in the *Commentaries* Caesar writ,
 Is termed the civilest place of all this isle;
 Sweet is the country, because full of riches,
 To people liberal, valiant, active, wealthy;
 Which makes me hope you are not void of pity.
 I sold not Maine, I lost not Normandy;   60
 Yet to recover them would lose my life.
 Justice with favour have I always done;
 Prayers and tears have moved me, gifts could never.
 When have I aught exacted at your hands,
 But to maintain the King, the realm, and you?
 Large gifts have I bestowed on learnèd clerks,
 Because my book preferred me to the King,
 And seeing ignorance is the curse of God,
 Knowledge the wing wherewith we fly to heaven,
 Unless you be possessed with devilish spirits,   70
 You cannot but forbear to murder me.
 This tongue hath parleyed unto foreign kings
 For your behoof –

CADE Tut, when struckest thou one blow in the field?

SAY

 Great men have reaching hands; oft have I struck
 Those that I never saw, and struck them dead.

BEVIS O monstrous coward! What, to come behind folks?

SAY

 These cheeks are pale for watching for your good.

CADE Give him a box o'th'ear, and that will make 'em red
 again.   80

SAY

 Long sitting to determine poor men's causes
 Hath made me full of sickness and diseases.

CADE Ye shall have a hempen caudle then, and the help of hatchet.

DICK Why dost thou quiver, man?

SAY

The palsy and not fear provokes me.

CADE Nay, he nods at us as who should say 'I'll be even with you'; I'll see if his head will stand steadier on a pole or no. Take him away and behead him.

SAY

90 Tell me: wherein have I offended most?
Have I affected wealth or honour? Speak.
Are my chests filled up with extorted gold?
Is my apparel sumptuous to behold?
Whom have I injured, that ye seek my death?
These hands are free from guiltless bloodshedding,
This breast from harbouring foul deceitful thoughts.
O, let me live!

CADE (*aside*) I feel remorse in myself with his words; but I'll bridle it. He shall die, an it be but for pleading so
100 well for his life. Away with him! He has a familiar under his tongue; he speaks not a God's name. Go, take him away, I say; and strike off his head presently, and then break into his son-in-law's house, Sir James Cromer, and strike off his head, and bring them both upon two poles hither.

ALL It shall be done.

SAY

Ah, countrymen, if, when you make your prayers,
God should be so obdurate as yourselves,
How would it fare with your departed souls?
110 And therefore yet relent and save my life.

CADE Away with him! And do as I command ye.

Exeunt some rebels with Lord Say

The proudest peer in the realm shall not wear a head on his shoulders, unless he pay me tribute; there shall not a maid be married, but she shall pay to me her maidenhead, ere they have it. Men shall hold of me *in capite*; and we charge and command that their wives be as free as heart can wish or tongue can tell.

DICK My lord, when shall we go to Cheapside and take up commodities upon our bills?

CADE Marry, presently. 120

ALL O, brave!

Enter one with the heads of Say and Cromer upon two poles

CADE But is not this braver? Let them kiss one another; for they loved well when they were alive. Now part them again, lest they consult about the giving up of some more towns in France. Soldiers, defer the spoil of the city until night; for with these borne before us, instead of maces, will we ride through the streets, and at every corner have them kiss. Away!   *Exeunt*

Alarum and retreat. Enter again Cade and all his IV.8
rabblement

CADE Up Fish Street! Down Saint Magnus' Corner! Kill and knock down! Throw them into Thames!

Sound a parley

What noise is this I hear? Dare any be so bold to sound retreat or parley, when I command them kill?

Enter Buckingham and old Clifford, attended

BUCKINGHAM

Ay, here they be that dare and will disturb thee;
Know, Cade, we come ambassadors from the King
Unto the commons, whom thou hast misled;
And here pronounce free pardon to them all
That will forsake thee and go home in peace.

CLIFFORD

What say ye, countrymen, will ye relent

And yield to mercy, whilst 'tis offered you,
Or let a rebel lead you to your deaths?
Who loves the King and will embrace his pardon,
Fling up his cap and say 'God save his majesty!'
Who hateth him, and honours not his father,
Henry the Fifth, that made all France to quake,
Shake he his weapon at us and pass by.

ALL God save the King! God save the King!

CADE What, Buckingham and Clifford, are ye so brave?
20 And you, base peasants, do ye believe him? Will
you needs be hanged with your pardons about your
necks? Hath my sword therefore broke through London
gates, that you should leave me at the White Hart
in Southwark? I thought ye would never have given out
these arms till you had recovered your ancient freedom.
But you are all recreants and dastards, and delight to live
in slavery to the nobility. Let them break your backs with
burdens, take your houses over your heads, ravish your
wives and daughters before your faces. For me, I will
30 make shift for one, and so God's curse light upon you
all!

ALL We'll follow Cade! We'll follow Cade!

CLIFFORD
Is Cade the son of Henry the Fifth,
That thus you do exclaim you'll go with him?
Will he conduct you through the heart of France,
And make the meanest of you earls and dukes?
Alas, he hath no home, no place to fly to;
Nor knows he how to live but by the spoil,
Unless by robbing of your friends and us.
40 Were't not a shame, that whilst you live at jar,
The fearful French, whom you late vanquishèd,
Should make a start o'er seas and vanquish you?
Methinks already in this civil broil
I see them lording it in London streets,

Crying 'Villiago!' unto all they meet.
Better ten thousand base-born Cades miscarry
Than you should stoop unto a Frenchman's mercy.
To France! To France! And get what you have lost;
Spare England, for it is your native coast.
Henry hath money; you are strong and manly;   50
God on our side, doubt not of victory.

ALL À Clifford! À Clifford! We'll follow the King and
Clifford.

CADE (*aside*) Was ever feather so lightly blown to and fro
as this multitude? The name of Henry the Fifth hales
them to an hundred mischiefs and makes them leave me
desolate. I see them lay their heads together to surprise me. My sword make way for me, for here is
no staying. – In despite of the devils and hell, have
through the very midst of you! And heavens and   60
honour be witness that no want of resolution in me, but
only my followers' base and ignominious treasons, makes
me betake me to my heels.   *Exit*

BUCKINGHAM
What, is he fled? Go some and follow him;
And he that brings his head unto the King
Shall have a thousand crowns for his reward.
                              Exeunt some of them
Follow me, soldiers; we'll devise a mean
To reconcile you all unto the King.   *Exeunt*

Sound trumpets. Enter the King, Queen, and Somer-   IV.9
set, on the terrace

KING
Was ever king that joyed an earthly throne,
And could command no more content than I?
No sooner was I crept out of my cradle

145

But I was made a king at nine months old;
Was never subject longed to be a king
As I do long and wish to be a subject.
Enter Buckingham and Clifford

BUCKINGHAM

Health and glad tidings to your majesty!

KING

Why, Buckingham, is the traitor Cade surprised?
Or is he but retired to make him strong?
Enter multitudes, with halters about their necks

CLIFFORD

10   He is fled, my lord, and all his powers do yield,
And humbly thus with halters on their necks,
Expect your highness' doom of life or death.

KING

Then, heaven, set ope thy everlasting gates
To entertain my vows of thanks and praise!
Soldiers, this day have you redeemed your lives,
And showed how well you love your prince and country;
Continue still in this so good a mind,
And, Henry, though he be infortunate,
Assure yourselves, will never be unkind.

20   And so, with thanks and pardon to you all,
I do dismiss you to your several countries.

ALL God save the King! God save the King!
Enter a Messenger

MESSENGER

Please it your grace to be advertisèd
The Duke of York is newly come from Ireland,
And with a puissant and a mighty power
Of gallowglasses and stout kerns
Is marching hitherward in proud array;
And still proclaimeth, as he comes along,
His arms are only to remove from thee

30   The Duke of Somerset, whom he terms a traitor.

KING

Thus stands my state, 'twixt Cade and York distressed;
Like to a ship that, having 'scaped a tempest,
Is straightway calmed and boarded with a pirate.
But now is Cade driven back, his men dispersed,
And now is York in arms to second him.
I pray thee, Buckingham, go and meet him,
And ask him what's the reason of these arms.
Tell him I'll send Duke Edmund to the Tower;
And, Somerset, we will commit thee thither,
Until his army be dismissed from him.   40

SOMERSET

My lord,
I'll yield myself to prison willingly,
Or unto death, to do my country good.

KING

In any case, be not too rough in terms,
For he is fierce and cannot brook hard language.

BUCKINGHAM

I will, my lord, and doubt not so to deal
As all things shall redound unto your good.

KING

Come, wife, let's in and learn to govern better;
For yet may England curse my wretched reign.

                                        Flourish. Exeunt

Enter Cade   IV.10

CADE Fie on ambitions! Fie on myself, that have a sword
and yet am ready to famish! These five days have I
hid me in these woods, and durst not peep out, for all
the country is laid for me; but now am I so hungry that,
if I might have a lease of my life for a thousand years,
I could stay no longer. Wherefore, on a brick wall have
I climbed into this garden, to see if I can eat grass or pick

a sallet another while, which is not amiss to cool a man's
stomach this hot weather. And I think this word 'sallet'
10 was born to do me good; for many a time, but for a sallet,
my brain-pan had been cleft with a brown bill; and
many a time, when I have been dry and bravely marching, it hath served me instead of a quart pot to drink in;
and now the word 'sallet' must serve me to feed on.

Enter Alexander Iden

IDEN

Lord, who would live turmoilèd in the court,
And may enjoy such quiet walks as these?
This small inheritance my father left me
Contenteth me, and worth a monarchy.
I seek not to wax great by others' waning,
20 Or gather wealth I care not with what envy;
Sufficeth that I have maintains my state,
And sends the poor well pleasèd from my gate.

CADE (*aside*) Here's the lord of the soil come to seize me
for a stray, for entering his fee-simple without leave.
(*To Iden*) Ah, villain, thou wilt betray me, and get a
thousand crowns of the King by carrying my head to
him; but I'll make thee eat iron like an ostrich, and
swallow my sword like a great pin, ere thou and I part.

IDEN

Why, rude companion, whatsoe'er thou be,
30 I know thee not; why then should I betray thee?
Is't not enough to break into my garden,
And like a thief to come to rob my grounds,
Climbing my walls in spite of me the owner,
But thou wilt brave me with these saucy terms?

CADE Brave thee? Ay, by the best blood that ever was
broached, and beard thee too. Look on me well; I have
eat no meat these five days, yet come thou and thy five
men, and if I do not leave you all as dead as a door-nail, I
pray God I may never eat grass more.

IDEN

Nay, it shall ne'er be said, while England stands, 40
That Alexander Iden, an esquire of Kent,
Took odds to combat a poor famished man.
Oppose thy steadfast gazing eyes to mine,
See if thou canst outface me with thy looks;
Set limb to limb, and thou art far the lesser;
Thy hand is but a finger to my fist;
Thy leg a stick comparèd with this truncheon;
My foot shall fight with all the strength thou hast;
And if mine arm be heavèd in the air,
Thy grave is digged already in the earth. 50
As for words, whose greatness answers words,
Let this my sword report what speech forbears.

CADE By my valour, the most complete champion that
ever I heard! Steel, if thou turn the edge, or cut not
out the burly-boned clown in chines of beef ere thou
sleep in thy sheath, I beseech God on my knees thou
mayst be turned to hobnails.

Here they fight and Cade falls down

O, I am slain! Famine and no other hath slain me; let
ten thousand devils come against me, and give me but
the ten meals I have lost, and I'd defy them all. Wither, 60
garden, and be henceforth a burying-place to all that do
dwell in this house, because the unconquered soul of
Cade is fled.

IDEN

Is't Cade that I have slain, that monstrous traitor?
Sword, I will hallow thee for this thy deed,
And hang thee o'er my tomb when I am dead;
Ne'er shall this blood be wipèd from thy point,
But thou shalt wear it as a herald's coat,
To emblaze the honour that thy master got.

CADE Iden, farewell; and be proud of thy victory. Tell 70
Kent from me she hath lost her best man, and exhort

all the world to be cowards; for I, that never feared any,
am vanquished by famine, not by valour.   *He dies*

IDEN

How much thou wrongest me, heaven be my judge.
Die, damnèd wretch, the curse of her that bare thee;
And as I thrust thy body in with my sword,
So wish I I might thrust thy soul to hell.
Hence will I drag thee headlong by the heels
Unto a dunghill, which shall be thy grave,
80   And there cut off thy most ungracious head;
Which I will bear in triumph to the King,
Leaving thy trunk for crows to feed upon.   *Exit*

*

V.1   *Enter York and his army of Irish, with drum and
         colours*

YORK

From Ireland thus comes York to claim his right,
And pluck the crown from feeble Henry's head.
Ring, bells, aloud; burn bonfires clear and bright,
To entertain great England's lawful king.
Ah, *sancta majestas*! Who would not buy thee dear?
Let them obey that knows not how to rule;
This hand was made to handle naught but gold.
I cannot give due action to my words,
Except a sword or sceptre balance it.
10   A sceptre shall it have, have I a soul,
On which I'll toss the flower-de-luce of France.
         Enter Buckingham
Whom have we here? Buckingham to disturb me?
The King hath sent him, sure; I must dissemble.

BUCKINGHAM

York, if thou meanest well, I greet thee well.

YORK

    Humphrey of Buckingham, I accept thy greeting.
    Art thou a messenger, or come of pleasure?

BUCKINGHAM

    A messenger from Henry, our dread liege,
    To know the reason of these arms in peace;
    Or why thou, being a subject as I am,
    Against thy oath and true allegiance sworn,   20
    Should raise so great a power without his leave,
    Or dare to bring thy force so near the court?

YORK (*aside*)

    Scarce can I speak, my choler is so great.
    O, I could hew up rocks and fight with flint,
    I am so angry at these abject terms;
    And now, like Ajax Telamonius,
    On sheep or oxen could I spend my fury.
    I am far better born than is the King,
    More like a king, more kingly in my thoughts;
    But I must make fair weather yet awhile,   30
    Till Henry be more weak, and I more strong. –
    Buckingham, I prithee pardon me,
    That I have given no answer all this while;
    My mind was troubled with deep melancholy.
    The cause why I have brought this army hither
    Is to remove proud Somerset from the King,
    Seditious to his grace and to the state.

BUCKINGHAM

    That is too much presumption on thy part;
    But if thy arms be to no other end,
    The King hath yielded unto thy demand: 40
    The Duke of Somerset is in the Tower.

YORK

    Upon thine honour, is he prisoner?

BUCKINGHAM

    Upon mine honour, he is prisoner.

YORK

Then, Buckingham, I do dismiss my powers.
Soldiers, I thank you all; disperse yourselves;
Meet me tomorrow in Saint George's Field,
You shall have pay and everything you wish.

Exeunt soldiers

And let my sovereign, virtuous Henry,
Command my eldest son – nay, all my sons –
50 As pledges of my fealty and love;
I'll send them all as willing as I live.
Lands, goods, horse, armour, anything I have,
Is his to use, so Somerset may die.

BUCKINGHAM

York, I commend this kind submission;
We twain will go into his highness' tent.

Enter the King and attendants

KING

Buckingham, doth York intend no harm to us,
That thus he marcheth with thee arm in arm?

YORK

In all submission and humility
York doth present himself unto your highness.

KING

60 Then what intends these forces thou dost bring?

YORK

To heave the traitor Somerset from hence,
And fight against that monstrous rebel Cade,
Who since I heard to be discomfited.

Enter Iden, with Cade's head

IDEN

If one so rude and of so mean condition
May pass into the presence of a king,
Lo, I present your grace a traitor's head,
The head of Cade, whom I in combat slew.

KING

The head of Cade? Great God, how just art Thou!

O, let me view his visage, being dead,
That living wrought me such exceeding trouble.   70
Tell me, my friend, art thou the man that slew him?

IDEN

I was, an't like your majesty.

KING

How art thou called? And what is thy degree?

IDEN

Alexander Iden, that's my name,
A poor esquire of Kent, that loves his king.

BUCKINGHAM

So please it you, my lord, 'twere not amiss
He were created knight for his good service.

KING

Iden, kneel down.
    Iden kneels
            Rise up a knight.
We give thee for reward a thousand marks,
And will that thou henceforth attend on us.   80

IDEN

May Iden live to merit such a bounty,
And never live but true unto his liege.
    Enter the Queen and Somerset

KING

See, Buckingham, Somerset comes with th' Queen;
Go, bid her hide him quickly from the Duke.

QUEEN

For thousand Yorks he shall not hide his head,
But boldly stand and front him to his face.

YORK

How now? Is Somerset at liberty?
Then, York, unloose thy long-imprisoned thoughts
And let thy tongue be equal with thy heart.
Shall I endure the sight of Somerset?   90
False King! Why hast thou broken faith with me,
Knowing how hardly I can brook abuse?

V.1

'King' did I call thee? No, thou art not king;
Not fit to govern and rule multitudes,
Which darest not – no, nor canst not – rule a traitor.
That head of thine doth not become a crown;
Thy hand is made to grasp a palmer's staff,
And not to grace an awful princely sceptre.
That gold must round engirt these brows of mine,
Whose smile and frown, like to Achilles' spear,
Is able with the change to kill and cure.
Here is a hand to hold a sceptre up,
And with the same to act controlling laws.
Give place; by heaven, thou shalt rule no more
O'er him whom heaven created for thy ruler.

SOMERSET

O monstrous traitor! I arrest thee, York,
Of capital treason 'gainst the King and crown.
Obey, audacious traitor; kneel for grace.

YORK

Wouldst have me kneel? First let me ask of these
If they can brook I bow a knee to man.
Sirrah, call in my sons to be my bail;

Exit an attendant

I know, ere they will have me go to ward,
They'll pawn their swords of my enfranchisement.

QUEEN

Call hither Clifford; bid him come amain,
To say if that the bastard boys of York
Shall be the surety for their traitor father.

Exit an attendant

YORK

O blood-bespotted Neapolitan,
Outcast of Naples, England's bloody scourge!
The sons of York, thy betters in their birth,
Shall be their father's bail, and bane to those
That for my surety will refuse the boys.

154

Enter at one door Edward and Richard with their army
See where they come; I'll warrant they'll make it good.
*Enter at another door Clifford and Young Clifford
with an army*

QUEEN

And here comes Clifford to deny their bail.

CLIFFORD

Health and all happiness to my lord the King!
He kneels

YORK

I thank thee, Clifford; say, what news with thee?
Nay, do not fright us with an angry look.
We are thy sovereign, Clifford; kneel again.
For thy mistaking so, we pardon thee.

CLIFFORD

This is my king, York; I do not mistake;
But thou mistakes me much to think I do.   130
To Bedlam with him! Is the man grown mad?

KING

Ay, Clifford; a bedlam and ambitious humour
Makes him oppose himself against his king.

CLIFFORD

He is a traitor; let him to the Tower,
And chop away that factious pate of his.

QUEEN

He is arrested, but will not obey;
His sons, he says, shall give their words for him.

YORK

Will you not, sons?

EDWARD

Ay, noble father, if our words will serve.

RICHARD

And if words will not, then our weapons shall.   140

CLIFFORD

Why, what a brood of traitors have we here!

YORK

Look in a glass and call thy image so;
I am thy king, and thou a false-heart traitor.
Call hither to the stake my two brave bears,
That with the very shaking of their chains
They may astonish these fell-lurking curs;
Bid Salisbury and Warwick come to me.

*Enter the Earls of Warwick and Salisbury with an
army*

CLIFFORD

Are these thy bears? We'll bait thy bears to death,
And manacle the bearard in their chains,
150　If thou darest bring them to the baiting-place.

RICHARD

Oft have I seen a hot o'erweening cur
Run back and bite, because he was withheld;
Who, being suffered with the bear's fell paw,
Hath clapped his tail between his legs and cried;
And such a piece of service will you do,
If you oppose yourselves to match Lord Warwick.

CLIFFORD

Hence, heap of wrath, foul indigested lump,
As crookèd in thy manners as thy shape!

YORK

Nay, we shall heat you thoroughly anon.

CLIFFORD

160　Take heed, lest by your heat you burn yourselves.

KING

Why, Warwick, hath thy knee forgot to bow?
Old Salisbury, shame to thy silver hair,
Thou mad misleader of thy brain-sick son!
What, wilt thou on thy deathbed play the ruffian,
And seek for sorrow with thy spectacles?
O, where is faith? O, where is loyalty?
If it be banished from the frosty head,

Where shall it find a harbour in the earth?
Wilt thou go dig a grave to find out war,
And shame thine honourable age with blood?   170
Why art thou old and wantest experience?
Or wherefore dost abuse it, if thou hast it?
For shame! In duty bend thy knee to me,
That bows unto the grave with mickle age.

SALISBURY
My lord, I have considered with myself
The title of this most renownèd Duke;
And in my conscience do repute his grace
The rightful heir to England's royal seat.

KING
Hast thou not sworn allegiance unto me?

SALISBURY
I have.   180

KING
Canst thou dispense with heaven for such an oath?

SALISBURY
It is great sin to swear unto a sin,
But greater sin to keep a sinful oath.
Who can be bound by any solemn vow
To do a murderous deed, to rob a man,
To force a spotless virgin's chastity,
To reave the orphan of his patrimony,
To wring the widow from her customed right,
And have no other reason for this wrong
But that he was bound by a solemn oath?   190

QUEEN
A subtle traitor needs no sophister.

KING
Call Buckingham, and bid him arm himself.

YORK
Call Buckingham and all the friends thou hast,
I am resolved for death or dignity.

CLIFFORD
　The first I warrant thee, if dreams prove true.

WARWICK
　You were best to go to bed and dream again,
　To keep thee from the tempest of the field.

CLIFFORD
　I am resolved to bear a greater storm
　Than any thou canst conjure up today;
200　And that I'll write upon thy burgonet,
　Might I but know thee by thy house's badge.

WARWICK
　Now by my father's badge, old Nevil's crest,
　The rampant bear chained to the raggèd staff,
　This day I'll wear aloft my burgonet,
　As on a mountain top the cedar shows,
　That keeps his leaves in spite of any storm,
　Even to affright thee with the view thereof.

CLIFFORD
　And from thy burgonet I'll rend thy bear
　And tread it under foot with all contempt,
210　Despite the bearard that protects the bear.

YOUNG CLIFFORD
　And so to arms, victorious father,
　To quell the rebels and their complices.

RICHARD
　Fie, charity, for shame! Speak not in spite,
　For you shall sup with Jesu Christ tonight.

YOUNG CLIFFORD
　Foul stigmatic, that's more than thou canst tell.

RICHARD
　If not in heaven, you'll surely sup in hell.　　*Exeunt*

Alarums to the battle. Enter Warwick　　　　V.

WARWICK
　Clifford of Cumberland, 'tis Warwick calls;

And if thou dost not hide thee from the bear,
Now when the angry trumpet sounds alarum,
And dead men's cries do fill the empty air,
Clifford, I say, come forth and fight with me.
Proud northern lord, Clifford of Cumberland,
Warwick is hoarse with calling thee to arms.

Enter York

How now, my noble lord? What, all afoot?

YORK

The deadly-handed Clifford slew my steed;
But match to match I have encountered him,   10
And made a prey for carrion kites and crows
Even of the bonny beast he loved so well.

Enter Clifford

WARWICK

Of one or both of us the time is come.

YORK

Hold, Warwick! Seek thee out some other chase,
For I myself must hunt this deer to death.

WARWICK

Then nobly, York; 'tis for a crown thou fightest.
As I intend, Clifford, to thrive today,
It grieves my soul to leave thee unassailed.   *Exit*

CLIFFORD

What seest thou in me, York? Why dost thou pause?

YORK

With thy brave bearing should I be in love,   20
But that thou art so fast mine enemy.

CLIFFORD

Nor should thy prowess want praise and esteem,
But that 'tis shown ignobly and in treason.

YORK

So let it help me now against thy sword,
As I in justice and true right express it.

CLIFFORD

My soul and body on the action both!

YORK

A dreadful lay! Address thee instantly!
They fight and York kills Clifford

CLIFFORD

La fin couronne les œuvres.   *He dies*

YORK

Thus war hath given thee peace, for thou art still.
30   Peace with his soul, heaven, if it be thy will!   *Exit*
Enter Young Clifford

YOUNG CLIFFORD

Shame and confusion! All is on the rout;
Fear frames disorder, and disorder wounds
Where it should guard. O war, thou son of hell,
Whom angry heavens do make their minister,
Throw in the frozen bosoms of our part
Hot coals of vengeance! Let no soldier fly.
He that is truly dedicate to war
Hath no self-love; nor he that loves himself
Hath not essentially, but by circumstance,
The name of valour.
He sees his dead father
40   O, let the vile world end,
And the premised flames of the last day
Knit earth and heaven together.
Now let the general trumpet blow his blast,
Particularities and petty sounds
To cease! Wast thou ordained, dear father,
To lose thy youth in peace, and to achieve
The silver livery of advisèd age,
And, in thy reverence and thy chair-days, thus
To die in ruffian battle? Even at this sight
50   My heart is turned to stone, and while 'tis mine
It shall be stony. York not our old men spares;
No more will I their babes; tears virginal
Shall be to me even as the dew to fire;

And beauty, that the tyrant oft reclaims,
Shall to my flaming wrath be oil and flax.
Henceforth, I will not have to do with pity:
Meet I an infant of the house of York,
Into as many gobbets will I cut it
As wild Medea young Absyrtus did;
In cruelty will I seek out my fame.   60
Come, thou new ruin of old Clifford's house;
As did Aeneas old Anchises bear,
So bear I thee upon my manly shoulders;
But then Aeneas bare a living load,
Nothing so heavy as these woes of mine.
                        Exit with his father on his back
            Enter Richard and Somerset to fight. Somerset is
            killed

RICHARD
So, lie thou there;
For underneath an alehouse' paltry sign,
The Castle in Saint Albans, Somerset
Hath made the wizard famous in his death.
Sword, hold thy temper; heart, be wrathful still;   70
Priests pray for enemies, but princes kill.   *Exit*
        Fight. Excursions. Enter the King, Queen, and soldiers

QUEEN
Away, my lord! You are slow. For shame, away!

KING
Can we outrun the heavens? Good Margaret, stay.

QUEEN
What are you made of? You'll nor fight nor fly.
Now is it manhood, wisdom, and defence,
To give the enemy way, and to secure us
By what we can, which can no more but fly.
        Alarum afar off
If you be ta'en, we then should see the bottom
Of all our fortunes; but if we haply 'scape –

80 As well we may if not through your neglect –
We shall to London get, where you are loved,
And where this breach now in our fortunes made
May readily be stopped.

> *Enter Young Clifford*

YOUNG CLIFFORD
But that my heart's on future mischief set,
I would speak blasphemy ere bid you fly;
But fly you must; uncurable discomfit
Reigns in the hearts of all our present parts.
Away, for your relief! And we will live
To see their day and them our fortune give.
90 Away, my lord, away!   *Exeunt*

V.3   *Alarum. Retreat. Enter York, Richard, Warwick,*
and soldiers with drum and colours

YORK
Of Salisbury, who can report of him,
That winter lion, who in rage forgets
Agèd contusions and all brush of time;
And, like a gallant in the brow of youth,
Repairs him with occasion? This happy day
Is not itself, nor have we won one foot,
If Salisbury be lost.

RICHARD   My noble father,
Three times today I holp him to his horse,
Three times bestrid him; thrice I led him off,
10 Persuaded him from any further act;
But still where danger was, still there I met him,
And like rich hangings in a homely house,
So was his will in his old feeble body.
But, noble as he is, look where he comes.

> *Enter Salisbury*

162

SALISBURY
Now, by my sword, well hast thou fought today;
By th'mass, so did we all. I thank you, Richard.
God knows how long it is I have to live,
And it hath pleased Him that three times today
You have defended me from imminent death.
Well, lords, we have not got that which we have;
'Tis not enough our foes are this time fled,
Being opposites of such repairing nature.

YORK
I know our safety is to follow them;
For, as I hear, the King is fled to London,
To call a present court of parliament.
Let us pursue him ere the writs go forth.
What says Lord Warwick? Shall we after them?

WARWICK
After them! Nay, before them, if we can.
Now by my hand, lords, 'twas a glorious day.
Saint Albans battle, won by famous York,   30
Shall be eternized in all age to come.
Sound drum and trumpets, and to London all,
And more such days as these to us befall!   *Exeunt*

COMMENTARY

THE chief sources of the play are the chronicles of Edward Hall, Raphael Holinshed, Robert Fabyan, and perhaps Richard Grafton. In this Commentary, Hall is quoted where all the chroniclers agree, Holinshed, Fabyan, and Grafton only where special use seems to have been made of them. References are to the following editions: Hall's *The Union of the Two Noble and Illustre Families of Lancaster and York* (1548–50), the reprint of 1809; Holinshed's *The Chronicles of England, Scotland, and Ireland* (2nd ed., 1587), the reprint of 1808; Fabyan's *The New Chronicles of England and France* (1516), the reprint of 1811; Grafton's *A Chronicle at Large* (1569), the reprint of 1809. Quotations from John Foxe's *Acts and Monuments* (1563) are from the edition of 1844, and biblical quotations are from the Bishops' Bible (1568 etc.), the official English translation of Elizabeth's reign. Quotations are normally given in modernized spelling and punctuation, with the exception of those from the 1594 edition of *The First part of the Contention betwixt the two amous Houses of York and Lancaster* (referred to as 'Q1') and from the first Folio, 1623 (referred to as 'F').

The Characters in the Play
For the family relationships between the principal characters, see the Genealogical Tables; and for the regularization of names in this edition, see the Collations, pages 283–7. Biographical facts about each character are given in the Commentary at his or her first appearance in the play or mention in the text.

I.1   The scene is located in the royal palace in London. The First Part of the play ended with Suffolk receiving from Henry VI his commission to depart for France to secure Margaret as Queen of England and swearing to rule the kingdom through his influence over Margaret. Historically Suffolk left England in November 1444 and returned with Margaret in April 1445. According to Hall, they landed at Portsmouth, from whence 'she was conveyed to . . . Southwick in Hampshire, where she . . . was coupled in matrimony to King Henry VI. After which marriage she was . . . conveyed to London and so to Westminster, where upon the thirtieth day of May she . . . was crowned queen' (page 205).

(stage direction) *Flourish* (a fanfare of trumpets)

hautboys oboes

the King. Born in 1421, Henry VI succeeded his father, Henry V, in 1422 under the Protectorship of the Duke of Bedford. He married Margaret of Anjou by proxy in 1445 at the instigation of the Earl of Suffolk and against the wishes of the Duke of Gloucester.

Gloucester. Humphrey of Lancaster (1391–1447), youngest son of Henry IV, was created duke in 1414 and fought at Agincourt. He claimed the Regency at the death of Henry V, but was allowed only to act as the Duke of Bedford's deputy. He was in constant strife with his uncle Henry Beaufort, Bishop of Winchester; he was Protector in 1427–9, and his influence over the King was strong until 1441. He had vainly advocated marriage between Henry VI and the daughter of the Duke of Armagnac.

Salisbury. Richard Nevil (1400–1460), first Earl of Salisbury and son of Ralph Nevil, first Earl of Westmorland, had as his second wife Joan Beaufort (the mother of Warwick), who was the daughter of John of Gaunt and the sister of Henry Beaufort. He joined Henry VI in France in 1431 and was one of the officers who arrested the Duke of Gloucester in 1447.

Warwick. Richard Nevil (1428–71), 'The Kingmaker', was the son of the first Earl of Salisbury. He succeeded to the Earldom of Warwick in 1449 by the right of his wife, Anne Beauchamp. He sided with the Duke of York when he claimed the Regency in 1453.

Cardinal Beaufort. Henry Beaufort (d. 1447) was the second illegitimate son of John of Gaunt and Catherine Swynford. He was created Bishop of Winchester in 1404 and was Chancellor on the accession of Henry V, who named him guardian to Henry VI; he was nominated Cardinal-Priest in 1426, and he crowned Henry VI in Paris in 1431. He was constantly at loggerheads with the Duke of Gloucester, whose efforts to deprive him of his see he defeated in 1432.

the Queen. Margaret (1430–82) was the daughter of René, Duke of Anjou and Count of Maine and titular King of Naples, Sicily, and Jerusalem. She married Henry VI in 1445 and as queen identified herself with the Beaufort–Suffolk party at the English court.

Suffolk. William de la Pole (1396–1450), fourth Earl and first Duke of Suffolk, served in the French wars under Henry V. At the death of the fourth Earl of Salisbury in 1428, he assumed command of the English forces in France. Inclined by his marriage to the widowed Countess of Salisbury to support the Beauforts, he emerged as the chief opponent of the Duke of Gloucester and was one of the instigators of Henry VI's marriage to Margaret of Anjou.

York. Richard Plantagenet (1411–60) was the only son of Richard Earl of Cambridge, and thus the grandson of Edmund Langley, the fifth son of Edward III. He became the third Duke of York in 1415 and was Henry VI's lieutenant in France from 1440 to 1445. He enjoyed the support of Warwick and was a strong opponent of Somerset.

Somerset. Edmund Beaufort (d. 1455) was the second Duke of Somerset, succeeding his older brother John in 1444. He was son-in-law of Richard de Beauchamp, the Earl of Warwick, and was a bitter enemy of the Duke of York. It was during his Regency that most of the English possessions in France were lost.

Buckingham. Humphrey Stafford (1402–60), first Duke of Buckingham, was the grandson of Thomas of Woodstock, the sixth son of Edward III. He accompanied Henry VI abroad in 1430 and was Captain of Calais in 1442 and Warden of the Cinque Ports in 1450. He was an opponent of the Duke of York.

1   *imperial.* Henry VI was ruler of the empire of England, Ireland, and France.

2   *had in charge* was commissioned
    depart departure

3–8   *As procurator . . . bishops.* This is based on Hall: 'This noble company came to the city of Tours in Touraine, where they were honourably received both of the French King and of the King of Sicily; where the Marquess of Suffolk, as procurator to King Henry, espoused the said lady in the church of Saint Martin's. At which marriage were present the father and mother of the bride, the French King himself, which was uncle to the husband, and the French Queen also, which was aunt to the wife. There were also the Dukes of Orleans, of Calabria, of Alençon, and of Brittany, seven earls, twelve barons, twenty bishops, beside knights and gentlemen' (page 205).

3   *procurator to* deputy for

4   *marry* (on Henry's behalf)

6   *France* (Charles VII (1403–61), who had succeeded his father in 1422)
    Sicil (Margaret's father, René I (Reignier; 1409–80) Duke of Anjou, Count of Maine, King of Naples, Sicily, and Jerusalem)

7   *Orleans* (Charles of Orleans (1391–1465), half-brother of John, Count of Dunois, 'The Bastard')
    Calaber Calabria (in the southern extremity of Italy)
    Bretagne (Francis I, who succeeded John V as Duke of Brittany in 1442)
    Alençon (John, second Duke (1409–76), ally of Charles VII in the wars against the English)

9   *espoused* married (in Henry's name)

11   *England* (Henry VI as representative of the nation)

12   *title in* (a legal term) rights to

13–14   *the substance | Of that great shadow I did represent* the
        real power behind the image I acted for. This is a
        common Shakespearian idea also used for dramatic
        effect in *Part One*, II.3.35–65.

15   *happiest* most fortunate

18   *kinder* more according to nature

19   *kind* loving (with a pun on *kinder*)

19–22   *O Lord . . . my soul.* Even while Henry is initially in-
        toxicated with Margaret, his religious cast of mind is
        stressed by Shakespeare.

19   *lends* grants

21–2   *in this beauteous face | A world of earthly blessings.*
        Henry is elaborating the proverb 'Beauty is a blessing'.

23   *sympathy* mutual feeling

25   *mutual* intimate
        conference communication (here by dwelling mentally)

27   *In courtly company* among courtiers
        at my beads saying my prayers (with the help of a
        rosary)

28   *alderliefest* (an archaic word in Shakespeare's day)
        most beloved

29   *salute* greet

30   *ruder* more unpolished
        wit intelligence

31   *overjoy* excess of happiness
        minister supply

32   *Her sight* the sight of her

33   *y-clad* (an archaic form in Shakespeare's day) decked

34   *Makes.* The singular verb form with a group of sub-
        jects was common in Elizabethan English.
        wondering admiring

39   *Protector.* Historically Gloucester had ceased to be
        Protector when Henry VI was crowned in 1429 in
        London.

40–42   *Here are . . . by consent.* Compare Hall: 'But in con-

clusion, for many doubts and great ambiguities which
rose on both parties, a final concord could not be
agreed; but, in hope to come to a peace, a certain
truce as well by sea as by land was concluded by the
commissioners for eighteen months' (page 203).

43–60   *Imprimis, it is agreed ... any dowry*. These articles are
based on Hall: 'The Earl of Suffolk ..., either corrupted with bribes or too much affectionate to this
unprofitable marriage, condescended and agreed ...
that the duchy of Anjou and the county of Maine
should be released and delivered to the King her
father, demanding for her marriage neither penny nor
farthing' (page 204).

43   *Imprimis* (the normal opening of an official document
initiating a series of items) in the first place

49   *Item* (a legal formula) also
it is further agreed between them. F omits this clause
here, although it has it in the Cardinal's speech at
line 56. Q1 has it in both Gloucester's and the
Cardinal's quotations.

51   *released* no longer controlled (by England)
(stage direction) *Gloucester lets the contract fall.* This
direction is found only in Q1 and probably reflects
contemporary stage practice.

53   *qualm* attack of faintness
54   *that* so that
55   *Uncle.* The Cardinal was actually Henry IV's half-
brother and hence great-uncle of the King.

59–60   *own proper cost and charges.* This was a legal formula,
indicating that Henry would bear all Margaret's
expenses.

61   *They* (the terms of the agreement)
62   *first Duke of Suffolk.* Historically Suffolk was created
duke in 1448, three years after his return from France;
see Hall: 'This Marquess, thus gotten up into Fortune's throne, not content with his degree, by the
means of the Queen was shortly erected to the estate
and degree of a duke and ruled the King at his pleasure'

(page 207). However, when the marriage contract was agreed, among the other celebratory elevations 'the Earl of Suffolk [was] made Marquess of Suffolk' (pages 204–5).

63   *girt* gird

63–5   *Cousin of York ... France.* Historically York was replaced as Regent the year after the King's marriage; see Hall: 'the Duke of Somerset was appointed Regent of Normandy and the Duke of York thereof discharged' (page 206).

63   *Cousin* (the monarch's form of address to a duke of the realm)

65   *parts* territories

66   *full* fully

70   *entertainment* welcoming reception

72   *her coronation.* See the quotation from Hall in the headnote to this scene.

73   *peers.* The pun is with 'piers' meaning *pillars*.

76   *my brother Henry* (Henry V)

78   *lodge* sleep

79   *In winter's cold and summer's parching heat.* Compare Hall: 'No cold made him slothful nor heat caused him to loiter' (page 112).

80   *his true inheritance.* Through Edward III's marriage with Isabella, daughter of Philip IV of France, England claimed the French throne. Henry V had secured the title with the Treaty of Troyes in 1420, although his father-in-law, Charles VI, actually wore the crown.

81   *Bedford.* John of Lancaster (1389–1435), third son of Henry IV, was Regent of France and Protector of England. He raised the siege of Orleans in 1429 and effected the death of Joan of Arc in 1431.
        toil his wits exercise his intelligence. As Regent of France after Henry V's death, Bedford had negotiated an alliance with Burgundy and Brittany against Charles VII and attempted to secure English rule in France by the establishment of trading relations and

171

sound administration. Compare Hall: 'the Duke of
Bedford, Regent of France, no less studied than took
pain ... to keep and order the countries and regions
by King Henry late conquered and gained' (page 115).

82   *policy* skilful political action (with overtones of
craftiness)

86–90   *Or hath mine uncle ... in awe.* In Hall, Gloucester
assumed the Protectorship 'as a man remembering
other and forgetting himself, called to him wise and
grave counsellors by whose advice he provided and
ordained for all things which either redounded to the
honour of the realm or seemed profitable to the public
wealth of the same' (page 115).

86   *Beaufort* (the Cardinal)

87   *Council* (the King's Privy Council)

89   *debating to and fro* discussing the arguments for and
against

90   *awe* subjection. Hall's phrase is 'brought to due
obeisance' (page 115).

92   *Crownèd in Paris.* See *Part One*, IV.1. Henry was
crowned in Paris in 1431 when he was ten years old
(Hall, pages 160–61).
      despite spite

96–101   *O peers of England ... had never been.* The full ex-
planation for Gloucester's opposition is found in
Part One, V.5, and in Hall: 'Humphrey Duke of
Gloucester, Protector of the realm, repugned and resisted as much as in him lay this new alliance and
contrived matrimony, alleging that it was neither con-
sonant to the law of God nor man, nor honourable to
a prince, to infringe and break a promise or contract
by him made and concluded for the utility and profit
of his realm and people; declaring that the King by
his ambassadors, sufficiently instructed and autho-
rized, had concluded and contracted a marriage between his highness and the daughter of the Earl of
Armagnac upon conditions both to him and his realm
as much profitable as honourable' (page 204).

96   *league* agreement

98   *books of memory* chronicles. Compare Hall's phrase
        'book of fame' (page 15) and *Part One*, II.4.101.

99   *Razing the characters* erasing the written records

100   *monuments* (in two senses: (1) memory; (2) stone
        memorials)

101   *as* as though

102   *passionate* excessively emotional

103   *peroration with such circumstance* rhetorical speech
        with so many illustrative details

104   *For* as for
        still for ever

107   *rules the roast* (proverbial)

109–10 *Reignier, whose large style | Agrees not with the leanness
        of his purse.* Compare Hall: 'King Reignier her father,
        for all his long style, had too short a purse to send his
        daughter honourably to the King her spouse' (page
        205).

109   *large style* impressive-sounding titles; see the note to
        line 6 above.

110   *Agrees* accords

111   *the death of Him that died for all* (a reference to 2
        Corinthians 5.15)

112   *the keys of Normandy.* Shakespeare seems to have
        taken this phrase from Fabyan; Hall calls Maine and
        Anjou 'the very stays and backstands to the Duchy of
        Normandy' (page 205).

117   *Myself did win them both.* Richard Nevil, who became
        the Earl of Warwick in 1449, is here credited with the
        military achievements of his father-in-law, Richard
        de Beauchamp (1382–1439), who appears in *Part
        One*.

120   *Delivered up* surrendered

121   *Mort Dieu* (a common French oath, literally 'by the
        death of God')

122   *suffocate.* The pun is with *Suffolk*.

125   *yielded* consented

126–29 *I never read . . . no vantages.* This seems to have been suggested by Hall: 'This marriage seemed to many both infortunate and unprofitable to the realm of England. . . . the King with her had not one penny' (page 205).

128   *own* own money and possessions

129   *match with* marry
        vantages profits, benefits

131-2   *Suffolk should demand . . . her!* Compare Hall: 'for the fetching of her the Marquess of Suffolk demanded a whole fifteen in open parliament' (page 205).

131   *fifteenth* (a tax of one fifteenth on all personal property. In *Part One*, V.5.92-3, Henry promises Suffolk a ten-per-cent tax levy for expenses.)

133   *starved* died

135   *hot* choleric

140   *proud prelate*. This phrase is twice used in the section on Humphrey of Gloucester in *A Mirror for Magistrates* (1559), lines 155, 205.

142   *ancient bickerings*. Gloucester's and Winchester's quarrels are dramatized in *Part One*, III.1. They are also stressed by the chroniclers; compare Hall: 'the Duke of Gloucester sore grudged at the proud doings of the Cardinal of Winchester, and . . . the Cardinal likewise sore envied and disdained at the rule of the Duke of Gloucester' (page 197).

143   *Lordings* (a form of address meaning 'my lords')

149   *next of blood*. As Henry V's only surviving brother and in the absence of a child of Henry VI, Gloucester at this time is next in line to the throne; see Table 1 (pages 304-5).

150   *heir apparent* (technically 'heir presumptive')

152   *the wealthy kingdoms of the west*. The reference is anachronistically to the Spanish possessions in America.

153   *he* (Gloucester)

154   *Look to it* beware
        smoothing flattering

156   *What* even

156–7   *the common people favour him, | Calling him 'Humphrey, the good Duke of Gloucester'*. Hall and Holinshed both give idealized portraits of Gloucester; but for the phrasing here Shakespeare seems to be indebted to John Foxe's *Acts and Monuments*: 'for the noble prowess and virtues . . . he was both loved of the poor commons and well spoken of of all men, and no less deserving the same, being called the "good" Duke of Gloucester' (III.713).

161   *flattering gloss* attractive appearance

162   *found* revealed to be

164   *He* (Henry VI)
    of age. Historically Henry was twenty-four at this time.

167   *hoise* remove by violence

168   *brook* allow

169   *I'll* I'll go
    presently immediately

171   *place* position in the government
    grief irritation

173   *insolence* overbearing pride

174   *the princes' in the land beside* that of all the other noblemen of the realm

175   *displaced* removed from the Protectorship
    he (the Cardinal)

176   *Or . . . or* either . . . or

178   *Pride went before; Ambition follows him*. Salisbury is adapting the proverb 'Pride goes before and ambition comes after'. *Pride* stands for the Cardinal, *Ambition* for Somerset and Buckingham.

179   *preferment* advancement

182   *bear him* conduct himself

185   *stout* proud
    as he as if he

186   *demean himself* act

187   *commonweal* state

188–90   *Warwick, my son . . . the commons*. Compare Hall: 'This Richard was . . . a man of marvellous qualities . . . but also from his youth . . . so set them forward

with witty and gentle demeanour ... that among all
sorts of people he obtained great love, much favour,
and more credence; which things daily more increased
by his abundant liberality and plentiful house-keeping
than by his riches, authority, or high parentage; by
reason of which doings he was in such favour and
estimation amongst the common people that they
judged him able to do all things and that without him
nothing to be well done' (pages 231–2).

189   *house-keeping* hospitality

191   *Excepting none but* except that which they have shown
to

192–3   *brother York ... discipline.* York is erroneously given
credit for having suppressed a rebellion in Ireland
before 1445. He actually did this in 1449, and his
appointment as English general in Ireland is dramatized in III.1; see the note to III.1.282–329, and compare Hall, page 219: '[York's] politic governance, his
gentle behaviour to all the Irish nation ... had brought
that rude and savage nation to civil fashion and
English urbanity.'

192   *brother.* York was Salisbury's brother-in-law, having
married Cecily Nevil, Salisbury's sister; see Table 1.

193   *them* (the Irish rebels)

194   *late exploits* recent military actions

201   *cherish* give support to

202   *tend the profit* serve the welfare

206   *look unto the main* (proverbial) have an eye to the main
chance

207   *main* (1) main chance; (2) most important business

208   *main force* overpowering strength

213–14   *the state of Normandy | Stands on a tickle point now
they are gone.* See the note to line 112 above.

214   *Stands on a tickle point* is in a precarious position

215–17   *Suffolk concluded ... fair daughter.* This is an echo of
Hall: 'that godly affinity which he had concluded,
omitting nothing ... of the nobility of her kin ...
that she was of such an excellent beauty and of so

high a parentage. . . . This marriage pleased well the
King and divers of his Council' (page 204).

215   *concluded on the articles* negotiated the final details of
the marriage contract

219   *thine* (York's)

220   *make cheap pennyworths* squander

222   *Still* continually

223   *While as* while
    silly pitiful

224   *hapless* unfortunate

225   *stands aloof* remains at a distance

228   *bite his tongue* (in order to hold his peace)

231   *proportion* relation

232–3   *the fatal brand Althaea burnt | Unto the Prince's heart
of Calydon.* Ovid in the *Metamorphoses* relates how the
Fates decreed that Meleager, Prince of Calydon,
should live only as long as a specified brand on the
hearth should continue to burn. His mother Althaea
snatched the brand from the fire and kept it alight for
many years until in a fit of anger she tossed it into a
heap of blazing wood.

233   *the Prince's heart of Calydon* the heart of the Prince of
Calydon

235   *Cold* unwelcome
    hope of France expectations of possessing the French
crown

238   *And therefore I will take the Nevils' parts.* Compare
Hall: 'When the Duke saw men's appetites and felt
well their minds, he chiefly entertained two Richards,
and both Nevils, the one of Salisbury, the other of
Warwick, being earl, the first the father, the second
the son' (page 231).

239   *make a show* give the appearance

240   *advantage* opportunity

241   *mark* target. The image is from archery.

242   *Lancaster* (Henry VI)

244   *diadem* crown

245   *Whose church-like humours fits not for a crown.* Com-

pare Hall: 'King Henry ... was a man of a meek spirit, and ... preferring ... quietness before labour .... He ... studied only for the health of his soul' (page 208).

245   *church-like humours* pious nature

246   *be still* remain politically inactive

247   *Watch* remain alert

248   *pry into the secrets of the state* probe governmental intrigues

249   *surfeiting* having become satiated through over-indulgence

251   *at jars* into dissension

252   *the milk-white rose* (the symbol of the house of York; see *Part One*, II.4)

254   *standard* battle ensign
       arms coat of arms

255   *grapple*. The word takes up the second sense of *arms* in line 254.

256   *force perforce* (a tautology for emphasis) by violent compulsion

257   *bookish* scholarly, interested only in religious books (hence 'ineffectual')
       bookish rule. This perhaps is an echo of Hall's depicting Henry 'like a young scholar or innocent pupil' (page 208).

I.2   This scene, which presumably takes place in Gloucester's house, is based upon an event recorded in the chronicles which took place historically in 1441, four years before the arrival of Margaret in England. Compare Hall: 'For first this year Dame Eleanor Cobham, wife to the said Duke, was accused of treason for that she by sorcery and enchantment intended to destroy the King, to the intent to advance and to promote her husband to the crown' (page 202). See also the headnote to I.4.
       (stage direction) *the Duchess*. Eleanor Cobham (d.

1446?) was originally Gloucester's mistress; she became his wife at some time before 1431.

2   *Ceres* (Roman goddess of agriculture)
        plenteous load rich harvest

5   *sullen* dark, dull

8   *Enchased* decorated

9   *grovel on thy face.* There may be a trace of Eleanor's interest in witchcraft in this phrase; compare I.4. 10–11.

12   *is't* is your arm

13   *heaved* raised

15   *abase* lower

18   *canker* spreading sore (here eating away at the mind)

19   *imagine ill* conceive evil intentions

21   *last breathing* final breath of life

22   *this night* last night

23   *requite it* repay you for it

24   *rehearsal* recital, telling
        morning's dream dream which will come true. (In folklore a morning dream was considered a favourable prophecy.)

25   *mine office-badge* the symbol of my Protectorship

29   *Edmund Duke of Somerset.* The duke at this time historically was John Beaufort (1403–44), the first Duke; but Shakespeare confuses him with his younger brother Edmund (d. 1455), the second Duke; see Table 1.

31   *bode* presage

32   *argument* proof

34   *presumption* (pronounced quadrisyllabically)

35   *list* listen

38   *chair* (the coronation throne)

42   *Ill-nurtured* poorly educated, badly bred

43   *second woman in the realm* (as the wife of Gloucester, who is heir presumptive)

46   *compass* range

47   *hammering* designing, shaping

49   *From top of honour.* This phrase appears to come from

A Mirror for Magistrates (line 4 of the section on Suffolk).

54   *checked* rebuked, scolded

56–8   *'tis his highness ... mean to hawk.* Compare Hall: 'Queen Margaret ... caused the King to make a progress into Warwickshire for his health and recreation, and so with hawking and hunting came to the city of Coventry' (page 236).

56   *pleasure* wish

57   *Saint Albans.* The town in Hertfordshire, twenty miles north of London, was the scene of two major battles of the Wars of the Roses.

58   *Where as* where

       hawk hunt with hawks

60   *presently* immediately

61   *Follow I must; I cannot go before* (proverbial)

       go before (take precedence over Queen Margaret)

67   *pageant* play, spectacle

68   *Sir John.* John is Hume's christian name in the chronicles; but 'Sir John' was also used as a type-name for a clerk of the church.

69   (stage direction) *Hume.* This spelling is found only in the account given in Foxe's *Acts and Monuments*; all the chronicles have the form 'Hum'.

71   *Majesty.* The term is an anachronism; as a form of address for the monarch it was first used for the Tudors.

       but 'grace' only a duchess

73   *Your grace's title shall be multiplied.* The pun is with *the grace of God*, and the allusion is to 1 Peter 1.2: 'Grace and peace be multiplied unto you.'

75–6   *Margery Jourdain, the cunning witch ... Roger Bolingbroke, the conjurer.* Compare Hall: 'counsellors to the said Duchess ... Roger Bolingbroke, a cunning necromancer, and Margery Jourdain, surnamed the Witch of Eye' (page 202).

75   *cunning* skilful

77   *do me good* cause me to prosper

88   *Marry* (a mild oath, originally meaning 'by the Virgin Mary')

88-9   *Hume ... mum.* There may be a vestigial rhyme here originating in the chronicles' spelling of the name, 'Hum'.

89   *no words but mum* (proverbial)

90   *asketh* demands

93   *flies from another coast* which comes from another quarter

97-106   *They, knowing Dame Eleanor's ... Humphrey's fall.* There is no historical evidence for this suborning of Hume by the Cardinal and Suffolk. The chronicles record only that Hume alone among the Duchess's confederates received a pardon (Hall, page 202).

97   *aspiring humour* ambitious character

98   *undermine.* This was still a military term in Shakespeare's day, meaning 'place explosives beneath a citadel's walls'.

99   *buzz* implant by means of whispers

        conjurations incantations

100   *A crafty knave does need no broker* (proverbial)

        broker agent, go-between

102-3   *go near | To call* come close to naming

105   *wrack* ruin

106   *attainture* conviction (and fall from grace)

107   *Sort how it will* let it turn out how it likes

I.3   The scene is located in the royal palace in London. The developing sexual intimacy between the Queen and Suffolk has no basis in the chronicles, but is dramatized in the Duke's capture of Margaret in *Part One*, V.3. The court rivalries and personal animosities are all historically based. For the chronicles' account of the episode of the armourer and his apprentice, see the notes to lines 24-6 below and to II.3.59-103.

1   *close* all together in a body

3   *supplications* petitions
    in the quill in a group

4   *the Lord protect.* The pun is with Gloucester's title.

6–12   *Here 'a comes ... for my Lord Protector.* The stage
    direction in Q1 makes the action clear: 'Enter the
    Duke of *Suffolke* with the Queene, and they take him
    for Duke *Humphrey*, and giues him their writings.'

6–7   *Here 'a comes ... sure.* The reprint of F in 1685 gives
    this speech to the First Petitioner and is followed by
    some modern editors. While there are arguments for
    making the change, the action as it appears in the first
    three editions of the Folio is understandable. As
    Suffolk and the Queen enter, the petitioners surge
    forward, with Peter aggressively trying to be first
    (lines 6–7). He is set right about Suffolk's identity by
    the Second Petitioner (lines 8–9) and Suffolk stops
    and addresses the First Petitioner, who is in the front
    of the group and from whom the Queen takes the
    petition.

6   *'a* (a common Elizabethan colloquial form of 'he')

10   *fellow* (a contemptuous, condescending form of
    address)

15   *an't* if it

16   *against John Goodman, my lord Cardinal's man.* This
    complaint indicates how the conflict at court between
    Gloucester and the Cardinal has seeped down to the
    lower levels of society. A similar point is made in *Part
    One*, III.1.
    man agent

18   *Thy wife too! That's some wrong indeed.* In view of
    Suffolk's relations with the Queen, he says this
    ironically, and probably with a knowing look at
    Margaret.

19–20   *Against the Duke of Suffolk ... Melford.* Compare
    Hall: 'the forenamed Duke of Suffolk, only for lucre
    of money, vexed, oppressed and molested the poor
    people; so that men's minds were not intentive, nor
    given to outward affairs and foreign conquests, but all

their study was how to drive back and defend domes-
tical injuries and daily wrongs done at home' (page
212).

20   *enclosing the commons.* This practice of landowners,
fencing in common land and making it their own
property, was a bitter social issue in sixteenth-century
England. In 1614 Shakespeare himself was involved
in a dispute over the enclosure of land he owned in
Old Stratford and Welcombe.

   Melford (Long Melford in Suffolk)

21   *sir knave.* Suffolk is being sarcastic in adding a
commonly used courtesy title to the term of abuse
knave.

23   *of* on behalf of

24–6   *Against my master . . . the crown.* Although the episode
of the armourer and his apprentice appears in the
chronicles, it is Shakespeare's invention that the Duke
of York is the subject of the treasonous remarks.

32–3   *pursuivant* (messenger serving the royal herald)

33   *presently* immediately

35   *protected* (another pun on Gloucester's title)

38   *base* of low birth

   cullions wretches (from the Italian *coglioni*, meaning
'testicles')

40   *guise* custom, habit

43   *Albion* England

44–5   *shall King Henry be a pupil still | Under the surly
Gloucester's governance?* Compare Hall: 'she had
neither wit nor stomach which would permit and
suffer her husband, being of perfect age and man's
estate, like a young scholar or innocent pupil to be
governed by the disposition of another man' (page
208). Margaret was advised by her father, King
Reignier, that 'she and her husband should take upon
them the rule and governance of the realm and not to
be kept under like young wards' (page 209).

44   *still* for ever

46   *style* the way I am addressed

48–50   *when in the city Tours ... of France.* This is an echo of Christopher Marlowe's *Edward II*, V.5.67–9: 'Tell Isabel, the queen, I looked not thus | When for her sake I ran at tilt in France'. Hall reports that at Margaret's marriage in Tours 'There were triumphant jousts' (page 205).

49   *rannest a tilt* competed in a jousting tournament

52   *courtship* (1) courtly manner; (2) wooing ability
      proportion bodily shape

53–8   *But all his mind ... canonized saints.* Hall notes about Henry 'there could be none more chaste, more meek, more holy, nor a better creature' (page 208). His pious nature is touched upon in *Part One*, III.1 and IV.1.

53   *bent to* directed towards

54   *To number Ave-Maries on his beads.* Compare *Part Three*, II.1.161: 'Numbering our Ave-Maries with our beads'.
      beads (rosary beads)

55   *champions.* The image is of the Christian as God's champion, which is developed at length in Ephesians 6. Margaret is also referring to the King's Champion, a warrior chosen to represent the king in single combat.

56   *saws* sayings

57   *tilt-yard* (arena in which knights jousted)

58   *brazen images* bronze statues
      canonized (accented on the second syllable)

59   *the College of the Cardinals* (the highest council of the Church of Rome, which is responsible for electing the Pope from among its members)

61   *the triple crown* (the diadem of the papacy)

62   *state* status
      his holiness (1) Henry's piety; (2) the title used to designate the pope

65   *work* bring about

68   *grumbling* discontented

72   *simple* ordinary. The allusion is to their relationship to

the royal family. See the note on Salisbury at the opening stage direction of I.1.

73–85   *Not all these lords ... his daughter*. Historically the Duchess of Gloucester had been accused of witchcraft and disgraced in 1441, some four years before Margaret became Queen of England.

75   *sweeps it* struts proudly

77   *Strangers* visiting foreigners

78   *on her back* in the clothes she wears

81   *Contemptuous* contemptible

    base-born of low birth

    callet drab

82   *vaunted* boasted

    minions (1) followers; (2) saucy women

83   *worst wearing* most unfashionable

84   *better worth* worth more

85   *Suffolk gave two dukedoms for his daughter*. Compare I.1.215–17.

86   *limed a bush* set a trap. The metaphor is from the practice of smearing twigs with bird-lime to catch young birds.

87   *enticing birds* decoys

88   *light* perch

    lays songs

90   *let her rest* bother yourself no more about her

    list listen

91   *am bold* presume, take it upon myself

92   *fancy* love

95   *late* recent. The complaint referred to is Peter's against the armourer (lines 24–30 above).

96   *make but little for his benefit* do him little good

98   *steer the happy helm* be in charge of the successful government. The metaphor is derived from the idea of the ship of state; compare *Part One*, I.1.177.

    (stage direction) *sennet* (a flourish of trumpets indicating a ceremonial entrance or exit)

100–104 *Or Somerset or York ... yield to him*. Shakespeare makes use of this rivalry in *Part One*, as well as here and later in III.1 and V.1. The chronicles refer to the animosity between the two peers and their competition for the Regency on several occasions (Hall, pages 179, 215–16).

100 *Or … or* either … or

101 *ill demeaned himself* behaved improperly

102 *denayed* denied

108 *field* (of combat)

109 *presence* royal receiving chamber
  betters superiors in rank

115 *censure* judgement

116–17 *If he be … excellence?* Hall discusses the Queen's attitude which lies behind these lines: 'This woman, perceiving that her husband did not frankly rule as he would but did all thing by the advice and counsel of Humphrey Duke of Gloucester, and that he passed not much on the authority and governance of the realm, determined with herself to take upon her the rule and regiment both of the King and his kingdom and to deprive and evict out of all rule and authority the said duke, then called the Lord Protector of the realm, lest men should say and report that she had neither wit nor stomach' (page 208).

121–35 *Since thou wert king … hop without thy head.* The combined attack on Gloucester by the nobles following the Queen's rebuke is based upon Hall's account of Gloucester's fall: 'by her permission and favour divers noblemen conspired against him, of the which divers writers affirm the Marquess of Suffolk and the Duke of Buckingham to be the chief, not unprocured by the Cardinal of Winchester and the Archbishop of York. Divers articles both heinous and odious were laid to his charge in open council' (page 209).

121–5 *Since thou wert king … sovereignty.* These charges are based upon those brought against Suffolk himself in 1449 (Hall, pages 217–18).

121 *Since thou wert king – as who is king but thou?* Compare Hall, page 208, where the Queen perceives 'that her

186

husband did not frankly rule as he would but did all thing by the advice and counsel of Humphrey' (page 208).

122   *The commonwealth hath daily run to wrack.* Compare Hall on Suffolk: 'the expeller from the King of all good and virtuous counsellors and the bringer in and advancer of vicious persons, common enemies and apparent adversaries to the public wealth' (page 217).

123   *The Dauphin hath prevailed beyond the seas.* Compare Hall on Suffolk's 'negligent provision and improvident policy of . . . the affairs and business in the parts beyond the sea. . . . the most swallower up and consumer of the King's treasure, by reason whereof the wars in France were not maintained' (page 217).
      Dauphin. This was the title of the heir apparent to the French throne, but it is used here to describe Charles VI, whose title the English did not recognize. The F spelling, 'Dolphin', reflects Elizabethan pronunciation and clarifies the quibble in the phrase *prevailed beyond the seas.*

125   *bondmen* slaves
126   *commons* ordinary people
      racked reduced to poverty by extorting money from them
      bags purses
128   *Thy sumptuous buildings.* The reference is to the Duke of Gloucester's residence, Greenwich Palace, which he had enlarged and embellished to satisfy his taste for Italian Renaissance architecture. Compare Hall: 'the Duke of Gloucester had not so much advanced and preferred the common wealth and public utility as his own private things and peculiar estate' (pages 208–9).
129   *treasury* wealth
130–31 *Thy cruelty in execution | Upon offenders hath exceeded law.* Among the charges brought against Gloucester, Hall singles out 'in especial one that he had caused men adjudged to die to be put to other execution than

the law of the land had ordered or assigned' (page 209).

133 *Thy sale of offices and towns in France.* Among the charges brought against Suffolk in 1449 were that he was 'corrupted by rewards of the French King' and that he purveyed 'his arms, furniture of his towns, and all other ordnances whereby the King's enemies ... have gotten towns and fortresses and the King by that mean deprived of his inheritance' (page 218).

134 *suspect* (accented on the second syllable) suspicion

135 *hop without thy head* (proverbial) be beheaded

136 *minion* hussy

137 *cry you mercy* beg your pardon

140 *my ten commandments* the marks of my ten fingernails (a proverbial expression thought to be derived from the legend that God scratched the commandments on the tablets with his nail)

141 *quiet* calm
  against her will unintentional

143 *hamper* (1) bind; (2) encradle
  dandle pet

144 *most master wear no breeches* (a proverbial saying indicating that the wife is master of the house)

147 *listen after* inquire about
  proceeds behaves

148 *tickled* (1) irritated, provoked; (2) almost caught (like a trout which has been 'tickled')
  fume smoking rage. Some editors read 'fury', which is defensible on the grounds of both sense and metre.

149 *She'll gallop far enough to her destruction.* The Duchess is viewed metaphorically as a maddened mare.

150 *overblown* dispersed

153 *objections* accusations

156 *duty* reverence

158 *meetest* the most suitable

160 *election* the choice

162 *unmeet* unfitting

164   *for* because
165–70 *if I be appointed . . . and lost.* Hall reports that in 1435
        'Although the Duke of York, both for birth and
        courage, was worthy of this honour and preferment,
        yet he was so disdained of Edmund Duke of Somerset,
        being cousin to the King, that he was promoted to so
        high an office (which he in very deed gaped and looked
        for) that by all ways and means possible he both
        hindered and detracted him, glad of his loss and sorry
        of his well-doing, causing him to linger in England,
        without dispatch, till Paris and the flower of France
        were gotten by the French King' (page 179). But there
        also seems to be some reliance on Holinshed's account
        of the events of 1446: 'But the Duke of Somerset, still
        maligning the Duke of York's advancement, as he had
        sought to hinder his dispatch at the first when he was
        sent over to be Regent, as before ye have heard, he
        likewise now wrought so that the King revoked his
        grant made to the Duke of York for enjoying of that
        office the term of other five years, and with help of
        William Marquess of Suffolk obtained that grant for
        himself' (III.208–9).

167   *discharge* making a proper financial settlement with me
        furniture military supplies
169   *danced attendance on his will* (a proverbial phrase)
171   *fact* crime, deed
174   *Image* model, embodiment
177   *for* of being
178   *what* who
186   *God is my witness* (Romans 1.9)
        falsely treacherously
188   *these ten bones* my fingers
191   *mechanical* (literally, 'engaged in manual labour')
        menial
194   *have all the rigour* experience the fullest severity
196   *prentice* apprentice
        correct punish
197   *fault* mistake

199   *cast away* destroy

200   *for* on account of

202   *doom* judgement, sentence

203   *Let Somerset be Regent o'er the French.* Compare Hall:
       'the Duke of Somerset was appointed Regent of
       Normandy and the Duke of York thereof discharged'
       (page 206).

204   *in York this breeds suspicion* this accusation arouses
       doubt about York's loyalty to the crown

205   *these* (Horner and Peter)

206   *single combat* a duel. Q1 specifies 'with *Eben* staues and
       Sandbags combatting in *Smithfield* before your royal
       Majesty.'
       convenient appropriate

208   *This is the law, and this Duke Humphrey's doom.* Some
       editors give this line to the King, on the grounds that
       Somerset and Horner both appear to reply to Henry;
       others insert two lines spoken by the King in Q1:
       'Then be it so my Lord of *Somerset*. | We make your
       grace Regent ouer the French'. But F's version may
       be implying that Gloucester's influence over the King
       is total, which illuminates the enmity of the Queen
       and the other peers. On stage the action would be clear
       if Henry were to nod in agreement at the end of
       Gloucester's speech.

215   *Sirrah* (the customary form of address for a social
       inferior)

I.4   The scene takes place in Gloucester's house. All of the
             accomplices of the Duchess are taken from the
             chronicles: 'At the same season were arrested, as aiders
             and counsellors to the said Duchess, Thomas South-
             well, priest and canon of Saint Stephen's in West-
             minster, John Hum, priest, Roger Bolingbroke, a
             cunning necromancer, and Margery Jourdain, sur-
             named the Witch of Eye, to whose charge it was laid
             that they, at the request of the Duchess, had devised

an image of wax representing the King, which by their sorcery a little and little consumed, intending thereby in conclusion to waste and destroy the King's person and so to bring him death' (Hall, page 202).

3 *therefore provided* equipped for that purpose

4 *exorcisms.* Technically these are rituals performed by the Church for expelling evil spirits; but here the word is used to mean ceremonies for conjuring up spirits.

5 *what else?* most certainly

Fear you not do not doubt

8 *aloft.* See the note to the stage direction at line 11.

below (i.e. on the main stage, though there may be a pun on 'below' meaning 'underworld')

10–11 *be you prostrate and grovel on the earth.* In Q1 Jourdain gives the reason for this: 'frame a Cirkle here vpon the earth, | Whilst I thereon all prostrate on my face, | Do talk and whisper with the diuels below.'

11 (stage direction) *aloft.* In Q1 the Duchess at this point 'goes vp to the Tower', presumably a raised area above the stage similar to that used in *Part One*, I.4.22.

12 *Well said.* The Duchess enters in time to catch Bolingbroke's words *let us to our work.* The phrase could also mean 'Well done'.

12–13 *To this gear the sooner* the quicker we get on with this business

14 *wizards* (practisers of black magic)

15 *silent.* In phrases like this the adjectival form was often used; compare 'the sweet o'th'night' (*2 Henry IV*, V.3.49–50).

16 *when Troy was set on fire.* The reference is to the *Aeneid*, Book II, in which Virgil describes the sacking of Troy by the Greeks.

17 *screech-owls* (birds of ill-omen whose cry was thought to herald death)

ban-dogs (watch-dogs chained up because of their excessive fierceness)

18   *break up* rise out of

20   *Whom* whichever spirit

21   *hallowed verge* magic circle

(stage direction) *Here do the ceremonies belonging* here perform the ritual proper to the raising of spirits. In popular plays of the period, such as Christopher Marlowe's *Doctor Faustus* and Robert Greene's *Friar Bacon and Friar Bungay*, similar supernatural rituals are used.

Conjuro te I conjure you

22   *Adsum* I am here

23   *Asmath.* This is not the name of any known spirit in magic. It resembles 'Asmenoth' and 'Asmodeus'.

24–5   *By the eternal God, whose name and power | Thou tremblest at.* The allusion is to James 2.19: 'the devils also believe and tremble.'

25   *that* that which

27   *That* would that. The tradition was that spirits were reluctant to answer human questions. Compare *Macbeth*, IV.1.71: 'Dismiss me. Enough.'

29–30 *The duke yet lives that Henry shall depose; | But him outlive, and die a violent death.* Presumably the reference is to the Duke of York, whose death at the Battle of Wakefield is dramatized in *Part Three*, I.4. In the manner of infernal prophecies the form of the utterance is quibbling: *shall depose* and *die a violent death* can apply to York or Henry.

30   (stage direction) *Bolingbroke.* Some editors have Southwell copying down the Spirit's answers as Bolingbroke asks the questions.

34   *Let him shun castles.* Hall notes, though not in connexion with the Duchess's magic practices, that at the first Battle of Saint Albans 'there died under the sign of the Castle Edmund Duke of Somerset, who long before was warned to eschew all castles' (page 233). See the treatment of this at V.2.67–9.

36   *mounted* (on mountains)

37   *Have done* finish quickly. See the note to line 27.

38   *the burning lake.* Compare Revelation 19.20: 'a pond of fire burning with brimstone'.

39   *False* treacherous
        avoid be gone
        (stage direction) *Sir Humphrey Stafford as captain.*
        This phrase is not in F. In view of line 51, I think
        Sir Humphrey Stafford, who appears in the play later
        (IV.2), is intended to be captain of the guard to whom
        the Duchess is committed.
        break in burst on to the stage (through one of the entry
        doors)

40   *trash* conjuring paraphernalia

41   *Beldam* hag
        watched you at an inch kept you under the closest
        observation. The phrase 'at an inch' is proverb-
        ial.

43   *this piece of pains* all this trouble you have gone to
        (ironical)

45   *guerdoned* rewarded
        these good deserts what you have well deserved

47   *Injurious* insulting

49   *clapped up close* securely imprisoned

50   *asunder* apart from one another

51   *Stafford.* See the first note to the stage direction at
        line 39. Some editors claim that here Buckingham
        (whose family name is Stafford) is addressing himself,
        and so do not include Sir Humphrey Stafford in this
        scene.

52   *trinkets* conjuring apparatus
        all forthcoming (a legal term meaning that the goods
        are properly confiscated and will be produced later as
        evidence)

54   *you watched her well* your surveillance of the Duchess
        was very successful

55   *plot* (1) trick; (2) piece of ground
        build upon (1) pursue to our advantage; (2) erect a
        structure

60   *just* precisely, exactly

61 *Aio te, Aeacida, Romanos vincere posse.* This was a classic example of the ambiguous statement. In *De Divinatione*, II.56, Cicero cites Ennius's *Annals* which records this answer given by the Pythian Apollo to the Greek Pyrrhus, who wished to know whether he would conquer Rome. Its two interpretations are (1) I proclaim that you, the descendant of Aeacus, can conquer the Romans; (2) I proclaim that the Romans can conquer you, the descendant of Aeacus.

65 *befall.* F has 'betide', but the emendation seems necessary in view of line 33.

70 *hardly attained and hardly understood* obtained with difficulty and not comprehended at all

71 *in progress* on a royal journey

73 *these news.* 'News' was often treated as plural in sixteenth-century English.

76 *post* messenger

II.1 The idea of a hawking expedition as the scene for a conflict between Gloucester and the nobles was probably suggested by a passage in Hall where Margaret persuades her husband to make a progress to Warwickshire 'for his health and recreation, and so with hawking and hunting came to the city of Coventry, where were divers ways studied privily to bring the Queen to her heart's ease and long expectate desire, which was the death and destruction of the Duke of York, the Earls of Salisbury and Warwick' (page 236). The location of the scene is the city of Saint Albans. (stage direction) In Q1 the stage direction is more explicit: the Queen has 'her Hawke on her fist' and the whole royal party is to act 'as if they came from hawking'.

1 *flying at the brook* hawking water-fowl. This was a sport favoured by the nobility.

2 *these seven years' day* for the past seven years

4   *old Joan had not gone out.* Presumably the meaning is
that this particular hawk would not have flown on
account of its age.

5   *point* (position, usually to windward, from which to
swoop on the prey)

6   *pitch* (the maximum height to which the hawk flies
before swooping)

8   *fain* fond

9   *an* if
         like please

10   *My Lord Protector's hawks do tower so well.* Gloucester's family crest was a falcon with a maiden's head,
which fact lies behind Suffolk's and the Cardinal's
gibes in lines 9–15.
         tower (fly in mounting circular spirals until the 'pitch'
is reached)

11   *aloft* (1) high in the sky; (2) in a high position in the
state

18–20   *The treasury of everlasting joy ... thy heart* (from
Matthew 6.19–21: 'Hoard not up for yourselves
treasures upon earth ... but lay up for you treasures
in heaven. ... For where your treasure is, there will
your heart be also')

20   *Beat* dwell

21–56   *Pernicious Protector ... this strife.* This seems to have
been suggested by Hall's account of the year 1442–3:
'You have heard before how the Duke of Gloucester
sore grudged at the proud doings of the Cardinal of
Winchester, and how the Cardinal likewise sore envied
and disdained at the rule of the Duke of Gloucester,
and how ... each was reconciled to other in perfect
love and amity to all men's outward judgements. ...
But venom will once break out and inward grudge will
soon appear ... for divers secret attempts were
advanced forward this season against the noble Duke
Humphrey of Gloucester afar off, which in conclusion
came so near that they bereft him both of life and
land. ... For first this year Dame Eleanor Cobham,

wife to the said Duke, was accused of treason' (pages 197–202).

21   *Pernicious* dangerous
       dangerous threatening

22   *smoothest it so* adopt such a flattering manner

23   *peremptory* overbearing

24   *Tantaene animis coelestibus irae*. The quotation is from Virgil's *Aeneid*, I.11, and means 'Is it possible for there to be so much wrath in the minds of heavenly creatures?'

27   *well becomes* is very appropriate to

28   *good* just

30   *An't like* if it please

31   *insolence* pride

33   *whet not on* do not encourage

34   *blessèd are the peace-makers on earth* (from Matthew 5.9)

35–6   *Let me be blessèd for the peace I make | Against this proud Protector with my sword*. Compare Matthew 10.34: 'I came not to send peace, but a sword'.

37   *that* (a single combat between us)

39   *Make up no factious numbers for the matter* do not bring supporters of your faction into the quarrel

40   *In thine own person* alone on your own behalf
       abuse insult, offence

41   *peep* even appear

44   *man* (falconer)
       put up the fowl raised the water-fowl

45   *two-hand sword*. It is not certain what effect Shakespeare was aiming at in specifying this weapon. The long two-handed sword was archaic by the time of Elizabeth, so it may be an anachronism intended to underline the fact that it is two old men who are proposing to fight with antiquated weapons; or Shakespeare may be naming a weapon appropriate to the date of the events he is dramatizing.

47   *Are ... grove*. F gives this line to Gloucester (see collations list 1), but some emendation is necessary,

as the King's words (line 48) indicate that it is
Gloucester who has spoken last.

Are ye advised is it agreed

50   *shave your crown*. The allusion is to the Cardinal's
      tonsure.

51   *fence shall fail* expertise at sword-play shall prove
      inadequate

      Medice, teipsum. This was proverbial: 'Physician,
      heal thyself', based upon the Vulgate: Luke 4.23:
      'Medice, cura teipsum.'

52   *protect* (another pun on Gloucester's title)

53   *stomachs* angry passions

55   *such strings jar* (1) such strings of a musical instrument
      sound in discord; (2) such high noblemen fall into
      dispute

      harmony (1) musical concord; (2) peace at court

56   *compound this strife* settle this dispute

      (stage direction) The episode that this direction intro-
      duces is found in the chronicles only in Grafton, from
      which Shakespeare may have derived his material; but
      some details suggest that he actually used the account
      found in Foxe's *Acts and Monuments*. See the notes
      below for quotations from this source.

61–80 *Forsooth, a blind man . . . have better told*. There are
      echoes throughout this exchange of the account of
      Jesus's restoration of the beggar's sight in John 9.

61–3 *a blind man . . . life before*. Compare Foxe: 'there came
      to Saint Albans a certain beggar with his wife . . .
      saying that he was born blind, and never saw in his
      life. . . . suddenly this blind man, at Saint Alban's
      shrine, had his sight again, and a miracle solemnly
      rung, and *Te Deum* sung; so that nothing was talked
      of in all the town but this miracle' (III.712–13).

61   *Saint Alban*. Alban was reputed to be the first British
      Christian martyr. He was executed by the Romans in
      A.D. 304 in Verulam (Saint Albans) for harbouring
      Christian converts.

64   *Now God be praised*. In Foxe it is Gloucester who is

delighted at the report of the miracle, 'showing himself joyous of God's glory' (III.713).

64–5   *to believing souls | Gives light in darkness.* Compare Luke 1.79: 'To give light to them that sit in darkness'; also Isaiah 42.16 and Psalm 112.4.

65   (stage direction) *the Mayor of Saint Albans.* Saint Albans was not incorporated until the reign of Edward IV. In Henry VI's time the town's chief officer was the bailiff.

66   *on* in

68   *this earthly vale.* Compare Psalm 84.6: 'the vale of misery'; and *Homily against Wilful Rebellion*, 490: 'this wretched earth and vale of all misery'.

69   *by his sight his sin be multiplied.* Compare John 9.41: 'If ye were blind, ye would have no sin, but now ye say "We see": therefore your sin remaineth'.

72   *circumstance* detail

73   *glorify the Lord* (from Matthew 5.16: 'and glorify your Father which is in heaven')

76   *Ay, indeed was he.* See the note to lines 96–102.

78   *like* please

82   *Berwick* (a Scottish border fortress town at the mouth of the Tweed. See the note to lines 88–9.)

83–5   *Poor soul . . . hath done.* In Foxe it is Gloucester who tutors the beggar about God's gifts, 'exhorting him to meekness, and to no ascribing of any part of the worship to himself, nor to be proud of the people's praise, who would call him a good and godly man thereby' (III.713).

84   *unhallowed* without saying prayers

85   *still* always

87   *of* for

88–9   *being called | A hundred times and oftener, in my sleep.* Compare Foxe: 'he . . . was warned in his dream that he should come out of Berwick, where he said he had ever dwelled, to seek Saint Alban' (III.713).

90   *Simon* (the name of which 'Simpcox' is a derivative)

91   *offer* submit an offering of money

94	*lame*. Simpcox's lameness is Shakespeare's addition to his source.
96	*plum-tree* (a slang term for the female genitals)
96–102	*How long hast thou ... of my life*. Compare Foxe: '[Gloucester] looked well upon his eyes, and asked whether he could see nothing at all in all his life before. And ... his wife, as well as himself, affirmed falsely "no"' (III.713).
97–9	*What! And wouldst ... very dear*. The proverb 'He that never climbed never fell' lies behind this exchange.
98	*But that* only on that occasion
100	*Mass* by the mass
101	*damsons* (a slang term for testicles)
103	*subtle* clever, crafty
	shall not serve is not good enough for him to get away with it
104	*wink* close your eyes
105–29	*In my opinion ... impossible*. Compare Foxe: '[Gloucester] said "I believe you very well, for me thinketh ye cannot see well yet." "Yea, sir," quoth he; "I thank God and his holy martyr, I can see now as well as any man." "You can," quoth the Duke; "what colour is my gown?" Then anon the beggar told him. "What colour," quoth he, "is *this* man's gown?" He told him also, and so forth; without any sticking he told him the names of all the colours that could be showed him. And when the Duke saw that, he bade him "walk, traitor", and made him to be set openly in the stocks; for though he could have seen suddenly, by miracle, the difference between diverse colours; yet could he not, by the sight, so suddenly tell the names of all these colours except he had known them before, no more than the names of all the men that he should suddenly see' (III.713).
106	*clear as day* (proverbial phrase)
108	*Sayst thou me so* that's what you are telling me, is it?
109	*red as blood* (proverbial phrase)
111	*black as jet* (proverbial phrase)

114	*many* multitude
124	*sit there* there you are
125–9	*If thou hadst ... impossible.* Compare the proverb: 'A blind man can judge no colours'.
128	*nominate* identify by name
130	*cunning* skill
134	*beadles* (minor church officials appointed originally to keep order in church and to deal with petty offenders, often by inflicting corporal punishment)
	things called whips. This phrase gained some notoriety after it was used by Ben Jonson in his additions to Thomas Kyd's *The Spanish Tragedy*, III.11: 'And there is Nemesis and Furies,	And things called whips'. Robert Armin in *A Nest of Ninnies* (1608) wrongly associates its popularity with *Hamlet*.
136	*presently* immediately
137	*straight* at once
138	*by and by* immediately
140	*me* for me, at my command
142	*go about* are trying
150	*bearest* endurest (the sins of the world)
152	*drab* slut
153	*pure need* sheer economic necessity
157	*the lame to leap.* Compare Isaiah 35.6: 'Then shall the lame man leap as an hart'.
159	*fly* be lost. The allusion is to Suffolk's bargaining away French towns as part of Margaret's marriage settlement.
161	*unfold* reveal
162	*A sort of naughty persons, lewdly bent* a gang of disreputable people disposed to evil
163	*Under the countenance and confederacy* with the patronage and complicity
165	*head* leader
	rout disorderly mob
166	*practised* conspired
168	*in the fact* redhanded, in the act
170	*Demanding of* asking questions about
171	*other* other members

172   *at large* in detail

174   *forthcoming* in custody waiting to be tried. Compare I.4.52.

175   *turned* blunted

176   *like* likely

        your hour the appointment you have made (for the duel; see lines 40–48)

177   *leave to afflict* desist from afflicting

180   *meanest* most socially inferior

181-2   *what mischiefs work the wicked ones, | Heaping confusion on their own heads.* Compare Psalm 7.17: 'For his travail shall come upon his own head; and his wickedness shall fall upon his own pate'.

182   *confusion* destruction

183   *tainture of thy nest* defilement of your own house. Compare the proverb: 'It is a foul bird that defiles his own nest'.

184   *look thyself be faultless, thou wert best* you had better make sure you yourself are free from connexion with the crime

185   *for myself* so far as I am concerned

187   *how it stands* what the circumstances are

190   *conversed* been associated

191   *like to pitch, defile nobility.* Compare the proverb: 'He that touches pitch shall be defiled'; also Apocrypha of the Geneva Bible, Ecclesiastes 13.1.

195   *repose us here* (stay in Saint Albans)

198   *answers* defence in court

199   *poise the cause in Justice' equal scales* weigh the case in the fair scales of Justice

200   *Whose beam stands sure* whose cross-bar (from which the scale-pans are suspended) is perfectly level (to ensure impartiality of judgement)

II.2   The scene takes place in a secluded part of York's garden and is based on Hall's account of the Duke's activities in 1448–9: 'Richard Duke of York . . . perceiving the King to be a ruler not ruling and the whole burden of the realm to depend in the ordinances of the Queen and the Duke of Suffolk, began secretly to allure to his friends of the nobility and privately declared to them his title and right to the crown' (page 210).

2   *supper.* York issued the invitation at I.4.78–9.

3   *close walk* secluded garden path

9–52   *Then thus ... I am king.* This is a fuller version of York's justification for his claim to the throne than that which appears in *Part One*, II.4 and 5. It is based on various passages found in Hall: the first is from the Introduction to the reign of Henry IV: 'Edward III ... had issue Edward, his first begotten son, Prince of Wales; William of Hatfield, the second begotten son; Lionel Duke of Clarence, the third begotten son; John of Gaunt, Duke of Lancaster, the fourth begotten son; Edmund of Langley, Duke of York, the fifth begotten son; Thomas of Woodstock, Duke of Gloucester, the sixth begotten son; and William of Windsor, the seventh begotten son. The said Prince Edward died in the life of his father, King Edward III, and had issue Richard, born at Bordeaux, which after the death of King Edward III, as cousin and heir to him, ... succeeded him ... and died without issue. Lionel Duke of Clarence ... had issue Philippe, his only daughter, which was married to Edmund Mortimer, Earl of March, and had issue Roger Mortimer, Earl of March; which Roger had issue Edmund Mortimer, Earl of March, Anne, and Eleanor, which Edmund and Eleanor died without issue. And the said Anne was married to Richard Earl of Cambridge, son to Edmund of Langley, Duke of York, the fifth begotten son of the said King Edward III, which Richard had issue the famous prince Richard Plantagenet, Duke of York' (page 2).

The second passage is from the account of the first year of the reign of Henry IV: 'Owen Glendower ... made war ... on ... Lord Grey of Ruthen and took him prisoner, promising him liberty and discharging his ransom if he would espouse and marry his daughter. ... The Lord Grey ... assented. ... But this false father-in-law ... kept him with his wife still in captivity till he died. And not content with this heinous offence, made war on Lord Edmund Mortimer, Earl of March, and ... took him prisoner' (page 23).

The third passage comes from York's oration to the parliament in 1460: 'Which King Richard, of that name the second, was lawfully and justly possessed of the crown and diadem of this realm and region till Henry of Derby, Duke of Lancaster and Hereford, son to John Duke of Lancaster ... wrongfully usurped and intruded upon the royal power and high estate of this realm and region, taking on him the name, style, and authority of king and governor of the same. ... After whose piteous death ... the right and title of the crown ... was lawfully ... returned to Roger Mortimer, Earl of March, son and heir to Lady Philippe, the only child of the above rehearsed Lionel Duke of Clarence, to which Roger's daughter, called Anne, my ... mother, I am the very true and lineal heir. ... Edmund Earl of March, my most well-beloved uncle, in the time of the first usurper, in deed but not by right called King Henry IV. ... he being then in captivity with Owen Glendower, the rebel in Wales, made his title and righteous claim to the destruction of both the noble persons' (page 246). See also Table 2.

10 *Edward the Third* (1312–77, eldest son of Edward II; he reigned 1327–77)

11 *Edward the Black Prince* (1330–76, eldest son of Edward III, so named because of the colour of his armour at the Battle of Crécy)

12 *William of Hatfield* (second son of Edward III; he died in infancy)

13 *Lionel Duke of Clarence* (1338–68, third son of Edward III, from whom the Mortimers were descended)

14 *John of Gaunt* (1340–99, fourth son of Edward III;

father of Henry IV by his first wife Blanche and of the Beauforts (including the Cardinal) by his mistress Catherine Swynford)

15   *Edmund Langley, Duke of York* (1341–1402, fifth son of Edward III, progenitor of the house of York)

16   *Thomas of Woodstock, Duke of Gloucester* (1355–97, sixth son of Edward III, probably murdered on the orders of his nephew, Richard II)

17   *William of Windsor* (seventh son of Edward III; he died in infancy)

19   *Richard* (Richard II, 1367–1400, younger son of Edward, the Black Prince; he reigned 1377–99, and was deposed and murdered by his cousin Henry Bolingbroke)

21   *Henry Bolingbroke* (1367–1413; he reigned as Henry IV 1399–1413)

25   *his poor queen.* Richard II married Isabella of France (*c.*1389–1409) in 1396.

26   *Pomfret* (Pontefract Castle, twenty-one miles from York, where Richard II was murdered)

    all you know. This way of addressing only two listeners may be due to the fact that the material Shakespeare is working from is York's oration to parliament in 1460, in which the same phrase occurs (Hall, page 246); but 'all' is used to refer to two people in *2 Henry IV*, III.1.35, and in *The Faerie Queene*, II.1.61.

35   *issue* a child

    Philippe (Philippa, 1355–*c.*1380, the daughter of Lionel Duke of Clarence, third son of Edward III; she married Edmund Mortimer, third Earl of March, and transmitted the claim of Lionel through her grand-daughter, Anne, to the house of York)

36   *Edmund Mortimer* (1351–81, third Earl of March)

37   *Roger* (1374–98, fourth Earl of March)

38   *Edmund* (1391–1425, fifth Earl of March; declared heir presumptive by Richard II in 1398)

    Anne (1388–*c.*1412; married Richard Earl of Cambridge, becoming mother of Richard Duke of York)

39–42   *This Edmund . . . till he died.* Following Hall, Shakespeare confuses Edmund Mortimer, the fifth Earl of March (see the note to line 38), with Sir Edmund Mortimer (1376?–1409), the brother of Roger Mortimer, the fourth Earl of March, who married Owen Glendower's daughter while in captivity.

41   *Owen Glendower* (Welsh rebel, born *c.* 1359, who refused Henry V's general pardon and is thought to have died of starvation in the mountains of North Wales *c.* 1416)

42   *Who* (Glendower)

45   *Richard Earl of Cambridge* (d. 1415, second son of Edmund Langley, Duke of York; he was executed for treason on the vote of his peers)

53   *proceedings* line of descent

56   *his* (John of Gaunt's)

57   *fails not* has not died out

58   *slips* cuttings. *Fails, flourishes, slips,* and *stock* are all terms suggested by the idea of the family tree.
    stock tree-trunk

60   *private plot* secluded area. *Plot* continues the gardening metaphor of lines 57–8.

62   *birthright* rightful claim according to the law of primogeniture

64   *We.* Notice York's immediate adoption of the royal plural.

65   *that* until the time that

67   *suddenly* quickly

68   *advice* careful consideration

70   *Wink at* close your eyes to

71   *Beaufort's pride . . . Somerset's ambition.* Compare I.1.178.

73   *the shepherd of the flock.* This is a phrase used by Hall in praise of Henry V (page 112).

77   *break we off* let us finish talking

82   *but* except for

II.3   Most editors locate this scene in a hall of justice, though this seems inappropriate for the Horner–Peter duel, which historically took place at Smithfield. F's stage direction, '*Enter the King and State, with Guard, to banish the Duchesse.*', and the Queen's lines 52–3 suggest an open public place.

3–4   *for sins | Such as by God's book are adjudged to death.* Compare Deuteronomy 18.10–12; Leviticus 20.6; Exodus 22.17: 'Thou shalt not suffer a witch to live.'

5–8   *You four ... the gallows.* Contrast the punishments detailed in Hall's account: 'for the which treason they were adjudged to die; and so Margery Jourdain was burnt in Smithfield, and Roger Bolingbroke was drawn and quartered at Tyburn, taking upon his death that there was never no such thing by them imagined; John Hum had his pardon, and Southwell died in the Tower before execution' (page 202).

7   *Smithfield* (a favoured London spot for the burning of heretics)

9   *for* because

10   *Despoilèd of your honour in your life* deprived of your good name for the rest of your life

11–13   *after three days' ... Isle of Man.* Compare Hall: 'Dame Eleanor Cobham ... was examined in Saint Stephen's Chapel before the Bishop of Canterbury and there by examination convict and judged to do open penance in three open places within the City of London, and after that adjudged to perpetual prison in the Isle of Man, under the keeping of Sir John Stanley, Knight' (page 202).

13   *With* in the custody of
Sir John Stanley. Historically it was Sir Thomas Stanley who was custodian of the Duchess of Gloucester. Among the chroniclers, Fabyan and Stowe (*The Annals of England*, 1592) have the name correctly. Sir Thomas's brother appears in *Part Three*, IV.5.

14   *were* would be

15–21   *Eleanor, the law . . . would ease.* In Hall, Gloucester at
         his wife's sentence 'took all these things patiently and
         said little' (page 202).

16   *justify* exonerate, excuse

19   *Will bring thy head with sorrow to the ground.* Compare
         Genesis 42.38: 'ye shall bring my grey head with
         sorrow unto the grave'.

21   *would* requires, would have

22–3   *Ere thou go, | Give up thy staff.* There is no historical
         evidence that Gloucester's loss of his Protectorship
         followed from his wife's conviction; but Hall does
         deal with the two topics in a single paragraph on page
         202 (see the quotation in the note to II.1.21–56).

23   *staff* (symbol of the Protectorship; compare I.2.25)

25   *My stay, my guide.* Compare Psalm 42.9: 'my guide
         and stay'.
         lantern to my feet. Compare Psalm 119.105: 'thy word
         is a lantern unto my feet'.

28–31   *I see no reason . . . his realm.* See the quotations from
         Hall in the notes to I.3.121.

28   *of years* no longer a minor, of age

29   *be to be* need to be

30   *govern* guide, control
         realm. There is a possibility that this is a misprint due
         to the F compositor's eye catching the word *realm* in
         the next line. The manuscript copy may have read
         'helm'; compare I.3.98.

31   *King his* King's

34   *Henry* (Henry V)

41   *That bears so shrewd a maim* who has suffered so severe
         a mutilation
         two pulls at once two things torn from him in a single
         moment (his wife and his office)

43   *raught* snatched, seized

45   *this lofty pine.* This is probably an allusion to the
         heraldic device of a pinetree adopted by Henry IV,
         Gloucester's father, from Thomas of Woodstock,
         Edward III's sixth son. The destruction of a lofty

pine is compared with those who 'are often snared with wiles, | And from aloft do headlong fall to ground' in one of Geoffrey Whitney's *Emblems* (1586), a book that Shakespeare knew.

45   *sprays* branches

46   *her youngest days* (when her pride was at its height. Eleanor is being viewed as one of Gloucester's *sprays* which is cut off at her sprouting stage)

47   *let him go* bother your heads no more about him
         Please it if it please

49   *appellant and defendant.* These were terms used in a trial by single combat to describe the challenger and the challenged.

50   *the lists* (literally the arena within which knightly combatants had to fight; here it merely means 'the place designated for the fight')

52   *therefore* for that reason

53   *quarrel* dispute, difference
         tried resolved by combat

54   *A* in
         fit properly arranged

55   *end it* settle the matter

56   *worse bestead* in such a bad state of preparedness

58   (stage direction) *drum* drummer
         staff with a sand-bag fastened to it (usually a mock weapon used in sporting contests)

59–103   *Here, neighbour Horner . . . for thy reward.* This episode is based on Hall: 'an armourer's servant of London appealed his master of treason, which offered to be tried by battle. At the day assigned, the friends of the master brought him malmsey and *aqua vitae* to comfort him withal; but it was the cause of his and their discomfort, for he poured in so much that when he came into the place in Smithfield where he should fight, both his wit and strength failed him; and so he being a tall and a hardy personage, overloaded with hot drinks, was vanquished of his servant, being but a coward and a wretch, whose body was drawn to

Tyburn and there hanged and beheaded' (pages 207–8). Shakespeare's making the armourer confess to treason is part of the dramatic build-up to York's rebellion.

60   *sack* (a general term used for sweet Spanish and Canary wine)

63   *charneco* (a sweet wine, possibly from Portugal)

64   *double* extra strong

66   *Let it come* pass the tankard round for the toast
      pledge you drink your health

67   *a fig for* (a proverbial saying related to an obscene gesture made by pushing the thumb between the first and second fingers)

71   *credit* honour and reputation

78   *fence* skill in fencing

87–8   *take my death* take my oath on pain of death, stake my life on it

89   *have at* let me get at

90   *downright* administered vertically (and thus with one's full force)

91   *Dispatch* let us get on with it
      double grow thick and slurred (with drink)

92   *alarum* the call to arms, signal to begin fighting

95   *in thy master's way* which hindered your master's ability to fight

96–7   *in this presence* in this place before the King

102   *Which* whom

II.4   The scene is located in a London street; Holinshed specifies Cheapside. For Hall's account of the Duchess of Gloucester's sentence and punishment, see the note to II.3.11–13.
         (stage direction) *mourning cloaks* (long black cloaks with hoods)

1   *Thus sometimes hath the brightest day a cloud* (proverbial: 'No day so clear but has a dark cloud')

4   *fleet* pass by rapidly

8	*Uneath* with difficulty
10	*abrook* endure
11	*abject* low, common
12, 35	*envious* spiteful, malicious
13	*erst* formerly.
15	*soft* stay, hold

16   (stage direction) *barefoot . . . verses written on her back and pinned on.* These details from Q1 are not in F's stage direction but are justified in its text; see lines 31, 34, and 105–7.

       taper. This detail is not found in Hall; Holinshed has a note that 'Polychronicon saith she was enjoined to go through Cheapside with a taper in her hand' (III.203), and Foxe has it also. The account in *A Mirror for Magistrates* specifies the bare feet, the taper, and the sheet.

       bills (weapons consisting of a staff terminating in a hook-shaped blade)

       halberds (weapons consisting of a battle axe and a pike mounted on a six-foot pole)

17	*take her* rescue her by force

19   *open shame.* The same phrase occurs twice in the portrait of Eleanor in *A Mirror for Magistrates.*

21	*giddy* fickle
23	*hateful* full of hate
24	*closet* private room, study
	pent up barricaded in, locked in
	rue grieve for
25	*ban* curse
31	*Mailed up* enveloped

       papers on my back. See the stage direction at line 16: *verses written on her back* describing the nature of her crimes.

32	*with* by
33	*deep-fet* brought from deep within my being
34	*ruthless* unpitying
35	*start* flinch with the pain
36	*be advisèd* take care

38   *Trowest thou* do you believe

45   *As* that

          forlorn ruined, disgraced

46   *wonder* object to be looked at with amazement

          pointing-stock object to be pointed at with scorn

47   *rascal* worthless, good-for-nothing

52   *her* (Queen Margaret)

54   *limed* smeared with bird-lime. See the note to I.3.86.

55   *fly thou how thou canst* no matter how you try to fly

          tangle ensnare

56   *fear not ... snared.* The Duchess is being sarcastic about her husband's unsuspecting nature.

57   *seek prevention of* take action to forestall

58–63   *Ah, Nell, forbear ... and crimeless.* This is based on Hall's depiction of one aspect of Gloucester's character at this time: 'he thought neither of death nor of condemnation to die, such affiance had he in his strong truth and such confidence had he in indifferent justice' (page 209).

58   *Thou aimest all awry* your conjectures are quite wide of the mark

59   *attainted* condemned for treason

62   *procure me* bring about for me

          scathe harm

65   *were not* would not be

67   *quiet* to endure uncomplainingly

68   *sort* frame, adapt

69   *These few days' wonder will be quickly worn* (proverbial: 'A wonder lasts but nine days')

          worn worn out (and thus forgotten)

70–73   *I summon your grace ... will be there.* Compare Hall: 'So, for the furtherance of their purpose, a parliament was summoned to be kept at Bury, whither resorted all the peers of the realm, and amongst them the Duke of Gloucester' (page 209). Historically the parliament at Bury did not meet until 1447, some six years after the Duchess's conviction.

71   *Holden* to be held

71   *Bury* (Bury Saint Edmunds in Suffolk)

73   *close dealing* secret plotting

75   *the King's commission* the royal warrant (specifying the punishment)

76   *stays* is ended

77   *Sir John Stanley.* See the note to II.3.13.

79   *protect* act as custodian of

80   *given in charge* ordered

81   *Entreat* treat
       in that just because

82   *The world may laugh again* (proverbial expression meaning better days may come again)

90   *this world's eternity* to enjoy this world for ever

95   *state* status, rank

96   *but reproach* someone deserving only censure. Eleanor is quibbling on *state* meaning 'condition'.

100   *better than I fare* may you prosper better than I

101   *conduct* conductor, guide

102   *office* duty, function

103   *is discharged* has been carried out

107   *shifted* altered, removed (with a pun on *shifted* meaning 'changed like an undergarment')

109   *attire me how I can* no matter what clothes I wear

III.1   The scene is located in the Abbey at Bury Saint Edmunds. The plotting of the downfall and death of Gloucester is based upon Hall's account of the events in 1447–8, as he details the Queen's resentment against the Protectorship and her plot to deprive the Duke of his office: 'This ... invention ... was furthered and set forward by such as of long time had borne malice to the Duke. ... Which venomous serpents and malicious tigers persuaded, incensed, and exhorted the Queen to look well upon the expenses and revenues of the realm and thereof to call an account, affirming plainly that she should evidently perceive that the Duke of Gloucester had not so much advanced

212

and preferred the common wealth and public utility
as his own private things and peculiar estate. . . . And
although she joined her husband with her in name . . .
yet she did all, she said all, and she bore the whole
swing . . . and first of all she excluded the Duke of
Gloucester from all rule and governance, not pro-
hibiting such as she knew to be his mortal enemies to
invent and imagine causes and griefs against him and
his; so that by her permission and favour divers
noblemen conspired against him, of the which . . .
the Marquess of Suffolk and the Duke of Buckingham
[were] the chief, not unprocured by the Cardinal of
Winchester and the Archbishop of York. Divers
articles both heinous and odious were laid to his
charge in open council, and in especial one that he
had caused men adjudged to die to be put to other
execution than the law of the land had ordered or
assigned. . . . But his capital enemies and mortal foes,
fearing that some tumult or commotion might arise if
a prince so well beloved of the people should be openly
executed and put to death, determined to trap and
undo him. . . . So, for the furtherance of their purpose,
a parliament was summoned to be kept at Bury,
whither resorted all the peers of the realm, and
amongst them the Duke of Gloucester, which on the
second day of the session was by the Lord Beaumond,
then High Constable of England, accompanied by the
Duke of Buckingham and other, arrested, apprehended, and put in ward, and all his servants se-
questered from him' (pages 208–9). Shakespeare also
allows the peers to accuse Gloucester of irregularities
in his handling of the French wars, which were
historically attributed to Suffolk and Somerset.

1 *muse* wonder why

5–17 *The strangeness of his altered countenance ... to us
belongs.* In John Hardyng's *Chronicles of England*
(1543) the change in Gloucester's demeanour is attributed to his sorrow at his wife's disgrace: 'He waxed

then strange each day unto the King, | For cause she was forejudged for sorcery . . . | And to the King had great heaviness' (1812 edition, page 400).

5	*strangeness* aloofness
7	*insolent* proudly overbearing
9	*since* when
12	*That* so that
	admired was amazed at
14	*give the time of day* extend a greeting
17	*Disdaining duty* refusing to show respect
	to us belongs is proper to us
18	*grin* bare their teeth
19	*the lion* (the heraldic symbol of England)
21	*near* closely related to. See the note to I.1.149.
22	*mount* ascend (the throne of England)
23	*Me seemeth* it appears to me
	no policy not prudent political tactics
24	*Respecting* considering
25	*his advantage* the good that will come to him
26	*come about* be in regular contact with
28–30	*By flattery . . . will follow him.* For the nobles' fears of Gloucester's popularity, see the quotation from Hall in the headnote to this scene.
29	*make commotion* cause a rebellion
31–3	*Now 'tis the spring . . . husbandry.* Imagery derived from the idea of the garden of state was extensively used by Shakespeare, his fullest treatment being in *Richard II*, III.4.
32	*Suffer* allow them to flourish
35	*collect* perceive, infer
36	*fond* foolish
38	*subscribe* agree (from the sense of signing a legal document)
40	*Reprove* refute
41	*effectual* decisive
45	*subornation* instigation
46	*practices* plottings
47	*privy to* aware of, informed about
	faults crimes

48   *reputing of* setting great store by

50   *vaunts* boasts

51-2 *Did instigate . . . fall.* Shakespeare has been careful to
      show the audience in I.2.1–60 that this is not the case.
      Suffolk is politic enough to allow that there is the
      possibility of no direct involvement by Gloucester
      (line 47) and to suggest that it was the Duchess's
      consciousness of Gloucester's royal birth which en-
      couraged her to plot against the King – which is true.

51   *bedlam* crazy (like an inhabitant of Bedlam, the London
      hospital for the insane)

52   *frame* plot

53   *Smooth runs the water where the brook is deep* (pro-
      verbial)

54   *simple show* innocent outward appearance

57   *Unsounded* with unrevealed depths

59   *Devise strange deaths for small offences done.* See the
      note to I.3.130–31.

60-63 *And did he not . . . each day revolted.* See the note to
      I.3.133. There may also be an echo here of Hall's
      suggestion that 'the Duke of Somerset, for his own
      peculiar profit, kept not half his number of soldiers,
      and put their wages in his purse' (page 216).

63   *By means whereof* because of which

64   *to* compared with

65   *smooth* plausible

66   *at once.* There are three possible meanings: (1)
      answering you all together; (2) without further dis-
      cussion; (3) once and for all.

67   *annoy* injure, wound

68   *shall I speak* if I am to speak according to

71   *sucking lamb* (1 Samuel 7.9)
      harmless dove (proverbial; compare Matthew 10.16)

72   *well given* kindly disposed

74   *fond affiance* foolish confidence

76   *he's disposèd as* he has a disposition like that of

77-8 *Is he a lamb . . . wolves* (proverbial: 'a wolf in lamb's
      skin')

77   *lent him* borrowed by him

79   *Who cannot steal a shape that means deceit* what man who is intent on deception is unable to assume a false outward appearance

81   *Hangs* depends
     cutting short (1) beheading; (2) forestalling
     fraudful treacherous

84–5   *That all your interest ... lost.* Somerset is referring here to events that took place historically in 1448–9, some two years after the parliament at Bury Saint Edmunds. Hall blames Somerset for the losses and corruption that Gloucester is accused of in lines 104–6 below: 'The Duke of Somerset ... made an agreement with the French King that he would render the town so that he and all his might depart in safeguard with all their goods and substance, which offer the French King gladly accepted and allowed, knowing that by force he might longer have longed for the strong town than to have possessed the same so soon. ... The other towns of Normandy, being persuaded, voluntarily rendered themselves vassals and subjects to the French nation. Now rested English only the town of Cherbourg, whereof was captain Thomas Gonville, which surely valiantly defended the town as long as victual and munition served; but when those two hands were spent and consumed, he, destitute of all comfort and aid, upon a reasonable composition, yielded the town and went to Calais, where the Duke of Somerset and many Englishmen then sojourned, lamenting their loss and desperate of all recovery' (pages 215–16).

85   *utterly bereft* completely seized from
     all is lost. In Holinshed's account of the French wars at this time (1448) there is a marginal gloss 'The English lose all in France' (III.215).

87–92   *Cold news for me ... glorious grave.* On Somerset's loss of the French territories, 'Sir Davy Hall, with divers other of his trusty friends, departed to Cherbourg and from thence sailed into Ireland to the Duke of York, making relation to him of all these doings,

216

which thing kindled so great a rancour in his heart and stomach that he never left persecuting of the Duke of Somerset' (Hall, page 216).

87–8   *Cold news . . . England*. Compare I.1.235–6.

89   *Thus are my blossoms blasted in the bud* (proverbial)

91   *gear* business

92   *sell* exchange

94   *stayed* stayed away

99   *for* on account of

100   *unspotted* innocent

104   *of* from

105–6   *stayed the soldiers' pay . . . lost France*. The same accusation is made at lines 60–63. See also the notes to lines 84–5 and to I.3.133 and 165–70.

105   *stayed* retained, kept back

107   *What* who

110   *watched the night* stayed up all night

112   *doit* (small Dutch coin worth about half an English farthing)

113   *groat* (coin worth 4d.)
      to my for my personal

115   *proper store* personal fortune

117   *dispursèd* paid out

119   *serves you well* is to your advantage

121–3   *In your Protectorship . . . by tyranny*. Compare line 59 and see the note to I.3.130–31.

123   *That England was defamed by* with the result that England became infamous for

124   *whiles* during the time

126   *should* was wont to

127   *lowly* humble
      fault offence

129   *felonious* wicked
      fleeced stripped by robbing, plundered
      passengers travellers

130   *condign* justly deserve

132   *Above the felon or what trespass else* more than the man convicted of a felony or any other kind of crime

133   *easy* insignificant

133   *answered* explained away

138   *keep* be guarded
        further future

140   *suspense* suspicion

145   *subornation* instigation to commit crime
        predominant (an astrological term) in the ascendant,
        ruling

146   *equity* justice
        exiled (accented on the second syllable) is exiled from

147   *complot* (accented on the first syllable) scheme, plot

149   *prove the period* mark the end

150   *expend it* pay the price (of my death)

151   *mine* (my death)

153   *conclude their plotted tragedy* bring an end to the
        tragedy they have planned

155   *cloudy* frowning

156   *unburdens* unloads, releases

157   *envious* malicious

158   *doggèd* (1) determined; (2) currish
        reaches at the moon (proverbial)

159   *overweening* overreaching

160   *accuse* accusation
        level aim (as with a weapon)

162   *Causeless* without reason

164   *liefest* dearest

165   *laid your heads together* plotted, contrived

166   *conventicles* secret meetings. This is the only occur-
        rence of the word in Shakespeare. He probably used it
        under the influence of Hall: 'The Earls of March and
        Warwick and other, being at Calais, had knowledge of
        all these doings and secret conventicles' (page 242).

167   *make away* destroy

168   *want* lack

169   *store* numerous accusations

170   *effected* shown to be true

173   *care* exercise care
        keep protect

175   *rated at* berated

218

176   *scope* full freedom

178   *twit* taunted

179   *clerkly couched* phrased in an educated way

180-81 *suborned some to swear* | *False allegations* procured some
        people to bear false witness. Compare Acts 6.11-13.

181   *o'erthrow his state* bring him down from his high
        position

182   *I can give the loser leave to chide* (proverbial)

184   *Beshrew* curse
        played me false deceived me

186   *wrest the sense* distort the meaning

188   *sure* securely

191-2   *Thus is the shepherd . . . first.* Compare Matthew 26.31
        and Ezekiel 34.8.

192   *gnarling* snarling over

194   *decay* downfall, ruin

200   *engirt* encircled

203   *map* image

206   *lowering* ominous
        envies thy estate shows malice towards your position

208   *subversion* destruction

211   *strays.* There are some arguments for the emendation
        'strains' here; but *binds* may mean 'pens in' rather
        than 'ties up'.

214   *dam* mother

219   *do him good* give him any assistance

223   *Free* magnanimous, honourable

224   *cold* uninterested

225   *show* display of innocence

226   *the mournful crocodile.* The allusion is to 'crocodile
        tears'. Hakluyt's account of Sir John Hawkins's
        second voyage (1565) includes a description of the
        crocodile's propensity for trickery: 'His nature is ever,
        when he would have his prey, to cry and sob like a
        Christian body, to provoke them to come to him; and
        then he snatcheth at them'.

227   *relenting passengers* sympathetic travellers (taken in by
        the crocodile's signs of sorrow)

228–9   *as the snake . . . child* (proverbial)

228   *rolled* curled up

229   *checkered slough* patterned skin

233   *rid* removed from

235   *is worthy policy* deserves shrewd planning

236   *colour* pretext, justification

237   *meet* fitting

238   *were* would be

239   *still* continually

240   *The commons haply rise to save his life.* Compare lines 28–30, and see the quotation from Hall in the headnote to this scene.

        haply perhaps

        rise (in rebellion)

241   *but trivial argument* only insubstantial evidence

242   *mistrust* suspicion

247   *Say as you think, and speak it from your souls* (proverbial)

248   *all one* just the same as if

        empty hungry

249   *kite* (scavenging hawk, frequently seen in Elizabethan London)

251   *So* if so

252–3   *were't not madness then | To make the fox surveyor of the fold* (proverbial: 'Give not the fox the sheep to keep')

253   *surveyor* guardian

254–6   *Who being . . . executed* the guilt of someone who has been charged as a cunning killer would be foolishly disregarded by a too rapid examination based on the fact that he has not carried out his plans

255   *idly posted over* foolishly disregarded (due to being hurried over)

256   *executed* accomplished

259   *chaps* jaws

260   *reasons* arguments. Some editors emend this to 'treasons', but the whole point is that Gloucester cannot be proved to have committed treason and so

the peers have to resort to giving the weak King
trivial arguments as justification for their animosity.

261   *stand on quillets* insist upon subtle legal arguments

262   *gins* traps

264   *So* so long as

264–5   *that is good deceit | Which mates him first that first
intends deceit* (proverbial: 'To deceive the deceiver is
no deceit')

265   *mates* checkmates, finishes off

267   *except* unless

269   *that* to show that

272   *be his priest* kill him (literally 'perform the last offices
for him'; a proverbial phrase)

274   *take due orders for* (1) make arrangements to procure;
(2) prepare yourself to be

275   *censure well* give your approval of

276   *And I'll provide his executioner.* Some editors see a
contradiction between this line and the First Murderer's words at III.2.1–2: *Run to my lord of Suffolk;
let him know | We have dispatched the Duke as he
commanded.* However, all the Cardinal is saying in
lines 273–7 is that he wants the murder carried out
more quickly than Suffolk's metaphorical way of
speaking implies. Suffolk (line 277) agrees that expedition is necessary and so accepts the Cardinal's offer to
supply him immediately with an assassin to do the
deed. This is also the sense of Q1's version: '*Suffol.*
Let that be my Lord Cardinals charge & mine. | *Car.*
Agreed, for hee's already kept within my house.'
Later, at line 326, the Cardinal underlines his working
together with Suffolk on the murder.

277   *tender so* am so solicitous over

281   *It skills not greatly who impugns our doom* it does not
matter much who questions our decision
(stage direction) *Post* messenger

282–329   *Great lords . . . for Ireland.* Compare Hall: 'It was not
enough the realm of England this season thus to be
vexed and unquieted with the business of Normandy,

but also a new rebellion began in Ireland, to the great displeasure of the King and his Council; for repressing whereof Richard Duke of York, with a convenient number of men, was sent thither as lieutenant to the King, which not only appeased the fury of the wild and savage people there, but also got him such love and favour of the country and the inhabitants that their sincere love and friendly affection could never be separated from him and his lineage' (page 213).

282   *amain* at full speed

283   *signify* report

      up in arms

285   *rage* outrage

      betime promptly

287   *being green, there is great hope of help* (proverbial: 'A green wound is soon healed')

      green fresh, new

288   *breach* outbreak

      craves requires

      expedient speedy

291   *meet* appropriate, proper

      lucky ruler successful governor. York is being ironical because of Somerset's lack of success in France; see the quotation in the note to lines 87–92.

293   *far-fet* far-fetched, deeply evolved

297   *betimes* sooner

299   *staying there so long* temporizing

300   *charactered* (accented on the second syllable) inscribed

301   *Men's flesh preserved so whole* unwounded men

302–3   *this spark will prove a raging fire | If wind and fuel be brought to feed it with* (proverbial)

304   *still* quiet

306   *happily* perhaps

308   *And, in the number, thee that wishest shame.* Compare 'Evil be to him that evil thinks', the motto of the Order of the Garter.

      in the number among them

310   *uncivil kerns* uncivilized, primitively armed Irish infantry

311	*temper clay* moisten the ground
314	*hap* fortune
320	*take order for* arrange
321	*charge* duty
322	*return we to* let us get back to the subject of
325	*break off* let us conclude
326	*event* business
328	*Bristow* Bristol
331	*Now . . . or never* (proverbial)
	steel harden
	fearful timid
332	*misdoubt* suspicion, mistrust
333	*that* that which
335	*keep* live
	mean-born of lowly birth
338	*dignity* the position of kingship
340	*tedious* laboriously intricate
342	*packing* on a journey
343–4	*you but warm the starvèd snake, | Who, cherished in your breasts, will sting your hearts.* The allusion is to the Aesop fable in which a man is stung by a snake which he had placed next to his chest to protect it from the cold; compare the proverb 'To nourish a viper in one's bosom'.
343	*starvèd* stiff with cold
347	*You put sharp weapons in a madman's hands* (proverbial)
349–54	*I will stir up . . . mad-bred flaw.* Compare Hall: 'to set open the flood-gates of these devices it was thought necessary to cause some great commotion and rising of people to be made against the King; so that, if they prevailed, then had the Duke of York and his complices their appetite and desire' (page 219).
350	*Shall* which shall
351	*fell* ferocious
352	*circuit* crown
354	*mad-bred* produced by madness
	flaw squall
355–9	*And, for a minister . . . Mortimer.* Compare Hall:

'because the Kentishmen be impatient in wrongs, disdaining of too much oppression and ever desirous of new change and new-fangleness, the overture of this matter was put first forth in Kent; and to the intent that it should not be known that the Duke of York or his friends were the cause of the sudden rising, a certain young man of a goodly stature and pregnant wit was enticed to take upon him the name of John Mortimer, although his name were John Cade, and not for a small policy, thinking that by that surname the line and lineage of the assistant house of the Earl of March, which were no small number, should be to him both adherent and favourable' (pages 219–20).

355   *minister* agent

358   *commotion* uprising

359   *Under the title of John Mortimer.* For Mortimer's connexion with the crown, see Table 2 and II.2.34–52. For Jack Cade's fictional descent, see IV.2.127–37.

360   *In Ireland . . . Cade.* The connexion between Cade and the Irish wars may have been suggested by Holinshed's note: 'John Cade . . . an Irishman, as Polychronicon saith' (III.220).

362   *till that* until. ('That' was often added after words such as 'if', 'after', 'when'.)

      darts arrows. A contemporary account of the Irish kerns notes that they were armed with 'darts and short bows'.

363   *porpentine* porcupine

365   *Morisco* morris dancer. The morris dance in Elizabethan England was apparently a good deal wilder than its modern counterpart, often involving play with weapons.

366   *as he his bells* (as the morris dancer shakes the bells attached to his shins)

367   *shag-haired* rough-haired

372   *For that John Mortimer, which now is dead.* Sir John Mortimer died by execution in 1424, after several years in prison, for urging his cousin Edmund

Mortimer's claim to the throne on the grounds that
Richard II had recognized him as heir presumptive in
1398. He has a long conversation with the Duke of
York about his lineage and claim in *Part One*, II.5.

372   *For that* because
375   *affect* favour, are inclined to
376   *taken* captured
378   *moved him to those arms* incited him to take up arms
       against the King
379   *great like* most likely
380   *strength* troops
381   *reap the harvest which that rascal sowed* (proverbial:
       'One sows, another reaps')

III.2   The scene is located in a room in the Cardinal's house
         in Bury Saint Edmunds. The chief source is Hall:
         'The Duke [of Gloucester] the night after his im-
         prisonment was found dead in his bed and his body
         showed to the lords and commons, as though he had
         died of a palsy or imposthume; but all indifferent
         persons well knew that he died of no natural death
         but of some violent force. Some judged him to be
         strangled; some affirm that a hot spit was put in at
         his fundament; other write that he was stifled or
         smouldered between two feather beds. After whose
         death, none of his servants ... were put to death: for
         the Marquess of Suffolk, when they should have been
         executed, showed openly their pardon, but this doing
         appeased not the grudge of the people, which said that
         the pardon of the servants was no amends for murder-
         ing of their master' (page 209).
         (stage direction) In Q1 Gloucester is killed on stage:
         'Then the Curtaines being drawne, Duke *Humphrey*
         is discouered in his bed, and two men lying on his
         brest, and smothering him in his bed. And then enter
         the Duke of *Suffolke* to them.'
2   *dispatched* done away with, killed

2   *as he commanded.* See the note to III.1.276.

3   *to do* to do again (so that we might refrain from doing it)

6   *dispatched this thing* taken care of this business

8   *well said* well done

9   *venturous* bold, daring

11   *laid fair* rearranged (so as to look normal after being upset in the struggle; see the note to the opening stage direction)

14   (stage direction) In F Suffolk enters with the royal party after exiting with the murderers after line 14. It is obviously more sensible for him to remain on stage after the murderers leave, as in Q1; see collations list 3.

15   *straight* immediately

17   *If* whether
        publishèd publicly proclaimed

18   *presently* at once

20   *straiter* more severely

21   *of good esteem* worthy to be believed

22   *approved in* proved guilty of
        practice conspiracy, plotting

24   *faultless may condemn a noble man* may condemn a good and innocent man. In view of the King's attitude to Gloucester the reading *noble man* should be retained as in F rather than changed to 'nobleman' as in most editions.

25   *acquit him* exonerate himself

26   *Meg.* Compare similar errors at lines 79, 100, and 120, for which see collations list 1. Referring to Margaret as Eleanor must have been Shakespeare's oversight in his manuscript, as such an error could not have survived in a theatre prompt-book.

30   *forfend* forbid

31   *tonight* last night

34   *Rear up* raise, support
        wring him by the nose (to restore him to consciousness)

40   *right now* a moment ago

raven's note. The cry of the raven was reputed to herald death; compare the proverb 'The croaking raven bodes death' and *Macbeth*, I.5.36–8.

41   *bereft* robbed me of
       vital powers human faculties (believed to be necessary to sustain life)

43   *hollow* deceitful

44   *first-conceivèd* previously perceived

48   *baleful* deadly

49   *murderous tyranny* the tyranny of murder

52   *basilisk* (a fabulous monster which killed with a glance, thought to be hatched by a serpent or toad from the egg of a cock)

54   *shade* shadow

56   *rate* berate

59   *for* as for

60   *heart-offending* doing injury to the heart

61   *blood-consuming sighs.* It was believed that every sigh drew a drop of blood from the heart.

63   *with* because of

65   *deem* judge

66   *hollow* false

67   *judged* believed that

69   *my reproach* blame of me

72   *woe* sorry

76   *like the adder waxen deaf* (a proverbial saying referring to the belief that the adder resisted the snake charmer by stopping one ear with its tail and pressing the other to the ground; compare Psalm 58.4–5)
       waxen grown

80   *statue* (pronounced trisyllabically)

82   *wrecked* shipwrecked

83   *awkward* adverse
       bank shore

84   *clime* country

85   *well forewarning* truthfully predicting

87   *unkind* cruel

89   *he* (Aeolus, god of the winds)

89   *loosed them forth* released them from
        brazen powerful. The allusion is to the bronze walls
        surrounding the isle of Aeolus in Homer's *Odyssey*,
        X.3–4.

94   *pretty vaulting* attractively rising and falling

97   *splitting* capable of splitting ships
        sinking sands sands which cause ships to sink

99   *Because* in order that
        thy flinty heart, more hard than they (proverbial)

100   *perish* destroy

101   *ken* (a nautical term) make out

105   *earnest-gaping* eagerly peering

110   *fair England's view* the view of fair England

111   *be packing* be gone
        heart (the heart-shaped ornament)

112   *spectacles* instruments of vision

113   *Albion* England
        wishèd longed-for

114   *tempted* induced

115   *The agent of thy foul inconstancy*. The allusion is to
        Suffolk's acting as Henry's proxy in the marriage
        contract arrangements.

116   *witch* bewitch. F's reading, 'watch', makes no sense in
        the context.

116–18 *as Ascanius did . . . burning Troy*. In Virgil's *Aeneid*
        (I.658 ff.) Venus transforms Cupid into the shape of
        Aeneas's son, Ascanius, so that he could bewitch
        Dido, the Queen of Carthage, with stories of his
        father's exploits at the siege of Troy.

117   *madding* becoming mad
        unfold disclose, relate

119   *witched* bewitched
        him (Aeneas, who deserted Dido and caused her
        suicide)

120   *I can no more* my strength fails me, I am capable of no
        more

122–9   *It is reported . . . of his death*. Compare Hall: 'When
        the rumour of the Duke's death was blown through

the realm, many men were suddenly appalled and amazed for fear; many abhorred and detested the fact, but all men reputed it an abominable cruelty and a shameful tyranny' (page 210).

126 *want* lack

127 *his revenge* revenge for his death

128 *spleenful mutiny* angry uprising

129 *order* details, manner

132 *breathless* lifeless

133 *comment then upon* then explain

135 *rude* uncivilized

136 *Thou that judgest all things.* Compare Genesis 18.25: 'the judge of all the earth'.
stay restrain

139 *suspect* suspicion

141 *Fain* gladly
chafe warm
paly bloodless, colourless

145 *unfeeling* incapable of feeling

146 *mean obsequies* insignificant funeral rites

147 *earthy image* (reflection of what he was, now only dead earth)

152 *my life in death* what my own corpse will be like when I am dead

154 *King* (Christ)
took our state upon Him became human. Compare the Collect for Christmas Day: 'to take our nature upon him'.

155 *To free us from His Father's wrathful curse.* Compare Galatians 3.13: 'Christ hath redeemed us from the curse of the law'.

157 *thrice-famèd* very famous

159 *instance* evidence, proof

160–78 *See how the blood . . . were probable.* Like Q1's opening stage direction for this scene (see the note above), this passage is clear about the manner of Gloucester's death. Contrast the variety of possibilities suggested by Hall in the passage quoted in the headnote.

229

160 *settlèd* congealed

161 *a timely-parted ghost* the body of a person who has died naturally

162 *meagre* emaciated

163 *Being all descended to* (the blood) having all drained into

164 *Who* (the heart)

165 *the same* (the blood)
   aidance assistance

166 *Which* (the blood)

171 *upreared* standing on end

172 *abroad displayed* spread wide apart

175 *rugged* shaggy, bristling

176 *lodged* beaten flat, levelled

178 *were probable* would be sufficient proof

183 *keep* protect, guard

184 *'Tis like* it is likely

185 *well seen* easily perceived

186 *belike* perhaps

187 *timeless* untimely

189 *fast* close

191 *puttock* kite

192 *was dead* came to be killed

198 *with ease* as a result of disuse

199 *scourèd* washed clean

202 *faulty in* guilty of
   (stage direction) The F text has no exit for the Cardinal and so the direction of Q1 has been adopted. It is appropriate that the Cardinal should leave the stage earlier than the general exit at line 299, perhaps after displaying signs of incipient sickness and guilt after seeing Gloucester's corpse.

204 *contumelious* slanderous

205 *controller* critic, detractor

212 *blameful* guilty

213 *stern* rough
   churl peasant
   stock tree-trunk

214 *graft* grafted

slip cutting (with possibly a pun on *slip* meaning 'moral lapse')

216   *bucklers* shields, protects

217   *deathsman* executioner

218   *Quitting thee* getting rid for you

219   *that* except for the fact that

221   *passèd* just uttered

224   *fearful homage* cowardly submission

225   *hire* payment (that is, death)

226   *Pernicious* destructive

227   *waking* awake

228   *presence* royal presence

230   *cope with thee* meet you in combat

232–3   *What stronger breastplate . . . just* (proverbial: 'Innocence bears its defence with it.' Compare also Ephesians 6.14: 'the breastplate of righteousness'.)

234   *naked* unprotected
       locked up in steel buckled in his armour

237–8   *Your wrathful weapons drawn | Here in our presence?* Drawing a sword in the king's presence was a serious political offence; compare *Part One*, I.3.46.

243–7   *the commons . . . lingering death.* Compare Hall: 'They . . . began to make exclamation against the Duke of Suffolk, affirming him to be the only cause of the delivery of Anjou and Maine, the chief procurer of the death of the good Duke of Gloucester, the very occasion of the loss of Normandy, the most swallower up and consumer of the King's treasure. . . . So that the Duke was called in every man's mouth a traitor, a murderer, a robber of the King's treasure, and worthy to be put to most cruel punishment' (page 217). At the parliament at Leicester later in the same year 'the commons of the lower house, not forgetting their old grudge, beseeched the King that such persons as assented to the release of Anjou and deliverance of Maine might be extremely punished and tormented; and to be privy to this fact, they accused as principal the Duke of Suffolk' (page 219).

244   *straight* immediately

250   *mere instinct of* pure impulse toward. *Instinct* is
       accented on the second syllable.

251   *opposite intent* antagonistic purpose

252   *contradict your liking* oppose your wishes

253   *forward in* insistent upon

256   *charge* give orders that

257   *In pain* under penalty
       dislike displeasure

258   *strait* strict

259   *Were there a serpent seen, with forkèd tongue*. This was
       probably suggested by Hall's description of Suffolk as
       'the abhorred toad ... of the realm' (page 219).

262   *suffered* allowed to remain
       harmful dangerous

263   *mortal worm* deadly snake

265   *whe'er* whether

266   *fell* cruel, fierce

268   *his worth* more worthy than he

269   *bereft* deprived

271   *like* probable (ironical)
       hinds boors, peasants

274   *quaint* skilful

277   *sort* gang, crew
       tinkers (a general term for vagabonds)

281   *cited* urged

284   *Mischance* disaster

285–97 *And therefore by His majesty ... for thy life.* Compare
        Hall: 'When King Henry perceived that the commons
        were thus stomached and bent against the Queen's
        darling, William Duke of Suffolk, he plainly saw that
        neither glozing would serve nor dissimulation could
        appease the continual clamour of the importunate
        commons. Wherefore to begin a short pacification in
        so long a broil ... he ... banished and put in exile
        the Duke of Suffolk, as the abhorred toad and common
        nuisance of the realm of England, for the term of five
        years, meaning by this exile to appease the furious
        rage of the outrageous people; and, that pacified, to

revocate him into his old estate as the Queen's chief friend and counsellor' (page 219).

287 *breathe infection in this air* pollute the air of England with his breath

289 *gentle* noble

290 *Ungentle* unkind

293 *said* pronounced it

299 *great* important

(stage direction) Neither F nor Q1 contains any direction for getting Gloucester's body off the stage. Presumably at this point the bed would be carried off stage by attendants or perhaps curtains would be drawn round it. The same bed would be needed for the Cardinal's death in the next scene.

303 *There's two of you, the devil make a third* (proverbial: 'There cannot lightly come a worse except the devil come himself')

304 *tend upon* follow, dog

306 *heavy* mournful

310 *the mandrake's groan.* Numerous superstitions attached themselves to this plant with the root shaped like a human body, including the belief that it shrieked when pulled out of the ground, which caused the hearer to die or go mad.

311 *searching* cutting

312 *curst* malignant, savage

313 *fixèd* gritted

315 *lean-faced Envy in her loathsome cave.* Envy was conventionally depicted as thin; compare Arthur Golding's translation of Ovid's *Metamorphoses* (1567), II.949–67:

She goes me straight to Envy's house, a foul and
    irksome cave,
Replete with black and loathly filth and stinking like
    a grave. . . .
There saw she Envy sit within, fast gnawing on the
    flesh. . . .

233

> Her lips were pale, her cheeks were wan, and all her
> face was swart;
> Her body lean as any rake.

318	*distract* mad
319	*curse and ban* excommunicate
322	*daintiest* most delicious drink
323	*cypress trees* (trees associated with death; compare *Twelfth Night*, II.4.50–51: 'Come away, come away, death, | And in sad cypress let me be laid')
324	*prospect* sight, view
	basilisks. See the note to line 52.
325	*smart* painful
	lizards' stings. The lizard was confused with the snake and thus thought to be poisonous.
326	*frightful* terrifying
327	*boding* presaging death
	screech-owls. See the note to I.4.17.
	make the consort full complete the group of musicians
331	*overchargèd* overloaded
333	*ban* curse
	leave stop
342	*woeful monuments* memorials of grief (that is, tears)
344–5	*thou mightst think upon these by the seal,	Through whom a thousand sighs are breathed for thee* you might think about my lips, which left their imprint on your hand and between which a thousand sighs pass for you
346	*know my grief* feel the full weight of my sorrow
347	*but surmised* only guessed at
348	*surfeits* overeats
	want lack of food
349	*repeal thee* get you recalled from exile. See the quotation from Hall in the note to lines 285–97.
350	*Adventure* risk
363	*several* separate, distinct
365	*joy* enjoy
366	(stage direction) *Vaux*. Sir William Vaux was a zealous Lancastrian who died at the Battle of Tewkesbury in 1471.

368   *signify* report

371   *That makes him gasp, and stare, and catch the air*. Note the similarity to Warwick's description of Gloucester's death in lines 160–76.

373   *Sometime* from time to time

375–6   *whispers to his pillow, as to him, | The secrets of his overchargèd soul* (proverbial: 'Take counsel of your pillow')

376   *overchargèd* overburdened (with guilt)

379   *heavy* sorrowful

381   *an hour's poor loss* the loss of a few hours of life (since the Cardinal, at his age, did not have long to live anyway)

382   *Omitting* forgetting about

384   *southern clouds* (commonly considered to be carriers of rain and fog)
        contend rival, compete

385   *earth's increase* growth of crops

387   *by me* at my side

393   *dug* nipple, breast

394   *Where* whereas
        from out of

399   *lived* would live
        Elysium (in Virgil, the region of Hades which housed the souls of the blessed after death; in Greek mythology, an island in the western ocean where the souls of the virtuous lived in perfect happiness)

400   *but to die in jest* not to die at all

401   *From* absent from

402   *befall what may befall* (proverbial: 'Come hap what hap may')

403   *fretful corrosive* gnawing painful remedy

404   *deathful* deathly, mortal

407   *Iris* (the messenger of Juno, queen of the gods)
        find thee out locate you

409   *into* in
        cask casket, jewel-box

411   *splitted bark* ship split in two
        sunder we do we separate

III.3   The scene is located in a bedchamber in the Cardinal's
house. His death occurred historically in 1447, a year
after Gloucester's murder. Hall's account differs
radically from Shakespeare's. Instead of the play's
picture of a guilty villain making a dreadful end, the
chronicle stresses the regrets of a very worldly prelate
for a life dedicated to power and material possessions:
'During these doings Henry Beaufort, Bishop of
Winchester and called the rich Cardinal, departed out
of this world and was buried at Winchester. This man
was son to John of Gaunt, Duke of Lancaster,
descended of an honourable lineage but born in baste
[bastardy], more noble of blood than notable in
learning, haught in stomach … rich above measure
of all men and to few liberal, disdainful to his kin,
and dreadful to his lovers, preferring money before
friendship, many things beginning and nothing per-
forming. His covetise insatiable and hope of long life
made him both to forget God, his prince, and himself
in his latter days. For Dr John Baker, his privy
counsellor and his chaplain, wrote that he, lying on
his death bed, said these words: "Why should I die,
having so much riches? If the whole realm would save
my life, I am able either by policy to get it or by riches
to buy it. Fie, will not death be hired, nor will money
do nothing? When my nephew of Bedford died, I
thought myself half up the wheel; but when I saw my
other nephew of Gloucester deceased, then I thought
myself able to be equal with kings, and so thought to
increase my treasure in hope to have worn a triple
crown. But I see now the world faileth me, and so I
am deceived, praying you all to pray for me"' (pages
210–11).
(stage direction) The Q1 stage direction gives an indication of how the scene was staged by means of the
use of a curtained area: 'Enter King and *Salsbury*, and
then the Curtaines be drawne, and the Cardinall is
discouered in his bed, rauing and staring as if he were
madde.'

236

4	*So if*
10	*whe'er* whether
15	*Comb down his hair ... it stands upright.* Compare III.2.171.
16	*lime-twigs.* See the note to I.3.86.
18	*of* from
19	*eternal mover* (God)
21	*meddling* interfering in the lives of men
24	*the pangs of death.* Compare 2 Samuel 22.5 and Psalm 18.3.
	grin bare his teeth (in pain)
25	*pass* die, pass on
28	*make signal* make a gesture, give a sign
30	*argues* gives evidence of
31	*Forbear to judge.* Compare Matthew 7.1.
	we are sinners all. Compare Romans 3.23.
32	*Close up his eyes* (the traditional last office for the dead)
	curtain (of the bed; see the Q1 opening stage direction for this scene, quoted in the note above)
33	*meditation* prayer

IV.1	The scene takes place on the coast of Kent. It is developed from Hall's account of Suffolk's death: 'But fortune would not that this flagitious person should so escape; for when he shipped in Suffolk, intending to be transported into France, he was encountered with a ship of war appertaining to the Duke of Exeter, the Constable of the Tower of London, called the *Nicholas of the Tower.* The captain of the same bark with small fight entered into the Duke's ship, and perceiving his person present, brought him to Dover road, and there on the one side of a cock boat caused his head to be stricken off, and left his body with the head upon the sands of Dover, which corpse was there found by a chaplain of his and conveyed to Wingfield College in Suffolk and there buried. This end had William de la Pole, first Duke of Suffolk, as men judge by God's punishment; for above

237

all things he was noted to be the very organ, engine, and deviser of the destruction of Humphrey, the good Duke of Gloucester, and so the blood of the innocent man was with his dolorous death recompensed and punished' (page 219).

(stage direction) The Q1 stage direction gives an indication of how the sound effects were managed in the Elizabethan theatre: 'Alarmes within, and the chambers be discharged, like as it were a fight at sea.'

1   *blabbing* revealing secrets, tell-tale
          remorseful conscience-stricken

2   *crept into the bosom* (proverbial)

3   *jades* wretched horses (but here referring to the dragons that drew the chariot of the night, driven by Hecate)

5   *flagging* drooping

6   *Clip* embrace, drape over. The sense is not altogether satisfactory and there is some case to be made for the emendations 'Clepe' ('summon') and 'Clap' ('bang on').
          their (the graves')

7   *contagious*. The night was considered unhealthy.

8   *of our prize* from the vessel we have captured

9   *pinnace* small, single-masted boat
          the Downs (an anchorage off the Kent coast, sheltered by the Goodwin Sands; see the quotation from Hall in the headnote to this scene)

10   *make* agree to

11   *discoloured* thus to be discoloured (with their blood)

13   *make boot of* make a profit out of
          this (the Second Gentleman)

16   *lay down* lose

18   *think you much* do you consider it a heavy burden

19   *port* demeanour, standard of living

22   *counterpoised* set against, balanced

24   *straight* at once

25   *laying the prize aboard* boarding the captured ship

28   *rash* precipitate in your decision

29   *George* (a badge depicting Saint George on horseback
      slaying the dragon, the insignia of the Order of the
      Garter, which Suffolk had received in Henry V's
      reign)

30   *Rate me* set my ransom, value me

33   *Thy name* (Walter, pronounced 'Water')

34   *cunning man* astrologer. The reference is to the
      prophecy at I.4.31–2.
      calculate my birth cast my horoscope

36   *bloody-minded* bloodthirsty ·

37   *Gualtier* (the French equivalent of 'Walter')
      sounded pronounced

41   *sell revenge* (for ransom)

42   *arms* coat of arms
      torn and defaced obliterated (the heraldic witness to
      disgrace)

48   *Jove sometime went disguised, and why not I?* This line,
      not in F, is adopted from Q1; it is obviously necessary
      in view of line 49.

50   *Obscure and lousy swain, King Henry's blood.* In F this
      line is assigned to the Lieutenant, which is obviously
      an error due to the misplacement of the speech prefix
      for Suffolk.
      lousy scurvy, contemptible. Some editors emend to
      'lowly'; but the word was probably adopted from
      Hall's account of Cade's slaughter of his old acquain-
      tances lest 'they should blaze and declare his base
      birth and lousy lineage' (page 221).
      King Henry's blood. This claim is false; Suffolk's
      mother was a remote cousin of Henry VI.

52   *jaded* base, ignoble

54   *Bare-headed* hatless (as a sign of respect)
      foot-cloth mule mule carrying the ceremonial hangings
      used to drape a horse

55   *happy* fortunate
      shook my head gave you a signal of approval

57   *trencher* dinner plate
      board dining-table

239

59   *crest-fallen* humble

60   *abortive* untimely and outrageous

61   *voiding lobby* (antechamber where petitioners waited for entrance to a lord's presence)

62   *duly* dutifully

63   *writ in thy behalf* provided you with letters of recommendation

64   *charm* silence
       riotous unrestrained

65   *forlorn swain* wretched fellow

67   *blunt* unable to inflict harm

69   *for thy own* because of the risk of losing your own head

70–71   *Poole! Sir Poole! Lord!* | *Ay, kennel*. The punning is on (1) Pole; (2) pool; (3) Sir Pol (parrot); (4) poll. Various attempts have been made to explain the unsatisfactory nature of the speeches in both F and Q1 at this point. Q1 indicates that the point of the exchange lies in the punning possibilities of Suffolk's name, which F appears to exploit more fully. Therefore both texts have been conflated for the reading of this edition.

71   *kennel* (open gutter in a street for drainage)
       sink sewer

74   *For swallowing* lest it swallow. This was one of the accusations against Suffolk; compare Hall: 'the . . . swallower up and consumer of the King's treasure' (page 217).

77   *Against* faced with
       senseless unfeeling
       grin grimace

78   *again* in return

79   *the hags of hell* (the Furies)

80   *to affy* to affiance, to wed

81   *worthless king* (Reignier, Margaret's father; see the note to I.1.109–10)

83   *policy* political trickery (which the Elizabethans associated with Machiavelli)

84   *Sylla*. Lucius Cornelius Sulla (138–78 B.C.) was

notorious for his ruthless persecution of his enemies
when he was dictator of Rome.

overgorged overfed

85   *gobbets* chunks of raw flesh

thy mother (1) Rome (in Sulla's case); (2) England (in
Suffolk's case)

87   *revolting* rebellious

thorough because of

88   *Picardy*. There is no record in the chronicles of a
rebellion in Picardy.

95   *a guiltless king* (Richard II, whose usurpation and
murder by Bolingbroke began the Lancastrian
dynasty)

98   *Advance* raise high

half-faced sun. Both Edward III and Richard II
sported the device of a sun's rays emerging from the
tops of clouds.

99   *Invitis nubibus* in spite of clouds

100 *The commons here in Kent are up in arms.* This is a link
between York's plans at III.1.348–59 and IV.2.

105 *drudges* slaves

108 *Bargulus* (a Balkan pirate referred to by Cicero in *De
Officiis*, which was used as an Elizabethan school text-
book)

109 *Drones suck not eagles' blood, but rob beehives.* Two
pieces of popular Elizabethan imaginative natural
history are alluded to here: (1) a drone or beetle that
was reputed to lodge under the eagle's wing and suck
its blood; (2) the drone bee was believed to devour
the honey of the hive.

111 *By* by the hand of

112 *remorse* compunction

113 *Ay, but my deeds shall stay thy fury soon.* This line is
adopted from Q1, where it is the reply to the equivalent of line 112 here. Suffolk clearly continues to act
highhandedly until the Lieutenant assures him he is
about to act, at which Suffolk introduces his mission
for the Queen as a new argument against his death.

The Lieutenant's reply is to give the order to Whitmore in the form that recalls the prophecy mentioned by Suffolk in lines 33–5. The arrangement of the type in F suggests that a complete line may have dropped out during imposition.

113   *stay* prevent, stop

114   *of message* as messenger
        France (the French King)

115   *waft* transport by water

118   *Pene gelidus timor occupat artus* cold fear almost completely seizes my limbs. This is not a classical quotation; it appears to be made up of a recollection of two passages: '*subitus tremor occupat artus*' (Virgil, *Aeneid*, VII.446); '*gelidos pavor occupat artus*' (Lucan, *Pharsalia*, I.246).
        Pene (Latin for 'almost'). F's 'Pine' makes no sense. The suggestion '*Perii*' ('I am lost') is attractive, but it is difficult to see how it could have produced 'Pine' palaeographically or typographically.

122   *fair* politely, courteously

126   *suit* pleading

129   *sooner dance upon a bloody pole* rather be displayed upon a bloodstained staff. The heads of traitors were so displayed on the gate-house ramparts of London Bridge. There is also a pun on 'Pole'.

130   *uncovered* with hat in hand (as a sign of respect)
        vulgar groom low-born servant

133   *Hale* drag

136   *Besonians* scoundrels (from the Italian '*bisogno*', meaning 'need')

137–8   *A Roman ... Tully.* Cicero (*Tully*; 106–43 B.C.) was actually killed on the orders of Mark Antony 'by Herennius, a centurion, and Popilius Laena, tribune of the soldiers' (Thomas North's translation (1579) of Plutarch's *Life of Cicero*).

137   *sworder* gladiator
        banditto bandit

138–9   *Brutus' bastard hand* | *Stabbed Julius Caesar*. According to Suetonius, Brutus was Caesar's illegitimate son, an erroneous belief based on the fact that Brutus's mother became Caesar's mistress after her husband's death.

139–40   *savage islanders* | *Pompey the Great*. Pompey was killed in Egypt in 48 B.C. by a group of his own former centurions who had gone into the service of King Ptolemy. The idea that he was murdered by *islanders* may have come from the belief that he was slain on Lesbos or from Plutarch's reference to the Egyptians being incited to the murder by 'Theodotus, that was born in the Isle of Chios'.

140   *by* at the hands of

142   *pleasure* desire that

147   *body* (as well as the severed head; see IV.4)

149   *living* while he was living

IV.2   The location of the scene is Blackheath. In the chronicles Cade inflames his mob with the possibility of seizing the government and abolishing taxes, and leads them to Blackheath to present their supplications to the King, who sends an army against them: 'This captain ... promising them that if, either by force or policy, they might once take the King, the Queen, and other their counsellors into their hands and governance that they would honourably entreat the King and so sharply handle his counsellors that neither fifteens should hereafter be demanded nor once any impositions or tax should be spoken of. These persuasions, with many other fair promises of liberty (which the common people more affect and desire, rather than reasonable obedience and due conformity), so animated the Kentish people that they, with their captain above named, in good order of battle (not in great number) came to the plain of Blackheath, between Eltham and Greenwich. ... Whereupon the King assembled a great army and marched toward them, which had lain on Blackheath by the space of seven

days' (Hall, page 220). Shakespeare combines these
events with those which happened after Cade had
retired to Sevenoaks and defeated the Staffords (for
which see the note to lines 105–13). Some details
of the scene are taken from Grafton's account of the
Peasants' Revolt led by Wat Tyler against Richard II
in 1381. See the Introduction, page 35.

(stage direction) *George Bevis and John Holland.* There
is some evidence that these may be the names of the
contemporary actors who played these roles originally.

1   *lath* piece of wood. A 'dagger of lath' was one of the
stock properties of the Vice character in the Tudor
Morality plays.

2   *up* in arms

3   *They have the more need to sleep now then.* Holland
takes the meaning of *up* to be 'out of bed'.

4   *dress* (1) put on clothes; (2) put in good order

5   *turn it* (1) renew it (by turning the material inside out,
as in repairing an old coat); (2) turn it upside down
socially

5–6   *set a new nap upon it* (1) improve the surface texture
of its cloth; (2) reform it

7   *threadbare* (1) worn out; (2) decadent, bankrupt

8–18   *it was never . . . we be magistrates.* Compare Grafton's
account of the words of John Ball (whom Grafton
calls Wall) in the 1381 revolt: 'that there be no
villains nor gentlemen, but that we be all as one and
that the lords be no greater than we be' (I.418).

8   *merry world* good times

9   *came up* became fashionable

10   *regarded* valued, highly estimated

12   *think scorn* think it beneath their dignity, disdain
go in wear
leather aprons (worn by workmen)

15–16   *Labour in thy vocation* (proverbial: 'Everyone must
labour in his own vocation')

18   *magistrates* rulers

19   *hit it* made a good point, hit the nail on the head

20   *brave* noble

       hard calloused (with manual work)

22   *Wingham* (a village near Canterbury)

24   *dog's leather* (inferior leather, used for making gloves)

29   *Argo* (a corrupted form of the Latin *ergo*) therefore

       their thread of life is spun (a proverbial phrase alluding to the Fate in Greek mythology who spun the threads of human existence)

31   *so termed of* thus named after

32   *of* on account of (with a quibble on *of* in line 31)

       cade of cask containing five hundred

33   *For* because

       fall (a pun with the Latin *cadere*, meaning 'to fall')

37   *a Mortimer*. See the note to III.1.355–9.

38   *bricklayer*. The quibble is on 'mortar'/*Mortimer*.

41   *Lacys*. Lacy was the family name of the Earls of Lincoln.

43   *laces* (a pun with *Lacys*)

44   *travel* (1) journey as a pedlar; (2) work ('travail')

45   *furred pack* (1) back-pack made from animal skins with the fur on the outside; (2) female genitals

       washes bucks (1) takes in laundry; (2) frees men from their cuckoldry (by giving them the opportunity to be even with their wives)

46   *honourable* noble

47   *field*. The quibble is on the heraldic term for the background against which the devices are set in a coat of arms.

48   *under a hedge*. The phrase 'hedge-born' was a colloquialism for the lowest kind of lineage.

49   *cage* (a small prison in the market-place where vagrants and minor criminals were exhibited)

51   *'A must needs* he must be

       valiant. The allusion is to the term 'valiant beggar', meaning one capable of work to whom it was illegal to give alms.

54   *whipped* (the punishment for vagabonds and minor criminals)

56–7   *of proof* (1) badly worn; (2) impenetrable (like good armour)

59   *burnt i'th'hand* branded with a 'T' on the hand (a common punishment for a thief)

61   *reformation* change of government

62–3   *the three-hooped pot shall have ten hoops.* A wooden drinking-cup holding a quart was bound by three equidistantly placed hoops; so that Cade's reform will make it three-and-a-half times as large as it is.

63   *small* weak

64   *All the realm shall be in common.* This detail seems to have been taken from Grafton, where John Wall (Ball) says 'Ah, good people, matters go not well to pass in England in these days, nor shall not do until everything be common' (I.417–18).
        in common community land
        Cheapside (the chief market area of Elizabethan London, just west of Saint Paul's Churchyard; under Cade's rule it will be empty and deserted)

65   *palfrey* riding horse
        go to grass graze

69   *on my score* at my expense (literally 'on my tavern bill')

70   *livery* (uniform indicating the household in which a servant is employed)

72   *let's kill all the lawyers.* Compare Grafton: 'and so kept on their way toward London ... spoiling and burning as they went all the houses that belonged to any man of law' (I.419); and Holinshed's account of the 1381 revolt: 'destroy first the great lords of the realm and after the judges and lawyers' (II.740).

76   *undo* bring about the ruin of

77   *the bee's wax* (the sealing wax used on legal documents)
        did but seal once to a thing put my name only once to a bond

79   (stage direction) *Clerk* (town clerk)

80–102 *The clerk of Chartham ... his neck.* Compare Holinshed's account of the 1381 revolt: 'The rage of the

commons was universally such as it might seem they
had generally conspired together to do what mischief
they could devise. As, among sundry other, what
wickedness was it to compel teachers of children in
grammar schools to swear never to instruct any in
their art? Again, could they have a more mischievous
meaning than to burn and destroy all old and ancient
monuments and to murder and dispatch out of the
way all such as were able to commit to memory either
any new or old records? For it was dangerous among
them to be known for one that was learned and more
dangerous if any man were found with a penner and
inkhorn at his side; for such seldom or never escaped
from them with life' (II.746).

80   *Chartham* (a village near Canterbury; but it is possible
      that 'Chatham' was intended)

81   *cast accompt* do arithmetic

83   *setting of boys' copies* giving schoolboys passages to
      copy out. A village clerk often doubled as the school-
      master.

85   *H'as* he has
      a book . . . with red letters (a book, perhaps a textbook
      or almanac, with certain capitals printed in red)

86   *conjurer* necromancer

87   *make obligations* draw up legal bonds
      court-hand (the handwriting used in legal documents,
      as opposed to the secretary-hand used for ordinary
      business purposes)

88   *proper* handsome
      of on

91   *Emmanuel* (that is, 'God with us'; often written at the
      opening of letters and legal documents)

95   *a mark* (a personal mark, used by illiterates in place of
      a signature)

104   *particular* private (a quibble on *general* in line 103)

105-13 *Fly, fly, fly . . . have at him.* In the chronicles the
        events of this scene take place in Kent: 'The subtle
        captain, named Jack Cade, intending to bring the King

farther within the compass of his net, broke up his camp and retired backward to the town of Sevenoaks in Kent . . . and made his abode. The Queen, which bare the rule, being of his retreat well advertised, sent Sir Humphrey Stafford, Knight, and William, his brother, with many other gentlemen, to follow the chase of the Kentishmen, thinking that they had fled; but verily they were deceived, for at the first skirmish both the Staffords were slain and all their company shamefully discomfited' (Hall, page 220).

105   *Sir Humphrey Stafford.* The Staffords were descendants of one of William the Conqueror's favourite captains.

105–6   *his brother* (William Stafford)

109   *'a* he

110   *No* (an answer to the negative implied in *but a*)

111   *presently* immediately

113   *have at* let me get at

114   *hinds* peasants

115   *Marked* destined

116   *groom* low fellow

117   *revolt* turn again to your previous condition

120–26   *As for these . . . gardener.* Compare John Wall (Ball) in Grafton: 'What have we deserved or why should we be thus kept in servitude and bondage? We be all come from one father and one mother, Adam and Eve. Wherefore can they say . . . that they are greater lords than we be? . . . They are clothed in velvet and chamlet furred richly, and we be clad with the poorest sort of cloth. They have their wines, spices, and fine bread, and we have the drawing out of the chaff and drink water' (I.418).

120   *pass* care

125   *a shearman* (a member of the cloth trade, the man who sheared the excess nap from cloth during its manufacture)

126   *Adam was a gardener.* This is a reflection of John Wall's theme in his sermon, which included (in

Holinshed's account) the couplet 'When Adam delved and Eve span, who was then the gentleman?'

132   *question* problem

142   *credit* believe

          drudge mean fellow

145   *Jack Cade, the Duke of York hath taught you this.* Hall's remarks about Cade's preparation for the rebellion may lie behind this line: 'This captain [was] not only suborned by teachers but also enforced by privy schoolmasters', with 'the intent that it should not be known that the Duke of York or his friends were the cause of the sudden rising' (page 220).

148–9   *Henry the Fifth . . . French crowns.* The reference is to Henry V's success in the French wars.

          went to span-counter played at the game of span-counters (a pastime in which the players used metal discs, normally employed for counting money, to see who could toss his 'counter' so that it fell within a 'span' of his competitors')

149   *French crowns* (1) French gold coins, *écus*; (2) bald heads (caused by venereal disease); (3) the French King's coronet

151   *Lord Say.* James Fynes (d. 1450) was one of Henry V's captains in France. He was made Sheriff of Kent in 1437 and Warden of the Cinque Ports in 1447. At the time of his death at Cade's hands he had recently been dismissed as Treasurer of England; see the note to IV.4.19.

153   *mained* crippled (with a pun on *Maine*)

154   *fain to go* obliged to walk

          puissance power

155–6   *gelded the commonwealth.* The phrase is from Cicero's *De Oratore*, III.41: '*Nolo dici morte Africani castratam esse rem publicam*'.

167   *up* in arms

170   *for* to serve as an

173–4   *'tis for liberty. | We will not leave one lord, one gentleman.* Compare Holinshed, where John Ball urges the rebels to destroy lords so that 'there should be an equality in liberty, no difference in degree of nobility, but a like dignity and equal authority in all things brought among them' (II.749).

175   *clouted shoon* patched-up shoes
179   *in order* lined up in formation
179–80   *out of order* disorderly, rebellious

IV.3   The scene is located in Blackheath. See the note to IV.2.105–13.

6–7   *the Lent shall . . . lacking one.* Cade clearly intends to reward Dick for his services by giving him a special slaughtering privilege during an extended Lent. Under Elizabeth's statute of 1563, slaughtering of animals was forbidden during the Lenten period so that more fish might be sold. It is not so clear what Dick's licence will amount to. F's phrase 'for a hundred lacking one', resembling as it does the usual legal formula for a lease, may mean that Dick's tenure of his right will be for ninety-nine years; or it may mean that Dick may provide meat for up to ninety-nine people who had dispensation from the Lenten statute; or it may be the number of beasts he will be allowed to slaughter. Q1 has '. . . licence to kil for foure score and one a week', which suggests that perhaps the number of the butcher's customers is meant.

9   (stage direction) *Sir Humphrey Stafford's coat of mail.* The phrase *This monument of the victory will I bear* requires this direction, which is based on information found in the chronicles. Hall has 'When the Kentish captain, or the covetous Cade, had thus obtained victory and slain the two valiant Staffords, he apparelled himself in their rich armour' (page 220); but Holinshed and Fabyan have additional details of Cade's prize: 'Sir Humphrey's brigandine, set full of gilt nails' (Holinshed, III.224); and 'the knight's apparel . . . his briganders, set with gilt nail, and his salade and his gilt spurs' (Fabyan, page 623).

10 *monument* memorial, testimony to success (Sir Humphrey Stafford's armour)

12-13 *we will have the Mayor's sword borne before us.* There is no evidence in the chronicles for this; but in Grafton's account of Wat Tyler, the rebel is killed with the Mayor's sword (I.425).

14-15 *If we mean . . . the prisoners.* Compare Hall: 'the lusty Kentish captain, hoping on more friends, brake up the gaols of the King's Bench and Marshalsea and set at liberty a swarm of gallants both meet for his service and apt for his enterprise' (page 222). Another source is Grafton's account of the 1381 rebellion, in which the mob 'set all the prisoners of Newgate and the Counters at large' (I.421).

14 *do good* prosper, succeed

16 *Fear not that* do not worry about our not doing that

IV.4 The location of the scene is the royal palace in London. Historically Cade's supplication was submitted to the King before the Staffords were sent against the rebels; otherwise the material for this scene is derived from Hall.

2 *fearful* full of terror

5 *throbbing* grief-stricken

7-8 *the rebels' supplication.* See the headnote to IV.2.

9 *I'll send some holy bishop to entreat.* Although this is not dramatized in the play, it is exactly the step Henry takes in the chronicles: 'to whom [Cade] were sent by the King the Archbishop of Canterbury and Humphrey Duke of Buckingham' (Hall, page 220).
entreat enter into negotiations

11-13 *I myself . . . Will parley with Jack Cade.* This is what Cade demands in the chronicles: 'These lords found him sober in communication, wise in disputing, arrogant in heart, and stiff in his opinion, and by no ways possible to be persuaded to dissolve his army except the King in person would come to him' (Hall, page 221). Richard II faced the Peasants' Revolt personally in 1381.

12   *cut them short* destroy them, cut short their lives

16   *wandering planet* (an astrological term) influential star

17   *enforce* force
    them (Suffolk's murderers)

18   *That* who

19   *Lord Say, Jack Cade hath sworn to have thy head.* In the chronicles, although Lord Say is not specified in Cade's supplication to the King, he is one of the 'traitors' that surrendered Maine, whose punishment Cade demands; and so the King agrees, 'to the intent to appease the furious rage of the inconstant multitude, to commit the Lord Say, Treasurer of England, to the Tower of London' (Hall, page 220).

27   *Southwark.* At this time Southwark was a suburb of the city.

32–3   *His army is a ragged multitude | Of hinds and peasants.* Compare Hall: 'a multitude of evil, rude, and rustical persons' (page 220).

37   *false caterpillars* treacherous parasites (in the garden of the state)

38   *graceless* deprived of divine grace
    they know not what they do. Compare Luke 23.34.

39   *retire to Killingworth.* Compare Hall: 'The King, somewhat hearing and more marking the sayings of this outrageous losel, and having daily report of the concourse and access of people which continually resorted to him, doubting as much his familiar servants as his unknown subjects . . . departed in all haste to the castle of Killingworth in Warwickshire' (page 221).
    Killingworth Kenilworth

40   *power* army

42   *appeased* rendered peaceful

51   *rascal people.* This is a phrase from Hall (page 29).

53   *spoil* despoil, loot

59–60   *The trust I have is in mine innocence,* | *And therefore am* *I bold and resolute* (proverbial: 'Innocence is bold')

IV.5   The scene is based upon the chronicles' account of the events during Cade's capture of London immediately after the King's departure for Kenilworth Castle.

(stage direction) *Lord Scales.* Thomas de Scales, seventh Baron (1399?–1460), was a staunch Lancastrian; he was hated by Londoners and was murdered by boatmen and his body cast ashore at Southwark. Compare Hall: 'The King . . . departed in all haste . . . leaving only behind him the Lord Scales to keep the Tower of London' (page 221).

the Tower (the Tower of London. The upper acting area used here would probably have been the same as that employed for I.4.)

3–4   *they have won the bridge, killing all those that withstand* *them.* In Hall, Cade, 'being advertised of the King's absence, came first into Southwark, and there lodged at the White Hart. . . . But after that he entered into London and cut the ropes of the drawbridge' (page 221). After Matthew Gough had been sent against the rebels, his troops attempted to 'keep the bridge'; but the rebels 'ran with great haste to open their passage where between both parts was a fierce and cruel encounter . . . for the multitude of the rebels drove the citizens from the stoops at the bridge foot . . . and got the drawbridge' (pages 221–2).

4–6   *The Lord Mayor . . . you shall command.* This is based on an event in the chronicles after Cade had already entered London: 'The wise Mayor and sage magistrates of the city of London, perceiving themselves neither to be sure of goods nor of life well warranted, determined with fear to repel and expulse this mischievous head and his ungracious company. And because the Lord Scales was ordained keeper of the Tower of London with Matthew Gough . . . they

253

purposed to make them privy both of their intent and
enterprise. The Lord Scales promised them his aid,
with shooting of ordnance, and Matthew Gough was
by him appointed to assist the Mayor and the
Londoners, because he was both of manhood and experience greatly renowned and noised' (Hall, page 221).

8   *assayed* tried

9   *Smithfield*. This was an open area outside the city
wall, north-west of Saint Paul's Church. It is not
associated with Cade in the chronicles, but was the
site of Richard II's meeting with the peasants and of
Wat Tyler's death in 1381.
gather head raise forces

IV.6   The location of the scene is Cannon Street, London;
see the note to line 2.
(stage direction) *and strikes his staff on London Stone*.
Compare Hall: 'he entered into London and cut the
ropes of the drawbridge, striking his sword on London
Stone, saying "Now is Mortimer lord of this city",
and rode in every street like a lordly captain' (page
221).

2   *London Stone*. This city landmark was a block of
ancient stone, thought to be of Roman origin, which
stood on the south side of Canwick (now Cannon)
Street.

3   *of the city's cost* at the expense of the city
the Pissing Conduit. This was a small conduit in
Cheapside near the junction of Threadneedle Street
and Cornhill.

5–6   *henceforward it shall be . . . Mortimer*. Compare Hall:
'He also put to execution in Southwark divers persons,
some for infringing his rules and precepts because he
would be seen indifferent, other he tormented of his
old acquaintance lest they should blaze and declare
his base birth and lousy lineage, disparaging him from
his usurped surname of Mortimer' (page 221).

14   *set London Bridge on fire.* During the fight between
Matthew Gough's troops and Cade's at London
Bridge, 'the multitude of the rebels drove the citizens
from the stoops at the bridge foot to the drawbridge
and began to set fire in divers houses' (Hall, page 222).

14–15   *burn down the Tower too.* In the chronicles there is no
attack by the rebels on the Tower; but see IV.5.8.

IV.7   The scene is located in Smithfield and is based upon
Hall's account of the deaths of Lord Say and Sir
James Cromer: 'And upon the third day of July [Cade]
caused Sir James Fynes, Lord Say and Treasurer of
England, to be brought to the Guildhall of London
and there to be arraigned, which, being before the
King's Justices put to answer, desired to be tried by
his peers for the longer delay of his life. The captain,
perceiving his dilatory plea, by force took him from
the officers and brought him to the Standard in
Cheapside, and there, before his confession ended,
caused his head to be cut off and pitched it on a high
pole, which was openly borne before him through
the streets. And this cruel tyrant, not content with
the murder of the Lord Say, went to Mile End and
there apprehended Sir James Cromer, then Shrieve
of Kent and son-in-law to the said Lord Say, and him,
without confession or excuse heard, caused there likewise to be headed and his head to be fixed on a pole;
and with these two heads this bloody butcher entered
into the city again and in despite caused them in every
street kiss together, to the great detestation of all the
beholders' (page 221).

(stage direction) *Matthew Gough is slain.* Compare
Hall's account of the fight for London Bridge: 'Yet
the captains . . . fought on the drawbridge all the night
valiantly; but in conclusion the rebels got the drawbridge and drowned many and slew John Sutton,
Alderman; and Robert Heysand, a hardy citizen; with

many other, beside Matthew Gough, a man of great wit, much experience in feats of chivalry, the which in continual wars had valiantly served the King and his father in the parts beyond the sea' (page 222).

all the rest (the royal forces)

1–2   *Now go some . . . them all.* These details probably come from Fabyan's account of the 1381 Peasants' Revolt: 'They . . . came unto the Duke of Lancaster's palace standing without the Temple Bar, called Savoy, and spoiled it was therein, and after set it upon fire and burnt it. . . . Then they entered the city and searched the Temple and other Inns of Court and spoiled their places and burnt their books of law' (page 530).

1   *the Savoy.* This house was the London residence of the Duke of Lancaster and was destroyed in the Wat Tyler rebellion of 1381. It was rebuilt in 1505.

2   *th'Inns of Court* (centres of the London legal profession)

4   *lordship* lord's domain

5–6   *the laws of England may come out of your mouth.* Wat Tyler made a similar pronouncement, 'putting his hand to his lips, that within four days all the laws of England should come forth of his mouth' (Holinshed, II.740).

11–12   *Burn all the records of the realm.* See the note to lines 1–2.

14   *biting* severe (with a quibble on *teeth*)

16   *all things shall be in common.* See the note to IV.2.64.

17–18   *the Lord Say, which sold the towns in France.* See the note to IV.4.19.

19   *one-and-twenty fifteens.* This was an enormously exaggerated rate of taxation (see the note to I.1.131). In Hall, one of Cade's promises to the mob is that 'neither fifteens should hereafter be demanded nor once any impositions or tax should be spoken of' (page 220).

20   *subsidy* (a special tax assessment)

22   *thou say, thou serge . . . thou buckram lord.* 'Say' was a kind of silk cloth resembling serge; and 'buckram'

was a coarse linen fabric stiffened with glue, used for making crude cloth articles for the stage. A *buckram lord* was a 'stuffed lord'.

23   *point-blank* easy range

25   *Basimecu* (anglicizing of the French *baise mon cul*, meaning 'kiss my arse')

26   *Be it known unto thee by these presence* (the standard formula in legal documents and proclamations; but Cade confuses 'presents' (meaning 'documents') with 'presence' (meaning 'in the company of the King'))

27–8   *the besom that . . . filth* (proverbial)

28   *besom* broom, sweeping-brush

29–30   *corrupted the youth*. See the note to IV.2.80–102.

32   *the score and the tally*. This was a method of keeping account of debts among the common people. A slat of wood was notched to indicate the sums of money owed, then split down the centre, one half being given to the debtor and the other half to the creditor.

     printing. This is anachronistic; the first printing press was not operated in England until Caxton's in 1474, twenty-four years after Cade's rebellion.

     used practised

33–4   *the King his crown and dignity*. Cade is again using a standard legal formula.

34   *paper-mill*. Paper was available in England from the beginning of the fourteenth century; but the first English paper-mill on record is John Tate's at Hereford in 1495–6.

35   *usually* habitually

39   *answer* acquit themselves of, explain away

40–41   *because they could not read, thou hast hanged them*. The allusion is to the practice of excusing criminals from hanging if they claimed 'the benefit of the clergy', which right was proved by their demonstrating that they could read Latin.

41–2   *only for*. This could mean 'were it not for'; but considering Cade's view of learning, the phrase probably means 'for that reason alone'.

43   *foot-cloth*. See the second note to IV.1.54. As it is a

sign of wealth to use a foot-cloth, Cade finds it an
especially blameworthy practice.

46–7 *hose and doublets* breeches and short-coats (with no
top covering, such as a cloak)

52 *bona terra, mala gens* (Italian for 'a good country, an
evil people'. This was apparently applied by Italians
to England.)

55–6 *Kent, in the Commentaries Caesar writ, | Is termed the
civilest place of all this isle.* Arthur Golding in his 1564
translation of Caesar's *De Bello Gallico*, V.14, has 'Of
all the inhabitants of this isle the civilest are the
Kentish folk'.

56 *civilest* most civilized

58 *liberal* refined, polished

59 *void of* without

62 *favour* leniency

64 *exacted at your hands* taken from you in taxes

66 *clerks* men of learning, scholars

67 *my book preferred me to the King* my own learning
enabled me to rise in the King's service

72 *parleyed unto* spoken with, negotiated with

73 *behoof* welfare

74 *in the field* during battle

75 *Great men have reaching hands* (proverbial: 'Kings
have long arms')
reaching far-reaching

78 *for watching* with staying awake (to work)

81 *sitting* (on the judicial bench)
determine decide
causes law-suits

83 *hempen caudle*. This was a cant term for the hangman's
rope.
caudle (a potion for an invalid, composed of sweet
warm gruel and wine. F's reading, 'Candle', is probably due to the fact that 'u' and 'n' were almost
indistinguishable in Elizabethan handwriting.)

83–4 *the help of hatchet* the assistance of the executioner's
axe. The emendation 'pap with a hatchet' (a pro-

verbial term describing the physical punishment of children for their own good) is attractive, as it balances *hempen caudle* metaphorically.

86	*provokes me* makes me tremble
87	*as who* like one who
91	*affected* loved
95	*guiltless bloodshedding* spilling the blood of innocent people
98	*remorse* pity
99	*an it be but* if only
100	*a familiar* (a personal devil he can call on to serve him, because he has sold his soul to Satan)
101	*a* in
102	*presently* at once
103–4	*Sir James Cromer* (son-in-law to Lord Say)
109	*it fare with your departed souls* your souls be treated after you are dead
114–15	*pay to me her maidenhead.* The allusion is to the *droit de seigneur*, the feudal right of the lord of the manor to spend the first night with the bride of any of his vassals.
115–16	*hold of me in capite* own the property that has been granted to them directly by me as their head (with possibly a pun on *maidenhead*)
117	*free* liberal (with their sexual favours) *as heart can wish.* Compare Psalm 73.7.
118–19	*take up commodities upon our bills* obtain goods on credit (with possibly a pun on *bills* meaning 'weapons')
121	*brave* splendid
125	*spoil* pillage
127	*maces* (public dignitaries' symbols of office)

IV.8   The location of the scene is Southwark. It is based upon the final stages of Cade's rebellion in the chronicles, where two prelates perform the task Shakespeare gives to Buckingham and Clifford in the play: 'The Archbishop of Canterbury, being then

Chancellor of England, and for his surety lying in the
Tower of London, called to him the Bishop of Winchester, which also for fear lurked at Holywell. These
two prelates, seeing the fury of the Kentish people, by
reason of their beating back, to be mitigate and
minished, passed the river of Thames from the Tower
into Southwark, bringing with them under the King's
Great Seal a general pardon unto all the offenders,
which they caused to be openly proclaimed and published. Lord, how glad the poor people were of this
pardon . . . and how they accepted the same, in so
much that the whole multitude, without bidding farewell to their captain, retired the same night, every man
to his own home, as men amazed and stricken with
fear. . . . a proclamation [was] made that whosoever
could apprehend the said Jack Cade should have for
his pain a thousand marks' (Hall, page 222).

1   (stage direction) *retreat* (signal for the recall of forces)
     Fish Street . . . Saint Magnus' Corner. In Hall, during
     the final battle for London 'for some time the Lon-
     doners were beat back to the stoops at Saint Magnus'
     Corner; and suddenly again the rebels were repulsed
     and driven back to the stoops in Southwark' (page
     222). Fish Street was on the north side of the Thames,
     across London Bridge from Southwark; and at the
     end of the street nearest the bridge stood Saint
     Magnus' Church.

2   (stage direction) *parley* (signal to request a conference)

4   (stage direction) *old Clifford.* Thomas de Clifford
     (1414–55) was the twelfth Baron Clifford and eighth
     Baron of Westmorland. He fought with the Duke of
     Bedford in France in 1435 and went to the relief of
     Calais in 1452 and 1454. He was slain at the first
     Battle of Saint Albans.

8   *pronounce* make proclamation of
     free generous

12   *rebel.* The F reading, 'rabble', may have been due to the
     compositor misreading 'rebbel' in the manuscript.

13   *embrace* welcome, accept

17   *Shake he his weapon* (make a sign of martial defiance)

19   *brave* arrogant, audacious

22–3   *therefore . . . that* to that end, for that purpose

23   *the White Hart*. After the King's flight to Kenilworth,
        Cade, 'being advertised of the King's absence, came
        first into Southwark, and there lodged at the White
        Hart' (Hall, page 221).

24   *given out* surrendered, given up

25   *ancient* former, historically sanctioned

26   *recreants* traitors

27   *dastards* cowards

29–30   *For me, I will make shift for one* (proverbial: 'Every
        man for himself')

30   *make shift* manage, look out

36   *meanest of* lowest in birth among

38   *the spoil* looting

40   *at jar* at odds with one another

41   *fearful* frightened

42   *make a start* (a hunting term) suddenly rouse them-
        selves to action

43   *broil* conflict

45   *Villiago* villain (from the Italian '*vigliocco*', meaning
        'coward')

46   *base-born* of low origin
        miscarry encounter disaster, die

47   *stoop unto* humble yourselves to beg for

51   *God* with God

52   *À Clifford* (rally) to Clifford (a cry like 'À Talbot',
        which was made famous during the French cam-
        paigns; see *Part One*, I.i.128)

55   *hales* draws, drags

57   *lay their heads together* (a proverbial phrase) conspire,
        plot

57–8   *surprise me* capture me

59   *despite* spite

60   *have through the very midst of you* I'll get through the
        centre of your party

63   (stage direction) The Q1 direction makes the action explicit: 'He runs through them with his staffe, and flies away.'

66   *a thousand crowns* (a very large sum of money in gold. The chronicles' 'thousand marks' is more realistic.)

67   *mean* method, means

IV.9   The scene is located in Kenilworth Castle, whence the King retired at the end of IV.4. It is based upon scattered events spread over two years in the chronicles following Cade's death.
        (stage direction) *on the terrace* (of Kenilworth Castle; the upper acting area was probably that used in I.4 and IV.5)

1   *joyed* enjoyed

4   *made a king at nine months old.* Henry was born at Windsor on 6 December 1421; Henry V died at Vincennes on 31 August 1422.

8   *surprised* taken prisoner

9   *him* himself
        (stage direction) *with halters about their necks.* This display is thought to have been based upon the anonymous play *Edward III*, where the citizens of Calais surrender in the same way in 1346.

10–22   *He is fled ... the King.* In the chronicles the King hears of Cade's death when he has left Kenilworth: 'After this commotion the King himself came into Kent and there sat in judgement upon the offenders, and if he had not mitigated his justice with mercy and compassion more than five hundred by the rigour of his law had been justly put to execution; but he considered both their fragility and innocency and how they with perverse people were seduced and deceived, and so punished the stubborn heads and delivered the ignorant and miserable people, to the great rejoicing of all his subjects' (Hall, page 222).

10   *powers* soldiers

12   *Expect* await
        doom judgement, sentence

13   *set ope thy everlasting gates.* Compare Psalm 7.9.

14   *entertain* receive favourably

17   *still* always

18   *infortunate* unfortunate

19   *unkind* cruel

21   *several* separate, different
        countries localities, districts

23–7   *Please it . . . in proud array.* In 1451 York 'returned
        out of Ireland and came to London in the parliament
        time, where he deliberately consulted with his especial
        friends, as John Duke of Norfolk, Richard Earl of
        Salisbury, and Lord Richard, his son, which after was
        Earl of Warwick' (Hall, page 225).

23   *advertisèd* (accented on the second syllable) in-
        formed

25–6   *with a puissant and a mighty power | Of gallowglasses
        and stout kerns.* In Hall, York, 'with help of his
        friends, assembled a great army in the Marches of
        Wales' (page 225).

25   *power* army

26   *gallowglasses* (Irish soldiers who were armed with axes
        and usually fought on horseback)
        stout strong, valiant
        kerns. See the note to III.1.310.

28–30   *And still proclaimeth . . . a traitor.* In the chronicles,
        York uses his enmity towards Somerset as a cover for
        his aspirations to the crown: 'After long consultation
        it was thought expedient first to seek some occasion
        and pick some quarrel to the Duke of Somerset, which
        ruled the King, ordered the realm, and most might do
        with the Queen' (Hall, page 225).

28   *still* continually
        comes along advances

29   *arms* armed men

30   *whom he terms a traitor.* Compare Hall, who has the
        Yorkists 'protesting and declaring . . . that their intent

263

was for the revenging of great injuries done to the
public wealth' (page 225).

31–5 *Thus stands my state ... second him.* Compare Hall:
'The King, much astonished with this sudden commotion' (page 225).

31 *state* situation

33 *calmed* becalmed. The F reading, 'calme', was probably due to 'd' being misread as 'e' by the com-
positor; the two letters were very similar in Elizabethan
handwriting.
with by

34 *But now* just now

35 *second* support

37 *of* for

38–40 *Tell him I'll send ... from him.* In the chronicles,
Henry leads an army to Blackheath and, once the two
forces are drawn up against each other, the King sends
the Bishops of Winchester and Ely to negotiate with
York, who informs the prelates that 'his intent was to
remove from him [the King] certain evil-disposed
persons of his Council ... amongst whom he chiefly
named Edmund Duke of Somerset, whom if the King
would commit to ward to answer to such articles as
against him should in open parliament be both pro-
poned and proved, he promised not only to dissolve
his army and dispatch his people but also offered himself like an obedient subject to come to the King's
presence. ... The King ... granted their requests,
caused the Duke of Somerset to be committed to
ward ... till the fury of the people were somewhat
assuaged and pacified' (Hall, page 226).

38 *Duke Edmund* (Edmund Beaufort, Duke of Somerset)

44 *be not too rough in terms* do not use violent language

45 *brook* endure

46 *deal* negotiate

47 *redound unto* turn out for

49 *yet* up till now

IV.10   The location of the scene is the garden of Iden's
house. It is Shakespeare's invention that Cade dies on
the property of the ideal English country gentleman.
The scene is based on a brief passage in Hall, which
describes Cade's death: 'John Cade, desperate of
succours which by the friends of the Duke of York
were to him promised, and seeing his company thus
without his knowledge suddenly depart, mistrusting
the sequel of the matter, departed secretly in habit
disguised into Sussex; but all his metamorphosis or
transfiguration little prevailed. For, after a proclamation made that whosoever could apprehend the said
Jack Cade should have for his pain a thousand marks,
many sought for him, but few espied him, till one
Alexander Iden, Esquire of Kent, found him in a
garden, and there in his defence manfully slew the
caitiff Cade, and brought his dead body to London,
whose head was set on London Bridge' (page 222).

(stage direction) Q1 makes the action explicit but gives
Iden an accompanying band of men: 'Enter *Iacke Cade*
at one doore, and at the other maister *Alexander Eyden*
and his men, and *Iacke Cade* lies downe picking of
hearbes and eating them.' See the note to line 37–8.

2   *famish* starve

4   *is laid for me* is circulated with orders for my arrest

5–6   *if I might have . . . longer* (proverbial: 'No man has a
lease of his life')

6   *stay* remain in hiding

8   *sallet* salad

8–9   *cool a man's stomach* (1) satisfy a man's hunger; (2)
pacify a man's anger

10   *sallet* (a light circular helmet)

11   *brown bill* (bronzed pike, usually carried by con-
stables)

14   (stage direction) *Alexander Iden*. A Kentish gentleman,
Iden came from a very ancient Sussex family and
married Lord Say's daughter when she was widow of
Sir James Cromer.

15   *turmoilèd* harassed, worried

18   *and* and is

20   *envy* malice

21   *Sufficeth that* it is enough for me that what
    maintains my state supports my way of life

22   *well pleasèd* (with the alms they have received)

23   *lord of the soil* (a legal term) landowner

24   *stray* stray animal (which a landowner had the right
    to impound should he capture it on his land)
    fee-simple (an estate belonging to a *lord of the soil* and
    his heirs for ever)

27   *eat iron like an ostrich* (a proverbial saying, based on
    the popular belief that ostriches ate iron for the sake
    of their digestion. Cade means 'be killed with my
    sword in your stomach'.)

29   *rude companion* rough fellow
    whatsoe'er whoever

34   *brave* defy, insult
    saucy terms insolent language

35   *best* most noble

36   *broached* let flow (like wine out of a cask)
    beard thee defy you to your face

37   *eat* eaten

37–8   *and thy five men.* This may be a sneering reference to
    the small size of Iden's estate and his few retainers.
    However, some editors take it literally and cause Iden
    to enter, as he does in Q1, with a group of men. In F
    Iden is clearly alone, the function of the scene being
    to show Cade the anarchist overcome by a single
    representative of a stable society.

38   *as dead as a door-nail* (proverbial)

42   *odds* advantage

44   *outface me with thy looks* stare me down

45   *Set* compare

47   *truncheon* stout club (Iden's leg)

49   *heavèd* raised up

51   *answers words* matches your words

52   *report what speech forbears* perform what words refuse
    to utter

53   *complete* accomplished

55   *burly-boned* hulking

       chines roasts

56   *God.* This is Q1's reading. The F reading, 'Ioue' (that is, 'Jove'), was probably due to a change made in accordance with the law of 1606 against blasphemy in plays.

64   *monstrous* unnatural (in rebelling against his king)

65   *hallow* bless

66   *hang thee* have you hung

       o'er my tomb when I am dead. The arms of a warrior were sometimes used to decorate his tomb.

69   *emblaze* publicly proclaim (as the device on a herald's coat announces the quality of a nobleman)

75   *her that bare thee* (your mother)

78   *headlong* unceremoniously

V.1   Historically the scene is located in the fields between Dartford and Blackheath. Shakespeare uses events some of which the chronicles place in 1452–3 on York's return from Ireland and some in 1455 immediately prior to the first Battle of Saint Albans.

       (stage direction) *colours* flag-bearers

1–11   *From Ireland thus ... France.* Compare Hall: 'the Duke of York, which sore gaped and more thirsted for the superiority and pre-eminence, studied, devised, and practised all ways and means by the which he might attain to his pretensed purpose and long-hoped desire' (page 231).

4   *entertain* welcome, receive favourably

5   *sancta majestas* sacred majesty. The phrase is from Ovid's *Ars Amatoria*, III.407–8: '*Sanctaque maiestas et erat venerabile nomen | Vatibus et largae saepe dabantur opes*' ('Sacred was the majesty and venerable the name of the poet; and often lavish wealth was given them').

7   *gold* (the golden royal regalia)

8   *give due action to my words* accompany my words with the appropriate action

9   *Except* unless
         balance give due weight to
         it (action)

10   *have I* as I have

11   *toss* impale and bear aloft
         flower-de-luce (fleur-de-lis, the heraldic three-leafed
         lily of the French royal coat of arms)

12–47   *Whom have we ... you wish.* In the chronicles it is
         two bishops who negotiate with York in 1452–3 rather
         than Buckingham. However, after hearing the King's
         promise to commit Somerset 'to ward', York 'dis-
         solved his army, and broke up his camp, and came to
         the King's tent' (Hall, page 226).

13   *sure* for certain

18   *of these arms* for these armed men

21   *power* army

23   *choler* wrath

25   *abject terms* despicable words

26–7   *like Ajax Telamonius, | On sheep or oxen could I spend
         my fury.* During the Trojan War the Greek hero Ajax,
         son of Telamon, became angry when Achilles' armour
         was awarded to Ulysses. As a result he was afflicted
         with a fit of insanity during which he attacked a flock
         of sheep before committing suicide.

27   *spend* vent

30   *make fair weather* (proverbial) accommodate myself to
         the circumstances by pretending to be pleasant

32   *prithee* beg you to

36–7   *to remove proud Somerset from the King, | Seditious to
         his grace and to the state.* See the note to IV.9.28–30.

41–4   *The Duke of Somerset ... my powers.* See the note to
         IV.9.38–40.

46   *Saint George's Field.* This open area, named after the
         church of Saint George the Martyr, which was near
         by, lay between Southwark and Lambeth on the south
         side of the Thames and was used as an assembly
         ground for the London militia.

49   *Command* demand

50   *pledges* hostages, guarantees
         fealty loyalty to the Crown

53   *use* call on for his use
         so provided

54   *kind* natural, correct

55   *We twain will go into his highness' tent.* See the note to
         lines 12–47.
         twain two

62, 106 *monstrous* unnatural

63   *discomfited* defeated

64   *rude* uncivilized, unpolished
         mean condition low rank

72   *an't like* if it please

73   *degree* rank in society

78–80   *Iden, kneel down . . . on us.* This episode may be based
         on the knighting of William Walworth, who slew Wat
         Tyler in 1381, as it is reported in Holinshed, or on a
         scene in the anonymous play *Jack Straw*, in which
         Walworth is knighted in a similarly abrupt manner.

79   *marks.* These were worth each about two thirds of a
         pound, although there were no specific coins of this
         denomination. A thousand marks is the amount men-
         tioned as a reward for Cade's death in the chronicles,
         but *crowns* are specified at IV.8.66 and IV.10.26.

80   *will* command

86   *front* confront

87–92   *How now? . . . brook abuse?* Compare Hall, where York
         visits the King after the dismissal of his army but,
         'beside his expectation and contrary to the promise
         made by the King, he found the Duke of Somerset
         set at large and at liberty, whom the Duke of York
         boldly accused of treason, of bribery, oppression, and
         many other crimes' (page 226).

89   *be equal with* express exactly what is in

92   *how hardly* with what great difficulty
         brook abuse endure deception

95   *Which* who

96   *doth not become* is not fit to wear

97   *palmer's staff* (carried by religious pilgrims and thus a sign of great piety)

98   *awful* awe-inspiring

99   *gold* (golden crown)

100   *Achilles' spear* (proverbial. According to post-Homeric legend, the spear of Achilles was used to wound Telephus, who was later cured by the application to the wound of rust from the spear itself.)

101   *the change* (from *frown* to *smile* and vice versa)

103   *act* enact, enforce

106–8 *O monstrous traitor . . . for grace.* Compare Hall: 'The Duke of Somerset not only made answer to the Duke's objections but also accused him of high treason toward the King his sovereign lord, affirming that he with his fautors and complices had consulted together how to obtain the crown and sceptre of the realm' (page 226).

109   *Wouldst have me kneel?* In the chronicles at this point York is arrested only to be released and march again on London three years later ·in 1455, which event leads to the first Battle of Saint Albans. Shakespeare here conflates the events of 1452–3 and 1455.
      these. As York has already dismissed his troops (lines 45–7), and his sons are not yet present with their forces, he probably gestures in the direction. of the door where his sons are to enter.

110   *brook I bow a knee to man* bear that I should humble myself to anyone

111   *sons.* Historically York's sons at the time of the first Battle of Saint Albans were young children, Edward being thirteen and Richard three. See the notes to the stage direction at line 121.

112   *to ward* into custody

113   *of my enfranchisement* in the matter of my freedom

114   *amain* quickly

117   *Neapolitan.* The reference is to Margaret's being the daughter of Reignier, titular King of Naples.

118   *Outcast of Naples.* Reignier had never managed to take possession of the throne his father had held.

120   *bane* destruction

121, 122   (stage directions) The direction in Q1 parallel with these conveys the confrontation clearly: 'Enter the Duke of *Yorkes* sonnes, *Edward* the Earle of *March*, and crook-backe *Richard*, at the one doore, with Drumme and soldiers, and at the other doore, enter *Clifford* and his sonne, with Drumme and souldiers, and *Clifford* kneeles to *Henry*, and speakes.'

121   (stage direction) *Enter ... Edward.* This may have been suggested by the rumour reported by Hall after York had been imprisoned in 1452: 'While the Council treated of saving or losing of this dolorous Duke of York, a rumour sprang throughout London that Edward Earl of March, son and heir apparent to the said Duke, a young prince of great wit and much stomach, accompanied with a strong army of Marchmen, was coming toward London, which tidings sore appalled the Queen and the whole Council. ... The King's Council ... set the Duke of York at liberty' (page 227).

        Edward. He was born at Rouen in 1442. After defeating the Lancastrians at Towton he proclaimed himself king and was crowned Edward IV in 1461. He died in 1483.

        Richard. He was born at Fotheringay in 1452, and created Duke of Gloucester in 1461. Parliament pro-. claimed him Richard III in 1483, and he was slain at Bosworth Field in 1485.

122   (stage direction) *Young Clifford.* John de Clifford (1435?–1461), thirteenth Baron Clifford and ninth Baron of Westmorland, was a strong Lancastrian. He was nicknamed 'The Butcher' after killing in cold blood the Earl of Rutland, the second son of York. He was slain six weeks after the second Battle of Saint Albans.

123   *deny* refuse

131   *Bedlam.* See the note to III.1.51.

132   *bedlam* crazy

132   *humour* disposition

135   *factious pate* rebellious head

142   *glass* mirror

143   *false-heart* treacherous

144-7   *Call hither . . . to me.* Compare Hall's description of York's reliance on the Nevils: 'the Duke of York had fastened his chain between these two strong and robustious pillars' (page 232).

144   *stake* (the post to which the fighting bear was chained in the popular Elizabethan sport of bear-baiting)
        two brave bears. The Nevils, father and son, are so referred to because the Warwick heraldic device was a bear chained to a ragged staff, inherited from Warwick's father-in-law, Richard Beauchamp.

146   *astonish* terrify
        fell-lurking curs cruelly waiting dogs (which attacked the bear in bear-baiting)

149   *bearard* bear handler, bearward

150   *baiting-place* bear-baiting pit

151   *hot* angry
        o'erweening overambitious, overreaching

152   *Run back and bite, because he was withheld* (proverbial: 'A man may cause his own dog to bite him')

153   *suffered* injured
        with by

156   *oppose yourselves* undertake resistance

157   *indigested* improperly formed. Richard of Gloucester's deformities are dwelt on in *Part Three* and in *Richard III.* Compare Hall: 'he was small and little of stature, so was he of body greatly deformed, the one shoulder higher than the other, his face small, but his countenance was cruel and such that a man at the first aspect would judge it to savour and smell of malice, fraud, and deceit. When he stood musing he would bite and chew busily his nether lip, as who said that his fierce nature in his cruel body always chafed, stirred, and was ever unquiet' (page 421).

158   *As crookèd in thy manners as thy shape.* All the

chroniclers and Shakespeare saw a symbolic relationship between Richard's twisted body and evil nature. See the quotation in the note to line 157.

159   *heat you* make you sweat with fighting
        anon soon

165   *spectacles* eye-glasses (a sign of Salisbury's age)

167   *frosty* white with age

172   *abuse it* put it to bad use

174   *That* (that is, *thy knee*)
        mickle much, great

177   *repute* consider

181   *dispense with* expect dispensation from
        for for breaking

182   *swear* pledge oneself

183   *greater sin to keep a sinful oath* (proverbial: 'An unlawful oath is better broken than kept')

187   *reave* bereave, rob

188   *customed right* (the portion of her husband's estate which a widow has the right to under law)

191   *sophister* skilful arguer

194   *I am resolved for death or dignity.* Compare Hall: 'The Duke of York and his adherents, perceiving that neither exhortation served nor accusement prevailed against the Duke of Somerset, determined to revenge their quarrel and obtain their purpose by open war and martial adventure and no longer to sleep in so weighty a business' (page 232).
        resolved for determined to possess
        dignity high place

196   *You were best to* you had better

200   *burgonet* (a small light Burgundian helmet)

201   *Might I but know thee by thy house's badge* if I can recognize you by your family crest (during the battle)

202–3   *my father's badge ... bear* (actually the crest of his father-in-law; see the second note to line 144)

204   *aloft* on top of

205   *cedar* (a tree associated with royalty because of its great height and strength)

207	*affright* terrify
212	*complices* allies
213	*in spite* spitefully
215	*stigmatic* branded (with deformity)

V.2   The location of the scene is the field of the first Battle of Saint Albans (1455), and Shakespeare develops in terms of personalities some of the events of the battle. In the chronicles, York with Warwick, Salisbury, and Lord Cobham leads his army towards London. On 20 May the King, accompanied by Somerset, Buckingham, Old Clifford, and the Earls of Stafford and Northumberland, leads his forces from Westminster to Saint Albans, where they are trapped by York three days later (Hall, page 232).

(stage direction) *Enter Warwick*. In the chronicles, the King sends messengers to York at one end of Saint Albans, commanding his obedience; meanwhile 'the Earl of Warwick with the Marchmen entered at the other gate of the town and fiercely set on the King's forward and them shortly discomfited' (Hall, page 232).

1	*of Cumberland* (one of the titles of the Cliffords)
2	*the bear*. See the second note to V.1.144.
4	*dead* dying
8	*afoot* on foot (without your horse)
9	*deadly-handed* murderous
10	*match to match* as opponent to opponent
11	*carrion kites* kites who eat carrion
12	*bonny beast* (horse. Q1 expands the allusion as 'the boniest gray that ere was bred in North.')
14	*chase* prey, game
20	*bearing* deportment, behaviour
21	*fast* firmly, unalterably
23	*shown ignobly and in treason* displayed in an ignoble and treasonous cause
26	*action* outcome of the action

27   *lay* wager
      Address thee prepare to fight
      (stage direction) *York kills Clifford.* This event is based
      upon (1) Hall's report that Clifford was among those
      slain at Saint Albans (page 233); and (2) Young
      Clifford's words to York's second son, the Earl of
      Rutland, before he stabbed him in 1461: 'By God's
      blood, thy father slew mine, and so will I do thee and
      all thy kin' (Hall, page 251).

28   *La fin couronne lès œuvres* the end crowns the works;
      the proverb 'The end crowns all'.

31   *confusion* destruction
      on the rout in disorderly flight

32   *frames* creates

34   *Whom angry heavens do make their minister.* Compare
      Ezekiel 14.21.
      minister agent

35   *frozen* (with fear)
      part side, faction

36   *Hot coals of vengeance.* Compare Psalm 140.10.

37   *dedicate* devoted, committed

39-40 *Hath not . . . valour* does not possess true courage,
      only the external signs of it owing to chance

41   *premised* preordained
      the last day doomsday

43   *the general trumpet* the trumpet which summons all men

44   *Particularities* individual affairs

45   *cease* put an end to
      ordained destined, fated

46   *lose* pass away, spend

47   *silver livery* white uniform (afforded by white hair)
      advisèd age wise and prudent old age

48   *reverence* venerable old age
      chair-days final days (appropriate to sitting in a chair)

51   *stony* without pity

52   *No more will I their babes.* This looks ahead to Young
      Clifford's notorious murder of the young Duke of
      Rutland; see *Part Three*, I.3.

52   *virginal* of young girls

53   *as the dew to fire.* Water drops sprinkled on to fire were believed to have the effect of making it burn more fiercely.

54   *reclaims* subdues

55   *to my flaming wrath be oil and flax* (a blending of two proverbs: 'Put not fire to flax' and 'To add oil to the fire')

56–60   *Henceforth, I will not ... my fame.* See the note to the stage direction at line 27.

57   *Meet I* should I encounter

58   *gobbets* chunks of meat

59   *wild* savage

    Absyrtus (the younger brother of Medea. In order to escape with her lover Jason from her father's kingdom of Colchos, Medea murdered Absyrtus and strewed the pieces of his corpse behind her so that her father, by picking them up, would be delayed in his pursuit of her.)

60   *seek out my fame* earn my reputation (of 'The Butcher'; see the note to the stage direction at V.1.122)

61   *new ruin of old Clifford's house* (his father's body)

62   *did Aeneas old Anchises bear.* In the *Aeneid*, Aeneas rescues his aged father from burning Troy by carrying him on his back.

64   *bare* carried

65   *Nothing* not at all

    heavy (1) weighty; (2) sorrowful

67–9   *underneath ... death.* See the note to I.4.34. The reference here is directly to I.4.65–8, where York reads the prophecies copied down from the Spirit's pronouncements by Roger Bolingbroke, who is thus made *famous* because Somerset died in the way he foretold.

70   *hold* maintain

    still always

71   (stage direction) *Excursions* sorties, sallies

72–83   *Away, my lord! ... be stopped.* Compare Hall: 'the

Duke of York sent ever fresh men to succour the
weary and put new men in the places of the hurt
persons, by which only policy the King's army was
profligate and dispersed and all the chieftains of the
field almost slain and brought to confusion' (pages
232–3).

73 *outrun the heavens* escape from the will of heaven.
Compare Psalm 139.7–12.

74 *nor ... nor* neither ... nor

76 *secure us* make ourselves safe

77 *what* whatever means
which who

78 *bottom* lowest ebb

79 *haply* by chance

80 *if not through* if we do not fail to do so owing to

81 *We shall to London get, where you are loved.* In Hall it
is York who has 'too many friends about the city of
London' (page 232). See the note to V.3.24.

86 *uncurable discomfit* irrevocable discouragement

87 *present parts* remaining forces

89 *To see their day and them our fortune give* to witness a
time when we shall gain a victory as they have now
and when they shall experience our bad luck

V.3 The location is still Saint Albans.

2 *winter* aged

3 *Agèd contusions and all brush of time* the bruises of old
age and the assault of time

4 *brow* peak, height

5 *Repairs him with occasion* takes advantage of the
opportunity to renew himself (by fighting)

6 *one foot* (of ground)

8 *holp* helped

9 *bestrid* stood over (while he was on the ground, in
order to protect him from the enemy)
led him off (from the battlefield)

11 *still* always

277

12   *hangings* tapestries, wall-hangings
           homely simple, humble

20   *have not got that which we have* have not yet made safe
           what we have won

22   *Being opposites of such repairing nature* since they are
           enemies who are able naturally to recover themselves
           quickly

23-4   *I know . . . to London.* York's confidence here is based
           on a political fact supplied by Hall: 'the Duke of
           York [was] had in more estimation among the citizens
           and communality [of London] than the King' (page
           236).

23   *safety* most prudent course

25   *present* immediate
           court of parliament (a parliamentary meeting consisting
           of the King and his Privy Council)

26   *writs* (summonses to attend parliament, issued by the
           King)

29   *by my hand* (a common oath)

31   *eternized* immortalized

AN ACCOUNT OF THE TEXT

THE Second Part of *Henry VI* exists in two versions. The first of these was published by Thomas Millington in quarto format in 1594 ('Q1') under the title *The First part of the Contention betwixt the two famous Houses of York and Lancaster*, which was reprinted by the same publisher in 1600 ('Q2') and in 1619 by Thomas Pavier, who combined it with a version of *Henry VI, Part Three* and called them together *The Whole Contention betweene the two Famous Houses, Lancaster and Yorke* ('Q3'.) The second version appears in the first Folio edition of the collected plays of 1623 ('F'), where it is the seventh play in the Histories section and is called *The second Part of Henry the Sixt, with the death of the Good Duke Humfrey*. It is obvious that there is a close relationship between these two texts; but its exact nature is still a matter of scholarly debate.

F is clearly the superior text and is about one third longer than Q. It seems likely that the two main compositors of the Folio volume, who divided the type-setting of the play between them, worked from a manuscript of theatrical origin. This manuscript may have been Shakespeare's own, because F reproduces features which are normally associated with the author's habits of composition. For example, it is unlikely that anyone but the writer would have been guilty of the slip of memory that caused Queen Margaret to be referred to as Eleanor (Duchess of Gloucester) four times in III.2 (lines 26, 79, 100, and 120). Certain stage directions appear to be authorial rather than theatrical (for example, '*Enter multitudes, with halters about their necks*' at IV.9.9, where '*multitudes*' is obviously impractical in the theatre); there is some uncertainty in the designation of characters (for example, Dick's speeches are indicated sometimes by '*Dicke.*', sometimes by '*But.*'); important speaking parts are sometimes covered by a block entry term (for example, at the opening of IV.1, where '*others*' stands for the Master, the Master's Mate, Walter Whitmore, and the two Gentlemen prisoners); and there is occasional indefiniteness in stage directions which would have been impractical in a theatre prompt-book (such as at I.4.21, where either Bolingbroke or Southwell can perform the incantation to raise the Spirit). It has also been suggested that Shakespeare's autograph may have carried theatrical annotations made with a view to the preparation of the prompt book. Some of the stage directions, particularly those specifying sound effects, strike one as being phrased with theatrical production in mind; and the names of Bevis and Holland who appear among Jack Cade's rebels in IV.2 are almost certainly those of the contemporary actors who first played the roles. However, features like these may well be the result of an actor-playwright composing with a knowledge of the resources of his company in mind.

Q is a much inferior text. In some sections its wording is very close to that of F; but at others material seems to have been transposed or appears to be a poor paraphrase of what is found in F. Q drops some minor characters, includes lines clearly recollected from other plays, and in general is poetically inferior to F. Q's stage directions often read like descriptions of what took place in a particular production rather than instructions of what should be performed.

Various theories have been elaborated to account for the features of these two texts and to explain the relationship between them and its origin:

1. Some scholars argue that Q is an original play which Shakespeare rewrote as *Henry VI, Part Two*. Passages where F and Q agree are viewed as having been taken over verbatim by Shakespeare from his source-play; passages in F which are superior to Q are seen as indicating rewriting; and those in F which have no parallel in Q are taken to be Shakespeare's additions.

2. A more generally accepted theory claims that Q is a memorially reconstructed acting version of the play F prints. The fact that some of the roles in Q are more full and accurate than others suggests that the actors who originally played the parts of Warwick, Suffolk, and Lord Clifford may have helped

in creating from memory the shortened and faulty version of
the text that Millington published.

3. The pattern of agreement and non-agreement in variants
between F and Q has been explained as being of printing-
house origin. Instead of working from Shakespeare's manuscript, the F compositors are seen to have set type from a copy
of Q3 (and possibly Q2) which had been corrected and added
to by reference to such a manuscript, following the amended
printed text whenever they could and consulting the hand-
written copy only when it provided substantial additional
material.

4. Many scholars believe that features of F and Q, whatever
their relationship, can be explained only by the play's being of
multiple authorship. Using mainly stylistic and some external
evidence, they argue that the play was originally the work of
Robert Greene, Thomas Nashe, and George Peele, and
Shakespeare working with them and/or revising the original
play to make it fit into a three-part sequence.

The purely textual features of Q and F versions are often
analysed in connexion with various pieces of external historical
evidence, which are themselves susceptible to very different
interpretations. For example, the first reference we have to
Shakespeare as a dramatist occurs in Robert Greene's pamphlet
Groatsworth of Wit (1592), where the dying writer appears to be
warning his fellow dramatists against Shakespeare, whom he
characterizes as 'an upstart crow, beautified with our feathers,
that with his *Tiger's heart wrapped in a player's hide* supposes he
is as well able to bombast out a blank verse as the best of you;
and, being an absolute *Johannes fac totum*, is in his own conceit
the only Shake-scene in a country.'

Clearly this allusion connects Shakespeare with the authorship of the *Henry VI* plays; but scholars differ as to the exact
nature of the charge Greene is making. Obviously he is angered
by Shakespeare's theatrical success; but is he implying that
Shakespeare plagiarized his and other men's work? Or is he
irate at the spectacle of a mere actor competing with university-
trained playwrights? Or is he being scornful of Shakespeare's
literary imitation of his contemporaries? And what exactly is

the point of the misquotation from *Part Three* (I.4.137)? With widely different interpretations of Greene's tirade possible, it can easily be seen that it may be used to support a variety of theories about the origins and relationship of the Q and F versions.

It is almost certain that the play belonged to the Earl of Pembroke's Men, a theatrical company which was forced to tour the provinces owing to the closure of the London theatres occasioned by the plague in parts of 1592 and 1593. Apparently these players went bankrupt as a result of this experience and were forced to sell up their effects. Some of their plays ultimately found their way into the repertoire of the Lord Chamberlain's Men, a company of which Shakespeare was to become the chief playwright and a leading shareholder. Like the Greene allusion, this tantalizingly incomplete theatrical history – involving as it does Shakespeare, Greene, Peele, Nashe, and Marlowe as playwrights, a company being disbanded, and plays changing hands – can be used in support of very different textual theories about *2 Henry VI*.

Thus at the moment there is no theory concerning the genesis and early history of the play which has won general acceptance; nor is there agreement about its date of composition (between 1588 and 1592), any estimate of which must obviously take into account much of the same evidence.

As F is the better version of the play it is this that the present edition follows. Only where F presents genuine difficulties has Q been used to make emendations. In the Commentary and in collations lists 1 and 3, Q's readings are recorded when they seem to throw light on possible meaning or stage practice, even where no emendation has been made in F. List 4 quotes the more substantial passages in Q which are noticeably different from those in F or constitute an addition to what is found there.

COLLATIONS

The following lists are selective. The quartos are abbreviated as 'Q1' (1594), 'Q2' (1600), 'Q3' (1619), and the editions of the Folio as 'F1' (1623), 'F2' (1632), 'F3' (1663–4), 'F4' (1685)

In lists 1–3 quotations from the early editions are unmodern-
ized, except that 'long s' (ſ) is replaced by 's'.

I

Emendations
Below are listed the more important departures from the text
of F1, with the readings of this edition printed to the left of
the square bracket. Those readings adopted from or based on
Q1 are identified, as are readings taken from the reprints of F.
Most of the other emendations were first made by eighteenth-
and nineteenth-century editors. Corrections of obvious mis-
prints and demonstrable mislineation, the straightforward
regularization of F's speech prefixes, the variant spelling of
proper names, and punctuation changes where the sense is not
significantly affected are not recorded.

THE CHARACTERS IN THE PLAY] *not in* F

I.1.　　49　*it is further agreed between them*] (Q1); *not in* F
　　　　51　*over*] (Q1); *not in* F
　　　　57　*duchy*] Duches (Q1); *Dutchesse*
　　　　　　the county of Maine] of *Mayne* (Q1); *Maine*
　　　　91　had] hath
　　　166　all together] altogether
　　　176　Protector] (Q1); Protectors
　　　205　And so . . . cause.] And so . . . Yorke, | For . . .
　　　　　　cause.
　　　206　Then . . . main.] Then . . . away, | And . . . maine.
　　　207　Unto . . . lost!] Vnto . . . maine? | Oh . . . lost,
I.3.　　29　master was] Mistresse was
　　　49　a tilt] at Tilt (Q1); a-tilt
I.4.　23–6　Asmath! | By the . . . power | Thou . . . ask; | For
　　　　　　till . . . hence.] *Asmath* . . . God, | Whose . . .
　　　　　　tremblest at, | Answere . . . speake, | Thou shalt
　　　　　　. . . hence.
　　　61　te] *not in* F
　　　65　*befall*] betide
　　69–70　Come . . . oracles | Are hardly . . . understood.]

Come . . . Lords, | These . . . attain'd, | And . . . vnderstood.

I.4.   73 Thither . . . them –] Thither . . . Newes, | As . . . them

        77 At your . . . ho?] At your . . . Lord. | Who's . . . hoe?

II.1. 23–5 What . . . peremptory? | *Tantaene . . . irae?* | Churchmen . . . malice;] What, Cardinall? | Is . . . peremptorie? | *Tantæne . . . hot?* | Good Unckle . . . mallice:

      32–3 I prithee peace, | Good . . . peers;] I prythee . . . Queene, | And whet . . . Peeres,

      41–2 Ay, where . . . darest, | This . . . grove.] I, where peepe: | And if . . . Euening, | On the . . . Groue.

      46–8 uncle. | CARDINAL . . . Are . . . grove. | GLOU-CESTER . . . Cardinal,] Vnckle, are . . . aduis'd? | The . . . Groue: | Cardinall,

      50–53 Now, by . . . for this, | Or all . . . *teipsum* – | Protector . . . yourself. | . . . The winds . . . lords.] Now . . . Priest, | Ile . . . this, | Or all . . . fayle. | . . . *Medice* . . . your selfe. | . . . The Windes . . . high, | So doe . . . Lords:

        83 Poor . . . thee.] Poore Soule, | Gods . . . thee:

      86–7 Tell . . . chance, | Or . . . shrine?] Tell . . . good-fellow, | Cam'st . . . Deuotion, | To . . . Shrine?

      88–91 God knows . . . called | A hundred . . . sleep, | By good . . . come; | Come . . . thee.'] God knowes . . . Deuotion, | Being . . . oftner, | In my . . . *Albon:* | Who . . . Shrine, | And . . . thee.

      92–3 Most . . . oft | Myself . . . so.] Most . . . forsooth: | And . . . Voyce, | To . . . so.

    101–2 Alas . . . my life] (*prose in* F)

      130 his] (Q1); it,

    133–4 My masters . . . whips?] My Masters . . . *Albones,* | Haue . . . Towne, | And . . . Whippes?

    146–7 I will . . . quickly.] I will . . . Lord. | Come . . . quickly.

II.2.   34–5 The third ... line | I claim ... daughter,] The third ... Clarence, | From ... Crowne, | Had ... Daughter,

        35, 49 Philippe] *Phillip*

        45–50 Married ... was | To ... son. | By ... heir | To ... son | Of ... Phillipe, | Sole ... Clarence;] Marryed ... Cambridge, | Who ... *Langley*, | *Edward* ... Sonne; | By ... Kingdome: | She ... March, | Who ... *Mortimer*, | Who ... Daughter | Vnto ... Clarence.

        46 son, son] Sonnes Sonne

        64–5 We ... king | Till ... stained] We ... Lords: | But ... Crown'd, | And ... stayn'd

II.3.   1 Stand ... wife] Stand ... *Cobham*, | *Glosters* Wife:

        3 sins] sinne

        22–5 Stay ... go, | Give ... himself | Protector ... hope, | My ... feet.] Stay ... Gloster, | Ere ... Staffe, | *Henry* ... be, | And ... guide, | And ... feete:

II.4.   83–4 And I ... if | You ... farewell.] And I ... her. | And ... farewell.

        105 Madam ... sheet,] Madame ... done, | Throw ... Sheet,

III.1.   104 'Tis ... France;] 'Tis ... Lord, | That ... France,

        107 Is ... it?] Is ... so? | What ... it?

        218 eyes] eyes;

        223 Free ... beams:] Free Lords: | Cold ... Beames:

        333 art] art;

        365 caper] (F2); capre

III.2.   26 Meg] *Nell*

        75 leper] (F3); Leaper

     79, 100 Margaret] *Elianor*

        116 witch] watch

        120 Margaret] *Elinor*

        174 Look,] Looke

III.2.   237 Why ... drawn] Why ... Lords? | Your ... drawne,

265 whe'er] where

318 on] (Q1); an

359 thence;] thence,

410 worth.] worth,

III.3.   10 whe'er] where

IV.1.   48 Jove ... I?] (Q1); *not in* F

50 Obscure ... blood,] (F *gives this line to Lieutenant*)

70–71 LIEUTENANT Yes, Poole. | SUFFOLK Poole? | LIEUTENANT Poole! Sir Poole! Lord! | Ay, kennell, puddle] *Cap.* Yes Poull. | *Suffolke.* Poull. | *Cap.* I Poull, puddle (Q1); *Lieu.* Poole, Sir *Poole?* Lord, | I kennell, puddle

85 mother's bleeding] Mother-bleeding

93 are] and

113 LIEUTENANT Ay . . . soon.] (Q1); *not in* F

114 SUFFOLK] (Q1); *not in* F

116–17 LIEUTENANT Walter! | WHITMORE Come, Suffolk] *Lieu.* Water: W. Come Suffolke

118 *Pene*] Pine

134 Come, soldiers . . . can,] (F *gives this line to Lieutenant*)

IV.2.   33 fall] (F4); faile

127–8 Marry ... not?] (*prose in* F)

127 this:] this

142–3 And ... what?] (*prose in* F)

IV.4.   58 be] (F2); *not in* F1

IV.5.   2–5 No ... rebels.] No. ... slaine: | For ... Bridge, | Killing ... them: | The ... Tower | To ... Rebels.

IV.6.   1–6 Now ... Mortimer.] Now ... City, | And ... Stone, | I ... cost | The ... Wine | This ... raigne. | And ... any, | That ... *Mortimer.*

9 SMITH] *But.* (i.e. 'Butcher')

13–15 Come ... away.] Come ... them: | But ... fire, | And ... too. | Come ... away.

IV.7. 14–15 Then . . . out.] Then . . . Statutes | Vnlesse . . .
out.

64–5 hands, | But to maintain] hands? | Kent to
maintaine,

83 caudle] (F4); Candle

122–8 But . . . Away!] But . . . brauer: | Let . . . well |
When . . . againe, | Least . . . vp | Of . . . Soldiers,
| Deferre . . . night: | For . . . Maces, | Will . . .
Corner | Haue . . . Away.

IV.8. 3–4 What . . . kill?] What . . . heare? | Dare . . .
Parley | When . . . kill?

12 rebel] Traitor (Q1); rabble

IV.9. 33 calmed] (F4); calme

IV.10. 19 waning] warning

56 God] (Q1); Ioue

V.1. 11 flower-de-luce] (F3); Fleure-de-Luce

109 these] thee

111 sons] (Q1); sonne

194 or] and

201 house's] housed

V.2. 19 What . . . pause?] What . . . Yorke? | Why . . .
pause?

28 *couronne les œuvres*] (F2); *Corrone les eumenes*

2

Rejected emendations

The following list records a selection of emendations and conjectures which have not been adopted in this edition, but which
have been made with some plausibility by other editors. Many
of these emendations are readings adopted from one of the
quartos or from the reprints of F. To the left of the square
brackets are the readings of the present text; to the right of them
are F1's readings where they differ from this edition, then readings adopted from the quartos and the F reprints, and other
suggested emendations. When more than one emendation is
listed, they are separated by semi-colons. All emendations made
to achieve metrical regularity have been ignored in this list;

and substantial passages from Q introduced by some editors at various points in the play, in accordance with their theories of the relationship between F and Q, are quoted in list 4 below.

I.1.	249	Henry, surfeiting in] Henry surfeit in the
I.2.	19	thought] hour
	38	were] are (Q1)
	75	witch] witch of Ely (Q1–2); witch of Rye (Q3); witch of Eie
I.3.	3	in the quill] in sequel
	6	PETER] FIRST PETITIONER (F4)
	20	Melford] Long Melford (Q1)
	66	haughty] haught (F2–4)
	88	the] their
	140	I could] I'd (Q1)
	148	fume] fury
	149	far] fast
	208	This] KING This
I.4.	15	silent] silence (Q1)
	33	*befall*] betide (Q1)
II.1.	48	GLOUCESTER ... Cardinal, I] CARDINAL I
	90	Simon] (F *Symon*); Simpcox; Saunder
II.2.	35, 49	Philippe] (F *Phillip*); Philippa
II.3.	19	ground] grave
	30	realm] helm
	46	youngest] haughtiest; highest
III.1.	140	suspense] suspect; suspects
	211	strays] strives; strains
	260	reasons] treasons
III.2.	393	its] his (Q1)
IV.1.	6	Clip] (F Cleape); Clap; Clepe
	32	What, doth death] What doth thee
	50	lousy] lowly
	118	*Pene*] (F *Pine*); *Poenae*; *Perii!*
IV.2.	80	Chartham] (F Chartam); Chattam (Q1); Chatham
	153	mained] maimed (Q1)
IV.3.	7	one] one a week (Q1)

IV.7. 57 because] beauteous; bounteous; pleasant; plenteous
      58 wealthy] worthy
      83 the help of] pap with a
IV.10. 37 five] fine
V.1. 10 soul] sword
      201 house's] (F housed); household (Q1)
V.2. 87 parts] part; party
V.3. 1 Of] Old (Q1)
      29 hand] faith (Q1)

3

Stage directions

The stage directions of this edition are based on those in F. The more important changes and additions to the F directions are listed below. The normalization of characters' names, minor adjustments in the order in which characters are listed, and the provision of exits and entrances clearly demanded by the action but omitted in F are not recorded. Asides and indications of characters addressed are all editorial, as are the correction of '*Exit*' to '*Exeunt*'. The readings of this edition appear to the left of the square brackets; to the right of the brackets are stage directions from Q1 wherever they have been adopted as or form the basis for those of the present edition, and the F readings. Quarto stage directions which have not been adopted in the present text, but which clarify the action or provide evidence of possible Elizabethan staging, are quoted and discussed in the Commentary.

I.1. 10 *He kneels*] *not in* F
      51 *Gloucester lets the contract fall*] Duke *Humphrey* lets it fall. (Q1); *not in* F
      56 *reads*] *not in* F
      72 *Gloucester stays all the rest*] and Duke Humphrey staies all the rest (Q1); *Manet the rest.*
I.2. 60 *Exeunt Gloucester and Messenger*] *Ex. Hum* (*after line 59 in* F)

I.3.   0 *four*] *three or foure*

       13, 19 *reads*] *not in* F

           24 *offering his petition*] *not in* F

           34 *servant with Peter*] with the Armourers man
              (Q1); *not in* F

           98 *Somerset*] (Q1); *not in* F

          135 *The Queen lets fall her fan*] The Queene lets fall
              her gloue (Q1); *not in* F

          174 *guarded*] *not in* F

I.4.   11 *Hume following*] *not in* F

     28, 31, 33 *reads*] *not in* F

           30 *As the Spirit speaks, Bolingbroke writes the
              answer*] *not in* F

           39 *Sir Humphrey Stafford as captain*] *not in* F

           51 *Exeunt above the Duchess and Hume, guarded*]
              Exet Elnor aboue. (Q1); *not in* F

           53 *Exeunt Jourdain, Southwell, Bolingbroke, escorted
              by Stafford and the guard*] Exet with them. (Q1);
              Exit.

II.1.   65 *with music*] (Q1); *not in* F
              Simpcox's Wife and others following] *not in* F

          137 *an attendant*] one. (Q1); *not in* F

          155 *Exeunt Mayor and townspeople, and the Beadle
              dragging Simpcox's Wife*] Exet Mayor. (Q1);
              Exit.

II.3.   0 *Enter the King, Queen, Gloucester York, Suffolk,
              and Salisbury; the Duchess of Gloucester, Margery
              Jourdain, Southwell, Hume, and Bolingbroke,
              guarded*] Enter King *Henry*, and the Queene,
              Duke *Humphrey*, the Duke of *Suffolke*, and the
              Duke of *Buckingham*, the *Cardinall*, and Dame
              Elnor Cobham, led with the Officers, and then
              enter to them the Duke of *Yorke*, and the Earles
              of *Salsbury* and *Warwicke*. (Q1); *Enter the King
              and State, with Guard, to banish the Duchesse.*

           17 *Exeunt the Duchess and the other prisoners,
              guarded*] Exet some with *Elnor*. (Q1); *not in* F

           92 *Alarum*] Alarmes (Q1); *not in* F

Horner] him

93 *He dies*] (Q1); *not in* F

II.4.   16 *Enter the Duchess of Gloucester barefoot, in a*
white sheet and verses written on her back and
pinned on and a taper burning in her hand, with
Sir John Stanley, the Sheriff, and officers with
bills and halberds] Enter Dame *Elnor Cobham*
bare-foote, and a white sheete about her, with a
waxe candle in her hand, and verses written on
her backe and pind on, and accompanied with the
Sheriffes of London, and Sir *Iohn Standly*, and
Officers, with billes and holbards. (Q1); *Enter the*
Duchesse in a white Sheet, and a Taper burning in
her hand, with the Sherife and Officers.

73 *Exit Herald*] (Q1); *not in* F

86 *with his men*] and his men (Q1); *not in* F

III.1.   194 *Exit Gloucester, guarded by the Cardinal's men*]
Exet Humphrey, with the *Cardinals* men. (Q1);
Exit Gloster.

222 *Exit with Buckingham, Salisbury, and Warwick*]
Exet King, Salsbury, and *Warwicke.* (Q1); *Exit.*

III.2.   0 *two Murderers*] two or three

14 *Exeunt   Murderers*]   *Exet*   murtherers.   (Q1);
Exeunt.
Sound trumpets. Enter the King, Queen, Cardinal,
and Somerset, with attendants] Then enter the
King and Queene, the Duke of *Buckingham*, and
the Duke of *Somerset*, and the Cardinall. (Q1);
Sound Trumpets. Enter the King, the Queene,
Cardinall, Suffolke, Somerset, with Attendants.

121 *Salisbury*] (Q1); *not in* F

135 *Exeunt Warwick, then Salisbury and the commons*]
Exet Salsbury. (Q1); *not in* F

148 *with Gloucester's body in it. Enter Warwick*] not in
F, *where ' Bed put forth.' follows line 146*

202 *Exit Cardinal*] (Q1); *not in* F

231 *Exeunt Suffolk and Warwick*] (Q1); *Exeunt.*

288 *Exit Salisbury*] (Q1); *not in* F

III.2.   299 *Exeunt all but the Queen and Suffolk*] *Exet* King and *Warwicke, Manet* Queene and *Suffolke.* (Q1); *Exit.*

          379 *Exit Vaux*] *Exet Vawse.* (Q1); *Exit*

          408 *She kisseth him*] (Q1); *not in* F

          412 *in opposite directions*] *not in* F

III.3.   28 *The Cardinal dies*] (Q1); *not in* F

IV.1.   0 *Alarum. Fight at sea. Ordnance goes off. Enter a Lieutenant, a Master, a Master's Mate, Walter Whitmore, Suffolk, disguised, two Gentlemen prisoners, and soldiers*] Alarmes within, and the chambers be discharged, like as it were a fight at sea. And then enter the Captaine of the ship and the Maister, and the Maisters Mate, & the Duke of Suffolke disguised, and others with him, and Water Whickmore. (Q1); *Alarum. Fight at Sea. Ordnance goes off. Enter Lieutenant, Suffolke, and others.*

          140 *and soldiers*] *not in* F

          143 *Exeunt all but the First Gentleman. Enter Walter Whitmore with the body of Suffolk*] *Exit Lieutenant, and the rest. Manet the first Gent. Enter Walter with the body.*

IV.2.   30 *Jack*] *Iacke* (Q1); *not in* F

          79 *Enter some rebels with the Clerk of Chartham*] Enter *Will* with the Clarke of *Chattam.* (Q1); *Enter a Clearke.*

          112 *He kneels*] *not in* F
               He rises] *not in* F

          171 *Exit with his brother and soldiers*] *Exet Stafford* and his men. (Q1); *Exit.*

IV.3.   9 *He puts on Sir Humphrey Stafford's coat of mail*] *not in* F

IV.5.   0 *three*] *two or three*

IV.7.   111 *Exeunt some rebels with Lord Say*] *Exet* one or two, with the Lord *Say* (Q1); *not in* F

          121 *Enter one with the heads of Say and Cromer upon two poles*] Enter two with the Lord *Sayes* head,

and sir Iames Cromers, vpon two poles. (Q1);
Enter one with the heads.

IV.8.   4 *attended*] *not in* F

IV.10.   57 *and Cade falls down*] (Q1); *not in* F

V.1.   47 *Exeunt soldiers*] (Q2); *not in* F

         78 *Iden kneels*] *not in* F

   111, 116 *Exit an attendant*] *not in* F

   121, 122 *Enter at one door Edward and Richard with their
              army . . . Enter at another door Clifford and Young
              Clifford with an army*] Enter the Duke of *Yorkes*
              sonnes, *Edward* the Earle of *March*, and crook-
              backe *Richard*, at the one doore, with Drumme
              and soldiers, and at the other doore, enter
              Clifford and his sonne, with Drumme and
              souldiers, and *Clifford* kneeles to *Henry*, and
              speakes. (Q1, *after line 122*); *Enter Edward and
              Richard. . . . Enter Clifford.*

         124 *He kneels*] (Q1); *not in* F

         147 *Enter the Earls of Warwick and Salisbury with an
              army*] Enter at one doore, the Earles of *Salsbury*
              and *Warwicke*, with Drumme and souldiers. (Q1);
              Enter the Earles of Warwick, and Salisbury.

V.2.   0 *Alarums to the battle*] (Q1); *not in* F

         27 *They fight and York kills Clifford*] (Q1); *not in* F

         28 *He dies*] *not in* F

         30 *Exit*] Exet *Yorke.* (Q1); *not in* F

         40 *He sees his dead father*] *not in* F

         65 *Exit with his father on his back*] He takes him vp
              on his backe. . . . *Exet* yoong *Clifford* with his
              father. (Q1); *not in* F
              Somerset is killed] *Richard* kils him vnder the
              signe of the Castle in saint *Albones.* (Q1); *not in* F

         71 *Exit*] (Q1); *not in* F
              soldiers] others.

293

4

Variant and additional passages in Q1

In general Q1 offers an inferior and truncated version of the text in F; but at certain points there occur passages in Q1 which either are noticeably different in content and expression from their counterparts in F or constitute genuine additions to what is found in F. Below are quoted, in modernized form, the more substantial of such passages, each printed below a reference to the appropriate point in the text of this edition.

I.1.24–31 Great King ... doth minister:

> Th'excessive love I bear unto your grace
> Forbids me to be lavish of my tongue,
> Lest I should speak more than beseems a woman.
> Let this suffice: my bliss is in your liking,
> And nothing can make poor Margaret miserable
> Unless the frown of mighty England's King.

I.1.135–6 My lord of Gloucester ... the King:

> Why, how now, cousin Gloucester? What needs this?
> As if our King were bound unto your will
> And might not do his will without your leave!
> Proud Protector, envy in thine eyes I see,
> The big swollen venom of thy hateful heart
> That dares presume 'gainst that thy sovereign likes.

After I.3.5:

> For but for him a many were undone
> That cannot get no succour in the court.

After I.3.206:

KING
> Then be it so, my lord of Somerset.
> We make your grace Regent over the French,
> And to defend our rights 'gainst foreign foes,
> And so do good unto the realm of France.

Make haste, my lord, 'tis time that you were gone;
The time of truce I think is full expired.

I.4.0–21 *Enter the witch . . . the Spirit riseth:*

> *Enter Eleanor with Sir John Hum, Roger Bolingbroke,*
> *a conjurer, and Margery Jourdain, a witch*

ELEANOR

Here, Sir John, take this scroll of paper here,
Wherein is writ the questions you shall ask,
And I will stand upon this tower here
And hear the spirit what it says to you;
And to my questions write the answers down.
> *She goes up to the tower*

SIR JOHN

Now, sirs, begin and cast your spells about,
And charm the fiends for to obey your wills,
And tell Dame Eleanor of the thing she asks.

WITCH

Then, Roger Bolingbroke, about thy task
And frame a circle here upon the earth;
Whilst I thereon all prostrate on my face
Do talk and whisper with the devils below
And conjure them for to obey my will.
> *She lies down upon her face. Bolingbroke makes a circle*

BOLINGBROKE

Dark night, dread night, the silence of the night,
Wherein the furies mask in hellish troops,
Send up, I charge you, from Sosetus lake
The spirit Ascalon to come to me,
To pierce the bowels of this centric earth
And hither come in twinkling of an eye;
Ascalon, *ascenda, ascenda.*
> *It thunders and lightens, and then the Spirit riseth up*

I.4.38–9 *Descend to darkness . . . avoid:*

> Then down, I say, unto the damnèd pool
> Where Pluto in his fiery waggon sits,
> Riding amidst the singed and parchèd smokes,

The road of Dytas by the River Styx;
There howl and burn for ever in those flames.
Rise, Jourdain, rise, and stay thy charming spells.
Sons, we are betrayed.

II.2.69–76 Do you . . . can prophesy:

WARWICK

Then, York, advise thyself and take thy time;
Claim thou the crown and set thy standard up,
And in the same advance the milk-white rose;
And then to guard it will I rouse the bear,
Environed with ten thousand raggèd staves,
To aid and help thee for to win thy right
Maugre the proudest lord of Henry's blood
That dares deny the right and claim of York.

III.1.281–7 Enter a Post . . . hope of help:

Enter a Messenger

QUEEN

How now, sirrah, what news?

MESSENGER

Madam, I bring you news from Ireland.
The wild O'Neil, my lords, is up in arms
With troops of Irish kerns that, uncontrolled,
Doth plant themselves within the English pale . . .
And burns and spoils the country as they go . . . .

QUEEN . . . Good York, be patient,
And do thou take in hand to cross the seas
· With troops of armèd men to quell the pride
Of those ambitious Irish that rebel.

YORK

Well, madam, sith your grace is so content,
Let me have some bands of chosen soldiers
And York shall try his fortune 'gainst those kerns.

QUEEN

York, thou shalt. My lord of Buckingham,
Let it be your charge to muster up such soldiers
As shall suffice him in these needful wars.

BUCKINGHAM
Madam, I will, and levy such a band
As soon shall overcome those Irish rebels.

III.1.322–6 But now . . . that event:

QUEEN
Suffolk, remember what you have to do,
And you, Lord Cardinal, concerning Duke Humphrey.
'Twere good that you did see to it in time.
Come, let us go, that it may be performed.

IV.2.21–30 HOLLAND I see . . . with them:

NICK But, sirrah, who comes more beside Jack Cade?
GEORGE Why, there's Dick the butcher, and Robin the saddler,
and Will that came a-wooing to our Nan last Sunday, and
Harry, and Tom, and Gregory that should have your Parn-
hill, and a great sort more is come from Rochester and from
Maidstone and Canterbury and all the towns hereabouts;
and we must all be lords or squires as soon as Jack Cade is
king.

IV.2.111–13 To equal . . . have at him:

Kneel down, John Mortimer;
Rise up, Sir John Mortimer.
Is there any more of them that be knights?
TOM Ay, his brother.
   He knights Dick Butcher
CADE
Then kneel down, Dick Butcher;
Rise up, Sir Dick Butcher.
   Now sound up the drum

IV.2.163–5 ALL No, no . . . the King:

STAFFORD Well, sirrah, wilt thou yield thyself unto the King's
mercy an he will pardon thee and these their outrages and
rebellious deeds?
CADE Nay, bid the King come to me an he will; and then I'll

pardon him, or otherways I'll have his crown, tell him, ere it be long.

After IV.3.17:

... London, for tomorrow I mean to sit in the King's seat at Westminster.

After IV.7.117:

Enter Robin
ROBIN O captain, London Bridge is afire.
CADE Run to Billingsgate and fetch pitch and flax and squench it.
Enter Dick and a Sergeant
SERGEANT Justice! Justice! I pray you, sir, let me have justice of this fellow here.
CADE Why, what has he done?
SERGEANT Alas, sir, he has ravished my wife.
DICK
Why, my lord, he would have 'rested me,
And I went and entered my action in his wife's paper house.
CADE
Dick, follow thy suit in her common place.
You whoreson villain, you are a sergeant! You'll
Take any man by the throat for twelve pence
And 'rest a man when he's at dinner,
And have him to prison ere the meat be out of his mouth.
Go, Dick, take him hence; cut out his tongue for cogging,
Hough him from running, and, to conclude,
Brave him with his own mace.
                              Exit Dick with the Sergeant

IV.7.120 Marry, presently:

Marry, he that will lustily stand to it
Shall go with me to take up these commodities following:
Item, a gown, a kirtle, a petticoat, and a smock.

IV.8.5–53 BUCKINGHAM Ay ... and Clifford:

CLIFFORD

Why, countrymen and warlike friends of Kent,
What means this mutinous rebellions,
That you in troops do muster thus yourselves
Under the conduct of this traitor Cade,
To rise against your sovereign lord and king,
Who mildly hath his pardon sent to you
If you forsake this monstrous rebel here?
If honour be the mark whereat you aim,
Then haste to France that our forefathers won
And win again that thing which now is lost
And leave to seek your country's overthrow.

ALL

À Clifford! À Clifford!
They forsake Cade

CADE

Why, how now? Will you forsake your general
And ancient freedom which you have possessed?
To bend your necks under their servile yokes,
Who, if you stir, will straightways hang you up?
But follow me and you shall pull them down
And make them yield their livings to your hands.

ALL

À Cade! À Cade!
They run to Cade again

CLIFFORD

Brave warlike friends, hear me but speak a word.
Refuse not good whilst it is offered you.
The King is merciful; then yield to him;
And I myself will go along with you
To Windsor Castle, whereas the King abides:
And on mine honour you shall have no hurt.

IV.9.1–21 KING Was ever . . . several countries:

KING

Lord Somerset, what news hear you of the rebel Cade?

SOMERSET

This, my gracious lord, that Lord Say is done to death,

And the city is almost sacked.

KING

God's will be done, for as He hath decreed, so must it be;
And be it as He please to stop the pride of those rebellious
men.

QUEEN

Had the noble Duke of Suffolk been alive,
The rebel Cade had been suppressed ere this
And all the rest that do take part with him.

*Enter the Duke of Buckingham and Clifford, with the
rebels with halters about their necks*

CLIFFORD

Long live King Henry, England's lawful king!
Lo, here, my lord, these rebels are subdued
And offer their lives before your highness' feet.

KING

But tell me, Clifford, is their captain here?

CLIFFORD No, my gracious lord, he is fled away; but proclamations are sent forth that he that can but bring his head
shall have a thousand crowns. But may it please your
majesty to pardon these their faults that by that traitor's
means were thus misled.

KING

Stand up, you simple men, and give God praise;
For you did take in hand you know not what;
And go in peace, obedient to your king,
And live as subjects, and you shall not want,
Whilst Henry lives and wears the English crown.

IV.9.48–9 Come, wife . . . wretched reign:

Come, let us haste to London now with speed,
That solemn processions may be sung
In laud and honour of the God of heaven,
And triumphs of this happy victory.

IV.10.1–22 CADE Fie . . . my gate:

IDEN

Good Lord, how pleasant is this country life;

This little land my father left me here,
With my contented mind, serves me as well
As all the pleasures in the court can yield;
Nor would I change this pleasure for the court.

V.2.15–30 For I . . . thy will! *Exit*:

YORK
Now, Clifford, since we are singled here alone,
Be this the day of doom to one of us;
For now my heart hath sworn immortal hate
To thee and all the house of Lancaster.

CLIFFORD
And here I stand and pitch my foot to thine,
Vowing never to stir till thou or I be slain;
For never shall my heart be safe at rest
Till I have spoiled the hateful house of York.
  Alarums, and they fight, and York kills Clifford

YORK
Now, Lancaster, sit sure; thy sinews shrink.
Come, fearful Henry, grovelling on thy face;
Yield up thy crown unto the prince of York.

                                        Exit York

V.2.30–65 Enter Young Clifford . . . his back:

    Alarums, then enter Young Clifford alone
YOUNG CLIFFORD
Father of Cumberland,
Where may I seek my agèd father forth?
O, dismal sight! See where he breathless lies,
All smeared and weltered in his lukewarm blood!
Ah, agèd pillar of all Cumberland's true house!
Sweet father, to thy murdered ghost I swear
Immortal hate unto the house of York.
Nor never shall I sleep secure one night
Till I have furiously revenged thy death
And left not one of them to breathe on earth.
    He takes him up on his back
And thus as old Anchises' son did bear

301

His agèd father on his manly back
And fought with him against the bloody Greeks,
Even so will I. But stay; here's one of them
To whom my soul hath sworn immortal hate.

> *Enter Richard; and then Clifford lays down his father,
> fights with him, and Richard flies away again*

Out, crooked-back villain; get thee from my sight!
But I will after thee, and once again,
When I have borne my father to his tent,
I'll try my fortune better with thee yet.

> *Exit Young Clifford with his father
> Alarums again, and then enter three or four bearing the
> Duke of Buckingham wounded to his tent*

Before V.3.1:

How now, boys? Fortunate this fight hath been,
I hope, to us and ours, for England's good
And our great honour that so long we lost,
Whilst faint-heart Henry did usurp our rights.

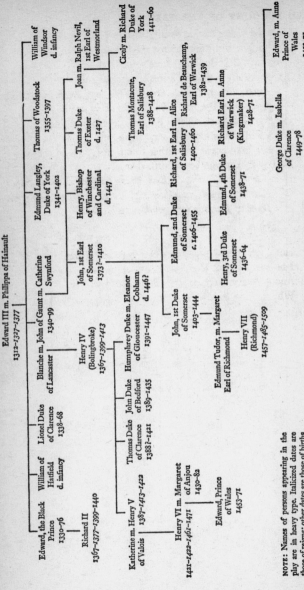

NOTE: Names of persons appearing in the play are in heavy type. Italicized dates are those of reigns; other dates are those of births and deaths.

TABLE 2: *The House of York and the line of the Mortimers*

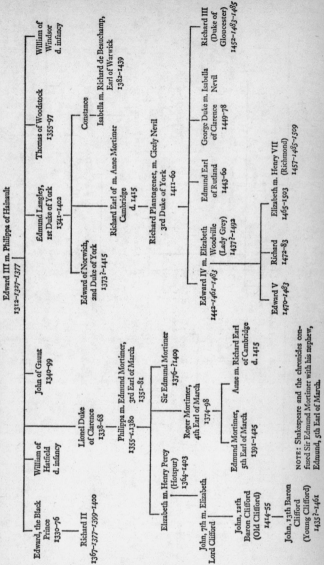

NOTE: Shakespeare and the chronicles confused Sir Edmund Mortimer with his nephew, Edmund, 5th Earl of March.